AN IMMODEST PROPOSAL

"Miss Dawkins," said the Earl of Clune, "ordinarily I suppose I would go about this much more delicately, but we've neither time nor opportunity. I find you lovely, clever, and personable. I can claim to be none of those delightful things, but neither am I perverse, cruel, or unhealthy. And I'm quite wealthy."

He paused, his dark and strikingly handsome face alert to Victoria's reaction. When she said nothing, he went on, "Briefly then, Miss Dawkins, I should like to offer you the position of companion . . . to me. That is to say, a house in a good district, a carriage, footmen, butler, clothes, and a quarterly stipend. Shall we say . . ." and he mentioned a number that caused Victoria to gasp.

When she recovered her breath, her voice was several registers higher than usual. "How dare you? How could you say such things, offer such things, when I have never, ever done such things before?"

Clearly the Earl of Clune's offer was not accepted. But that would not deter a lord who always got what he wanted. Now he merely had to alter his proposition into one Victoria could *not* refuse. . . .

Lady of Spirit

Edith Layton

A SIGNET BOOK

NEW AMERICAN LIBRARY

NAL BOOKS ARE AVAILABLE AT QUANTITY DISCOUNTS WHEN USED TO PROMOTE PRODUCTS OR SERVICES. FOR INFORMATION PLEASE WRITE TO PREMIUM MARKETING DIVISION, NEW AMERICAN LIBRARY, 1633 BROADWAY, NEW YORK, NEW YORK 10019.

SIGNET TRADEMARK REG. U.S. PAT. OFF. AND FOREIGN COUNTRIES
REGISTERED TRADEMARK—MARCA REGISTRADA
HECHO EN CHICAGO, U.S.A.

SIGNET, SIGNET CLASSIC, MENTOR, ONYX, PLUME, MERIDIAN AND NAL BOOKS are published by New American Library, 1633 Broadway, New York, New York 10019

First Printing, October, 1986

1 2 3 4 5 6 7 8 9

PRINTED IN THE UNITED STATES OF AMERICA

1

It was not quite the meanest street of the lowest slum in London town. After all, the crowd of humanity that thronged the street, impeding traffic and overspilling from the crowded pavements into the cobbled road, clearly had change to jingle in their pockets and were obviously intent on buying some of the many goods and services being loudly hawked all about them.

No, it wasn't quite the meanest street. For even though the used dresses on the carts, loudly touted as having once adorned titled ladies, looked so well worn and weary that those noblewomen must have existed three centuries before, still their potential purchasers fingered the garments with a confident proprietary air, and made shrewd offers that never rose from empty purses or idle speculation. Similarly, those carts filled with thrice-descended gentlemen's garments, the barrows loaded with displaced, chipped, and strangely mated sets of china, the wagons brimming with hats that had known so many heads that they had quite lost their own and sported mad and mischievous shapes, and the lines hung with quilts that had covered so many sleepers that now it took three of their number to comfort one, were all surrounded by interested, eager, possible customers.

It was not the most degraded slum. There, there would be apathy and despair; here, there was custom and trade. It was also evident the citizens here had the money to eat. The scents that arose from the pavements even managed to transcend the natural ones emitted by such a press of closely packed humanity so clearly unacquainted with soap, so plainly unfamiliar with any quantity of water.

However, the stench was not quite so unpleasant that the young servant in livery who rode on the side of the gentleman's sporting curricle really had to hold his nose so high in the air as his master's two chestnuts picked their way down the road. He certainly didn't need to hold his free hand over that freckled protuberance as though he'd never encountered the like, especially since he'd been raised in just such a district himself. But now he wore a uniform, and acted in the heady position of tiger, or postboy, to his employer when he went out driving, and so rejoiced in the exalted duties of holding his lordship's reins and watching his carriage whenever asked. And he had to have some response for the jeering, taunting, snickering packs of children who hooted and catcalled as they saw the expensive equipage creeping down their streets, and knew that his employer certainly wouldn't countenance his doing what he itched to do, which was to leap down and plant each and every one of them a facer they wouldn't forget.

His master, driving the equipage, had no expression but cool polite amusement on his dark handsome countenance. But there was no way his tiger could hope to emulate that—his master was, after all, an original, a man among men, a complete object of worship to his youthful employee—and a fellow couldn't mimic a god; it was enough that he was noticed by him. His master, after all, was the reason why no more than taunts reached the carriage, and no physical thing had touched them at all, although they'd traveled this day through districts where most men of property seldom returned with as much as they had set out possessing, in property or in person.

For his master had more than a cold dark eye and a knowing manner, and any wise man would note it. He might only be in his third decade of life, and dressed in the latest fashion of closely tailored jacket, tightly knit buckskin inexpressibles, and high polished boots. But he wore an air of experience as well, and the garments were well cut enough to show the long lean body was thoroughly muscled everywhere, more than padding could simulate, and from far more than the gentlemanly pursuits of dancing, riding, or even sparring could account for. The hands on the reins were broad and strong, and though well tended, their clearly marked sinews and long thick traceries of veins showed that they were no strangers to hard work. His thick straight jet hair might be swept back from his high forehead in Corinthian fashion, the clear skin on his clean-shaven dark face might be scented with bay rum, his decisive chin might be graced with a deep cleft in the ball of the center of it to tempt the ladies to lose their good sense, but one look into the obsidian eyes beneath their strongly inverted V's of black brows would warn any man to think twice about attempting to divest him of anything he wished to keep. No, his tiger thought proudly, a fellow wouldn't fear driving through the teeth of hell with this master.

But the other gentleman could not be more of a contrast to the vehicle's driver. He was a young man, and the tiger, though several years younger, knew he had never been so young himself. For the curricle's passenger, sitting straight on its high seat and looking with awe about him, made no attempt to disguise his blatant wonderment and enthusiasm as he watched this enthralling new world swirl past him.

The young gentleman was either nearing adulthood or had already entered it—one could decide which was true from whatever expression his open countenance wore at the given moment. From the way he carried himself it was clear that he hadn't had the time to grow used to his new-size lanky body and long limbs as yet. He was slender with fine straight light brown hair arranged fashionably about a long, pale, even-featured face that obviously had only recently lost the last of its spots. His eyes were a light pale blue and they gazed with wide unconcealed fascination on the crowds that milled about him.

"I dislike ruining your pleasures, Theo," the older gentleman said softly as he slowed his horses even more to avoid their marching over a merchant who took it into his head to follow a potential customer out into the road, waving a pair of striped trousers as an inducement to lure him back to his stall, "but I begin to think we should head back. I doubt you can find your needle in this haystack, especially since your recollection of her is sketchy at best."

"No, no," the young gentleman replied enthusiastically, "I recall very well. Anyway, she don't look anything like anyone I've seen here yet. She'll stick out like a sore thumb, 'pon honor, I promise you."

A trio of brilliantly dressed young women chose that moment to shriek and pout and blow kisses and curtsy to the dashing gentlemen they suddenly spied on the high seat of the curricle, and then each decided to outdo the others in her entreaties to the fine gents to come down and have a closer look—by pulling up skirts, lowering bodices, and showing generous peeks of ankles and thighs. They drew an amused crowd of onlookers to watch their attempts at public seduction, and the driver's face assumed an expression of sardonic resignation. But he flashed a white-toothed smile of regret to the trio, and though seated, made a sketch of a bow to them, which pleased the crowds enormously, and there were cheers of "Well down, guv," and " 'E's a man of taste, all right." As his equipage passed them by, the trio of flyblown sirens was even louder in their own regrets.

"Theo," the driver said coolly to the back of his young passenger's head as they left the young women behind and the crowd dispersed again, "put them out of your mind and be grateful fleas can only jump, not catapult. Now, set your eyes back into their sockets, take a breath to get your heart started again, and tell me how any female could stick out like a 'sore thumb' in this place."

"That's just it," the young man said cheerfully, "she don't look nothing like that. She's old, for one thing, and her hair's always all skinned back, and devil take it, Cole, she looks like what she is, a governess. Now, wouldn't a governess stick out in a place like this? No one here even knows what a governess is," he continued blithely, sweeping his hand to encompass the scene, "so since her landlady said she's out shopping, why, let's have a look about before we go home, since we've come this far. There's a few more streets to go yet. And you were right, Cole: now I feel a dog for having reduced her to this. So let's give it a try. I don't see how someone like her can get on here. She'll starve—why, this is the meanest slum."

The young tiger smiled when he heard that, because it was absurd to imagine this might be the meanest slum. For there wasn't anyone in the crowd who didn't have at least the price of a meal or the coins for one of those heavy, succulent meat pasties, for example, which could see a fellow though an entire day, and half the night as well if he didn't chew it well enough.

It was true. A street away, the young woman who stood, irresolute, to the side of one of the barrows, locked in place even though she was continually buffeted by hurrying passersby, staring at a beef pasty as though the baker had miraculously heaped the crust up in such a way to spell out her own name, certainly had the money in hand to purchase one as well. But she held the coins in her hand until they grew as warm as the piping crust on the little meat pie, and yet made no move to let them cool in the baker's wide stained apron pocket. For the rent, she was thinking despairingly, the rent surely needed the coins equally as much as she needed that pasty.

When the baker turned to her with a wide gray-toothed smile, having let her look her fill until he decided it was time to make a sale, she smiled back and stepped back, and then melted away to be lost in the swirling crowd as though she'd never stood there longing so long for his wares. By the time he'd shrugged and turned to a livelier customer, who joked with him and gave him smiles and an opportunity to pinch her cheeks or any other portions of her dimpled person he chose, for a penny off a pie, he'd almost forgotten her, although he'd been plotting a way to give her a more extravagant discount. As a businessman he thought it only fair, since after all, she'd been more extravagantly lovely.

He'd noted her all the while she'd thought herself unobserved, for he prided himself on being wide-awake, and never let an opportunity slip past him. She'd had masses of thick, wavy hair the color of his richest beef gravy, with bits of gold glinting in it in the sunlight, just the shade, he thought hungrily, of his own best chicken stock. Her eyes were huge and clear and of the lightest brown, near to almost gold as well. She'd been dressed soberly in blue, not expensive like a lady, he'd decided, but well, like an upper servant, almost prim. But she didn't put off a fellow even when she didn't smile, for her cheeks were jolly, round and pink, her lips pink and curved as well. Her figure was so trim, yet lavish where it ought to be, where he most liked it, that he quite willingly would have closed his stall for the entire quarter-hour, just as he'd planned, despite the trade lost as he made the trade he'd planned. But she was gone, and as a businessman he absorbed the loss, took stock of his less desirable new opportunity, and got on with business.

The young woman appeared from out of the crowd again, quite unnoticed by the baker, for now she was all of three barrows down the street from him and so was obscured from his view by all the people walking, eating, and browsing at the other food stands. This time she looked quite wistful as she wishfully gazed upon a different vendor's tray of mutton pies, still bubbling with juices as they simmered down to an edible; salable temperature on their rack. But this time too, she reckoned their cost, and knew again that they cost too dearly for her to contemplate buying.

Still, she had to eat, that was clear. For, she argued silently with herself, what was the point of having two weeks' rent money in hand if she couldn't live to enjoy the rental of her room for that space of time? And she might find a position this very day, she thought, and so by the time that second week was done, she'd laugh thinking back on her unnecessary frugality today. Then, she suddenly decided, unconsciously stepping closer to one particularly nicely browned and softly puffing little pie, certainly there would be coins and to spare for such a treat.

But though she withdrew her hand from a pocket of her skirts, it froze closed over her coins as she tore her gaze from the pasty and waited for the proprietress of the stall, a thick red-faced female, to finish with a customer, notice and then serve her. For, she then realized, she might not get a position this day or the next or the next, and those two weeks would come and then pass, whether she did or not. And, a silent voice scolded, she'd certainly be able to live out those weeks on her usual one meal a day. Then too, she well knew that by this evening, as usual, whatever was leftover merchandise would go far cheaper, since no butcher or baker fancied carrying home broken, stale, and unsold goods.

The young woman sighed and put her hand back into her pocket, her resolute fingers still knotted tightly around the coins so that they wouldn't be tempted by her frivolous nose or eyes to open up for such a strictly self-indulgent treat. So when the proprietress of the stall finished her transaction and turned around at last, pushing damp strands of hair away from her overheated face so as to better see her next customer, the young woman, in her embarrassment, dropped her gaze to the street at once, hoping she'd look as if she were searching for something she'd dropped there as well.

And then she found it.

It was as though she'd found a pirate treasure, and she stood quite still, not believing her eyes. It wasn't a coin, which would have presented her with more of the problems she already had with those few coins she did possess, causing her to debate whether to spend it or hold it against the day when she had no more of its fellows. It was both more valuable and desirable to her just now than that. For what she saw was one orphaned, broken pasty that must have fallen from the rack and then rolled halfway under the rumpled meat-juice-stained cloth that hung over the table. Only one golden end of it peeked out from under the cloth, to hint at its presence, and it seemed no one knew of it but herself.

It would be a simple matter, the work of a moment, to stoop, as though taking a pebble from a slipper, or picking up a dropped coin, or straightening a stocking. Then, casting one's own shawl negligently over it, just as though the shawl had happened to slip off one's shoulder as one bent down, one could scoop it up and carry it, still unnoticed, away.

Had she done it at once, she would have done it. But her second's hesitation brought the word "thief!" to her mind, and while she argued with herself that it was not theft to take something broken and forgotten, and that it was, moreover, foolishness to ignore such a gift from the gods, another self shrieked that it was her stomach making such ludicrous claims, for her conscience, which had been to Sunday school, knew better. Nothing was ever free here; anything dirty might be dusted off, anything damaged might be marked down a few pence. In a district where some squeezed out livings by culling burnt coal from the gutters, and others by foraging for cast horseshoe nails among the cobblestones, anything might be sold, whatever its condition. Anything free, like charity, was not only incredible, it was instantly suspect. Torn by such reasonings, she was, of course, immobilized.

While a worn matron bought three pies with carefully counted pennies, and an old toothless fellow squabbled with the proprietress, claiming similar treats could be gotten at tuppence less each just up the aisle, and a bright-eyed young boy eyed the pies and the altercation knowledgeably, the young woman still stood quite still, and with the scent of pasties adding their own pertinent argument, debated the exact meaning of "theft" over and over with herself.

No one noticed her, save for the bright-eyed boy, who was in the habit of noticing everything. That wasn't strange, for lovely as she was, the young woman was only one of the hundreds of persons loudly going about their business this pleasant spring morning. Food, clothing, furnishings, pets, papers, pots, rags, and even persons—everything was being vended on this teeming street. All manner of humanity pushed and paraded past. A wise man kept one hand on his pocket and the other over his heart, for if it were true that there was nothing new under the sun, certainly all of it could be seen here, and most of it was for sale. But still, it was decidedly odd to see the two elegant gentlemen in their dashing high curricle pulled by two blooded chestnuts, as they slowly turned the corner and hove into plain sight.

"They must o' come fer a taste of yer apple dumplings, m'pretty," a harridan cackled as she pushed her penny at the baker's wife she'd done business with for all of her life.

"Aye, me dumplings is famous, luv, just ask m' old man," that equally ancient dame laughed, glancing down smugly at her formidable bosom before she dropped an extra biscuit into the paper for the compliment's sake.

"Hoo!" cried a clothing vendor, pointing a lady's pink chemise at the vehicle in his glee. "Look who's got lost! Eh, lads, Windsor Palace's t'other way!"

"Ain't you the card though," a triple-chinned owner of a soup-and-stew cart bellowed. "Never listen to 'im," she shouted, to the pleasure of her customers. "I'm right 'ere, gents, 'er Majesty 'erself at yer service! Move over, Georgie, and give the gents some room."

But it was doubtful the gentlemen heard her disrespectful reference to their king, for even though the woman had a voice so loud it caused the surfaces of her soups to ripple when she roared at her own wit, they could scarcely hear her above all the laughter and talk and all the boastful, pleading, and promising calls of all the tradesmen crying all their wares together. Even the driver of the curricle scarcely heard his companion, close as he was, when he gasped and then when he gave a sudden shout.

Certainly the young woman, mesmerized by the vision of the fallen pasty under the cloth, heard nothing but her own interior dialogue. The scents around her had turned mere hunger into something profound and painful in its intensity. She noted the pasty had suffered a few cracks and bruises in its escape from its rack, and as she studied the black stains it bore on its crust from its travels, she told herself that it would be best to leave it, if not for honesty's then for her own health's sake. Anything rolled on these well-trodden cobbles would be carrying plague at worst, stomach distress at best, she reasoned. Yet still she could not help but see that withal, it was whole, even damaged it was beautiful, and it was free and it was there for her taking. She stopped thinking then.

She stepped closer to the barrow. She wavered. Then she inclined one shoulder, as if in a subtle shrug. She began to list very slightly to that side. And her arm, as though of its own volition, began to reach down and toward the truant, hidden meat pasty.

And then she felt a firm hand clap on her shoulder and clasp it hard, and she looked up to see a man grinning down at her. If her heart did not precisely stop then, her breath certainly did, as did her brain, abandoning all its complex duties so that she could at least remain standing and not sink to the ground in a dead faint.

The gentleman on the seat of his high curricle muttered a swift curse and threw the reins to his startled tiger. Then in one swift motion he was down to the ground, and seconds later at the side of the young woman who looked as though she were about to fall dead at the feet of his erstwhile passenger, who was now just standing and beaming at her companionably. The older gentleman put out his hands to hold the stricken young woman upright, but at his touch she seemed to come to her senses. He could feel her shoulders stiffen in his clasp and she wheeled about and gave him such a look of bright, blazing, wild indignation that he let his hands drop to his sides again.

"I found her. This is Miss Dawkins," the younger gentleman explained triumphantly, and then went on as she turned in amazement to face him. "We've been looking for you everywhere, Miss Dawkins. Your landlady said you might be out shopping here today. I say, don't you recollect me?"

The young woman shook her head, and then seemed to let out all of her breath in a long sigh. Her face, which had gone white as chalk a moment before, now blushed pink, but when she spoke, it could be heard that it was not pleasure or coquetry which had made her color up, but suppressed violence of feeling.

"Ah yes," she breathed in a low, well-modulated voice and refined accents, which could be heard clearly, since all those in the vicinity had quieted, the better to hear this interesting drama unfold. "It is Lord Malverne, is it not?"

"Ooo 'Lord,' is it?" a middle-aged female whispered, poking her companion in the ribs, whereupon, "Aye, 'Lord,' " he agreed, and the sound of the word repeated at once by most of the enthralled spectators set up a long low moan that the young woman could swear caused prickles to stand up on the nape of her neck.

"Oh, good, you remembered me," the young gentleman replied, oblivious, but then, seeing his former companion wince, he added hastily, "Oh, and this is my cousin, Lord Colin Haverford, Earl of Clune."

At this, an excited babble immediately broke out around the trio, and as the circle of interested parties grew, some even pushing to get closer to the players of the impromptu drama, the earl frowned and put up his hand. But before he could speak further, his young cousin, seeing his look of exasperation, went on to say hurriedly:

"Ah, but here's no time and place for introductions, you're dead right, Cole. It isn't a social matter. The crux of it is, Miss Dawkins, that I'm devilish sorry I got you your position lost, for I told them again and again that you wasn't after me for my money or to marry me, and they wouldn't listen, is what it was, you see. But I heard they dismissed you from your post—it was the earl here who told me of it, and made me see that it was bad of me not to set you up nice and right and tight again. So here I am, and if you'll give me your hand on it, I'll get you a new position, and everything will be fine again."

"Oohoo," spoke up the baker who had once drawn his own designs on the young woman, and who'd just abandoned his barrow and shouldered through the crowd to see the show that he discovered was featuring her. "I've got a nice tight position for you here as well, lovey. And I don't care if you're after my money, luv, you're welcome to it, if you give me more than your hand on it, that is."

A great deal of laughter greeted this, and the earl said quickly in an undervoice, as he saw the young woman's cheeks grow feverish, "Good grief, Theo, this is not the place to speak. Miss Dawkins, if you will be so kind as to meet with us, at your pleasure of course, we may yet remedy this matter."

"No," Miss Dawkins blurted, and several onlookers applauded as a few others cried encouragement.

She was so mortified by the enraptured audience she'd drawn that she seemed to see the gentlemen through a fine red veil. When the young gentleman had accosted her, she'd been sure she was about to be arrested for the theft of a meat pie, and the only thought that she'd been able to muster was that it was amazing how a thief-taker could have known what her ambitions were before she'd even done the terrible deed. But a moment later, when the other gentleman had held her steady, her nerves had calmed enough for her to comprehend just who the original young man was. A sense of brilliant relief had flooded through her. Then oddly, she'd felt an immediate reaction which was the opposite of her original gratitude that he knew nothing of her nefarious designs on the pasty, for it was an overwhelming sensation of outsized affront that she experienced.

He'd never voiced the denunciation she'd expected to hear. He hadn't even thought of the crime he'd inadvertently aborted, so this anger at an accusation that was never made, except in her own mind, was, she dimly perceived even then, nothing to do with him. It was only her own guilt crying out, too loudly, for concealment, but it was no less profound for all that.

Then too, as she at last registered just who the gentleman was, and began to remember all her grudges against him, he began spouting embarrassing nonsense that made her very real distress seem banal, and made her a figure of fun for the world to see. He had offered her a post, but then it was only right that he do so, for as he said, in all honor, he owed her one. And she needed such help badly; indeed, she had been entertaining little dreams of glory these past sleepless nights in which just such an apology and precisely such an offer were tended to her. But right now it wouldn't have mattered if he offered her a throne, or a kingdom, or even a plate full of fresh meat pasties. All she wanted now was to be let alone, to be away at once from all the sniggering spectators, and the scene of her intended crime.

"I mean . . . I meant," she said in confusion, "we cannot speak now, not here, in this place. Please, you know my direction, can we meet later? Oh, we must meet later," she cried, staring round at all the interested crowd. "Please."

Then she turned away blindly, pushed her way through the throng which had surrounded her, evaded the baker's open arms, and fled into the crowds.

The two gentlemen remaining might have found themselves in some difficulty, able-bodied though they were, if the crowd had decided the pretty young miss had a real grievance against them. But though the baker felt she should be avenged, a fair portion of the female audience held that she'd had a fair offer and given them a rare set-down, and so it was the gentlemen that ought to be supported. While they debated this theme, and fringes of the crowd shredded off to find better amusement, the two gentlemen returned to their curricle and drove off.

"Old!" was all that the earl said, shaking his head.

"She wore her hair differently," argued his young cousin nervously, "and devil take it, Cole, but she was a governess. How should I know how old she was? Who looks at a governess? Damn it, I ain't a queer nabs, and they ain't like females exactly."

"Old!" the Earl of Clune muttered again, and though his face was black as thunder, so dark that even his tiger felt pity for his young passenger, the earl would not venture another word for all the ride home.

When the sky began to dim and the crowds to dissipate, beginning to head home to taverns or rooms or alleyways, and the vendors began to dispose of the last of their goods so as to lighten their barrows for the homeward push, the old, the destitute, the very young, and the infirm haggled for the last rags and crumbs. The young woman returned to the pasty barrow in time to see the proprietress auction off the last of her merchandise. But of the several pies offered, none of them was the one Miss Dawkins had almost carried off, for that one was gone, neither on the table for auction nor lying, where it had first enticed her, half-hidden on the pavement. Someone else had doubtless spirited it away. Seeing that, she was too dispirited to even bid on the other pasties, inexpensive as they were. For now that her temper had cooled, she could see that she had been punished for her evil intentions.

Her desire for a free but ill-gotten gain had cost her dearly: she'd lost a dinner and a chance for employment together. And while she might have been able to afford the one, she very much doubted she could bear the expense of the other much longer.

" 'Ere," said the weary proprietress, looking over the heads of the small collection of her last motley, ragtag customers to the lovely, sad, aloof young woman who was gazing at her so solemnly from a little distance away, as though she feared venturing closer. " 'Ere," she said roughly, gesturing with the small, cold, broken brown pie she held out in her work-reddened hand to her, "take it. That's all right, dearie, pay me next time."

"What? Oh. Oh, no, thank you," the young woman said, surprised, ashamed.

"Don'cha want it?" the vendor asked, amazed.

"No. That is . . . oh dear," said the young woman, and then since she didn't know how to accept charity any more than she knew how to look for it, she shrugged her shoulders and, smiling sadly, turned and walked away, with a great deal of dignity but little else, for the second time that day.

2

Miss Victoria Eliza Dawkins paused on the landing of the fourth floor of her lodging house to catch her breath. She was a young and reasonably agile female, but the stairs were steep and the stairwells seemed to grow increasingly narrow, winding more tightly around the core of the house as they ascended, as if the rooming house were the interior of some giant snail's shell. But since even in times of broad daylight they were dim and dank as well, she started at a shadow and then quickly stepped up the last stairs to the last floor, where her own room hugged a corner directly beneath the eaves.

She let herself into her room and bolted the door behind her at once, and then dropped her reticule upon a small dented dressing table and then sank to the only other article of furniture in the room, her bed, to regain her breath at last. It was a rule of thumb that the higher the floor, the lower the price of the room, and in her present financial state Miss Dawkins would not have scorned lodgings on the roof itself, directly under the chimney pots, if the rent had been small enough.

Luckily, Mrs. Rogers, the landlady, had offered this one vacant room at an absurdly low price. And although Miss Dawkins realized it was closer to the heavens than most pigeons ever got, and though it was so small that she made sure the door was always bolted, since if she fell out of bed in the night she'd have been in the hall if it weren't, and though the neighborhood was such that it was dangerous to step into the street on a cloudy day, still, the young woman counted herself fortunate to have found it.

Because, unlike so many of her neighbors in this section of the city, Mrs. Rogers at least still clung to some rudiments of propriety. She allowed no females to conduct business in their rooms unless it was to do with sewing or knitting or handiwork that had nothing to do with bringing clients back to rooms for services rendered. She allowed no one to sleep in her halls, drunken or sober, and permitted no more than six persons to each room. And she always locked the main door at midnight each night. Although in this neighborhood this was only a symbolic gesture, Miss Dawkins appreciated it.

It was true that the upper floors had not felt a broom upon their scarred surfaces for decades, and some of the windows looked like thin walls, it had been so long since a cloth had been taken to them, but then, Mrs. Rogers could scarcely be blamed for that, having over the years grown to a size which precluded her fitting onto her own stairways, and then too, some of her lodgers were not inclined to be fastidious. Still, Miss Dawkins had got herself a room with a roof, and a bed, and a door that she could close against intrusion, and it was extremely cheap. And it came with a bowl of gruel, available between seven and half-past each morning in the kitchen downstairs, if one could swallow it, all included in the price.

It was not what Miss Dawkins was used to, in fact she shuddered to think of a person who might be used to such. But she prayed it was temporary, and as she sank back upon her lumpy bed she shivered just a little, for just a moment, because she'd allowed herself to wonder in that moment if there would not be a time, and soon, when she would look back at this meager refuge and wish she were lucky enough to have it back again. For it seemed to her that just as the stairs which brought her here today grew more constricted as they spiraled upward, so her life of late grew more convoluted as it relentlessly bore her downward.

She was no stranger to London, since she'd been born and raised here for all her twenty years, although this section she found herself in now had been the stuff of myths to her for all her young life, and the persons she found herself among had been the sort she'd always been warned not to speak to in the streets. She'd not been raised to nobility, nor to excessive riches. But she'd lived in a neat, comfortable, safe section of town, with many luxuries, for her father had been an apothecary, and her mother from a family fortunate in their dealings in dry goods. There had been, some century past, a grandfather who was a younger son to a minor baron somewhere in the south. And there were tales of an ancestral female favored by the royal lecheries of King Charles, but as that could be said of almost any other comely lass of her time, the family had no pretensions, and little to show for it save for some warm apocryphal stories and a little antique brooch with half its seed pearls gone.

The Dawkins family—Papa, Mama, Grandmother, son and heir Richard, and lovely little Victoria—had been content to live in unrenown and modest comfort. They may have existed in tastefully furnished, spacious rooms above their apothocary shop just city blocks from where noblemen squandered thousands on excesses like diamond buckles for their shoes, and the same number of streets away from impoverished wretches who could not even sell themselves for coppers, but the doings of either world, from either pole, were completely alien to them. In fact, those in the *ton* might have had more in common with those in the gutters than they did with Victoria Eliza's family, for each of those other sets, it was understood by the scandalized Dawkins clan, countenanced, as they would have never done, illegitimacy, promiscuity, insobriety, and gambling from those within their ranks.

In time, if times had been allowed to run their course smoothly, the family expected that one day Victoria Eliza might have caught the eye of some other worthy apothecary, or perhaps a young man at law, or even some youthful physician, and settled down with him (only if her eye had been similarly dazzled, for she had a fond papa) in pleasant, unremarkable bourgeois bliss. There might have been some difficulty with these expectations in time, for Victoria grew to be as clever as she was lovely, and with the education her doting papa brought her, she had been developing some rash and liberal fancies about a woman's lot, but that conflict, happily, and unhappily, never came to pass. For when she was in her seventeenth year, Victoria's papa succumbed to an infection of the lungs that none of his great jars and many vials of roots and powders and salves could cure.

She had been at a respectable boarding school for young females of moderate means and aspirations all through the unhappy events, and when she came home for the funeral it was made clear to her by her grieving mama that she was to finish up her last year at the school. If she didn't, she couldn't complete all the schooling her father had contracted for and it would be a waste, and the Dawkinses disliked waste above all things. And also, in that way she could always earn her own livelihood as a teacher herself, if, heaven forfend, she should ever have to do so.

When Victoria returned to London at eighteen years of age, with certificates of competency in three languages, passing aptitude in music, history, and art, and one for pretty behavior as well, in her hand, she was just in time to see to the sale of her home and her father's shop. There might have been some truth to that story about the ancestor who'd been King Charles's lady after all, since it appeared some reckless blood had been secretly percolating in the veins of the family down through all the years. For it transpired that all unbeknownst to his horrified family, Papa Dawkins had been making clandestine investments in all manner of schemes by which he'd hoped to make a great fortune and amaze and astound the world.

He'd placed money on stocks for developing gold mines that produced sand, and had put good coin of the realm in schemes to dig diamonds from the rich soil of Surrey. It seemed there was no illusion he hadn't been willing to back with his hard-earned money, if only the tale was told glibly enough. Mostly, it appeared he fancied himself a medical expert, and in his papers there were discovered dozens of patents for curing colds, removing stones without surgery, and manufacturing blood in bottles. What he *had* succeeded in discovering was a foolproof way to lose all his money, his property, and everything the family had owned, except for the antique brooch with half the seed pearls missing, for no one would buy that at all.

It was odd, Victoria thought now, sighing and stirring on her bed, how inheritance will out. For if one saw how the themes of personality ran in her own little family, then it wasn't too difficult to believe Papa had descended from some wayward lady no better than she should be. And although her mama had been a good, meek, indulgent woman, Victoria had always been closest to her grandmother, a fiercely independent managing female who'd run her son's hapless wife as she ran his family, until the day she died, still shouting instructions, when her granddaughter had been thirteen. It was not surprising, then, that after Papa's funeral, Richard, for all he was three-and-twenty and tall, straight, and stalwart-looking, had looked about, just as Mama had done, just as they both always did when tragedy struck, waiting for someone to take charge and tell them what to do. So Victoria, the only one left who was able to, did.

Mama was told, of course, she mustn't hesitate to take Cousin Beatrice's kind offer, and that she must do so at once and without a backward look. Though a pinchpenny, Cousin Beatrice was well enough off, and lived nicely on the profits of her husband's dry-goods store in Manchester. And if she were kind enough to take Mama in as a companion, and unkind enough to insist there was no room for her daughter as well, well, what of it, Victoria had insisted, it was a generous offer, and she could take care of herself. Mama, of course, used to having life ordered for her, went, though, despite all orders, with many a backward glance, and, despite all assurances, with many a reservation. But there was no help for it.

Richard was urged, just as he wished to be, to take Cousin Josiah's cousin's best friend's offer of employment, with an eye to eventual partnership, in an apothecary shop in Virginia, in the United States of America. It was the best of all the offers, and however many miles away the position, its opportunities stretched further. He might venture far, his sister reminded him, but his money would return by post with alacrity, to keep their tiny family solvent and perhaps one day buy them all freedom from worry again. So, with only a few nervous backward glances, he too went.

Victoria went through the only door open to her. She went to Mrs. Valentine, known to the family through her patronage of their shop. She was a draper's wife who lived in London and had a beautiful, precocious daughter who needed polishing. It turned out she needed a thrashing more, but before anyone could discover that, she'd decamped to Paris without either baggage or benefit of clergy, with a dissolute young man she'd met at Vauxhall, departing precisely three weeks after she'd met Miss Dawkins. Therefore, Miss Dawkins, of course, had to depart the day after that.

Fortunately, Master Edward Richmond, age seven, and known to the Valentine family through their draper's shop, was in need of strong discipline, being a great trial to his mother due to his waywardness and passionate spirit. But unfortunately, as Miss Dawkins soon discovered, so was his father. And so it was not long before she found herself in need of a new position once again. That was how she discovered the Misses Parkinson, Employment Counselors, and that was how she found her next post.

Now, of course, even the estimable Misses Parkinson seemed unable to help her, though only just this morning Miss Lavinia Parkinson, senior counselor, had condoled with her and then added pithily that she ought not to worry, as it was only to be expected that there be many a slip till a good tight fit was found. A governess or companion, after all, she reminded Victoria, could look forward to twenty years or more of employment with the same family if she suited. Although sometimes luck played a hand, Miss Parkinson had said wisely, seeking such an adoption by a family was much like finding any other kind of permanent position in life, such as housekeeper or wife, and so it took more than luck, it took patience and time as well. Victoria tried to find some comfort from that advice, reminding herself that it was given by a shrewd, experienced woman who ran one of the best employment bureaus in London.

But for all her experience, though Victoria was not to know it, the redoubtable Miss Parkinson had been dreading her interview with Miss Dawkins. Very little could discomfit Miss Lavinia Parkinson, but, as she told her sister later when they were having tea, just the sight of that lovely Miss Dawkins entering her chamber distressed her. In fact, the first glimpse that morning of that slender child, she vowed, looking at her hopefully with those great slanting golden eyes of hers in that sweetly smiling face, had fair sent chills through her, she moaned.

Because the stunning ones, she'd sighed, were the devil to work with. If they weren't being molested by members of the household after they'd finally been placed, like that poor Miss Hastings frequently was, they were turned down roundly when prospective employers got one look at their pretty faces, like that lovely Miss Robins had been for so long. And though she'd heard remarkably cheerful rumors of Miss Robins' magnificent change of fortune just this spring, this Miss Dawkins, she'd groaned, almost upsetting her tea in her exasperation, now had a far greater problem than just a beautiful face and form to handicap her.

But at least, she'd exclaimed, oversugaring her tea in an unconscious effort to sweeten more than her cup, she'd given the child hope by telling her it might take time. And it was only true, she told her sister, as that lady snatched the sugar pot away before Miss Lavinia could unwittingly do herself an injury by drinking pure syrup due to her distress, that in time, anything might happen.

But for all she'd nodded at the sage Miss Parkinson's every syllable, Miss Dawkins seriously wondered at how much more time was left to her now that she had to count her hours and her funds together, as if some giant meter were running, charging her so much per breath, so much per moment. She'd sent the lion's share of her earnings for the past two years to Mama for safekeeping, though she knew all too well that share was scarcely enough to keep a cub in comfort, just so that poor Mama could look at the reckoning whenever her own duties became too onerous, and have some hope for the future. For though Mama's letters claimed she lived comfortably enough with Cousin Beatrice, Victoria could read between the lines and tell that a steady diet of toads was never nourishing to the spirit, and that a dependent in that household might dine well only if she remembered to take her daily portion of humble pie.

Richard had not contributed anything as yet to the family, but then, he was saving up for the partnership and at least his letters showed great promise. She couldn't apply to her brother for funds, would not apply to Mama, and, Victoria thought, rising from her bed in agitation to gaze out her window at the rooftops, even her modest hopes might prove too expensive for her to indulge in any longer.

This morning Miss Parkinson had encouraging words and some clever ideas, but Victoria knew words and ideas were not sovereigns or pence. Worst of all, enough time had passed so that they'd both known neither words nor ideas counted for anything when there was no reference of good character for an employment counselor to work with. For Miss Parkinson had at last to admit that Miss Dawkins was in the most unenviable of positions, since few sane persons would take a strange young woman into the very bosom of their family, into the entrails of their household, if that person had no avowal of good character from her last employer. For all Miss Parkinson couched it in tenderer terms, it was becoming clear to Victoria that a person without such a reference was simply unemployable.

And it was that blithe young gentleman that had accosted her this morning after she'd left the employment bureau unemployed again, and been reduced to contemplating theft because of it, who had lost her last post and that reference for her.

The two young daughters of the Colfax family had been neither beautiful nor wayward; they were two stodgy, plump, and uninspired little girls, and though teaching them was neither challenging nor thrilling, it had paid very nicely. Blessedly, the gentlemen in their family could not have cared if the new governess had resembled a gorgon or an angel. It wasn't due to their superior morals. Mr. Colfax was a very successful ironmonger with investments far more interesting to him than any female could be. Two sons were safely away at school, and the one adolescent youth at home, like so many rackety young gentlemen, clearly regarded governesses with such loathing that he would never note their age or physical condition. Mrs. Colfax had aspirations to the Quality, as well as another adolescent daughter who she hoped might help her achieve those aims, and schemes for the child's brilliant marriage took up all her time. Victoria had been governess in the Colfax establishment for all of seven months and it had seemed bidding fair to become a permanent post.

Then she had done a small favor for a friend of the young gentleman of the house and lost her position, her good name, and any chance of an unexceptionable reference for it.

Young Lord Theodore Malverne was a noble youth, and though James Colfax was a cit, they had a commonality. Not only were they of an age, they'd discovered they shared the same cultural tastes. For they both frequented the same gaming hells, taverns, and bawdy houses. When they finally noted this amazing coincidence, they were convinced they were soul mates and spent increasingly large amounts of time in each other's riotous company. Lord Malverne's noble clan frowned when they noted it, but waited resignedly for the new university term to begin in the autumn and hoped the young man might lose his taste for wild oats even before then. It is doubtful Mr. Colfax noticed it more than he regarded anything going forth in his household, except expenditures, but Mrs. Colfax certainly did and was in ecstasies at how her clever boy was rising in the social world.

Then one day, an evil day that had dawned as clear as any other, with no premonitions of disaster, a day unfortunately unmarked for her by comets or rains of frogs, young Master Colfax bearded Miss Dawkins in the schoolroom and asked a favor of her. There was nothing remotely immoral or immodest about the encounter. The only ones who noted it with any emotion were his two sisters, who were pleased at having been woken from their slumbers in time for tea, for they'd been listening to their governess read them a history lesson and they had the uncanny ability, Victoria had noted, to doze like fishes, with their small bland eyes wide open.

Young James Colfax had a friend, he explained, and at this utterance he'd guffawed, as was his wont after any statement, and then waved his friend, who'd been hovering in the hall, into the room. Victoria had often seen young Lord Malverne running tame about the Colfax household, but had never spoken to him before and so was impressed that this young blade was at least as glib and conversational as the heir to this house was not. Charmingly, respectfully, and shyly he'd told her a tale and asked her a favor.

The lady of his dreams was, he explained, not only modest, virtuous, and entirely lovely, but also, alas, entirely French. No matter how he sought to make his feelings clear to her, he failed, for, he'd admitted ruefully, he couldn't get his tongue around frog-talk and hadn't his grades this term shown it! But his best chum, Jamie, had said his sisters' governess, Miss Dawkins, was whizbang when it came to jawing foreign language and a rare hand at knowing poetry and such too. The long and short of it was, he'd said bashfully, looking at his booted toes, just as he'd avoided her gaze all the while, could she copy out a poem in French for him, something to do with love eternal and that sort of rubbish, so he could give it to his lady and convince her of his intentions?

It was such a small thing, she agreed of course, a trifle amused, and a little touched by his youthful amours. She would have been much less so if she'd heard what the young nobleman had said cheerfully to his boon companion as they left the room.

For, "If this don't bring LaPoire around to my bed, Jamie, I swear I don't know what will!" he chortled. "Between the garnets and the poem, I'll have her by next midweek, see if I don't!"

"A crown you don't, Theo, 'cause I heard the Duke of

Austell's got his eye on her, and your paltry garnets and cat yodel in French don't stand a chance against one look from him," his friend claimed, and before they'd even gotten down the stairs the wager was laid, though two days later it was forgotten. For by then, of course, the female in question had bestowed her expensive favors elsewhere, courtesans being notably more prone to be more prone for mature, handsome, wealthy noblemen than for callow young swains, however noble, and who, moreover, exist on modest allowances from quarter to quarter.

So when Miss Dawkins, having sought and discovered a tender touching little sonnet to do with hopeless love, roses, nightingales, languishing knights, and hems of virtuous ladies' skirts, and having copied it out in her fairest hand, and signed it with encouraging best wishes, and sealed it, addressed to Lord Theodore Malverne, finally delivered it to the gentleman, she was surprised at his attitude. For he looked at it, said, "Oh, yes," stuffed it into his pocket with a cursory thank-you, and went whistling out of the house. Miss Dawkins was a little put out by his cavalier attitude.

But that was nothing to compare to his mother's reaction when she met with his valet, whom she regularly paid an extra sum to keep track of her eldest son, and discovered the missive that had been sent to him that he'd obviously been carrying close to his heart.

"Who," his mother demanded a week later, as she pounced on him as he was on his way out to a late dinner with his cronies, "is Miss Victoria Dawkins?"

The young gentleman looked blank for a moment and then said cheerily, remembering, "Oh, m' friend Jamie's sisters' governess."

"Governess?" shrieked his parent. "And what have you to do with her?"

"Why, she's a very good sort of female, Mama," her son answered earnestly, frowning in surprise at her wrath and wanting to set matters straight. "Always glad to do a chap a favor. She's devilish accommodating, actually," he mused, and then, being a fellow of few words, at least for his parent, added three more, "Good night, Mama," and went out the door.

Miss Dawkins went out the door of the Colfax domicile not a day later, with a great many more words at her back. Lady Malverne, stung into a vast uncharacteristic disregard for social station, had deigned to come to the Colfax home, and while her amazed and gratified hostess poured tea and plumped pillows and tittered in nervousness and excitement at her guest, she had waved about the paper with the fateful sonnet and delivered herself of her grievances against the cozening, conniving, social-climbing villainess of a governess, a *servant,* who'd been casting out lures to her foolish boy. An hour after Lady Malverne left with a sigh of great vindication, Miss Dawkins left with no recommendation.

That had been all of five weeks ago. First Victoria had gone to Mrs. White's, a respectable lodging house in a decent area, but after a week's time she'd realized with sorrow that it had grown quite beyond her touch. The following week she'd stayed a few streets further down the social ladder and the town, and at last, two weeks past, she'd engaged this room. She'd been aghast at her circumstances then, and now only hoped she could afford to stay on just a few weeks more.

Now the long dim twilight of late spring was upon the rooftops of London and Miss Victoria Dawkins realized, with a little jolt of surprise, for whenever she relived those horrid moments she quite lost touch with actual time, that it had grown too dark, too late, to walk these streets in safety in search of her dinner. Only the sort of female Lady Malverne and Mrs. Colefax had taken her for would do so alone at his hour, for then they wouldn't be alone for very long. She shrugged and turned to her table; the biscuits she kept in a tin there would have to do for her evening meal, and would, she thought in an attempt to cheer herself up, be far more economical as well.

It wasn't quite so bad, Victoria rationalized. There were, she knew, always the charitable institutions, the workhouses, the river. No, she thought, squaring her shoulders resolutely, nothing so dramatic; there was, after all, always the possibility of seeking quite different employment, if she could only overcome her own wretched dignity. She could ask to assist some honest tradespersons, like the bakers and barrow mongers she'd seen today. There were, she told herself bracingly, avenues she hadn't even explored as yet.

And as for those other roads, those other proposals for employment that had so frequently been called to her, or whispered to her by males in the streets, and certain females of the district who'd offered to assist her to enter that quite different, quite old, lucrative profession that flourished here in this neighborhood, why, they didn't bear wondering about. She knew herself well enough to realize, almost to her regret, that some things would simply not be possible for her, even the river being more possible and preferable, for there were some matters of dignity she accepted that she could never learn to surmount, even for her life's sake.

The worst part of all of this, Victoria thought, rising and wishing there were enough room to pace in her tiny room, was the silence. Anything, she thought sadly, would be easier to bear if one could only speak of it to someone. The last person she'd had coherent speech with was Miss Parkinson, and that was hours before, and since she didn't wish to be bothersome or considered an object of pity, it might be a day more before she ventured back to the employment office again. Even a little caged bird's company would be welcome, she sighed, but then, she thought, perversely cheered by the dreadful idea, she doubted she could afford the seed for it. Tomorrow, she decided, she would rise in time for Mrs. Rogers' gruel, and try to eat it as well, and have a chat with its creator, even though she knew it would be all to do with bunions, the price of giniver these days, and what a terrible curse problems of wind were to females of a certain age.

Her next morning's activities decided, Miss Dawkins sat upon her bed again, and leaning over her dressing table, began to compose an encouraging letter to her mama, filled with all the brilliant job possibilities she was considering. She'd already written and given Mama to understand that since she'd not decided as yet, it would be best to write to her in care of the Misses Parkinson, for she'd known that if she'd divulged her present address her mama would have fainted on the spot. She was describing a splendid illusionary position of companion to a kindly widow that she'd been offered, when she heard, incredibly, a tapping upon her door.

Victoria waited a moment to be sure her ears were not playing tricks, and a second longer to be sure it was not the wind. Then she took the two steps to her door and said at once, before whoever it was changed his mind, "Who is it?"

"Ah, miss," a very youthful voice replied hesitantly, "our mum was wishful to know if you'd care to come next door and have a bite of dinner with us, us being neighbors and all."

Victoria paused only long enough to promise the deity her future strict obedience to all the commandments and any others he might have thought up since and cared to add, she was so stunned and grateful, and then she drew the door open.

There was, she remembered, a large and confusing family, comprising mostly children, occupying what Mrs. Rogers euphemistically called a "two-room suite" just down the hall from her, between the consumptive old man's room and the old woman who wore three sweaters, as she had come to think of the other tenants who dwelt on her floor. This lad who stood before her in her doorway looked oddly familiar, until Victoria realized that she must have seen him a dozen times, along with his siblings, as they flashed up and down the long stairwells as they went about their business, as frequently and effortlessly as though the stairs bore them along on silent, swiftly moving runners.

He was about eleven or twelve years of age, she decided, as she thanked him and then threw a shawl over her shoulders to do courtesy to the invitation. The wise blue eyes in his thin face declared he was done with childhood, in the manner of all the older children who dwelt in this midden, but by his size and smooth face it was obvious he was not yet near to manhood. He had pale skin and light fair hair, damp and obviously combed so recently that it still bore regular even furrows from a comb's teeth. He was dressed neatly if shabbily in threadbare nankeens, frequently darned hose, and a jacket that his thin wrists eloquently declared no longer fitting.

"My mum," he said conversationally as he led Victoria down the dim hall, after reminding her to bolt her door behind her, and waiting courteously for her to do so, "isn't feeling up to par just now. So she's having a bit of lie-down in the other room, but," he said at once, as gallant and cool as though he were handing her into a castle rather than his shabby attic rooms, "we'd be pleased at your company, and my mum says to go ahead with dinner, and p'raps she'll see you later on."

The room Victoria entered seemed at first stare to be filled entirely with children. But that was because it was such a small room, and the children were so similar in appearance. There were, she saw after only seconds, only three others: another boy, both a little darker and smaller than her escort, an even smaller girl, blond and fair as her bigger brother, and when the doll the child had thrown over her shoulder wriggled and cooed, it could be seen that it was an infant of indeterminate age and gender.

The other children stood very silent and large-eyed and seemed to be awaiting Victoria's judgment of them, so she said at once, "How do you do, I am Victoria Dawkins, and you . . . ?"

As her escort, who promptly named himself Alfie Johnson, introduced her along the line to his siblings Bobby, Sally, and then, dismissively, to Baby, Victoria began to take note of the other features of the room. Mrs. Johnson might be sleeping in the other room, but this one obviously served as bedroom as well, for there were two sad little heaped-up mounds of coats and shawls serving as bedclothes on the floor that still clearly bore the imprints of small curled-up bodies, and as Victoria watched, Baby was deposited in a wooden crate lined with similar castoffs that was on one end of the long table where dinner had been set out.

For all her attempts at politeness, Victoria's gaze was relentlessly drawn over the heads of her youthful hosts to that promised repast. A ragged but surprisingly complete cornucopia of a cold collation awaited her. The cracked dishes bore an assortment of foodstuffs, a wealth of victuals, an oddly lavish sampling of all that she had coveted this morning at the market: bowls of stew, assorted breads, slabs of fried fish, several pasties, half-puddings and whole ones, and a truly prodigious array of cakes and sweet breads and cookies.

The children remained very still, and seeing only one chair, Victoria was about to ask where she ought to sit, when she saw one particular item of food upon the table that caused the words to catch in her throat. There was no mistaking it. She'd gazed so long and hard at it this morning, it had precipitated such a maelstrom of feeling, that she didn't doubt she'd see it in her dreams for all her days. But tonight, certainly, there was no mismarking that peculiar jagged crack in its crust, that odd pattern of soot on its browned side where it had kissed the paving stones. Seeing that damaged mutton pasty was like seeing the face of an old lover who had never loved in return; it was embarrassingly unforgettable.

"Aye," her escort, Alfie, said, grinning at her reaction, "I thought you'd remember it. Well, it's yours, miss," he said expansively, "and it's only fair. For you saw it first. I wouldn't have twigged to it without you. And that one at least, not like the rest of this lot, took no planning at all to bring in. Naw, it wasn't no trouble to me at all in the getting, and never the least danger to me once it was in m' pocket."

"But that is to say," Victoria gasped, bewildered, "do you mean to imply that half of this . . . feast is stolen?"

"O' course not!" Alfie snapped, looking so wounded she could have bitten her tongue off in dismay at her rash accusation. " 'Alf of it nicked indeed!" He sneered. "Do you think I'm a flat? Why, every blessed bit of it is!"

3

The gentleman was shown into the sitting room just as though such a thing happened every day. It had actually been decades since any male had adorned the room, though his hostess's manner did not reflect that, and centuries since anyone entitled to the name "gentleman" had entered the premises, though his hostess never had any idea of that at all. For had she known any such gentleman had ever crossed her threshold before, doubtless she would have given herself airs and become insufferable toward those few neighbors she spoke with.

But Mrs. Rogers was to enjoy no such felicity; she was, after all, no historian. She hadn't an inkling that her lodging house had once been owned by no less a personage than a baron. That gentleman, however, had been dust for some three hundred years and had dwelt in the house when it had been located in what was then the suburbs of London. That had also been in a bygone time when noblemen commonly came to the district for sociability and conversation, rather than for low amusements and a chance to acquire some interesting diseases along with the several vices that were now the only thing they ever sought here.

This gentleman, however, did not have the look of a man seeking pleasures, strange or otherwise, and certainly he would have been hard pressed to find any of any sort in

Mrs. Rogers' establishment. Instead, it was reasonable to assume that he'd come, just as he'd said, to speak with a lodger, one Miss Dawkins. But it wasn't propriety then which sent Mrs. Rogers puffing up the stairs she'd not climbed in years to fetch the girl down, nor was it an attempt to keep her house's name virtuous which decided her against sending the gentleman, who was after all not only much younger than herself but obviously in fine physical fettle, straight up to her tenant's bedchamber. It was the fact that in all her fancies she'd always imagined opening her sitting room to such a visitor.

For Mrs. Rogers entertained, as do all mortals, dreams of grandeur, even though she'd never been daring enough to dream of ever actually entertaining such a perfect vision of a Corinthian, or rather, as she babbled to her hapless neighbors for months after, such a complete swell, and if what was printed on his card was to be believed, an 'onest-to-gawd earl, no less.

Dreams of glory aside, there was also the practical consideration that she'd not have a prayer of hearing a word passed between her lodger and the gentleman if he was to go upstairs to meet with Miss Dawkins, but if a body was clever enough to crouch right outside the door to the sitting room during the encounter, she'd be likely catch every syllable uttered.

If houses can be said to possess ancestral auras—and there are those who say brick and mortar can collect more than grime over the centuries, even to the point of absorbing spiritual essences—then it was possible that the walls of the sitting room sighed with gratitude when the visitor stepped across its doorsill. For this was obviously a gentleman of the Quality who paced its narrow confines. It was undoubtedly a nob of the first stare whose impatient black gaze took in the room in all its threadbare splendor in one cursory glance, and then turned his back to the door and gazed out through the yellowed lace panels which mercifully obscured the view to the street.

Even if it were possible that subsequent, socially inferior occupants of the house had also left traces of their less affluent and well-bred ectoplasms in the wood and plaster warp of the room, it still might be said that all the several spirits would be at peace with this particular visitor. For the Earl of Clune had only come into his honors a year previously, and moreover, had never expected or wished to achieve his noble state. He'd been a mere "Mister" Colin Haverford for the previous seven-and-twenty years of his life, although anyone who'd ever known him would argue that the gentleman had never been "mere" at any time in his existence. Still, an earl to the title born and raised might not have undertaken the mission he had. But even as the hands that were folded behind his broad, immaculately tailored back were not yet accustomed to idleness, so too this gentleman was not yet in the habit of sending others to do his bidding, and would never think of leaving affairs of conscience for others to resolve.

However, his young cousin, Lord Malverne, perhaps because titled since his christening, obviously had no such compunctions. The earl scowled as he thought of his feckless young relative. A week had passed since young Theo had come raging into his study complaining at the injustice of the fact that the crass interference of his mama had lost some innocent governess her livelihood. Until that moment the earl hadn't thought much of the young sprig of fashion he seemed to have inherited along with his honors and properties when he'd come into his own title.

Colin Haverford had become head of what he'd always considered to be a singularly unpleasant family at the same moment that he'd acceded to the earldom. He'd known of their existence, of course, and had met with them now and again where it hadn't been possible for them to avoid him, at funerals and weddings, but they'd not tossed him a look when there had been four persons between himself and the title, and in all, he'd been glad of it. But with the title had come responsibilities, both moral and legal. And since it rapidly became apparent that Theo's mama saw her son only through rose-colored glasses, just as she'd once viewed her ideal, his father, the young baron who'd died too soon for her to discover otherwise, and his uncle, her brother, saw him only, as he saw all else, through the bottom of a wineglass, it seemed someone must take on some responsibility for him growing to a decent manhood. Lady Malverne was old-fashioned enough to believe in the absolute authority of the head of the family. And since the new earl was appalled to discover that the lady's idea of manhood was only noblemanhood, he accepted the unpleasant duty as the lad's mentor with the same resignation with which he'd accepted all else about his new position.

He'd taken some time with the lad, and so had been tremendously pleased that day to find that Theo seemed actually to be concerned that his actions had caused some innocent underling distress. He'd been gratified that the young lord appeared aggrieved when he'd learned that a governess who'd penned a love note in a foreign language for him had lost her position due to a misunderstanding of the favor. He'd been, however, far less than charmed when he'd finally discovered that the entire incident had taken place some five weeks past, and had, as the young villain had casually admitted after interrogation, quite slipped his mind because of the splendid mill he'd gone to, the races he'd attended, and the new roan he'd had his eye on, until that very morning, when something said at breakfast had reminded Mama, and she'd gloated over it all over again.

It had taken time for the concept that five wageless weeks could be a matter of life or death to a servant to sink into Lord Malverne's privileged head, but the hope for the lad, his relative thought, was that once the message had come clear, he'd been on fire to find the poor old soul and right matters for her once again. Nothing would do but he must seek her out, reimburse her for time lost, and help find her a new position. For even he could understand that a person, however humble, might not wish to be reemployed in an establishment she'd been peremptorily and unjustly bounced out of, however matters might now be explained to everyone's satisfaction.

As the earl had some notion of young Theo's attention span, and since after he'd made the inquiries Theo had no idea of going about, he'd also known the sort of neighborhood the unfortunate governess's employment counselors said she now resided in, he'd decided to accompany the lad on his mission of mercy. One look at the rapt expression on the youth's face as they'd driven through the noisome streets had convinced him of his wisdom in the matter. If Theo had gone alone it was very possible he might never have returned, or if he had, it might have been with the sort of problems, or at the least, parasites, that the noble Malvernes had never encountered. Slumming with cronies might bring Theo to some dicey straits, but these streets were ones where few young sporting gents, however lively, ever ventured alone. After all, it was thrills and pleasure the youth of the Quality were after, not actual suicide.

The earl had also privately thought that Theo might have a hard time of it when he did find the rejected governess. The poor old lady he said he sought might have been so abjectly grateful and embarrassingly servile in her delight at having been found and vindicated that she could have brought too much of the wrong sort of attention to the lad from others in the area who had their own grievances against rich and thoughtless young gentlemen and their treatment of helpless females. Or she might still be so angry and swollen with insult and the sort of smoldering rage that proper old females who have nothing else to their names subsist upon, that she could have also caused Theo harm or brought some sort of indignity upon him when he finally located her and tried to mend matters.

The last thing the earl had expected of the journey was that it would cause him sleepless nights. But the wretched cast-off aged governess, Miss Dawkins, it transpired, was one of the loveliest young creatures his wondering eyes had ever chanced upon in all his wandering. When Theo had voiced his unheard shout and leaped down to the street and the earl had seen whom he'd accosted, there was even a mad moment when he'd thought the lad as overwhelmed by the girl's beauty as he was, but, being younger, was unable to control himself and his desires. Then when the glowing girl had grown pale and that charming face had blanched and become wide-eyed with terror as Theo accosted her, the earl had known that whatever the reason for the incident, it must be stopped at once. He'd then been so overwhelmed by the revelation that this graceful beauty was the pedantic old governess Theo had been seeking that he'd stood by, leveled by amazement as he'd not been in years, mute as a callow boy himself, while Theo proceeded to thoroughly muddy matters further, insult the girl more profoundly, and embarrass her into flight.

It was that, and the fact that only this morning the earl had learned that Theo had once again confused good intentions with good works, and had neglected to follow up on the matter in all the past weeks' time, that caused the barely suppressed anger so apparent in the earl's dark face. But if he'd been completely successful in his attempts at concealing his chagrin, if he'd been less tense, if he'd been all asmile and charming when he'd come to call here, Mrs. Rogers mightn't have believed him for a moment, and certainly never for long enough to allow him into her house, much less her beloved sitting room. For true gentlemen, she knew, with the surety of someone who has always been downtrodden, do not chat up commoners, nor spare a grin for those they deem beneath them. Nor, she thought with the unswerving devotion to distinctions of class of the truly oppressed, as she huffed up the last steps and held her hand to her wide and wildly thumping bosom before she rattled Miss Dawkins' door, should they.

And so it was that she demanded that Miss Dawkins descend to greet her guest at once, with no further delay. Because when the young woman heard it was a gentleman, and a real one at that, come to call on her, she hesitated, she prevaricated, she almost refused at once. Then Mrs. Rogers, with all the authority vested in her as proprietress of Miss Dawkins' last refuge, lost all her patience with such revolutionary behavior. It was a nob, a *nobleman*, that were cooling 'is 'eels, she shouted, and as Mrs. Rogers lived and had trouble breathing after all those flights of stairs, Miss Dawkins would receive him or receive her marching orders. Visions of whatever errand the gentleman was embarked upon being far less ominous than her landlady's present glittering eye, Miss Dawkins, being wise as she was hesitant, capitulated. She descended with as much grace as was possible, with Mrs. Rogers hard on her heels, panting and crowding and prodding her all the way down the stairs.

She'd not been sleeping well, no, nor eating well either since he'd seen her, he thought after his first look at her when she entered the room. She wore the same blue frock he'd seen, but he thought it fitted a bit more loosely around her slender frame. Although hers was not a beauty composed of contoured cheeklines and strong bones, and would never be, still her round cheek was paler and her fair complexion had a more translucent look. And though the earl doubted anything short of plague itself could dim her beauty or take the glow from out those odd, tilted golden eyes he remembered so well, he worried for her, this female he scarcely knew, and cursed the circumstances that had brought her to this pass.

And she, irrationally, thought only that temper suited him, and that she'd rather see it than the smooth sardonic look he quickly assumed as she gave him good-day. She'd known who he was at once. Not only were earls not thick in her acquaintance, but it would have been impossible to forget that distinctive form and countenance. Lord Malverne was a fairly tall and reedy youth, but his cousin, though equally tall, and certainly not heavyset, was a substantial man. The gentlemen of fashion that young Lord Malverne and his cronies aped were languid fellows, all airs and graces, and if they had expertise with sword or fists, they practiced to make it both subtle and discreet. The earl was not cut to that pattern. His muscularity was clearly deliniated by his fashionable clothes; strong passions flickered beneath the surface of those knowing onyx eyes. Withal, Corinthian or not, she'd never seen his like before.

Then she lowered her own eyes, for he was addressing her and she was a servant and he a gentleman, and she knew her place, and it was not for her to judge him, at least not here, beneath his very gaze.

"My graceless cousin was supposed to have visited with you again, Miss Dawkins," he said, and she noted with surprise that it was a warm and soothing voice, with a small odd endearing slur in its sibilants and a soft Welsh burr to give it weight and timbre. When he had spoken to her in the street, she'd not heard a great deal above the echoes of her own guilt crying out for discovery, except, unfortunately, for every embarrassing comment from the enthralled crowd that had gathered about them.

"He was supposed to right matters, and in far less public and far more comfortable fashion that he did when he surprised you in the marketplace," the earl continued. Then he paused, and she glanced up to see why he'd done so. A smile which quite transformed his face caused her to drop her gaze in confusion, as he said ruefully, "I don't know half the details, I confess, his mama sings one song, he another, but from what I've ascertained, our family's done you a disservice, and I'm here to remedy it."

He reached into his jacket and withdrew an alarmingly large packet of banknotes and held it out to her.

"Not half enough, I know," he said with regret, "but there's never been a way insult and inconvenience can be paid for. I hope, however, that this illustrates, at the least, our earnest intent."

She couldn't move for a moment, she was so fascinated by the amount of money before her. But then she whipped her hands behind her back before they could escape her vigilance and snatch the bills from his hands. Perhaps, she was later to think, if he'd been stout, or ancient, or laughably mannered and effete, she would have taken it without a second thought. But he was so very attractive to her, he was so magnetic and powerful a personality that she found herself reacting as no servant ought. Perhaps, she attempted to excuse herself later by imagining, she'd wanted at that moment to be an equal in his eyes, perhaps that was why her wretched pride had been stung. It might have been the way the money had been proffered; had it been decently shrouded in a parcel, she was to think afterward, she could have taken it, counted it, and then demurred. But then it would have been in her clasp, and once there, she knew for a certainty she would not have parted with it.

But the bare, naked notes he held out to her so negligently in that large tanned hand . . . at that moment she could only think that was how he would pay off a tradesman, a hackney driver, it was how she'd seen the ladies of joy in the district being negotiated for, though none had ever commanded so much money, no, not for a month's services. But it was how a person would reimburse a servant, and in that odd, prideful moment she did not want him to think her a servant. Which was, of course, as she recalled later as she damned her stiff-necked arrogance, what she was.

"Not enough?" he asked, mistaking her gesture, and raising one dark, already arched brow in amazement.

"No, no, too much," she said, when she could, after she'd licked her suddenly dry lips. "I've only been unemployed six weeks. And no," she said at once as he began to speak, cutting him off although she knew that too was not done by an inferior when her master spoke, "one cannot pay for insult. I don't expect it."

"And so you infer that I incur another debt even as I seek to pay one?" he mused, but he withdrew his hand and held the bills before him between two hands then, turning the packet over and over, before he asked bluntly, though in pleasant tones, "What is it you want, then?"

She hesitated, still staring at the notes, for at that moment she wasn't sure. She surely wanted the money, and employment, and her independence back again. But just then she didn't want to be merely a pitiable governess in anyone's employ. Then she became distraught when she suddenly saw that she could never have pride in herself so long as she was ashamed of what she unalterably was.

"A good character," she blurted then, seizing on her utmost hurt, "my reference of character from Mrs. Colfax. Lady Malverne advised her not to give it to me," she explained to his look of puzzlement. "I cannot find employment without it."

At that he sighed. "But, Miss Dawkins," he said gently, "you increase my debt. There's the reason I've come armed with so much blunt. I'm afraid the lady's taken herself off to Bath with her family in tow, leaving our Theo temporarily orphaned and in my care. I doubt his reference will suit, nor will mine. And as you might guess, Mrs. Colfax, who I understand is a socially thrusting person, won't lift a pen without the lady's permission. Our interference with Mrs. Colfax would only blacken your name further with her, I suspect, so I'm afraid it's the money or nothing, at least until Lady Malverne returns.

"I can convince her to have Mrs. Colfax write an unexceptionable one for you," he said, staring down at her consideringly as he weighed the packet of bills in his hands, "but," he sighed, "it's never the sort of thing to do by post. Even if she complied, it wouldn't do. No, she'd have your last employer damn you with faint praise and play the innocent when I objected. We'd have letters whizzing back and forth, up and down the Bath road for weeks. She believed you were after dear Theo's name or protection, and she's renowned for her firmly held principles. Which is," he said, smiling that curiously gentle smile, "another way of saying that she has the flexibility of a slab of pine. Come, Miss Dawkins, take the money until matters are mended."

It was an eminently reasonable argument, a clear and logical request. Victoria swallowed down a bitter taste, which must have been the dregs of her pride, and reached for the notes, which this time he laid down carefully upon an adjacent table for her. And then he said, as her fingers closed over them, in oddly light and unconcerned accents:

"It scarcely matters, you know. Only for my own information. But why the devil did you pen those verses?"

"He," she said, drawing back, with the money in hand, in her surprise omitting young Lord Theo's title, "that is, Lord Malverne, said there was a Frenchwoman he wished to impress, but that he didn't know the language, nor any poetry suitable for her."

"The jingling of coins is the most poetic thing Lucille LaPoire ever heard." The earl laughed. "Come, Miss Dawkins, I've said it makes no difference now. It's over. When Theo told me of it, I assumed you were an elderly female nearing retirement, willing to do anything for a sum to add to your nest egg, even to copying out passionate sonnets for boys to deliver to demireps. Theo said nothing to dissuade me. Thus when Lady Malverne bent my ear, I believed her addled, or overprotective to the point of mania. Had I seen you first, I would have believed her completely. You're all of what . . . twenty-one? Less? And entirely lovely. It can't have been easy for you."

He said this with seeming sympathy, he said it with such concern in his deep, soft, slightly slurring accents that she forgot what he'd called Lord Malverne's lady-love. But for all his charm, she could not forget, as he seemed to wish her to, that he was no less than an earl and she no more than a servant, and money was changing hands between them even as they spoke.

"But no, I should have disbelieved Theo's mama as well," he commented, gazing down at her with troubled eyes. "You're entirely too wise to stalk him. It's ludicrous, only a mother could think it. If you'd tried, you could have nabbed far better. But what I can't understand is why on earth you aided him in his pursuit of his expensive demimondaine. Money must certainly have been a consideration. No matter," he sighed, shrugging, "we all make mistakes. As I," he breathed as if to himself, "may yet prove."

He remained silent for a brief moment, collecting his thoughts. He'd given her the money, he'd settled accounts as best he was able, and yet she still stood and stared at him as though she were awaiting something he'd forgotten to say. There was something he'd not said. But it wasn't that he'd forgotten it, for the thing hadn't been far from his mind or his lips since she'd entered the room. It was only that she was such an accomplished actress she'd almost defeated her own purposes, he realized, playing the innocent so well he'd begun to doubt himself enough to refrain from broaching the matter entirely.

But she never belonged in this dingy, dusty parlor in this low slum, he thought, she was as incongruous as a rose in a rubbish heap here. The thing was so obvious it was no wonder she stood hesitantly, waiting to give him the chance to realize the truth of it. She'd noted him as a man; he was no peacock, but when there was so much tension between a man and woman there was little doubt of it, he knew he couldn't be wrong in that. Even now as she waited for him to speak she chanced a glance to him, and what she saw in his returned and interested gaze caused her to veil her eyes with her lashes and close her hands spasmodically over his money. It was then he realized she obviously wanted him to take the initiative, she'd some idea of the refinements of the matter.

After all, he thought, she'd had enough discretion to forego young Theo's protection, despite her obvious pressing financial needs. Theo was very young and callow, and an experienced female of taste, or certain tastes, might well pass over such an unformed youth, no matter what his worldly endowments. But was she puzzled now about what gave rise to his own hesitancy in the matter? he wondered with rising desire, as he decided that further shilly-shallying was unnecessary and impolitic, for not only might it make him lose esteem in her eyes, it might even win him her mockery. Since he found himself disliking the idea of that very much indeed, he decided to proceed immediately, but warily.

For all he appeared to be unique, when he wished he could disguise all emotion upon his expressive face like any other well-bred gentleman of fashion, she thought, because he wore an unfathomable look as he spoke again.

"Miss Dawkins," he said hesitantly, "in the ordinary way of things, I suppose I could go about this much more delicately, but we've neither time nor opportunity. I should not like to visit here again; I'm convinced you're used to better as well. So I'll be straightforward about it, though I should rather, if circumstances were different, put my proposition to you slowly and by tender and sensitive degrees. In short, it's clear your career as governess has hit a considerable snag. You can't have found any of it pleasant or profitable in any event. I don't doubt you've just earned more for being summarily dismissed than you ever did when you were employed."

She could not reply to this, for it was entirely, disgracefully true. She only continued to gaze up at him, turning his bundle of bills in her hands mindlessly, and it was as if her silence satisfied him, for he seemed easier in his mind, and he nodded and went on,

"I find you, as I said in a more roundabout way, lovely, clever, and personable. I can claim to be none of those delightful things, but neither am I perverse, cruel, or unhealthy. And I'm quite wealthy. Ah, this is not easy, perhaps that's why I've not attempted just such a formal arrangement since I've come to London, though Lord knows," he murmured, shaking his head, as though he spoke half to himself, "I've been told often enough that it's expected of a man in my position.

"Briefly then, Miss Dawkins, I should like to offer you the position of companion . . . to me. That is to say," he said carefully, as she gaped at him, "ah, a house in a good district, a carriage, footmen, butler, clothes, and a quarterly stipend, shall we say," he said ruminatively, and then he quickly mentioned a number which caused Victoria to gasp almost louder than Mrs. Rogers did at her hidden station behind the door.

"And," he said, smiling tenderly at her now that he'd done with recounting the details of his offer, "I don't require any letter of reference. It is enough that I've heard you and seen you."

He stepped close to her and touched her cheek gently.

"I'm very attracted to you," he admitted. "I don't know when I've ever felt such an instantaneous longing for any female. Come, Miss Dawkins—absurd name, Victoria, isn't it? Well, then, come, Vixen, admit half as much to me, I've been a gentleman, but I've not been insensible to your reactions to me. Although I can't promise anything, of course, without sounding like a braggart, I can't help but feel we'll deal very well together. And though I mentioned I haven't set up just such an arrangement here in town before, I'm not at all inexperienced in dealings with your gender, rather the reverse I should say.

"But why am I listing my achievements"—he grinned—"when it's you, in all fairness, who'd be expected to present credentials to me, which right I waive, and when there's a far simpler way to make my point, that I'll be delighted to demonstrate."

And then, as Mrs. Rogers held her breath at the prettiness of the gentleman's speech, he stepped forward, took the dazed Miss Dawkins, still clutching the money to her breast, into his arms and kissed her with a concentration and thoroughness Mrs. Rogers had only ever dreamed upon. Until Miss Dawkins erupted like a fury, spitting and clawing, and tore herself from his clasp.

"How dare you?" Miss Dawkins cried, several registers higher than her usual dulcet, modulated tones. "How could you say such things, offer such things, when I have never, ever done such things before?"

But, "Obviously," was all the gentleman commented dryly, crossing his arms in front of his wide chest and looking, Mrs. Rogers thought at least, from her keyhole vantage point, a good deal more ill-at-ease than his cynical tones let on.

This brief comment, rather than fueling the fire, as her hidden landlady hoped, seemed rather to achieve the reverse, and Miss Dawkins grew very still. A dozen vile epithets flew to her lips, a half-hundred accusations hovered at the edges of her consciousness, but all she said then, having rapidly reviewed them all and found them all wanting, was, "Oh!"

Then, "Take your money," she cried, making a gesture as if to fling the packet of banknotes to the floor, and only then noticing that she must have somehow dropped them all during his embrace.

So then, "Bother me no more," she shrilled, turning on her heel.

"Wait!" the earl commanded coolly. "My card," he said calmly, presenting it to her, "for though you may have rejected one offer, we still have unfinished business."

"Ha!" Miss Dawkins replied, unimaginatively, even to her own ears. She methodically tore the small white placard into tiny bits and tossed them, like an insult, if not into his face, for she had an upbringing she couldn't surmount, then into the air, so that at least they fluttered down very nicely, she thought, between them. Then she spun round and flung open the door, shouldered past Mrs. Rogers, and then fairly flew up the staircase.

Everything they said of the Quality wasn't quite true, Mrs. Rogers thought glumly, for they clearly weren't blind to expense, since the earl thought nothing of promptly stooping and calmly gathering up all the bills the ungrateful ninny had dropped at his feet. But still, there was everything to be said for breeding. For then he gave another card to Mrs. Rogers, along with one of the notes, and said, so aloof and icy that it thrilled her to bits, "Here, my good woman. She may yet change her mind. Keep this for her against the day.

"Yes," he added so cynically, just as he ought when addressing an inferior such as herself, that it made her heart swell with happiness, "just the card, the money's for you. This time," he added obliquely, before he donned his high beaver hat, touched it in a sort of salute, and left her, impressed to near tears, and wondering at how any mortal girl could be so hardhearted and stupid as her lodger Miss Dawkins.

The seventh Earl of Clune had left an enormous, gloomy, lavishly furnished multiroomed town house in the heart of London for his successor, so naturally the eighth Earl of Clune passed most of his time in a smaller, comfortably furnished, and cheerful town house several blocks away. The smaller house was actually the more expensive one, the Earl of Clune's entailed property being in a neighborhood that was not quite so newly fashionable as the one he'd bought for himself shortly before he'd come into the title, and its simpler furnishings being more expensive because they were in the highest kick, his architect had assured him, of the latest fashion. But what he'd actually paid for was the comfort of chairs not so antique that their embroideries repelled booted feet, and carpets and furnishings that needed no protection from the sunshine his high wide new windows admitted, and paintings not so elderly that they refused to celebrate the same light and air he considered vital to his comfort.

His widowed mama and her companion dwelt in the ancestral mansion when they were in town. Not for reasons of status, for his mama didn't care a fig for such nonsense, but because she decided *someone* ought to inhabit the old place, and someone also had to be hostess at the formal dinner parties the new earl obviously could not give in what she considered to be his more rakish private bachelor quarters.

It would have disappointed his mama almost as much as it would have disillusioned such a dissimilar female as Mrs. Rogers, had they known it, but the earl had passed the last week in unremarkable fashion in his less-than-raffish quarters, doing nothing more shocking then reading a few racy books, and nothing more scandalous than having a few old army cronies over to reminisce with sottishly, a few nights past. Warm, saucy, yielding female companionship, the earl brooded as he settled down in his chair in his study on the fifth night of the less-than-hilarious week he'd just endured, was the last thing he'd exert himself for just now, though it was undoubtedly the foremost thing upon his mind.

She'd looked at the money as though it were manna, by God, he thought again; she'd scarcely looked anywhere else through the whole interview. Except into his eyes. He shifted uncomfortably and reminded himself yet again that despite her refusal, it was obvious that the chit was no better than she should be. For she was, as he continued to remind himself defensively, the unlikeliest-looking governess he'd ever seen, so she couldn't possibly have actually been one. Plus there was the incontrovertible evidence that she'd either no morals at all or extremely flexible ones, since if she hadn't designs on Theo herself, it was clear she'd been callous enough to take the boy's money for writing out a love letter she ought to have been ashamed to know he was sending to an even more experienced tart than herself. She never belonged in that low slum, he thought moodily, and never mind she kissed like an innocent, she'd never stopped him when he'd begun his offer, and a stone-deaf woman would have known what he was about by then. Probably, he thought self-righteously once again, she'd gone through the whole pantomime for spite, and turned him down only because she'd had a better offer.

He'd gotten through three pages of his book on Roman history, and a few dozen explicit fantasies of his own on quite a different subject, when the clock struck two chimes into a new day, and he heard his cousin Theo attempting to steal into the house. As the butler had come to the door and greeted him loudly, as instructed, and a footman was quick to inform him that his lordship awaited the pleasure of his company in the library, Lord Malverne wore a sulky expression as he came in to greet his cousin, having been, his cousin judged wisely, thwarted in more than his obvious attempt to get to his guestroom unnoticed.

"Is it cards, dice, horse- or womanflesh you've been unlucky with tonight, Theo?" the earl asked, barely raising his eyes to the young man who slouched into the room and settled sullenly into an adjacent chair.

"Sometimes," the young gentleman said unhappily, "nothing goes right."

"Too true," his cousin commented sagely, reaching into the pockets of his dressing gown and withdrawing a clutch of papers, "which is why I assumed you've avoided me so assiduously this past week. So I made a few inquiries, and can you guess what I discovered? All these, just imagine! Theo, my love, your revels now are ended."

"Now . . . but, Cole," Lord Malverne protested, wincing at the sight of all his unpaid chits from bootmakers, bookmakers, and tailors, come to haunt him in the night, "I get my quarterly in a matter of days. I'll make it up, I vow I will."

"True, true," the earl agreed, "but you'll not add to them any longer, either. I'm sorry, Theo, I said I'd look after you, but I'm no chaperon. I look foolish in crepe, for one thing, and I can't abide sitting by the wall while all the rest of you dance, for another. No, I can't forcibly keep you from your favorite haunts, and obviously I can't trust your word either. So it's off to Bath to your proud mama, my boy. I'm tossing you back to your family."

"Ah, Cole, beat me, stab me, but don't exile me, for love of God. I'm devilish sorry, I'll reform, promise," his cousin babbled in his dismay.

"Nothing so drastic. A few cups of the waters and a few

weeks in the countryside until school begins will do you a world of good. No, Theo," he said, his voice and face suddenly cold and serious, and thus effectively cutting off the young man's pleas, "it's to be done, and there's no hope for it. I'll allow you to make your own excuses to them, but that's the extent of my charity.

"By the by, Theo," the earl commented without seeming to look up from his book as his cousin began to creep, utterly dejected, from the room, causing the young man to look up with some sudden hope, "as I haven't seen you in a spell, only tell me one thing. I've been attempting to clear up that unfortunate business with Miss Dawkins. The governess," he said testily to his youthful relative's blank stare. "Ah yes, I see you remember now that you forgot to remember to settle that score as well. All I should like to know, to complete the business, is how much you paid her to write out that ridiculous love poem to the devine LaPoire for you."

"Money?" Theo said foolishly.

"I understand you don't recall faces, lad, but sums, I should think you'd be more careful of . . . how much did you pay her for the favor? I hardly think she'd risk copying out cloying love poems to an expensive harlot for an underage nobleman solely out of consideration for your big blue eyes, no matter what your doting mama claims."

The young gentleman paused, obviously thinking feverishly. He'd gotten a bit confused himself. He'd told Mama it was a debutante he'd had the governess write the poem out for; he'd told Cole it was for the heavenly LaPoire, which was only true, he thought indignantly; and he'd told the governess . . . yes, now he remembered.

"Well, ah, you see, Cole," Theo began in a tone of voice which made the earl sit up straight with a terrible sense of dark foreboding, which showed upon his face and made his cousin stammer the more, until the earl said, "Out with it," in such clear cold accents that his cousin's blood chilled enough to cool his overheated face, and he said, when he was able:

"I didn't precisely pay her, Cole, for she didn't know what she was doing, you see. It was more in the line of a favor to me. I never actually told her about LaPoire, as I told you, now you mention it, why, how could I? She was very ladylike, Cole,'' he added censoriously, much affronted at his relative's opinion of his ethics, ''and a governess, to boot. So instead I told her,'' he said, avoiding his cousin's dark black stare, ''that it was for a very young French girl I'd just met, a true lady, born in France, and young and innocent, but French too, that is to say . . .'' His voice trailed off in the silence which greeted his statement.

Lord Malverne noted, even in the yellow glow of dancing gaslight his cousin had just installed, that the earl's face was grim, and for such a dark-complexioned fellow, oddly white.

''Ah, Theo,'' the earl closed his eyes and said, whispering each word like the shivers they sent up his listener's spine, ''I think I shall beat you after all, and stab you too. For I begin to think exile's far too kind a fate for either you, or,'' he added so quietly his cousin was sure later it was only a low echo of the moan of the late-night wind outside that he'd heard, ''me.''

4

"Yer hair," the young boy said knowingly, "too tight. Much too tight. You'd scare crows."

The young woman spun around and faced toward where her critic sat, legs swinging, upon the kitchen table. He missed not one bite from the apple he was untidily devouring as she made a face at him.

"Alfie," Victoria then said patiently, "a governess or a companion is *not* an opera dancer or a woman of the streets. I'm supposed to look competent. Respectable. Worthy."

"Aye," Alfie said as best he could around a very large portion of apple that he'd bitten off in one piece, "but I never heard that respectable is the same as ugly. And no one," he added wisely after he'd somehow miraculously managed to completely swallow down the mouthful of fruit, "wants a nasty bit of goods littering up their house, no matter how 'worthy.' " He mimicked the word in the precise accents the young woman had used. " 'Cause," he went on impeturbably in the more usual accents he affected, "there's no law as says a good woman has got to be an 'orrful-looking one, is there? Now," he added generously, "I ain't saying you'd be quick to be hired if you was to grab the eye the minute you walked in the door. But I am saying there's no harm, and only a good bit of good, in looking yuman. Pleasant-like," he explained ruminatively, in response to Miss Dawkins' thoughtful expression.

"Oh yes, Miss Victoria," the little blond girl beside her said. "Oh yes, just so, oh it's much better," she sighed as Victoria loosened some of her heavy hair from its tightly bound knot so that it bloused out in freedom, in soft swelling waves around the sides of her face, "but wouldn't it be nice if you could go looking like a princess, with your hair hanging loose altogether, all about your shoulders like it ort . . . 'awt' to do," the child corrected herself quickly, looking up to Miss Dawkins for approval.

It was Alfie who nodded his pleasure at his sister's correct diction, and he grinned back at Victoria conspiratorially after she'd smiled fondly at the girl. Alfie had a remarkable gift, an uncanny ability to reproduce any sort of speech he heard, so that he spoke in the cant of the neighborhood when he wished, and could ape the best-bred boy in London when it suited him. But he recognized that his siblings did not have such a talent. And so, as he told Victoria that very first night, after they'd cleared the table of the crumbs of their meal, one of the best reasons for their friendship was precisely that it was clear she was used to better than slum brats, for then she could teach Bobby and Sally, and maybe even eventually Baby, respectable ways to speak and act.

That was the reason he hadn't been in the least offended when, in her initial shock at the sight of the bounty laid out for their dining pleasure, she'd accused him of having stolen half the meal he'd provided her. Similarly, he'd simply beamed when she'd been staggered at his proud claim that every last bit of it had been thieved. For, as she discovered later, the entire evening had been set up as a bizarre sort of interview. The proper young lady next door's repugnance for dining on contraband, her horror at the insanitary conditions that prevailed in the room, and her wincing at every mispronunciation the children used was precisely what Alfie had been looking for in a confederate.

"Now, miss," he'd said, resting his elbows on the table beside her as she finished up the meal she was at least flexible enough to realize ought not to be wasted, however gotten, since it couldn't be returned anyhow, "what it is, is that Mum's been sick, still is sick, and the children needs seeing to bad, they need some grown-up caring for them, they needs schooling best of all. I can see to the food in their bellies, and I can scrag anyone's got dirty plans for them, y'see. But if they's got education, they can get good posts when they're able, so they ought to speak good and look good and use all the right words and cutlery, if you get my meaning. And though I can copy, mind, I can't know everything, for there ain't too many of the Quality comes here I can learn too much good manners from. They don't exactly come down here," he said wryly, "to use their best bibs and tuckers, if you follow."

As Victoria sat and listened and wondered at the child who spoke so confidently and knowingly about "the children" he wished her to instruct, Alfie went on to outline his master plan. He'd provide the food, and see to the ready for her rent, if she would take up her duties with them. The argument that ensued lasted until near dawn, growing both more heated and more hushed as the night progressed, in consideration of the other children, so that they could creep off to their beds when they wearied of watching the two combatants with wide and wondering eyes.

In the end, as all wise adversaries will, they reached a workable compromise. Victoria would provide the instruction for the children. Alfie would provide food and the blunt for the rent. But the stealing would stop, because Victoria had brought up the pithy point that no matter how clever a dipping cove, as Alfie bragged he was, an Alfie in Newgate could provide for no one at all. And she'd won the point entirely by stopping his protests of excellence with the observation that aptitude had nothing to do with luck. She tossed away examples from the Good Book, which she realized wasn't the sort of literature Alfie was impressed with, bucolic vineyards and rural shepherds being worlds removed from the grim realities of the slums of London town. Putting it bluntly and in terms he could see the logic in, she pointed out the fact that luck had an evil way of running out, or else there wouldn't be so many clever men hanged, or stupid runners with pearl pins to fasten cravats, instead of ropes, about their own fat necks.

Sally would continue to peddle flowers and ribands and anything else that could be gotten cheap and sold high on the street, Bobby would continue to assist Mr. Mercer, the greengrocer, in his stall at the weekly market, and Mrs. Gibbs, the laundress, in her rooms, every day. And Alfie would forage and deal and trade, as he did best, in order to bring in some money. For her part, Victoria insisted, she would also give whatever lessons local inhabitants wanted, at an hourly rate. But she would continue to look for a steady position with a good family, for if she secured one, she could contribute far more to their partnership.

And partnership it would still be, she insisted, overriding all of Alfie's protests at her not having to continue their association if she could find a prime place again, as he wasn't the sort of layabout such as thrived in the neighborhood, the kind of fellow who would live on a female's earnings and do nothing in return. He didn't use terminology quite that polite, but Victoria didn't chastise him for it; his emotions about the matter were too painful and sincere for that. But she won her way for two reasons. The one they both acknowledged aloud was her claim that she considered Alfie and his siblings to already be family, which she needed, since she had so little family of her own left now, and sorely missed them. The other, remaining unspoken, was moot, since neither of them knew how she'd ever get a decent position without a letter of good character to recommend her, anyway.

But now, more than a week after Miss Dawkins had received her second unorthodox job opportunity, that one refused as it was proffered by the Earl of Clune, she was dressing to go out for an interview for another post, this one again offered by the Earl of Clune. This one, she hoped, was a respectable offer. But in any case, there was, she thought, gazing into the looking glass Alfie had somehow procured for her, no help for it. She must go and find out.

Without theft, the new association between the Johnson

children and the governess next door was proving to be an unprofitable venture. In fact, it was rapidly going into bankruptcy. No one in Tothill Fields had any use for lessons in deportment, elocution, watercolors, or pianoforte. Not one of them had the slightest interest in history, unless they knew some rich cove would pay if they promised to keep it under their hat. Since all life here was negotiated down to the ha'penny, mathematics was too fine an art in the streets for it to need to be taught, English itself was enough of a foreign language for most of the residents to get their tongues around, literature that rose above caricature was too deep to even contemplate. And dancing was the Lord's own gift to the poor; it would be pure madness to pay for the teaching of it. Besides, little resembling the art of the dance as Miss Dawkins recognized it was practiced in her new surroundings.

There was no work to be had governessing for Miss Dawkins, aside from her hire from Alfie. He, in turn, found as so many others, adult and child, had done before him, and exactly as he'd tried to explain to Miss Dawkins it would be, that hereabouts, honest employment never paid enough for an honest living.

The children did their tasks, Miss Dawkins took her daily constitutional to the employment bureau, but their evening meal, their main repast, grew smaller every day.

Victoria knew it wouldn't be long until the other major shareholder in her newly incorporated trust began secretly plying his trade again. She couldn't bear the thought of Alfie in irons, Alfie in captivity, or Alfie transported or hanged for his sin of providing for his family's hunger in he way he knew best. The law of the land was as harsh as the deprivations which caused such crimes, for malefactors of any age. It had also become absolutely true that Victoria now felt herself a member of the little clan, and loved her newfound family as profoundly as though she'd known them from the cradle onward. Now she felt the full weight of her responsibility for them, even it were a self-imposed duty. She gazed at herself in the glass and heaved a heartfelt sigh that turned to a cough, for the task before her.

"You didn't drink up all the lemon and honey," Alfie accused, stung by her carelessness into completely disregarding the last of his apple. Both Sally and Bobby looked up at her in horror at that, for they both knew only too well the terrible fate that could befall a person who began to cough and couldn't stop it.

"No, no," Victoria assured them, "I finished every last drop of it, and I feel quite the thing this morning. Heavens," she said, staring down into all the little white faces filled with concern, "can't a person clear her throat without all of you playing nursemaid?"

They chuckled at that, but it was true that they had helped her when she'd been ill earlier in the week, as they'd helped her, it seemed, since the hour she'd met up with them. For she'd gotten a streaming cold, and seeing that, they'd hurried to concoct and urge her to drink hot mulled wine, and donated heaps of blankets for her to pile over her bed to "sweat 'er all out," as Sally had inelegantly put it as she'd bustled about her room filled with importance, like a miniature ministering angel. And it would have worked, too, and she'd have been cured in a trice, Victoria admitted, if it weren't for her inexperience with life as she found it, and her own missishness.

Alfie wasn't far wrong when he'd claimed in disgust that she washed more often than the family cat, even though Sally defended her by allowing as how Miss Victoria smelled very good for all, before Miss Victoria stifled her giggles and corrected Sally's grammar. But it was certainly silly for her to have washed her hair in the evening, for all she'd felt grubby after she'd woken from her wine-soaked and heavily blanketed slumbers, entirely forgetting she'd have no sunlight, nor any fire to simulate it, to dry it in. Because the night had turned chill and then it had been impossible to sleep with that great damp, cold weight set upon her head. And then, of course, to sit up all the next night, trembling with disgust and terror, that was, in the clear light of morning and the children's amazement, foolishness itself, it seemed.

For "o' course there was rats 'ere, great walloping big 'uns too," Alfie said in exasperation. Why else did she think Baby slept in his box on top of the table, " 'stead of 'neath it, where he'd be less likely to fall down and break somethin' important?" And didn't she know that one of them always kept awake while the others kipped out? She might have only noticed the local livestock that night she'd sat up with all that wet hair on her head, but they'd always known who they'd shared rooms with, and Miss Victoria was only lucky her unknown roommates hadn't thought to take a nip out of her pretty little nose, Alfie scoffed. Then it was decidedly lowering for Miss Victoria to have Sally shyly pluck at her dress and whisper to her to never mind Alfie, miss, they never took after grown-ups much, they truly didn't.

So the cold in the head slowly took firmer hold, and perhaps it was the broken, sleep-starved nights that made matters worse. Or it might have been the additional fact that Miss Victoria claimed it was the cold that caused her dwindling appetite when she didn't eat her share of their diminishing dinners that contributed to the problem. But after only a week, she feared she was growing very ill indeed.

Her throat ached almost as much as her head did, she would have gladly donated her stuffed nose to any rats that might relieve her of the burden of breathing through it, and each word she uttered felt as though it were being torn from out her throat, it left it so sore, that is, until she lost her voice entirely. But at least, then when it came back, she thought with a certain gallows humor, she had a nice new cough to give it resonance.

Thus it was five days, a full five days passed and wasted, until she felt able to drag herself out to haunt the estimable Misses Parkinson's employment bureau again. Despite the way she felt, Victoria dressed as nicely as she was able and hauled herself out-of-doors because she firmly believed that the only way to better things was to attempt to better things. The only new thing that awaited her was the offer of a post as a companion, paying an astronomically high salary, and it was offered by, of course, no less a personage, Miss Lavinia Parkinson had crowed, than the Earl of Clune.

Two days after Miss Dawkins had laughed hollowly in her employment counselor's face, thereby effectively, she later realized, diminishing her chances to find gainful employment there ever again, or at least until she felt well enough to explain herself at length and most contritely, Mrs. Rogers appeared, for the second time in a decade, upon the upper floor of her boardinghouse. This time she bore a message which her grim look told her lodger she would do well not to ignore. It was a brief note, of the nonmonetary sort, from Mrs. Rogers' new favorite, a noble rascal whose exploits now quite eclipsed Prinny's in her humble estimation. It was, of course, from the Earl of Clune.

It said, with a brevity and lack of grace that would have thrilled Mrs. Rogers had she been able to read it, or do more than caress the heavily embossed crest it bore:

"Miss Dawkins, I have a position to offer you. One that is unexceptionable. Clune."

At the bottom, the stiff page bore yet one more item scrawled in heavy black ink: "There is also the matter of a reference."

For such a summons, Miss Dawkins thought, princes and popes would rush to obedience.

And so would governesses who'd taken on responsibility for four delightful children who had so far actually taken on all the responsibility for a great lump of a useless girl who couldn't lift a finger to help them as yet, Victoria thought as she dressed for the visit.

"You'll do," Alfie admitted at last, and Victoria spun round and bestowed such a smile upon him that he ducked his head and pretended that he'd dropped the apple core that he'd swallowed seconds before. But the dark green walking dress that was supposed to make her appear to be dignified and proper did just that, though the folds draped about her slender body could not deny the shapely form beneath, nor could its cool and mossy hue help but point out all the gold light that danced in her clean brown hair, as well as the vivid purity of her white complexion. It must have been the excitement that sent high color to her cheeks and caused her oddly saffron-hued eyes to glow.

"You just take care, 'ear?" Alfie said gruffly.

Then he went once again into the litany he chanted at his employee and partner every time he saw her about to set her foot outside the door. She had more book learning than anyone he'd ever known so well, he thought with exasperation each time he spoke to her, but about the things that *counted,* she was a complete flat. There were instructions she must get through her pretty head, if she were to come back safely to them each night. And as Miss Dawkins placed her bonnet atop that neatly coiffed head, Alfie went over the warnings again, as the other children nodded wisely.

She must walk quickly and with purpose, since a female loitering was clearly advertising her wares. She must never stop when spoken to, unless she wished to be more than spoken to, by anyone, of any age or sex. For any female might know, Alfie had pointed out innumerable times, that there were gents who looked like toffs who were anything but. But here, there were also other females who looked like ladies, or even gentle grandmothers, who'd be on the lookout to snare her for their own evil uses.

Miss Dawkins had looked blank the first time her young mentor attempted to subtly inform her of such dangers. Then Bobby had spoken up to whisper huskily, "Them as run an accommodation 'ouse is what 'e means, miss."

"Er, a nunnery, Miss Victoria, is what 'e's speaking of," Sally had volunteered helpfully, in low nervous tones.

"A snoozing ken, a grinding 'ouse, a pushing school, can't y'see?" Bobby had cried desperately, to Victoria's continuing expression of ignorance.

"A bawdy 'ouse!" Alfie had finally shouted.

"Ooo, Alfie, what you said!" Sally had exclaimed in shock, as Bobby too looked grieved at his brother's language in front of the lady, and even Alfie himself had seemed embarrassed.

After that, Victoria had agreed to let Alfie take her out upon the streets with him so that he could identify some of those deceptive females for her. Most of them, he'd admitted, would be unwilling to actually kidnap a female from this district, because they'd be afraid of what sort of retribution the girl's possibly equally vicious and violent family might exact from them. In a way, Alfie had said wisely, a stray rich young lady had more to worry about from the likes of them than a poor local girl did. But some, he'd warned, to keep her from overconfidence, were so powerful as to be extra daring, and might reckon a poor family would settle for money in the hand for a girl stolen and then started in business at higher wages than they could ever have hoped to negotiate for her themselves.

So he described the best, or worst, of them to her: the deceptively kind, elderly, and highly respectable-looking Mother Carey, who made occasional forays into the district for recruits for her expensive house of pleasure. He described her so many times that Victoria almost saw the wicked woman reaching out for her constantly in her broken nightmare-glazed sleep. That imagined falsely benevolent, genteel aged face crowned with gray hair became worse to her at those times than did the reality of the rats rustling in the walls. Miss Dawkins was easily able to reassure her anxious little clan as she stepped out the door to go to her interview that she'd be cautious, very cautious indeed.

But she was not so cautious as to actually take a hackney to the interview as they'd requested her to do. The children, after all, watching her departure from the window, wouldn't be disappointed, since they'd know that she'd have to walk on a fair way until she reached a district respectable enough to have carriages prowling for hire. Once she'd left the grim streets far behind, she decided that considering their finances, the cost of riding would be so high a price to pay for indolence that she'd rather crawl all the miles to the Earl's elegant address than summon such an extravagance.

True, it was a mizzling damp day, and true also that she'd not felt very well when she'd risen this morning. But now the walking seemed to be doing her some good, for she could swear she felt lighter with each step she took, and it didn't seem to be only because the prospect of finally getting a position or a suitable reference cheered her. Perhaps the moisture in the dank air had eased her previously constricted chest, or it might have been that the motion of her limbs as she paced forward drove the chills from her body, but now she began to feel as warm as if it were a fine summer's day, as blithe and light-headed as though she'd sipped fine French wine this morning instead of the chocolate Alfie brought in for the family. Indeed, she almost removed her pelisse, until she realized it wouldn't look right, however unusually, unseasonably warm it seemed to have become.

He'd written that it was an unexceptionable offer he had to make to her this time, but with such a gentleman, with the nobility as wild as she'd always heard it was, one could never be sure. That was why she hadn't told the children about his previous offer; she didn't wish to get their hopes up. Then too, in some small corner of her mind she'd also wondered if they, with their benighted background, wouldn't consider her an idiot for not taking him up on it, then or now, whatever it had or still entailed. But then, she wondered much the same herself.

He was wealthy; she was almost starving. He was youthful, undeniably attractive, well-bred, and cleanly. Although she was young and adequately educated, she was, she considered, only passing fair. This not very outstanding virtue was certainly transitory, but while it lasted, right now it couldn't be denied that it seemed she had little else to make her way in the world with any longer. And there was no denying the fact that the gentleman had been honest with her, and if she were to be honest with herself, he had appealed to her no little bit.

But she certainly was an idiot, she almost giggled to herself as she walked the miles to the best part of town, if she even seriously considered such a thing for the space of a moment. She knew nothing of the talents he would require of her. Although she was well-educated, she had the uneasy feeling that in such matters the youngest of the Johnson children, save of course for Baby, knew more, if only from observation and hearsay, about the particulars and specifics of such activities than she did. It was only her real hunger for sustenance for both the body and the spirit, she told herself, combined with her overactive imagination, that could account for her countenancing such an arrangement for even one mad moment.

For she realized that however pleasant her wild fancies might paint such an occupation in the frightening, lonely hours of the night, it would be in actuality much the same employment as the dreaded, dangerous Mother Carey might have in store for her. Her innate practicality also told her that even if the earl's shocking offer were to be initially different, only a fool would expect fidelity from such an employer, and were she to be that fool, were she to go that route, it wouldn't be long until she were little different from any of the females who practiced similar arts in dark doorways near Mrs. Rogers' rooming house.

She began to walk still more rapidly when she realized that even if the post the earl had offered were to become a lifelong situation for her, performed faithfully until retirement, she would still be little different morally than any of those lost back-alley trollops.

But this time he'd implied that he'd summoned her forth for actual respectable employment, and so she believed him, or so she had to do. In truth, in her innermost secret thoughts, the idea of continuing poverty for herself and the children was so frightening she couldn't promise herself that what she refused today she would not be only too eager to accept tomorrow. This was especially so, she thought as she hurried onward, despite how difficult it had suddenly become to breathe in the damp morning air and the sharp pain that grew in her ribs as she walked faster, when one considered an offer that came from a fellow as powerful and persistent as this gentleman, the Earl of Clune.

The dark gentleman tried to retain his civility, and so he took a turn around his desk again, refusing to look back immediately at the small, scrawny white-haired old female who had just attacked him. She hadn't taken a step toward him or shied any lethal object at him, except for the accusations she made in her high, shrill accents. If only she were a gentleman, he thought angrily, he might have leveled her; if she were only a lady he would have done the same with one wry comment. But she was only a very old female, a dependent at that, and so the Earl of Clune could do no more than to cast one beleaguered look toward his mama, standing at the old harridan's side.

"Oh, come now, Comfort dear, you shouldn't say such things to Cole," that handsome, stately middle-aged woman said reasonably. "He'd have to be loose in his loft to bring such a female here. This is the earl's house, not his bachelor quarters," and then, realizing from her son's muted groan of displeasure that she'd once again said the thing she'd thought rather than the thing she ought, Mrs. Haverford continued rapidly, "and it isn't for us to tell him what to do, you know. Not even I," she said a bit more forcefully, "I, who am his mother, have the right to do so, for it is his home, my dear."

Mrs. Haverford cast a sly look toward her son after she said this, and awaited his acknowledgment of a mission nicely accomplished.

"Oh indeed," the pinch-faced little old female agreed at once, before the earl could respond with a grateful smile, as she drew her shawl more tightly around her meager shoulders, "no, no, of course not, he's a grown man, as well as a great nobleman, he's entitled to do as he wishes. I should never presume to dictate to him, indeed, I should never dream that I had the right. But then too, *I* do not have to stay on to be insulted and victimized, even though I am obviously his inferior, only a poor old female, entirely dependent upon his and your good graces. So of course I shall not argue, Roberta, and if you wish to let me go, I shall leave at once, and you may take on this young *female* in my stead. I don't doubt she'll be able to run to your bidding faster than I can ever hope to do, any longer at least," she concluded, then pressed a handkerchief to her face to stifle a sob, and thus effectively stifled all other comment and movement in the room for a few moments.

"I did not say," the earl repeated wearily, "that I planned to hire Miss Dawkins as your replacement as my mama's companion. I only mentioned in passing that as I've had more difficulty than I thought, finding another decent post for the girl, and as our family owes her a post, and as obviously, I too hastily summoned her here in the expectation of presenting her with one, you might consider visiting with Cousin Emma, whom you've said you're fond of, or another of your cousins, for a short time. While you were gone, the young lady could stay on here with Mama. Then, when we found her a position, she could move on, and you could move back. It would simply ease matters for me. That is all."

"All," the elderly woman whimpered, putting a world of sorrow into that simple utterance before she whipped the handkerchief away from her grief-ravaged face and cried, "all! I've been with your mama for years, my lord, and I realized from the beginning of it all last year, that now the family's been elevated, I might no longer suit. But I implore you, my lord, think hard before you do this thing. This female may have been wronged by young Theo, but from what I can see, you may be more grievously harmed. I know the address that summons went to. In fact, the footman whistled when he was told where to deliver it, and the staff were all wondering if he'd return in one piece.

"What sort of young woman resides in such a low slum? What sort of diseases, what types of uncleanliness of mind or body shall you bring to your mama by bringing such a creature here?"

"At least I can see that I scarcely have to bring my mama to the theater this season, seeing the sort of tragedy her companion can enact at the drop of a hat," the earl replied, much goaded.

"Unkind, Cole," his mama said gently. "It's just that Comfort is high-strung and very protective of me. But he's right, you know," she said, turning to the older woman. "He's given his word and it's a debt he must honor. If she's obviously a low creature, he can give her a sum of money and let her go back from whence she came. But I suggest that if the child is decent, there's no reason why she can't stay on here, as well as you, for a space, Comfort. She can assist you, but if you find that too objectionable, my dear," Mrs. Haverford added, with the rare but effective control she could sometimes summon, "why, then, it might not be wrong for you to visit your cousin for a few weeks now, after all."

Miss Comfort, companion and distant relative to Mrs. Haverford, paused, and then swallowed what she was about to say. She avoided the dark and fulminating stare of the earl, and looking up at her kinswoman, sniffed and said only, almost meekly, "Very well, Roberta."

"And I believe we ought to go and let you get on with it, Cole," Mrs. Haverford said quickly, seeing that her companion was now about to take up a position in a nearby chair so as to watch the interview with the unfortunate young unemployed governess, which was to take place in a very short while, as it went forth. Then, as her son shot her an undeniably grateful look, she drew her companion along with her as they left the earl's study, however unwilling that old female seemed to be as she went with her.

Thus when Miss Dawkins finally arrived at the earl's town house, only ten minutes late despite her difficulty in walking, she discovered, after the lofty butler took her pelisse and her bonnet and most of her courage, and showed her into the earl's private study, that he was quite alone.

The earl, rising to greet her, quite forgetting her inferior status, found that though she'd obviously been shedding weight she didn't seem particularly deprived, since she was in glowing good looks. In fact, her color was so high it was almost as if twin spots of rouge had been rashly applied to her cheeks, and her eyes positively glittered with light.

He sat again and motioned her to take a seat in a chair he'd placed to the side of his desk.

"How do you do, Miss Dawkins. I'm glad you answered my cryptic summons," he said calmly.

She only nodded.

"I apologize for putting it so curtly," he said abruptly when she ventured no greeting in return, "but then, I couldn't very well put it charmingly. Not after our last conversation, for then I didn't think you would've come. So I tried to put it in the least seductive manner possible," he said, becoming a little annoyed at her silence, since he'd paused sufficiently for her to comment after each statement he'd made.

"Oh, you succeeded," she finally said in a lower, huskier voice than he remembered.

He frowned, wondering now if her high color wasn't due to more than cosmetics, and if her silence weren't the sort of protective muteness a person affects when she knows she can't trust a spirits-loosened tongue. It certainly wasn't a chilly enough morning to account for that bright flush upon her cheek.

"But I'm sorry to say," he went on, deciding that he would try to give her the money and then send her on her way after all, for although he still didn't know her game, it looked as though Old Cold Comfort was right, as he'd been right originally, and the chit was no better than she should be, "that the post I thought I had secured for you when I sent you the note has fallen through. Once again, I've something else to offer you, though, and it won't be a wasted trip if you don't insist that it be," he said, opening a drawer, preparing to write her a bank draft, when she suddenly arose.

"Oh no," she cried in agitation, "I can't, I could not, indeed, you don't know how much I wish I could, if only for the children's sake, but I can't, I won't be your mistress, your lordship, not today. But perhaps in a week or two . . ." She wavered on her feet as she seemed to contemplate something very confusing, and then she said weakly, "Though I can't promise that either, I'm afraid. It is very warm in here, I think," she whispered in a panicky voice, and she turned to go. Then she seemed to stumble, before she fell to the floor in front of his desk.

When he reached her and drew her into his arms, raising her head and supporting it, he realized he could scent nothing on her person but a faint lilac perfume, and nothing at all of the aroma of juniper berries, or malt or hops or grain, or any of the several spirits he'd thought he would detect. But in the space of a few moments as he attempted to rouse her, he could feel the intense dry heat emanating from her body, and realized suddenly to his shame both why she had seemed so distracted and why she'd looked to be in such high good health, for the girl burned with fever.

He bore her up in his arms and strode out into the hallway. He asked the butler to fetch the housekeeper to show him which bed to lay her in, and then ordered a footman to summon the doctor. His mama appeared from the hallway, a hundred questions apparent on her distressed countenance, and Miss Comfort, at her side, gazed upon the girl in his arms as though she was doing something unspeakably vulgar there.

The housekeeper spoke of a room close by his mama's, and he was about to bear Miss Dawkins there, when she stirred in his clasp and opened her eyes and then struggled to be set down. He stood her on her feet carefully, taking care to keep his arm about her shoulders.

"You're not well," he said slowly and distinctly, as she gazed fearfully at the strangers that crowded about her. "You must stay here with us for a while, until you feel more the thing."

"Oh no, I cannot," she cried. "The children, I must get back to the children. Oh, my poor children, they'll be all alone, they'll worry after me."

The earl opened his eyes wide and his hand tightened on her shoulder, but then he said gently, "I'll send to them, you cannot go now."

But, "The children!" gasped Miss Comfort. "*Miss* Dawkins, is it? *Unemployed* governess. Ha, what did I tell you!"

Before the earl or his mama could hush the exultant old woman, Miss Dawkins, shaking her head to clear it, turned to gaze at the speaker.

"Ah!" she cried then in great fright, drawing back. "Oh no, only let me go from here. What do you want of me? Ah, please, let me loose, for see, it's Mother Carey who seeks to imprison me!"

Blind terror showed in Miss Dawkins' eyes before they closed again and she sank again into the earl's waiting arms. As he lifted her, to follow the housekeeper to the chamber being readied, he heard Miss Comfort ask wonderingly, "Who is this Mother Carey she takes me for?"

"A notorious whoremonger," the earl replied, tossing the remark over his shoulder as he ascended the stair.

"Oh, Cole," moaned his mama, as her companion grew livid with indignation before she checked, and then cried out triumphantly.

"Aha! See? *Just* as I said!"

5

The carriage was pulled down the street by a team of blooded horses who stepped proudly and held their noble heads almost as high as their liveried driver did. The coach bore a crest upon its shining sides, and its polished surface threw back the light of the sun so brilliantly that it was jarring to see that the reflections caught and held upon its gleaming exterior were only those of some of the lowest streets in the slums of town.

The elegant conveyance was not a common sight in such a district, and so perhaps only because two sizable stalwart footmen clung to the rear step, and an uncommonly aggressive-looking young tiger shared the high seat with the driver, the coach attracted no more than envy from those that beheld its passage. Since there was obviously no profit to be taken from merely seeing such a vision, those that noted its passage tended to dismiss it after a few blinks, and some muttered comments about "nobs out for a bit of fun."

For the coach, with all its fittings, proclaimed that it was the property of a nobleman of high rank in the realm, with all the might and rights and funds that such a position commanded. In this England of 1815, in this impoverished corner of London, this meant that the fortunate gentleman who sat within its velvety depths had countless choices: he might do anything here, from purchasing children to selling his soul, with little expectation of interference from any other mortal man. It was only wasteful, then, the Earl of Clune thought wryly, that all he was about to attempt to be was a superior sort of removal man.

Miss Dawkins, the doctor had said, must be easy in her mind if she were to have any fair chance at recuperation. It was, the fellow had said with a shake of his head for the limits of his art, yet too early to ascertain whether she had contracted a dangerous mortal pneumonia, or an inflammation of the lungs, or merely congestion that rest and medication might soon put right. Therefore it was fortunate that she'd obviously had a good start in life with proper care and nourishment before she'd come to her present state of health, or her current living conditions. He'd added this last bit, along with an odd look to Miss Comfort, when she'd helpfully supplied that piece of residential information, even interrupting him as he'd been attempting to inform the earl and his mama of the young woman's condition to do so. But he insisted the evidence of such a superior upbringing was unmistakable. It had been a strong young heart he'd laid his ear to, the feverishly warm skin was clear and clean, and it was rich red blood that caused the blush she'd borne all through his examination.

For, as he'd then patiently explained to Miss Comfort, there was no question the lass would have little chance at survival if she'd originally sprung from such poverty. There was no truth, he'd sighed, to the fallacy current among the upper classes that held the poor were more vigorous, and, growing weedlike, were naturally less susceptible to diseases than their betters were. If Miss Comfort wished to see that for herself, he added bitterly, she might visit the infirmary he ran in the poorer section of town one day, or better still, come with him now to potter's field, to see the amazing number of all of those supposedly thriving slum-bred rudely healthy babes and their mamas, and their siblings and papas, where they all slept arow, in hundreds of rows, forever.

And again, no, he'd stated, grinning as though extraordinarily pleased with Miss Comfort's next question, even though by then he'd have had every right to be annoyed with her constant interjections, he believed what the girl claimed was true. Because, although he couldn't swear to it of course, since he hadn't carried out that intimate an examination (not having been told of the necessity for such), he very much doubted that the child had ever borne a child, or had ever even been in that happy state of expectation. Then in reply to her further doubts on the subject, he'd laid down his hat as though preparing for a lecture, and lowering his voice confidentially as though speaking to a colleague, he'd informed Miss Comfort that he based his opinion upon sound observations. There was, for example, he'd explained, the fact that he hadn't observed any of the usual signs of such a past history, such as enlarged or darkened nipples, for example, or stretched marks on her . . .

And then the earl cut him off in mid-sentence before the horrified Miss Comfort became his next patient. The earl had to struggle to conceal the same delight that the doctor showed at his foolproof method of ending importunate inquiries, and as Miss Comfort gasped for air at the indelicacy of the discourse and resorted to her salts, he escorted the chuckling physician to the door.

But the good doctor had told him privately and seriously as he'd left that there was no question but that the girl needed to be made more comfortable in her mind if ever any of his broths and potions were to have even a chance to be of any benefit to her.

Miss Dawkins seemed as appalled as Miss Comfort was when the earl entered her bedchamber. But that may have been because Miss Comfort had been reduced to hovering in the hall, having been banned from the sickroom because of the fright her imagined resemblance to a procuress produced in the patient. For the earl's mama only nodded with satisfaction as he came in. Then she continued telling the young woman sitting in the guest bed, wrapped in one of her own dressing gowns, that it was useless to argue against staying on with them, since she and her son were convinced they were entirely responsible for the sad pass she'd come to. And to deny this, she said haughtily, was to imply that the noble Haverford family did not honor their debts. The earl smiled at how suddenly top-lofty and regal his mama, who still grumbled whenever Miss Comfort reminded her that she ought to call her eldest "Clune" instead of "Cole" in front of strangers, could become when trying to prove a point. But a look into Miss Dawkins' eyes, glittering with fever and glassy with her attempts to sit upright and speak sense, robbed the moment of all its humor for him.

She'd had only two wishes, and when he'd sincerely assured her that they'd immediately be seen to, she'd finally allowed herself to lie back against the pillows, and then let her trembling hand be guided around the glass that held the sleeping draft, and obediently drank it all down. Then, with the repeated echoes of his promises in her ears, she closed her eyes in repose at last.

Only two wishes, the earl mused as he was driven to his destination to do her bidding. Even Aladdin had presumed to beg three. The first was that "my children," who were, as she'd explained, an assortment of infants she'd been looking after who dwelt in rooms near to her in her lodging house, be advised of her fate and assured that she'd return to them as soon as she was able. That, the earl was prepared to send a footman to accomplish.

But then she'd spoken almost shamefacedly of the box in her room that contained her treasures, and he'd known he must perform the errand himself. They were "rubbishy treasures," she'd admitted with the ghost of a smile, trinkets and mementos signifying nothing in worldly terms, but they were hers and all she had and she didn't want to lose them or leave them to the discretion of strangers who might paw through them after invading her empty room. And so she wished they might be given to the children to keep safely until her return. It wasn't only because she'd not, perhaps because of her feverish state, named him a "stranger" that the earl was being driven to a district wherein even his thoroughbred nags disliked to set their hooves. It was because in that moment she'd reminded him of his own lost treasures that he hadn't preserved as carefully as she attempted to keep hers, although it might have been that he'd loved them twice as well.

His had been, he recollected even now as precisely as if he'd just opened the lid of the old ornate bonbon tin he'd carefully hoarded them in over the years, a wonderful trove. He could still list them, even as he could see them still in his mind's eye so perfectly he could almost touch them as he'd so often done when he'd lifted them out to finger in wonder at his luck and taste in finding them, for each had its story and reason for being, as much so as any human thing had.

There had been: a brass button from his father's regimental coat (for his mama had all his medals); a bent and burnished half-coin which bore the imprint of a half-face, the old golden profile, he was sure, of the Roman ruler of the long-vanished centurion who'd carried it on his travels to the barbaric isles of Britain; a singularly lovely tiny thread-waxing reel, with, to be sure, some nicks on its flowery enameled front, an odd thing for a boy to value, until you turned it over and saw the only slightly damaged enameled view of Venice, where that boy dreamed of going one day; a faceted steel marcasite shoe buckle, taken for diamonds when it was found in the road, kept for its glitter when its face was washed, in the innocent hopes that one day its mate would be found so they might be presented to mama as a gift; a small warped gilt frame that had lost its portrait somewhere in history; and other similar choice items, as well as a staggering assortment of unique natural found objects—feathers, shells, oddly shaped nuts, bizarre glinting stones.

They'd been actual treasures, he'd thought when he'd been fourteen, and even now, in his voluptuous coach, tended by all his servants, the eighth Earl of Clune continued to regard them as such.

Those fifteen years ago, when he'd realized that all hopes were dashed and that he would have to leave the home he'd known since birth, he'd taken some comfort from the fact that the box would go with him. Nothing else except his memories would. The manor, the home farm, the stables with whatever few cattle remained, the furniture, the art on the walls, the draperies, carpets, and furnishings even to the bed in which he'd slept since he'd been breached, all, all would remain, save for his dog, and he allowed to go only because he'd had no more pedigree than the chap who'd purchased everything the family had to sell in order to go on as a family together.

"Face it, Roberta," the seventh Earl of Clune had said impatiently to his mama as she sat before his desk, "Paul is gone, you've four children to feed and educate, and no man to help you. The manor can't support you, the sale of it can, and nicely too, in the cottage at Weyhill. It makes perfect sense, your solicitors were right, Paul left you nothing but the children. I recommend your putting the place on the block immediately, with all its contents. Unless," he'd said easily, too easily, so easily that even her young son, sitting quietly in a corner of the study, looked up from contemplation of coming personal disaster at his words, "unless of course you're willing to try something else, something more venturesome perhaps, some other kind of arrangement?"

Mama had been lovely then, the earl thought now, remembering again the rage which had warred with the shame he'd felt at the earl's words, and the look he'd surprised for a moment on the heavy, broad face of the older man. Mama had never been beautiful—no woman so tall, however shapely and graceful, so dark, however pure her skin, with such marked features, however classical, could be called "beautiful" in the same way petite, pink, curved, and fair-haired ladies like the earl's own lady-wife, the Countess of Clune, could be considered so. No, "handsome" was the word they'd used for her, but it scarcely mattered what they called her, for it wasn't the first time Colin had seen men look at her the way the earl had done. But those usually were sidewise glances, cast warily from men in markets and in the fields.

The Earl of Clune, distant head of their family, looked at her just so that day they came to him for advice or possible aid, but he did so straightly and without disguise. Then for the first time Colin realized that nobleman did not necessarily mean gentleman, and knew also why his mama had so feared this visit, this last desperate attempt to save her home. He also, in that revelatory moment, knew why, though he was sure he hadn't entirely then, he'd insisted, as her eldest son, on the right to accompany her to High Wyvern Hall, the earl's home.

The earl's half-open heavy-lidded eyes had lowered at last, as though against his will, under the force of the lady's angry stare. Then, looking about his sumptuously furnished study, as though for something he sought, in an effort to deal with his rare moment of defeat and embarrassment, the earl saw her boy Colin's face. And then gave a bark of genuine laughter.

"Oh, here's a fire-eater! Never fear, my dear, for I believe your future and your virtue will be safe with this young one at your side."

The earl looked hard at Colin then, and in that brief time, all scorn and contempt was erased from the older man's jowled, mocking face, and a fleeting spasm of displeasure replaced it, as a passing light of some bitter inner admission lit his pale green eyes.

"Aye," he said almost to himself, still staring at the unblinking boy, "I shouldn't sleep easy if we lived in ancient days, for though I've a quiverful of boys between you and the title, lad, still you've the look of a master about you."

And then he laughed, and then his habitual look of lazy pleasure was back upon his face, and so Colin believed the whole of it had been mockery. For he was only fourteen, and far too tall, his flesh hadn't had time to cover his newly lengthened bones, and he was swarthy as a Gypsy and had been silent and sullen throughout the visit. And the earl had three fair sons, two already grown men, and one of an age with Colin, and all lithe and richly clad and self-important, for though all had known their distant cousin, all had ignored him this time, as though they'd known he'd come to call with hat in hand and nothing in pocket. And all, even the one of an age with Colin, had looked at his mama as their father had done. For they were the infamous Haverfords of High Wyvern Hall, and knew they were expected to be precisely as they were.

Proud Harry, Wicked John, Secretive Maxmillian—their distant cousin Colin could well believe they might enact bloody scenes from a bygone age in their attempts to oust one another and sit upon their father's throne chair in the ancient stone main hall. But as for himself, he wanted nothing to do with the title with all its majesty and money, or the Hall, for all its size and history. He wanted only to keep his small family's roof over their heads, but knew in that moment the agony and frustration of being too young to make any difference in their or his own fate.

Papa had been an only son of a younger son, the Midland Haverfords, only a cadet branch of the noble line. Papa had been a career soldier, and though the little French Corporal had provided employment for him for the past years, in the last year, in Holland, Bonaparte had accounted for his death as well. Mama had a good background, but only a respectable, not a wealthy or titled one, and Welsh at that.

The earl was close-fisted, but he was right and the solicitors were right, the manor would have to be sold. After all, the cottage was never so small as the name implied; it had enough bedrooms and fifteen acres with it, and as it was the one thing entailed upon Papa, it was theirs and they'd owe no living man for the living to be had, however meager, from it. There was also the matter of a small allowance from the earl, to be given for the look of it in the world's eyes, since they were his relatives. For incredibly enough, as the earl had said, since none of his own sons had wed as yet, and because of some uncles who'd failed to do so, and some others who'd been barren or female-producing, Colin was fourth in line for the title. And, Colin had thought all the long bleak way home from High Wyvern Hall, about as likely to inherit it as he was to be able to solve his family's financial woes.

He'd said good-bye then, in his own way, to all the things he'd known since birth. He'd shooed away his eight-year-old sister, discouraged his five-year-old brother's company, and been grateful the baby was still in the cradle, for a fellow didn't want anyone seeing how badly his older brother was taking the remove. It was true he'd been away at school since he was eight, but "home" had only one meaning to him, and now he'd never be entitled to set foot upon the place where his family had lived forever, ever again. So he said good-bye to the stream he cooled himself with in summer, and bade farewell to the towering oak that always whispered threats to him every stormy night outside his bedroom window, and bid adieu to that small clearing on the rise where he'd buried, in their time, Jasper, the spaniel, Fancy, the hound, and Beau, the turtle.

He'd known that the morning the family loaded their clothes and few personal possessions into their carriages was going to be difficult, but he'd steeled himself for it so that he could be a support to Mama and an example to the children. The servants had blotted their eyes as they stood in the doorway to say good-bye, and it was ironic, he'd thought, that they could choose to stay on in Eden if they wished, and he could not.

Mr. Yarrow, the new owner, and owner of a mill and a thriving new manufactory, stood in the dooryard with his man at law and watched the Haverfords depart. His wife and young children were there as well, and Colin had thought it was because they were so anxious to move in. It wasn't until he'd seen the Yarrows eyeing each trunk that left, whispering together, and ticking off items on a list that he realized they were counting the trunks and watching to see that nothing they had bought, which was almost everything they'd seen, was taken from their grasp. Colin had stiffened in indignation, but he'd continued to stand dry-eyed and cold, supervising the remove.

When the last coach had been loaded, and the children boarded, with Nurse and Mama shaking hands all round, Colin had come out of the house for the last time, with his tin box of treasures in hand, almost as if it were the last security he held. And Mr. Yarrow had cried out at once, as Colin made to enter the lead coach, "Here, hold on, laddie. What you got in hand, eh?"

How to say what it was? The earl stirred in his coach, miles and years removed from the event, still wondering at how he would describe it even now. There was pride to consider, and insult, and honesty, all together. He'd stolen nothing, but was angry at the accusation, yet aware that though the items he held were his own, they were totally unknown to the rest of the world. In the end, he'd tried to be so supernaturally blasé, civilized, and urbane that he had, of course, failed utterly. For, "Oh," he'd said dismissively, waving a hand as he imagined one of his noble cousins might, "nothing to speak of, sir."

"I'll be the judge of that, laddie," Mr. Yarrow snapped, with a quick sharp look to his wife, who nodded excitedly, for here was precisely what they'd been expecting. It was unheard of, and thus very suspicious, that the Haverfords thus far seemed to have kept to their bargain. For the Yarrows knew no one of their acquaintance who wouldn't try smuggling out something valuable, something they ought not, under cover of the confusion of a major removal.

"I'll just have a look," Mr. Yarrow said briskly, striding to Colin and putting out his hand for the box.

It was unthinkable to struggle, and yet equally appalling to think of his closely guarded valuables exposed to everyone's gaze, for somehow then, for the first time, he dimly recognized that his goods were foolish, even laughable items to have hoarded so diligently for all those years.

"They're nothing," he'd said, backing away, laughing a false laugh that cracked even as his voice had been doing lately, "only," he said in a last anxious attempt to be adult and casual, so that what he meant to sound amusing and ironic came out a little frantic, "my little treasures, you see."

"Oh, I see very well, thank you!" cried Mr. Yarrow, and pounced, and while all the family and servants and neighbors stared, snatched the tin box away from him. He pried the ornate lid off as Colin began to murmur for its return, and then, dragging his fingers through the contents, Mr. Yarrow grew an increasingly confused expression. Then, a second later, a hundred years later, Colin heard him cry in vast chagrin, disguised as amusement, for he'd expected to discover all manner of exquisitely expensive worthy things hidden so as to be spirited away from him.

"Oh, treasure indeed. A boy's treasure. A magpie's hoard. Look," he shouted, holding up his hands as the objects fell from his fingers back into the box. "What a cache! Broken bits and lost ends, shining gewgaws and old buttons, rotten acorns and pieces of shells! Here—take back your treasure, laddie, here, here, didn't you hear me? Take back your rubbish, and good day to you, sir."

He'd never answered, not then, nor even when his mama had gently tried to broach the subject again, miles from home. But when darkness had fallen, before the coaches had pulled up for the night, quietly, so as not to awaken Mama where she'd dozed in her corner, he'd opened the window and tossed the box, the shameful box filled with rubbish, out, somewhere on the road between home and exile.

When he'd finished with school, the earl bought him colors in his father's unit. He sold out after a year, taking great care to return the money whence it had come. Then, on advice from a friend, he shipped out to the Caribbean islands, to make his fortune. He'd made the acquaintance of hunger there, even in that lush and tropic place, hunger of a sort that came from more than having missed his tea. And he'd become familiar with weariness too, the bone-bred exhaustion that came from more than exertion in the social whirl. But he'd been glad of it, for it strengthened his purpose, reminded him of his situation, and kept him from the seductive easy style of life he might have followed in that green and easy land. He worked at anything he could turn his hand and his broad back to, and invested everything he made, save for that which he sent home to help the family. It transpired that he had a very strong back, and just as important, a strong talent for investments.

He worked in the fields of sugar plantations, he bought shares in a distillery. He managed the workers in the fields of sugar plantations, he bought sugar and rum for export. He bought sugar, coffee, and spice plantations, he bought distilleries, he even bought, at the last, shares in the very ship which carried him home, enormously wealthy, after seven years, to prepare to take on the title Earl of Clune.

The old earl, the disease which he'd contracted from one or two of his many forgotten pleasures now ascendant, slumped in his chair in his opulent study and looked out of pale green eyes at the dark young man who was to be his heir.

"I knew it in my blood then," he croaked, his voice already ruined by that which was slowly taking his life. "I did. A chill, something in the air, a feeling, call it what you will, that day, I knew. I've lived with ghosts too long not to know one, even when it comes from the future, not the past. It's yours now, lad, or as soon as may be. I wish you well with it. I do, you know. And do you know," he said with the travesty of a laugh, "I do believe you'll do better with it than we would have done, any of us. I do believe it's time for someone like you to be master here. Someone who can master himself might take the curse from this place, this name."

There was nothing to be said in reply. The night before his own wedding, Proud Harry had taken another proud man's wife and then a ball in his chest for it. Wicked John's drinking would have ended him more slowly if it had not dazed him enough to fall into the frozen Thames one riotous night in town, and while all his boisterous companions giggled and tried to remember what to throw to a drowning man, besides quips, he'd drowned. And Secretive Maxmillian had a row with one of the many lovers he'd been wise enough to be secretive about, thus enabling the gentleman to run him through before his father found out about the liaison.

Now, a year after becoming the eighth Earl of Clune, an honor as unwished for as it was still improbable to its recipient, the eighth earl rode to a mean slum to pick up a box of trinkets for an impoverished governess, and not for one moment did he believe his actions to be either singular or unworthy of him. He'd been poor, he'd been unemployed, and he had once owned such treasure. With all he had now, earned and chance-gotten, he still would have given much to have that tin box, which was more than likely part of an east-bound roadway now, perhaps even enshrined forever by the efforts of Mr. Macadam, even as it was in his memory.

His servants, however, were appalled at the street where they were told to wait for him. The footmen stared in horror as their master insisted on entering the hovel alone, and his young tiger and the coachman began to theatrically and with many elaborate wasted gestures clean the firearms they'd brought with them for the edification of the crowd of urchins and their elders who materialized from out of the shadows to goggle at the stationary carriage.

Mrs. Rogers ducked and bowed and scraped so many times, her chins quivering in excitement, that the earl grew impatient with her, and abandoning the manners he'd begun with, demanded to be let up to Miss Dawkins' room. This appeared, oddly, to be precisely what she wished, for with a sigh of repletion and sheer adoration now shining in her small eyes, she immediately handed over the key and even managed to look blissful when he flatly ordered her to remain belowstairs, after she'd ignored all his hints that she needn't bother accompanying him.

But, he thought, when at last alone with Miss Dawkins' door shut behind him, if her belongings were as he'd imagined them, it wasn't fair that any others see them. He even felt guilty himself as he stood and gazed around the small room. The place almost fitted him as close as one of Weston's jackets, and the only lifting of his spirits came when he realized that it was scarcely likely he'd miss anything hidden here.

Little time elapsed before he'd gotten all her belongings, clothes as well as the sampler on the one bureau, and a tray with a bottle of lilac scent, combs, soap, ribands, and a sewing case, into her portmanteau. He knew, as she did not, that in such surroundings, these items were most likely to be the first to disappear when their owner was missing for more than a day. And then, and only then, when all else was accounted for, did he lift the small gilt casket from the bureau top and take its key from underneath it. He ought, he knew, to immediately see to giving it, along with her message, to the children down the hall.

He hesitated with the little gold box in hand. He'd no more right to see what it contained than Mr. Yarrow had to pry into what he had collected those years before. But perhaps because he thought no one else would ever know, and perhaps precisely because he thought of that incident again and so in some small unexamined corner of his mind almost believed he'd find half a Roman coin, a marcasite buckle, or an acorn shaped remarkably like the king's own head, he inserted the key, cracked the lid open, and stared at what lay within.

It was not very much, as he expected, but it was of better quality than he'd anticipated. There was no gimcrackery, no nuts or stones; she was, after all, a grown young woman and not a child. But there was nothing of very great value either: a military medal and ribbon, an amethyst ring, a cameo brooch, and a silver locket. There were a few calling cards, and an elegant old miniature of a lovely golden-eyed lady who must have been some ancestor, painted on ivory, set in a circle of seed pearls, most missing, the whole suspended from a worn back riband. Yes, he thought, not realizing he was nodding affirmatively even as he cradled the delicate piece in his palm, treasures, yes, these certainly were treasures.

"Now, I'd put that back very slow, I would, and I'd keep my hands in sight all the while too," a hard young voice declared stridently.

The earl spun round to look to the door. He blinked. An assortment of children completely filled the doorway. And they were all glowering at him. There was a pretty blond little girl holding a doll almost as big as herself against her shoulder, an older, darker-haired boy with a broom in hand, and the speaker was a fair-haired youth only a little senior to the others. He had his mouth set grimly and was cradling the bulk of a large cudgel in the crook of his elbow, while gripping on to it tightly with his other hand.

"Now, you're bigger, true, but there's more of us, and you'll never get us all at once. And think of the 'oller we'll set up," the boy said loudly, and the others nodded, while the girl's doll, the earl was surprised to note, now began hiccuping gently.

"I'm a friend of Miss Dawkins'," the earl explained.

"Aye, and I'm 'er dad, I am," the boy said sweetly.

"She sent me here to pick up her things, and to speak with you, as well," the earl said patiently.

"All I'm listening for is the sound of you . . . leaving,"

the boy answered, trying to tap the cudgel against his arm in a threatening manner.

"I assume you're Alfie," the earl said thoughtfully, watching the child and taking his measure. "All right," he said suddenly, loudly enough so the children all winced and shuddered back for an instant before they squared their shoulders and stepped forward again.

"Now, listen," the earl said, setting his booted feet apart, standing straight, and crossing his arms in front of his chest, so that he appeared to dominate the small room. "Do you honestly think I need these trifles I appear to be stealing?"

"Who's to say?" the boy replied angrily. "P'raps you made your bundle from stealing little things, like. Lots of little things add up," he said.

"True," the earl answered, a smile making a fleeting appearance on his dark face. "And I suppose you think I crept up here to make my fortune."

"Nah," the boy said scornfully, "spider couldn't creep up by old Rogers on rent day, she'd be waiting at the door to collect from everyone. But you could of tossed 'er a tuppeny piece and got up 'ere for it."

"I am Colin Haverford, Earl of Clune," the gentleman stated coolly. "Miss Dawkins came to my home seeking a position I'd advertised. She collapsed, she's ill. I'm letting her stay on until she's recovered, and she asked me to collect her things and send to you with the news of this."

The younger children seemed impressed and not a little disturbed with this information, but the older boy appeared to be even angrier.

"Ooo, 'eavens, sir, wot a lovely story you do tell." He sneered. "And I'm s'posed to be lummakin enough to believe a belted earl would 'op to a servant's bidding? Oh, pull the other one, luv, to make 'em even."

The dark gentleman's face seemed to grow even blacker. His ebony brows dipped downward and almost met over his narrowed jet eyes. His strong jaw set hard. The little girl trembled, and the older boy took a tighter grip on his makeshift club.

"My nephew," the gentleman began in cold flat tones,

"who's a spoiled young idiot, misused her good nature and then ill-spoke her to save his own worthless neck, and so lost her a good position. Then, soon as I clapped eyes on her I made it worse by offering her a bad one, if you get my drift. Now she's sick and I'm feeling guilty as bedamned, you miserable whelp, and I'm trying to make it up to her, you see? And furthermore, when I came to get her things, I snooped, even as you would, because earl or not, I'm human too, damm it!" the earl shouted.

"Oh, well," said the boy equitably, laying down the cudgel, "why din't you say that in the first place?"

6

" 'Ere we are, your lordship," the boy said magnanimously, flinging the door to his rooms wide. "Now I expect you'll be a bit more comfortable 'ere. And a deal more private too. Now, Bobby, you fetch that carpetbag down to 'is lordship's carriage, smartly now. And, Sally, you take Baby in t'other room, I think 'e needs seeing to."

"Oh, but, Alfie," the little girl said at once, hoisting the baby higher on her shoulder, "I just did, 'member? Just afore we came into Miss Victoria's room, 'cause you said as he smelt high as last week's fish then."

"That was then," her brother said pointedly, glaring at the girl, "and this 'ere is now, if you catch my meaning."

"Yes, Alfie," Sally replied at once, instantly obedient, turning to go into the other room, and then, catching herself, paused and dipped such a low curtsy to the gentleman that she wavered and bobbed under the weight of Baby as she attempted to straighten from it. But as soon as she had, she turned around and went directly into the next room. Baby bobbled over her shoulder, giving the gentleman a glimpse of a lone emergent white tooth in an enormous damp smile of farewell, before his sister turned to present his round rump and her own wistful face as she closed the door behind her.

"Now, then," the fair young gentleman said decisively, pushing the one chair in the room to his guest, " 'ave a seat, your lordship, and we'll see if we can't sort things out.''

The earl seated himself, crossing his legs as casually as if he were in his club instead of a low-ceilinged cramped and ill-furnished hovel, and politely waited for his host to speak what was obviously on his mind. The boy took a few turns around the room, which, considering the size of it, was not a very long time, and then he spoke.

''Now, as I understand it, she's sick as a 'orse, right?''

''She's ill, yes,'' the earl replied seriously, ''but we have every hope that it's not a mortal taking. We haven't even bled her yet, for if some sleep and potions bring the fever down first, the doctor thinks it best to let nature mend her. He is a very good physician,'' the earl mused.

''And speaking man to man, if you don't mind the liberty, your lordship,'' Alfie said gravely, ''I understand she din't take up your dishonorable offer neither?''

''Not that offer, no, most emphatically not,'' the earl replied just as calmly, ''and I haven't had an opportunity to proffer my second, more correct one to her.''

''Ah well,'' the boy breathed sadly, shrugging his thin shoulders as if nothing in the strange old world could surprise him any longer, ''can't say as I'd blame you for being put out wiv 'er. There's not many around 'ere as would nay-say you. You're a fine-looking gent and it prolly was a fair arrangement you'd set up. But she's a lady, see, even if she ain't precisely one. It's just that 'er sort would rather starve to death in a gutter than take up wiv you in silk and satin, if you get my meaning. But I'm sure she din't mean insult.''

''I quite understand, no insult taken,'' the earl replied with an admirably solemn expression.

''When do you suppose she'll be able to come back to us?'' Alfie asked after completing another turn around the room.

''It's difficult to say precisely when,'' the earl replied, and was about to say more when the door to the room burst open again.

''Oh, Alfie, you ort to see!'' the young boy who'd been introduced to the earl as ''m' bruvver Bobby, 'e's eight,'' cried as he rushed as breathlessly into the conversation as he'd entered the room. "What a rig, 'e's got! Four fine Arabians 'e's got, matched blacks, black as midnight they are, spanking 'uns, and a 'normous carriage wiv curtains and red velvet cushions, and a raft of servants dressed fine as guards at t' Tower. Oh, Lud, Alfie, 'alf the street is out, lookin' their eyes out. Come see!"

"I am talking to 'is lordship, thank you," Alfie said with barely contained fury, "and I'll thank you to get in t'other room wiv Sally and Baby if you please, till I'm done, if you know what's 'ealthy for you, that is."

"Yes, Alfie," the other boy said, deflating immediately and creeping off meekly into the other room, as wretchedly as though it had been brickbats and not words his brother had thrown at him.

"It's not easy dealing wiv 'em, but they're very young, don't you know," Alfie said apologetically as the door closed softly behind his brother, and the earl nodded sympathetically, waiting for him to go on.

"Well," the boy finally sighed, "I'm glad as you've got 'er now as she's sick, for there's not much we could do for 'er 'ere. But the thing of it is, your lordship, that she and us, well, we 'ad an arrangement too, y' see."

Alfie folded his arms and stood before the earl in almost the same attitude as the earl had stood before him not moments before, legs apart, and frowning. It was such excellent mimicry of a mature gentleman with a poser on his mind that in that moment the earl almost forgot it was a pale fair youth of an admitted eleven years of age, dressed in threadbare castoffs that confronted him, and not his own mirror image.

"So though I'm glad that she's fallen on 'er feet, so to speak, I'm sorry too," Alfie went on, " 'cause the truth of it is, your lordship, that she can't rightly take you up on any offer 'cause she's got a *prior*"—he paused to let the deliciously legal sound of the word he'd dredged up sink in before he went on—"a prior arrangement wiv us. We're in the way of being 'er employers, that is to say," he explained.

When the gentleman only gazed at him quizzically, the

boy said with great care, "That is, you see, we arranged that she instruct my sister and brother and Baby in gentle ways, and in return I'd see to her room and board, meanwhile. It's a sad blow," he said, shaking his flaxen head, becoming more the gentleman employer by the moment, even to the point of now enunciating his "aitches" exquisitely, "to find she's not to be with us for some time."

"Aha. I believe I see the whole of it now," the earl said, nodding wisely, "but surely you would let her out of her contract if certain financial details were worked out so that you could find a replacement?"

The earl reached into his jacket and withdrew a purse, and then withdrew a sum from that purse. The sight of the bills in the gentleman's hands seemed to catch the boy's breath up in his throat, for he had to clear it and swallow once before he was able to speak again. But when he did, it was the earl who became speechless. For, "No," Alfie said firmly, "I can't sell Miss Dawkins' contract to you, my lord, much as I can use the blunt, as well you know it.

"Thing of it is," the boy said at last, and boy he seemed now, for he'd become very pale and his voice was far less confident, "the way I sees it, you've a use for her one way or t'other. And that's your business and her business, never mine. But whichever business it is, there's no way I can match it. So I'd tell her to go wiv you, one way or t'other, both ways leads to a good life for her, no mistake, and I've a care for her. Even if I din't, I ain't going to pretend to sell you somethin' we both know I ain't got, not really. But mark me well, I'm not a beggar. Not me. I don't take nothing for nothing in return. But I can sell you something you ain't got. And it's not her. It's me.

"Listen, your lordship," Alfie said quickly and quietly, deadly earnest and extremely pallid now. "It's certain you've a grand house and stables and what-all. It's sure you've got a job of work, some position somewhere in there for me, maybe two, maybe one for my brother too. There ain't nothing I can't learn to do, and quick, too. I could handle your horses or clean up in the kitchens, or what-all, I could."

"And the money?" the earl asked softly.

"Ah, the money's good, no mistake," Alfie said in agitation, his blue eyes never leaving the earl's face. "And there's a lot of folks hereabouts would call me a nodcock for not snapping it up. In fact, they'd be reserving a nice room in Bedlam for me right now if they heard me. But I ain't lived here all my life, and I know a few things they don't. I'm no Miss Dawkins—it ain't just my noble nature makes me turn it down. But don't you see, that money's just a one-time thing, no matter how much it is. And when it's done, it's gone. But a job means money on the barrelhead every month, and a future, and I've got a family to think of."

"Ah," the earl said, appearing to think deeply. "And if you come with me, for it is indeed quite possible that I can find some sort of useful employment for you, what of the others? Who'd look after them?"

"Gawd, with money in hand, there ain't no one I couldn't get the hire of to look in on the little ones," Alfie said fervently, all intent, bending forward, as if he wished the earl to commit himself immediately through the sheer tension of the moment.

"And your mama, of course, will agree to this?" the earl asked softly, watching Alfie closely.

"Ah, yeah, oh sure, o' course," Alfie answered quickly.

"Well then, I think we may indeed strike some sort of bargain," the earl said, rising to his feet. "May I just have a word with your mother before I say more? It's only right, after all, and though you did say she was resting in the other room, as your brothers and sister are already in there, surely she must be awake now."

"Ah, it ain't necessary. She's feeling so poorly these days, you see," Alfie said nervously, backing toward the closed door to the other room, "I know she wouldn't want a fine gent such as yourself seeing her, as bad as she looks now, don't you know."

The dark gentleman stood very still and then asked gently, "How long has she been gone, Alfie?"

"She tole you?" the boy asked in disbelief, despair plain on his thin face.

"Miss Dawkins? No, not a word. But it was the fact that there was not a word that tipped me the clue, Alfie. For she sent her love to all of you and never mentioned your mama, and Miss Dawkins," he said with a wry smile, "as we all know, is most proper. Then too," he added, "if your mama were here, I should think you'd very much want her to meet me. I'd think seeing your employer would comfort her, no matter how she felt about her lost looks."

"Lawd," Alfie sighed, settling back till he rested against the worn table, "you ain't just whistling. A real earl in 'er own 'ouse? She would o' been amazing pleased."

Then he stood and faced the earl, a certain sad dignity upon him, and he looked up straight into the dark gentleman's fathomless eyes as he spoke, for the first time with neither affectation nor guile. "She died January past. It was a fierce winter, remember, and she hadn't been feeling too clever since Baby was born. It was consumption, I think, or it could've been something else, it don't matter really. But the lucky thing in it was she din't die here. She was taking in sewing, piecework, to do at home. I was to meet her across town, at the dressmaker's, to help her carry the goods home. But when I got there, she was already down in the street, with a great crowd gawking at her.

"Well," Alfie went on, dry-eyed, all emotion firmly suppressed, "she din't last long after they got her inside. The luck in it was that no one round here knew of it. She's in potter's field under her born name, so's nobody could find out. I figure she don't mind, and 'er maker knows 'er, whatever name I gave to the beadle. But that way I could keep us all together, don't you see."

When Alfie paused, for inspiration or for the purpose of getting himself in control again, the earl reflected that the boy could speak very well when he wished, but that emotion of any sort caused him to lapse into the argot of the streets.

"There were no relatives?" the earl said gently.

"Nah, none, she came to town from the country when Da died, 'e was a sailor, she was once a lady's maid, and there was only just the two of them. And don't tell me about the orphan 'omes,'' Alfie blazed, before he remembered that this was a gentleman and someone he wished to please. He quickly subdued himself so that he could go on in a quiet, almost wheedling voice, ''Have you seen them, sir? Workhouses are better, I think. I even went up to Guildford Street to have a look in at the best one, the foundling hospital there. Gawd, give me Newgate instead! So I decided that since no one knew our mum was gone, no one had to know. Mrs. Rogers and t'others could believe they always just missed her coming in and going out, and when they began to ask too much, why then Mum could always get sick with something they din't want to get too near.

''Do you know what 'appens to kids who 'ave no one to look after 'em, your lordship?'' Alfie asked, before he answered himself in a voice of disgust. ''Our Sally's only six, and yet there's a 'ouse not two blocks from 'ere, where they'd be 'appy to have 'er wiv others just like 'er they got on staff. 'Cause there's gents find little girls 'er age just right for their pleasure. And they ain't blokes from round here, neither. And Bobby, 'e's small for his age, but if they din't find him pretty enough for bedwork, or if he wasn't snapped up for a thieves' ken, why it would be up the chimney wiv him in a trice, and a nice fire under his feet, for the sweeps is always looking for likely lads wiv no one to speak for 'em. And Baby? 'Oo wants another baby? Lucky if 'e'd last out a month, 'e'd be. And me, why I can take care of myself, but the thing is, I got to take care of them.

''But January's a long time gone,'' Alfie said, brooding, ''and I began to see that Mum couldn't stay in her room forever. When Miss Dawins moved in I watched her close, and it wasn't long before I decided she'd do, she'd do fine. We needed a grown woman with us for the look of it. And since I soon saw she didn't know the time of day around here, it was clear she needed us just as much as we needed her. In a few weeks, I thought we'd all move along to new rooms together, to a lodging house a long way away, and we'd put it about that she was our sister and that she had a rough young husband in the navy, so's no one would get funny ideas, and we'd have done fine. Yes, we would've. But now I s'pose that's all over."

Complete quiet settled over the room then. Sally and Bobby, both with their ears to the door, looked at each other in wild surmise as the silence grew, but neither the tall gentleman nor the fair-haired boy noted it, each being too busy with his own thoughts.

"The foundling hospital is a worthy place. I've donated money to it myself," the earl said at length, and went on, oblivious of the snarl forming on the boy's lips, "but aside from the fact that I doubt you'd be around long enough for the ink used in your name to dry on their register, I've a fondness for the place and hardly think it right to bring it down about all those innocent children's ears.

"Alfie," the earl then said decisively, slapping his gloves against his palm before he extended one long well-tended hand to the boy, "I believe I understand you very well and that I've a position for you, if, that is to say, you're willing to sign on with me."

"I believe," Alfie said with admirable control, as he spat in the palm of his own chapped hand and proffered it to the earl to shake to seal the bargain, "that I am. Aye, sir, I believe that I am."

The eighth Earl of Clune's town carriage pulled up in front of the door to his London residence. When his tiger let the steps down, an odd little procession disembarked. A usually stolid footman swung the ornate doors to the town house wide, as his eyes seemed to open wider, and even the earl's butler, one of the best men in London town, a man who had once seen a previous employer run through by a swordsman and had only drawn in his breath sharply as the weapon was withdrawn, with all the life's blood, from his master's breast, now forgot himself so much as to gasp aloud.

"Mama," the Earl of Clune said pleasantly, with a great deal of high humor lurking in the depths of his black eyes as his mother paused on the stair to stare at the new arrivals in her son's train, "may I present to you the

Johnson family? This is Alfred . . . and here is Robert . . . may I make known Miss Sally Jane . . . and this is Baby, more properly known as . . . ah . . ."

" 'Arold!" cried Robert, rising from his bow as his brother called out, "James!" even as the little girl holding the infant stammered, "R-Roger, mum."

"Harold James Roger Johnson," the earl repeated with great pleasure. "Children, this is my mother, Mrs. Haverford. The Johnsons will be staying on with us for a while, Mama."

And as his mother eyed the quartet of children with something very akin to her son's vast pleasure in her own dark eyes, he bent to her and whispered softly, "They followed me home, Mama, may I keep them? I promise to take care of them, and I swear they won't eat much."

A small fire grumbled comfortably in the grate in the study, warding against any slight chill in the late-spring evening. A few lamps were lit to burnish the long twilight, and the gentleman at his ease in the deep leather chair looked up from his book lazily as his guest entered, bringing drafts and noise and a sulky expression in with him.

"Oh, no, don't get up, why trouble yourself," the young man complained as he flung himself down upon a chaise, causing the piece of furniture to squeal in protest at his invasion. "You can be easy, sitting and looking as though you hadn't a care in the world, and no doubt you haven't, for your mama is snug in another house, while you live as you please here, rich as Croesus. It's not fair," the young gentleman moaned, looking to the table where a decanter filled with something ruby red sat surrounded by crystal goblets.

"Life is seldom fair," the earl commented, putting a mark in his book and shutting it carefully, "as witness the fact that your family decided to return you to me forthwith, like a letter that hadn't been properly franked. I still wonder how you managed that," he sighed. "A promise of reformation, no doubt. Odd, your mama has her moods, but I'd judged her eminently sane. And touch one drop of port my dear Theo," he added casually, "and I'll break your arm. It's enough that your enchanting parent is always running to me with tales of your dissipation; it would be more than I could tolerate if you made yourself free here before my very eyes, for then I could not pretend ignorance as I so often must do."

"Ho! As if a fellow could become dissipated on only two guineas in his pocket," the young man said gloomily, still eyeing the tray thirstily.

"Two arms, then, if I must," the earl said, his dark eyes so hooded by the shadows that it might have been either laughter or displeasure which colored his voice. "Elevate your thoughts, Theo, for you shan't have a drop tonight, not from my hand. What happened to your allowance this time?"

"It's all your fault anyway, Cole, for I went round to visit with your mama this afternoon," the young gentleman mumbled as if that were explanation enough.

"Oh," the earl said, and unmistakably, even in the darkness, his white teeth could be seen gleaming in a smile. "What was it this time? Hazard? Evens and odds? Basset? Faro?"

"It was the bones, the devil's teeth, b'god," young Lord Malverne cried in agitation, "and the boy has the devil's own luck with the dice, Cole, you never saw the like, they dance for him, they sing for him, they all but speak for him. I left while I still owned my own hat!"

"That at least was wise of you. But, Theo, gambling with children is a terrible vice, it corrupts them," the earl said with a great deal of censure.

"Can't corrupt that whelp Alfie Johnson any more than you can corrupt old Nick himself," Theo mumbled.

"This visit to my mother wasn't all family duty, then. It's clear you were only trying to win back last week's allowance this time." The earl sighed, taking up his book again.

"No, wish I was, Cole," the young gentleman said, sitting up and sounding so genuinely wretched that this time his cousin looked at him sharply and put down his book. "Thing of it is, my mother sent me a letter asking me to trot over to see what I could see. There's been talk . . . well, dammit all, Cole, since you've taken the title there's been talk, because they don't know what to expect of you. It's stupid stuff, I know. Everyone knew what villains the Earls of Clune before you were, and here you are, more decent than our family has any right to expect, and they watch every move you make even more carefully.

"The short of it is, Cole," the younger man said earnestly, "everyone wonders what the deuce is going on. They talk of little else. Yes, they know I caused Miss Dawkins to lose her post, and she's said to be ill, but for the life of them they don't know why your mama is putting her up, nor why a parcel of infants is included in the bargain. Miss Dawkins ain't going to work for your mama, that's clear, for Old Cold Comfort is still there, and so what's the gal doing there, my mother wants to know."

"And? Go on, Theo, there's more, I can tell, spill it," the earl said wearily.

"Well, they wonder if she's going to be your mistress or your wife," Lord Malverne said unhappily.

"What?" the earl shouted, coming to his feet. "What sort of idiocy is that? The girl was at death's door. She's only been with my mother two weeks, and scarcely ever out of bed, and in that bed alone the whole time. I've never so much as seen her alone in all that while."

And to cover the unmistakable note of grievance that even the speaker detected in his own last statement, the earl said quickly, "And what sort of degenerate do they think me, that I would land my mistress on my mother's doorstep?"

The earl fell silent then, hearing his own question and remembering that if Miss Dawkins had breathed "yes" at that long-past moment she would indeed have been his mistress. But then, recollecting that the wish was never the deed, he glowered at his young cousin again. "And do they believe the children to be mine, as well?" he added sardonically.

Seeing his young relative's reddened face, the earl turned away, his own stern features more rigid with anger.

"Blast!" said the earl, throwing his book down upon

the chair he'd just vacated, and wrenching his dressing gown off.

"It's all very well," he said gruffly, standing in his shirtsleeves and ringing for his valet so that he might get dressed to go out, "to say that gossip does not bother me, for it doesn't you know. But I won't have anything bothering my mother, and since my sister wed Axelham last autumn, and his family's as priggish a bunch of puritans as I've ever had the misfortune to meet, I don't like controversy swirling about her head either. I've lodged the girl with my mother until she's well enough to take up a decent post again, and for more reasons than I care to go into, the children are part of the bargain—they're her responsibility as well. And I am not related to them by the furthest stretch of fevered imagination. And I am in the meanwhile actively seeking a position for Miss Dawkins to take on as soon as she can stand on her own two feet—and not with or under me either, for that matter, is that understood?" he roared, pointing at his cousin.

"Oh, understood, Cole," Theo said happily. "I'm glad to see you mean to straighten the matter out. For I've a wager on at the culb that your mistress is to be Melissa Careaux, the filly from the opera, the one with all the jet curls, you know, the one everyone said you ogled the other week at the theater? Most chaps have laid odds it's to be Lady Lambert," he went on smugly, never seeing the arrested look of horror in his cousin's dark eyes, "and a few are still holding out for Amy Farrow, for since she's had a tiff with the Baron Hyde she's been saying she fancies your sort of looks. But I think you've better taste than that," Theo said loyally, "and then too, Melissa Careaux has the biggest, most enchanting . . . ah, er . . ." He paused with his hands still sketching something prodigiously curved in midair as his cousin's valet entered the room. ". . . prominences, you understand," he ended weakly, quickly inspecting his fingernails, as both his cousin and his cousin's valet gazed at him in amazement at his sudden fit of discretion.

The earl dismissed his young relative, and then went to his room and dressed rapidly. He uttered not one word to his man after he announced his change in plans and prepared for an evening out, which was unusual. For he was an employer who seldom stood upon ceremony, never spoke down to a servant, and tended to treat all his fellowmen with the same easy graces. This was, his valet felt, unfortunate but understandable, since it was known that the earl had not been brought up in expectations of his title. The lapse could be excused, since in sum he was a fair employer and a credit to a valet when he cared to be turned out properly.

But for all the sensitivity to his fellowman which his servant found deplorable, this evening the earl hadn't a care for his valet's sensibilities, he was too bedeviled with his own thoughts. This was the first night he'd planned to pass at home in the past weeks, and he'd been expecting to spend it in the way that suited him best, reading and relaxing before his own fireside. This was, after all, the first evening that the physician had declared Miss Dawkins entirely out of danger. Her fever had gone, the continuance of life was thus assured, and at last he could spend a night in his own quarters, and one without pacing or broken snatches of sleep stolen between vigils. But surprisingly, with all the danger and drama of the sick young woman struggling for her health upstairs in his mama's best guestroom, it hadn't been that unrelentingly grim at the Haverford town house where his mother held state. For he'd had the children to deal with, and had discovered that they entertained him far more than he'd diverted them from their worries about their governess and friend.

He'd thought his mama had been inordinately pleased at their arrival, for few society matrons would countenance, much less celebrate, a pack of slum brats being landed upon them. But his mama was never a society matron, and since they'd come to her, he'd come to realize how flat she must have found life now that his sister was wed and in the North Country, and his brothers had gone off, respectively, to a naval career and to university, and he to his own lodgings. She'd taken charge of the situation at once, and lodged the four of them in the disused nursery in the attics without hesitation. Then, in the past week, between fretting over "poor Miss Dawkins" and fussing over the Johnson ménage, he'd seen that she'd seemed to positively bloom, rather than flag, from all her unaccustomed activities.

This morning Miss Dawkins had looked up at them, her face little more colorful than her pillow slip, save for those enormous golden eyes, shining with intelligence and not fever at last, and she'd smiled wanly, sensible at last, and thanked him at the last, before he'd left the room, for seeing to her. Then he'd gone to round up Alfie from the stables, where, after what must have been a shocking confrontation, to judge from the evidence of blackened eyes and bruised knuckles on the pair the first day they'd met, he'd obviously found a kindred spirit and boon companion in Jack, the earl's tiger. After Alfie had been summoned and his siblings sent with him to Miss Dawkins' bedside, the earl hadn't thought it odd in the least that the sight of the five of them reunited to celebrate Miss Dawkins' recovery brought tears to his mama's eyes, or even a certain mistiness to his own. But then too, he had never doubted his responsibility to her, or to the children, for a moment.

Boarding and succoring a nonentity of a governess and a pack of grubby urchins did not seem to him to be irregular in the least. And this, as his valet flinched to contemplate, was not just a charming eccentricity such as one often found among the nobility, although the servant steadfastly maintained otherwise when chatting up his fraternity in the tavern.

For the earl knew that his relative had lost Miss Dawkins her means of livelihood and indirectly but definitely brought her low. If he and his family had had no direct hand in reducing Alfie and his siblings to their circumstances, once having seen them and met them directly, there was no possibility that he could have turned his back upon them. Although this was singular behavior for a nobleman, the earl, after all, as his valet sadly acknowledged, had not been bred to his title.

But he had been raised as a gentleman, and he knew how pernicious gossip could be. Miss Dawkins was on the road to recovery. The Johnson children were out of immediate danger. It was as well then that young Theo dined out on gossip and drank in every nuance of it. It was time to prepare for the determination of all of their futures; it was past time to set matters right again. And this very evening, the earl thought, checking his appearance in the glass and approving of the sober but correct evening garb he'd donned, he would at least make a beginning. He would start scotching the worst of the rumors.

He'd offered Miss Dawkins the post as his mistress on that distant afternoon, and the only thing he found shocking in it now was that he'd offered the position so quickly. For it had been a valid offer, the situation was vacant, it would have paid well, and if he'd not read her character wrongly, there would have been nothing amiss but for the speed with which he'd made up his mind, without so much as a fair trial, that she'd suit him. But, he reasoned now, he'd been very much taken with her, she'd caused an instantaneous response in him, he'd thought he'd caused a similar reaction on her part, and he'd believed her eligible for such a post. She was not, he had not, she would not, so be it; he shrugged now, inadvertently causing his valet to worry about whether it was his response to his cravat, which was, as the fellow thought with some trepidation, a "Trompe d'amour" tonight and not the "Waterfall" he usually wore.

There was a planet full of willing females, the earl thought, never noting the change in cravat style, and dismissing his man, he went down the stairs musing that there wasn't the slightest need for him to pine for one, however tempting, who had the impediment of virtue to hinder a possible relationship. He'd not set up a mistress in town, and had come to know a man of his position was expected to. But that wasn't why he'd been interested in filling the void. When he'd seen and spoken with Miss Dawkins, he'd suddenly realized he was weary of having to go out to seek a new companion to fill his bed each night that the spirit moved him. He discovered he was tired of all the arrangements he had to make in order to provide for each evening's sport. No matter it hadn't worked out, it was as well that she'd started that chain of thought; it was time, he believed, that he had such a convenience available for himself.

There had been, after all, he reminded himself, even as he called for his carriage, the steady arrangement with Genevieve, the planter's wife, his first year in the islands, and then Marie, in the small apartments in Kingston Town, and then Sukey, who had been a constant inconstant lover for an entire two years, until they'd both been bored to tears by each other despite all their games. He'd always preferred such dealings in intimate matters to intermittent impersonal transactions. The only reason he hadn't set up such an accommodation since he'd taken the title, he imagined, was that he hadn't the time for it. Then too, perhaps in the back of his mind he'd considered the predecessors to his earldom, and hadn't wished to heap even more scandal upon the name. And by so depriving himself, he thought now, as he entered his carriage and directed it to the opera, he'd caused even more.

It was even more ironic, he realized, grinning to himself in the darkness, that all his proper meetings with the proper Miss Dawkins, and every respectable gesture he'd made toward her since that improper offer she'd refused, were precisely what were sending him out into this night in search of improper diversions to end gossip.

Miss Melissa Careaux could not dance a graceful step onstage and had a voice much like an ill-tuned bagpipe, so it was as well that she had nothing to say and only simpered frequently. But she did have curls as black as night, and when they were upon his pillow it was hard to see where his head left off and hers began, but since there were no spectators and as they were seldom apart for most of the night anyway, it hardly mattered. And once they were entangled there, the earl discovered that everything else young Theo had claimed about the young woman was similarly true, even down to the impressive prominences he'd stammered over. She was an obliging armful, dusky, perfumed, supple, all pouting lips and accommodating in every particular of her mind and body.

And not a thing that happened between them through the

night was remotely proper, not one minute that passed, nor any action undertaken. But then too, neither was any of it any enormous pleasure to him either, or at least, never so much as he wished it to be. None of it was the eager opera dancer's fault, if fault there was in it. It was only that the gentleman found that incredibly enough, despite both their laudable efforts, he couldn't seem to keep his mind on improper matters.

Perversely, when he understood the nature of the difficulty, he tried even more valiantly to achieve bliss, so much so that the young woman never forgot him, nor did she ever wish to, even though the morning brought her only a handsome sum and never the offer of the more permanent employment that she'd been hoping for and that he'd originally hinted at.

It was a most unlucky night for young Lord Theo Malverne too, for his cousin lost his wager for him. But then, no one won immediately, since the morning after Colin Haverford had done interviewing Miss Careaux for the vacant post of mistress to the Earl of Clune, it seemed he hadn't a thought to conducting further auditions for the position. It was also decidedly odd that after such an evening, he bathed and dressed again with not a thought of getting a wink of sleep to separate his days. Then he left his bachelor fastness and went to visit his ancestral town house again.

For Miss Careaux hadn't failed him at all. She'd indeed been everything he'd expected, and less. The night had brought him more than pleasure. It had convinced him that whatever else transpired, he must see to it that the unemployed governess, Miss Victoria Dawkins, left town, and very soon, as soon as she was able, if there were ever to be any peace for him, or surcease from gossip for his family.

7

The room was flooded with sunshine, light streamed in and lit the silken cerise peonies as though they rioted in a country garden rather than upon a lady's boudoir walls. The tiny golden roses and ivory rosebuds that paraded on the bed hangings, flourished along the carpet's edges, and trimmed every porcelain fitting on the washstand glowed in the bright spring light as well. There was no way anyone, save for a dead person, could lie still in bed while all the world shone with spring, Victoria thought the moment she opened her eyes to the glorious light that poured into the room as the maid pulled back the curtains.

But because she feared the doctor's wrath, dimly remembering him to be a fiercely opinionated person from the hazy recollections she had of him forcing her to quiet and insisting on her drinking down his evil drafts, she remained beneath the coverlets. All her body yearned to be up and out from this bed. Now that she could think clearly at last, she ached to be out entirely from this elegant room where she lay, feeling more prisoner than patient, awaiting the doctor's visit. It was never that she was ungrateful. No, she felt she could live out another lifetime and not be done with her gratitude to the doctor and her hostess and all within this house for what she was convinced was the gift of her very life. But now that she could reason, she couldn't bear to increase her debt to them.

She'd been mortally ill; she understood that now. That day she'd arrived here, she'd almost turned back at the door when the knocker had spun around so many times she'd wondered if she could ever catch it to lift it to ask to come in. Then, when she'd seen the earl and supposed him still planning to entice her, with no respectable chance to earn her keep in sight, it seemed that was the last bit she'd needed to overset her entirely. The rest was still a jumble. But first she'd blazed with heat, then she'd been sure she'd seen the infamous Mother Carey leering at her, and then she'd seen dragons and angels and phantoms everywhere.

There had been moments when she'd known there was a good physician in attendance, she'd seen a calm and lovely lady who talked good sense, and she'd realized it was really the children at her bedside. Although, to her dismay, she couldn't fathom why the children had been summoned to her at the earl's own home if she were not just about to die. So in her fear she'd fled reason entirely for a space, only knowing she must fight out the illness in order to come to her senses again. And through it all, always in dream spasms and often in what she knew must have been reality, she'd seen his face. The Earl of Clune's stern visage was her one sure touchstone, for it never altered in fact or in fancy, and so much as he'd deceived her she welcomed him, for the sight of his dark face was sanity and sanctuary for her wandering wits.

Yesterday, she'd opened her eyes to a cool, real world at last. Today she was ready to leave, though there were a great many questions she needed answered, and a great many answers she feared. Yesterday she'd been told that the children had been brought to the earl's house not only to be with her, but because he'd realized it was inhumane to leave them alone. She privately thought it was more likely that if Alfie had decided he must be taken up by the earl, there was little chance that he, or any other living man, however imperious, could have resisted. The earl, she'd decided late last night as she'd finally slipped into her first sweet healthy sleep in this bed, had simply been kidnapped by the Johnson children, just as she'd been commandeered in her turn, and she'd smiled as she drifted to sleep, pleased that in this, at least, he was as vulnerable as anyone.

Early this morning the arrival of her first visitors had enabled her to get a hard look at the shadowy figures she'd seen hovering over her bed when she'd been so ill. Miss Comfort was a sour-faced old lady, to be sure, small and angular, with delicate but pinched features and light blue eyes. But far from being a seducer of lost girls, she was so prim that Victoria wasn't sure the lady knew precisely what it had been about this wicked "Mother Carey" she'd been taken for that was so dreadful. Mrs. Haverford was a tall, handsome female with hardly any silver in her dark hair, and a wealth of awareness in her large deep, dark eyes. She'd laughed when Victoria stammered a thank-you to the "Countess" when she'd realized the lady urging her to drink her chocolate was none other than the Earl of Clune's mother. The lady had said, as she'd corrected her guest, that though her eldest was a belted earl due to hereditary law, she herself was certainly no more than she'd ever been before. But even after knowing her for only the space of an hour, Victoria believed there was actually little more any woman could possibly be than the lady already was, since any title, in her case, could never be so wonderful as its subject.

Victoria Dawkins had fallen on her feet, to be sure, just as Alfie had whispered to her last night when he'd been allowed to come in to see that she was herself again. They all had. But she wasn't eleven years of age, and she knew that everything she saw, touched, and tasted now was as transitory as the fevered dreams she'd experienced just hours before had been. She was not a lady, and she still had nothing, not even a chance to pay her benefactors back. If he should care to offer again, she supposed she could be the gentleman's mistress, but to be so now would not even be free choice, it would be in the nature of a debtor working off a debt. That would make it worse than immoral, it would lose even that spicy savor, it would be at the last, only unendurable, a pathetic attempt at payment for superior services rendered. Truly, the house of Haverford owed her nothing any longer, Victoria thought, sitting up straight in bed, and she must leave it as soon as she was able.

But when that could be, and what would become of the children, and how she could show her gratitude, and how she could abide receiving even a word more in charity, knowing all she did—these were all questions Victoria struggled with in the bright new morning. Now that everyone had let her alone to prepare for her interview with the doctor, she had the time to sort out her questions. Because she knew she could ask only a few; the rest she'd have to answer for herself.

"Aha. Up and bright as a penny. Do you know me, Miss Dawkins? Of course you do. Wouldn't shrink back as if you'd just seen something nasty if you didn't. Needn't fear. I've nothing for you to swallow just now, and won't bleed you again. There, just open wide. Ah, good. Let me listen a moment. Good. Clear as a bell. Cough, please. Ah. You'll do," the doctor said heartily, having invaded the room and her privacy with all the brusque and busy cheer she remembered.

"Thank you," she said as he pulled her coverlet high again, "but when may I leave, sir?"

"Voice always that husky?" he asked suspiciously, and when she nodded, he left off frowning as he took her hand and asked her to grip his. "As I thought," he replied, nodding, and releasing her hand, "no more strength than a day-old kitten. Leave bed in a week, I should say, *if* you behave yourself."

"A week?" she gasped. "But no, surely not. I'm quite recovered. I've excellent restorative powers. I must go sooner. I'd meant . . . I'd thought . . . that I might leave this house and return to my own lodgings this afternoon."

"Certainly," the doctor thundered, "and by so doing, by this evening you might quit this world! You've just come through a crisis, young woman. If you leave this room, I leave you to your own destiny, I'll wash my hands of you. I'm a physician, not a mortician. Take one step through that portal and it would be like stepping off London Bridge," he bellowed.

"Oh, wonderful, doctor," an amused voice cut in. "Now you've cured her lungs, you'll have to treat her for shock. Or is this the latest treatment for convalescents, frightening them to their feet so that they won't malinger?"

"Wicked, ungrateful chit wants to go home," the doctor explained in a roar.

"Indeed?" the earl said, looking in from the doorway, much interested.

"I do not believe one ought to attempt to do anything for quite some time after such a taking," Miss Comfort said briskly, materializing from the hallway and entering the room. "I recall my poor Uncle Samuel, pronounced fit as a fiddle by his physician one February morning, after just such an illness, and yet discovered by his housekeeper to be entirely dead in his bed that night. Isn't that frequently the case, doctor?" she asked, folding her hands and staring down dolefully at Victoria.

"Aye, it might be, but I imagine it depended on just what he was doing in bed with the housekeeper," the doctor barked, seeing Victoria's expression.

As the import of his reply began to register upon Miss Comfort and the tip of her sharp little nose turned white, the earl's mama came into the room, seemingly borne in upon a moving platform of children. Victoria gave a glad little cry and held her arms out, and an astonishingly well-scrubbed and beautifully dressed Sally flew into them.

"Oh, Miss Victoria," Sally sobbed from her idol's circling arms as Victoria looked down, amazed and delighted to see that the child's hair was not just a dirty-blond shade, but rather a lovely light subtle golden-red color. Bobby's shaggy hair was only a shade darker, she noted as she looked up from the girl burrowed into her embrace. Alfie, however, had almost silvery-white tresses. There was much to be said for the merits of hot water and pure French soap over those of cold water and laundering soap, Victoria realized. No matter what the moralists said of cleanliness and godliness, though the Lord doubtless didn't mind the difference, it was clear that mortals oughtn't to forget to consider economics when they applied the old adage. For she'd scrubbed at their hair and faces when they'd been in her custodial care and never gotten such glowing results.

And she never could have envisioned how they'd appear in new clean clothes. Though they hadn't been dressed as little fops and dandies, the boys looked like young gentlemen in their white shirts and short jackets, and Sally like a miniature heiress in her white muslin dress sashed with pink and her new white stockings.

"You look capital," Alfie pronounced with pleasure, "and 'ere, Sal, leave off sniveling all over 'er, or she'll think you've been beaten 'stead of fed and 'oused like a queen."

" 'Here,' and 'her' and 'housed,' Alfie, as I told you," Miss Comfort said at once in perfect governessing tones, as Alfie grinned widely and dropped an enormous wink to Victoria at how successfully he'd diverted both Miss Comfort and Sally at one stroke.

"It's only that I'm so glad to see 'er . . . her," Sally sniffed, drawing back and bestowing a watery smile on Victoria.

"May I come in?" the earl asked politely, but pointedly from the doorway.

"But you are in already, Cole," his mother laughed, "all but for your boots, which are still on the doorsill. Why ask permission? But, my dear," she said at once, understanding her son's comment at last and turning a worried face to Victoria, "we've been most inconsiderate, you've no more privacy in here than you'd have in a dooryard, no wonder you yearn for home!"

"Oh no, ma'am, never!" Victoria gasped. "I've been treated magnificently. It's not that I've ever found any fault here, it's only that I don't wish, I cannot wish to be a burden upon you, indeed I only want to repay you for all your kindness, and I know that lying here and battening upon your good offices is not the way to do it."

Miss Comfort nodded her satisfaction with a statement she completely agreed with, the doctor frowned and cleared his throat for another harangue, and the children fell silent. Mrs. Haverford spoke up at once.

"Nonsense," she said sharply. "I hope we know our

debts. It was a certain poetry lover in our own family," she said, never even glancing at Theo, who had quietly come into the room unannounced after the others, and who, upon hearing himself mentioned, now turned to exit just as silently, only to find himself blocked by the substantial frame of his cousin Colin, "who set all these unfortunate events into motion. Although," she added consideringly, "search as I may, I can't find anything unfortunate in making your acquaintance or coming to know the children, however unpleasant the circumstances that caused our meeting may have been."

"It's an ill wind that blows no good," Miss Comfort said, nodding in concurrence again.

"And how are you feeling this morning, Miss Dawkins?" the earl asked, coming into the room and taking the patient's hand in his, behaving entirely properly in every respect, as if by his example he might bring some order to the rapidly filling sickroom.

Victoria sat up sharply as he approached, and it may have been that which accounted for her becoming quite pale as he neared her. But then when he took up her hand, healthy color rose in her cheeks again. As the earl mused on whether the sudden pallor was more flattering to her because of the way it pointed up her large golden eyes, or whether the rosy blush was more attractive for the way it gave animation to her face, she hesitantly assured him of her restored health and thanked him for his concern. All he could clearly see of her were her face and her hand, for a voluminous blond lace morning robe covered over her bedgown, and coverlets hid all else, and her long wavy brown hair was pulled back in a single heavy plait. But he found he wasn't attending to her reply, he was so caught up with the sudden bizarre discovery that despite her wrappings, in a room filled with people, even after his arduous night, he found himself more entranced and in a way more deeply stirred by her than he'd been by the unclad female with whom he'd passed the entire night alone.

For once he was grateful to Miss Comfort when she began to speak of false dawns, and warn of mistaken recoveries, thus drawing the doctor into heated debate again, for as he tore his gaze from Miss Dawins' rose-suffused face, he realized that he'd been staring at her too pointedly, and for far too long.

"I think," he said firmly, effectively silencing the other argument, "that at least I'll be able to temporarily relieve the room of some crowding. Mama, I've family business to discuss. You may stay on, Theo, until I return, if you promise to play nothing more advanced than pick-up-sticks with the children, although I don't doubt that they could relieve you of next month's allowance, even at that."

While Lord Malverne protested his uninterest in any games of chance, Mrs. Haverford detached herself from the children, bade the doctor wait upon her return, and drew her son out of the room with her. She took his arm in hers and led him down the hall to her sitting room, hoping that the children and young Theo might divert Miss Dawkins from the tales of false remissions and sudden ghastly demises that Miss Comfort immediately continued to regale the doctor with.

"Gad, Mama," the earl sighed, once he'd firmly closed the door behind them and joined his parent on a settee in her sitting room, "I can't understand why you keep her on. She's merry as a churchyard at midnight."

His mama didn't pretend not to know whom he was speaking of, but only said with gentle censure, "I'll agree Comfort's not to your taste, Cole, and perhaps not even to mine any longer. But it's no good your continuing to say that I should let her go, for I can't. She's a good soul, dear. No, don't sneer, truly she is. Don't forget, since I cannot, that she stayed with me when I had very little, remember?—when you were out making our fortune. There were other relatives with better prospects she might have gone to. All we could offer her then was a tiny room, and she shared whatever little else she had with us. She's earned her ease now. I cannot, no, it's simply not possible for me to toss poor Comfort out now.

"It isn't a matter of money, either, for just the other day I hinted at how time was passing and mentioned the considerable pension you'd provided for her, only to set her mind at rest on the subject, should she wish to leave us, you understand. But then I took one look at her face, and I vow, Cole, I thought she'd sink as fast as that unfortunate uncle she was just going on about. But only think, where would she go? She's made her life with me, this is her home now. Life is not kind to aged, unmarried, unpropertied females,'' she added sorrowfully.

''And there's no need for her to go, either,'' she said more forcefully. ''You don't live with her, Cole,'' she reminded her son, tapping his knee lightly to make him attend to her, ''and then too, things aren't so bad now. Victoria's here, poor child, and even though she's been ill and won't be herself for some time, I like her very well. And the children! Who could resist those children? Comfort quite likes them all too—even Victoria, I know, though she'd rather perish than admit to it. Sally's her especial love, she dotes on the child, though not a soul who didn't know poor old Comfort as I do could guess it, since it's true her fondest smile looks vinegar-begotten. But we'll all rub on together very well now, I think, Cole. Who would have thought such a muddle could have worked out so well?'' she asked in wonder. ''Why, I haven't been so entertained in ages.''

The earl smiled at his mama's enthusiasm, and wondered again just why she'd never cared to remarry. At any age, she was still a fine-looking woman. Some gray shone in her dark tresses, true, but the silvering only served to soften her strongly marked features, and her dark eyes, which he forgot were mirrors of his own, could still speak volumes in a silent language that many a younger woman would have given her own eyelashes to learn.

''Ah, but how well you do rub on together, there precisely is the rub, my dear,'' he said softly, and then very swiftly, for they often didn't need to waste words between them, he explained that which Theo had said was the world at large's latest pleasure to gossip over.

''But how stupidly cruel!'' his mother exclaimed at last. ''And, Cole, only think, you'd have to have been . . . what? Oh, Lud, I'm such a nit with mathematics . . . ah, seventeen, I think, to have fathered Alfie. I suppose it's possible,'' she muttered thoughtfully before she jerked her head up from the fingers she'd been counting on to cry, "oh, Lud! Just look where such reasoning gets even me. It's shocking. And as for your intentions toward Victoria . . ." But here she stopped and lowered her dark lashes over her eyes.

"Dear discreet Mama," her son laughed, "I do look a great deal, I'll admit. I'm alive, you know, and she's very good to look upon, even in a sickbed. But I scarcely know the girl! And I've never exchanged a private word with her since she's come here, and I promise you, I'd never land a mistress of mine upon you."

"But a wife . . . ?" his mama said slowly, peeping up at him as mischievously as a girl herself.

"I am not in the market for a wife," the earl said in beleaguered tones, "so since I haven't any of the delightful plans for her that the world seems to think I cherish," he continued rapidly, "I've come this morning to have you help me think of some way, short of marriage, mistress-ship, or murder, that I can honorably dispose of the problem of Miss Dawkins."

Before she could voice her outrage at his cold assessment of the situation, he went on calmly, "Now, what I've been wondering and wanting to ask is if you have anything against ghosts?"

"Ghosts?" she asked, confused and silent for a moment before she laughed gleefully and cried, "Ghosts! Of course, the very thing! Clever Cole. It's time you took up residence at High Wyvern Hall, whether it's supposed to be ghost-ridden or not. It's been deserted since the old earl died. And what a perfect place for Victoria and the children, far from the city, far from tattle-bearers."

"But not far from me, and so never far from gossip if I lived there too, dear noodlehead," her son said affectionately. "The same conditions would prevail, because so long as your dear Comfort stays on with you, Miss Dawkins remains clearly redundant in the world's eyes. I'd thought rather that I might go there and discover whether there are any families in the area that could use a governess-companion. Then she could be near the children, because I also believe we might find some family living on the estate willing to foster a parcel of infants as well. There's room for a legion of them at the Hall, and we could continue to look after them there."

"Likely," his mama said shrewdly, remembering that part of the country, "there'd be a great many families who'd wish to get themselves into the new earl's good graces. And a great many more with marriageable daughters who might need to add governesses or companions to their households almost as much as they'd need a noble husband to add to the family."

"And you certainly need a new diversion," her son said crossly. "Since you've got my sister popped off and my brothers have evaded your clutches, you've become a fiend for matchmaking."

As his mama then promptly proposed any number of improbable matches for him, to coax him out of the sullens she'd seemed to cast him in, he laughed along with her. All the while he ruefully admitted to himself that it had been his own actions which spurred both the gossip and her own expectations. He had goggled at the girl. All the while she'd lain ill he'd visited every day, and paced, fretted, and then sat keeping a vigil at her bedside through the worst of it. But he'd only felt guilt for her state, and a natural male's interest in such a lovely face, for he had no more matrimonial ambition for her than he had for Miss Comfort, whom his mama next proposed as a possible bride for him.

As he'd said, he wasn't in the market for a wife, and class aside, and birth and fortune aside, he certainly wasn't about to tender such an offer to any female he scarcely knew. The fact that he'd offered Miss Dawkins a position as mistress upon even shorter acquaintance didn't signify. A mistress was one matter, a wife entirely another. This was so much the case that many men, he knew, kept both at hand. For the one was a pleasant diversion, like a rich dessert to be taken at the end of each day. The other was a source of constant nourishment if one were lucky in one's choice, but a steady diet nevertheless, partial to the menu or not, if one were less fortunate. He didn't know if he himself would care to dine out frequently once he was wed, but then, he seldom seriously thought of marriage at all.

It wasn't that he disapproved of the state in theory. It certainly wasn't that he had no interest in the pleasures to be found with that other delightful sex. It was just that the matter had never come up. He'd been too busy trying to repair his fortunes when he'd been younger and more susceptible to transitory passions of the heart and lower regions, and so at the time had expended them all on lightskirts and passing fancy women. The sort of titled females he was supposed to keep company with now, he supposed, likely wouldn't have countenanced being in the same room, much less marital bed, with him had his noble relatives not met with misfortune. The sort he might have taken up with before those unhappy events were now often too awed, if not by him, then by the name which had been appended to him. It was a problem, he often thought—but a problem that he could sort out later, as much later as was possible. He was not, just as he'd claimed, in the market for a wife.

The earl and his mama were still chortling together companionably when they emerged from the lady's sitting room, and their great humor had its contagious effects upon the others at Miss Dawkins' bedside. Miss Comfort stopped arguing with the physician and he in turn did not actually ever call her the name he had on the tip of his learned tongue. Theo and the children had amused Miss Dawkins admirably, and when they all left the sickroom to give her some rest, she looked relaxed, if wan. This time the earl had taken great care not to stare at her, but she scarcely noticed, for never once did she look directly at him. Until he said, as he took her hand in farewell, that it would be some weeks until they met again, since he was off to the country to do, as he said with a glance to his mama, some prospecting.

". . . And 'ow," Alfie continued, shaking his fair head in puzzlement, "you could 'ave taken 'er for Old Mother Carey, I do not know. 'Cause Mother Carey used to be in the business 'erself, and so still looks a treat for an old besom, that is, while Miss Comfort frightens 'orses in the street on 'er bad days, she does."

"You could say it right, you could say 'her' and 'horses,' and all the rest of it, and you could be kinder, for she's been very kind to you, you know," Victoria said repressively, putting down the book she'd been reading to him.

" 'Course I could." He grinned. "I always could, you know. But then she'd have nothing to aim for, nothing to gloat over when I finally do get it right. Anything comes too easy to hand, Miss Victoria, ain't valued. And how good it really is don't count, else you'd have to pay a fortune for potatoes in the market, and you'd get a heap of nightingale tongues thrown in for nothing. And it isn't being unkind to say she's got a face would freeze bow bells at forever noon, 'cause it wouldn't be anything but a lie to say else. Anyhow, how she looks has nothing to do with how she is, ain't that 'zactly what she's always trying to teach us with those Bible lessons?"

Then he turned such a bland and innocent face to her that Victoria grinned at him, and shaking her own head, said on a sigh, "Alfie, my lad, you terrify me, you do."

They were sitting in her room, reminiscing about the early days, the days when they'd first come to live at the Earl of Clune's London town house. A month had passed since then, and though they both knew their fates weren't settled as yet and their present state was exceedingly tenuous, a month, after all, had passed. A month held four weeks of time, time enough for the children to have put on color and weight and begin to walk upon the earth as though they belonged upon it. A month contained thirty days, days in which a young woman might regain her poise and her self-respect, and with thirty nights to pass in easy sleep, begin to grow in confidence as she grew in health. Now, whatever was yet to come, still they could look back and chat about those early days as though they'd happened to someone else, as though they'd been amusing.

They knew that the Earl of Clune had returned to town

last evening, and though they didn't know what his visit to his mama today portended for either of them, they could sit in Victoria's room and discuss it together. Indeed, perhaps they had to sit in her room and discuss it together, so that they could retain, at least with each other, all that they had gained in the past thirty days.

Sally was with Miss Comfort, learning French, of all the amazing things, Bobby was being fitted for a new pair of boots, and Baby was asleep in his cot, upon clean linen sheets, in an earl's nursery, just as though he were a valuable child. Alfie lounged in an elegant lady's chamber, and the lady in attendance upon him chatted and joked with him as they both tried to believe that when they were summoned at last to audience with the earl, whatever transpired they might keep some shred of what they had right now, in these last moments that were fast fleeting from them.

The boy had just launched into a scandalous tale of how he'd first won both the earl's groom's respect and his pocket watch, when there was a scratching at the door. He was still such a naturally milky-white-complexioned boy that only Victoria saw how minutely paler he became when the maidservant at the door told them the earl wished to see Miss Dawkins and then, after he'd done with her, he'd be pleased to see Master Alfie and the other children.

And so for Alfie's sake if nothing else, reflecting privately on how brave and proud a person might be if there were always someone else to be that for, Victoria casually shook out her skrits and smiled and calmly said she'd send to Alfie the moment she was done talking with the earl. Then she went, head high and stepping as smoothly as a swan moves upon still waters, down the stair to the study where the earl awaited her.

He had not changed in thirty days, she thought at once when she rose from her curtsy. He still caused her to stare and then drop her gaze in confusion at how splendid, how powerful and magnetic a man he was. He wore the usual sort of gentleman's daytime attire, dove-colored buckskin breeches, shining black hessians, a white cravat over a gleaming white shirt and striped waistcoat, and a tight-fitting blue jacket over that, but he wore it all as he wore the look of appraisal he turned upon her, with complete assurance, with natural certitude.

"You look very well," he said at once, his dark gaze never wavering. "Mother tells me you're completely recovered. I can believe it."

She wore one of the new frocks his mother had insisted on acquiring for her. One like all the rest that she'd begged to be fashioned in not too forthcoming a style for a governess to presume to wear, but one, like the others his mother had insisted the seamstress make not too frumpy for a young lady to wear as well. It was a high-waisted deep-rose-colored day dress, sashed with an old-rose-hued riband, which alone had cost more than a governess would earn for a day's wages. But Mrs. Haverford had claimed, and even Miss Comfort had agreed, that a young woman who looked as though she did not necessarily need her salary to live would eventually live much better in any position she undertook.

The earl did not see any of this discussion in the product of it, he only saw that Miss Dawkins looked more lovely than even he'd remembered. The sight of her was like a blow to his stomach and took both his voice and his thoughts momentarily away. Her hair was parted in the middle and was pulled back, but allowed to form soft wings to either side of her face. For all that it was a modest style, he thought it suited her to perfection, emphasizing the sheer delicate beauty of her face as no more elaborate fashion could have done. Her form was similarly enhanced by the gown she wore, and when he found himself gazing at her high breasts and then down at the outline of her rounded hips and then further downward at the folds that hinted at the shapely limbs beneath, he looked away at once to the papers he'd spread upon the desk.

Since he'd not attempted polite chatter, she thought him brusque, impatient with the trivialities of dealing with the governess he'd been saddled with, and anxious to see to the disposal of her future. So for all she'd wished to make some small talk, and for all she'd wanted to thank him for the kind treatment she'd received at his hands, she held her tongue and waited to hear of what would be her future.

"It's summer, we're very fortunate," the earl said at last, "since most of the *ton* are repairing to their country estates now. My principal seat, High Wyvern Hall, is in the south. It is your great good fortune, I believe, that one of my near neighbors, Squire Ludlow, has two unwed daughters. And their governess has seen fit to retire."

He didn't mention that he didn't doubt that the poor creature had been retired as soon as he'd mentioned that he knew of a young woman of good family he'd be pleased to see secure such a post. In fact, he wondered if the woman hadn't been given her marching orders the very night he'd taken dinner with the squire, and it hadn't helped his digestion of his host's mutton to wonder if some old indigent female hadn't been let go even as he poured cream over his apple cake. For he'd been told of the possibility of such a vancancy as the butler had handed him his hat and cloak as he'd left, and it had been confirmed by messenger the very next morning. But he didn't tell that to the young woman standing before him now.

She hadn't taken a seat—he hadn't remembered to invite her to do so, being too involved with what her reaction would be to what he was about to tell her. She never noted the omission, being too anxious herself to know whether she was standing or seated.

First he told her how close Squire Ludlow's estate was to his own. Then he told her of the generous salary they offered, the lovely home they had, and the two charming young ladies she'd instruct. Then he told her that his own factor, Mr. Stanley, and his good wife, Mary, being childless, had agreed to take in and foster the Johnson children, so that they'd continue to be sheltered beneath his own roof. He then mentioned again how near she'd be to High Wyvern Hall when she was with the squire, how often she'd be able to see the children, how lucky the children were to find such a good couple to watch over them, and how delightful the Ludlows were, until even to himself it sounded as though he were trying to sell her the position, rather than present it to her as what it was, a generous gift.

When she didn't reply at once, he began thinking how absurd it was actually, that he, an earl, should feel uncomfortable and regretful when he was doing something so benevolent as offering some friendless, homeless young creature a cloudless future. It was the only way that he could keep from focusing upon how her lovely mouth was trembling; it was a sure way to remind himself how she'd thrown his money in his face that day after she'd refused his kiss, after he'd touched those soft pink lips with his own.

And she, even knowing that she was very fortunate, still couldn't bring herself to answer him as yet. For with all her good fortune, she could feel only a terrible emptiness. Because, she realized, by finding her a post, he'd denied her her fondest secret daydream: that she'd be offered a post taking care of the Johnson children for him, thus being paid to do what she wanted most in the world. By handing her such a proper offer instead, he'd also forced her to see at last that her other, most private night-fancy, that he'd again offer her a chance to be his mistress, but this time by some unknown chicanery force her to it, was only that—a foolish, conceited, and wicked fancy. They'd been absurd dreams, but even so, it was hard to relinquish them, for both had sustained her for thirty beautiful days and thirty oddly comforting nights.

"Well?" he asked impatiently, when she didn't answer him at once. "Is there something amiss?"

"Oh no," she felt constrained to say at once, but speaking too soon, so said at once again, without properly thinking, "But it's only, I had thought, I know it isn't wise, but I had hoped that perhaps . . . perhaps your factor might want a governess to look after the children, and so I might stay on with them."

"You cannot stay on with them. It is quite impossible for you to stay on in my home," he said abruptly.

"Oh," she said, shrinking back, not looking at him now, hurt and humiliated and wishing only to leave at once, "I see."

"No, you don't," he replied angrily, and coming out from behind the desk, he took her in his arms and after looking down into her disbelieving eyes, he stared at her quivering mouth and then lowered his head and kissed her, very hard, and for a very long time.

And then he raised his head and released her lips, and said gruffly, for his benefit as well as hers, before he let her go entirely, "Now. Now I think you see."

8

There were a great many good things to be said for living and working at the Old Manor. And Miss Dawkins made sure to include each and every one in each of her letters to her mama. She never failed to cite the fact that the Old Manor was a historic and noble home, for all that its owners were merely country gentry. For, just as she copied out in her neat hand, quoting directly from the book the seventeenth-century parson, one of the Ludlows' ancestors, had written, it had been erected in the fourteenth century upon the burnt ruins of the house built in the twelfth century, and all manner of wings and ells and chimneys, walls and gateways and gables had been added onto its original E-shape ever since.

It might well have been true that no one more important than the bailiff of High Wyvern Hall had resided there centuries before, and that royal feet had never trod its passages as they'd done at High Wyvern Hall, but for all that it never achieved the fame or prominence of its lofty neighbor, the Old Manor was now so unique that touring gentry often requested leave to sketch it to better preserve its memory in their diaries and notebooks. Miss Dawkins might have privately thought it was because no one could quite believe that any edifice could be such a hodgepodge of styles and fashions, for she believed the Manor was a one-building museum of architectural fads and conceits.

But she never wrote of that, for she always tried to pen cheerful letters, full of hope, brimming with content.

So she wrote about how Squire Ludlow was such a merry fellow, never mentioning that half his merriment was poured from bottles each night, and she told her mama how charming Mrs. Ludlow was, omitting the fact that the lady of the house never felt it necessary to exhibit such charm to an employee. The young ladies, her charges, Miss Charlotte and Miss Sophrina, she wrote, were bright and beautiful and clever. But of course, she did not put a word to paper that hinted at how that brightness was all surface glitter, the beauty was what they considered foremost, and the cleverness was cutting and spiteful, not only to each other but to their governess as well.

But the air in the shire was more potent than Squire Ludlow's wine to Victoria, and being London born and bred, the quiet and the beauty of the countryside was a revelation and a joy to her. And so that, and only that, was the sum and the substance of all the truth in all her letters. Almost all those letters went only to her mama, her brother being, just as he so ruefully admitted in his infrequent responses, a very poor correspondent. It might have been comforting, Victoria often thought as she bit on the end of her pen, seeking inspiration for another artificially optimistic bit of news, to be able to write of her loneliness, her longings, and her frequent concealed sieges of desolation. But since the many letters she received from her parent were so determinedly pleasant, so scant of actual incidents, and yet so full of things unsaid, she thought it only fair that she write only fair news to solace her mama, who might even, she felt, be half as unhappy as she herself was.

She'd come to the Old Manor on the twenty-fifth of May. Mrs. Haverford had taken her there in the same carriage that was bringing the Johnson children to High Wyvern Hall with her. There had been a great deal of weeping and hugging and snuffling when they'd finally parted; even Miss Comfort had looked regretful and had presented a lean, powdery, lavender-scented cheek for Victoria to kiss in a gesture of farewell. The Ludlows had been impressed to silence by the way the new earl's mama had embraced their new governess at the last, and that good impression had made life endurable for Victoria for a good three weeks. But now it was the second week in July, and Mrs. Haverford had not visited with Miss Dawkins again, and so their new governess was being treated just as all their old governesses had been. And Victoria didn't know how much longer she could bear it, although there was nothing else for her to do but bear it.

Her promised recommendation from Mrs. Colfax, doubtless prized from her by Lady Malverne, had finally come by post. But it was such a poor, feeble thing that Miss Parkinson had been entirely right to send it back to Victoria with a terse note about seeing if she might not ask the woman to work up some more enthusiasm, as the testimonial (if it could even be called such) wouldn't do for a new employer at all, the halfhearted way that it was worded. The Ludlows had accepted it without looking at it for their neighbor the earl's sake. And for the earl's sake, Victoria wouldn't send it back nor would she attempt to have it written anew in any way. To do so would be to contact the Earl of Clune again, and that she wouldn't do even if she were to learn that he held her personal fortune in his hands, and was waiting to present it to her just for the asking.

He'd said she was not welcome in his home; then he'd kissed her. Which meant, she understood, that she was only good enough for his bed.

It was true, for Victoria had heard of it, that some gentlemen regarded some females just as they might regard certain public conveniences, as things necessary to bring physical easement, but therefore also as insensate objects fashioned for the sort of lower functions one did not discuss in polite company. Certainly, then, they wouldn't regard such receptacles as being remotely human. She'd not thought that of him, though she'd scarcely known him. But she'd imagined him wise and kind. Now she saw that had been only her wish overlaying the truth of the man, even as all the complicated fretwork and brickwork overlaid the few rooms that had been the original whole of the house she now resided in.

But he'd kissed her with passion to show her why she was not acceptable in his home, and so as he'd wished, she saw the whole of it now. And nothing, nothing in the mortal world, would induce her to cross his path again, even as nothing could erase the thought of him or his touch from her mind ever again.

When Victoria thought of how her life had run since her papa had died, except for that one brief month's interlude under the earl's care in London, which turned out to have been unreal as a dream, she found it hard to know how she was supposed to get through the next several decades she was supposed to have coming to her. The children were the last pleasure she had left, and she couldn't even go to see them, for she never knew when the earl was in residence at High Wyvern Hall and dared not risk being seen by him.

But Alfie would often visit her; as a known familiar of the earl, he was always welcome at the Manor, and sometimes he'd have Bobby or Sally and even Baby in tow. That was almost the whole of what she had to look forward to for personal pleasure. When she thought that she was only twenty years old, she wondered if the earl had done her any favor, restoring her to life and health. So it was fortunate that she had so little time to think in her new position.

Miss Charlotte was seventeen and supposedly had needed a companion, but all she really required to make her happy was a large enough looking glass or a suitor who'd tell her what her mirror could not when she had to leave it. And Miss Sophrina was sixteen, and supposedly needed a governess, but since she'd somehow already learned to read love letters and could sign her name to a dance card, she had no interest in further scholarship. So Miss Dawkins, her employers firmly believing that the only idle servant ought to be a dead one, had many other duties to fill up the vacant hours when her charges eluded her, rejected her, or locked her out of their rooms and lives entirely. This soft summer's morning found her in the gold salon carefully tracing out the needlepoint design on a tall-back chair onto a piece of parchment so that she could then work it on a hoop and repair the damage to the tapestry covering there.

"Now they 'ave you teaching the chairs to chat, do they?" a cheeky voice inquired, and she spun around, letting the stiff sheet of paper slip to the floor so that she could bend to embrace the fair-haired boy who stood before her.

"Ah, Alfie, don't you look fine?" she sighed, holding him at arm's length as he suffered both her embrace and her inspection with admirable fortitude. But he did, she thought. He wore a blue jacket remarkably like the sort a gentleman such as the earl might choose for such a day's visit, his shirt was still pristine, and his pantaloons were uncommonly clean and of a fine nankeen. Even his boots retained a vestige of a shine. His hair was clipped and combed, his face was clear, and his eyes the shade of the summer's sky she'd seen at dawn. In all, she could see that one day he'd grow to be the magnified image of the miniature fine gentleman he appeared to be now.

She beamed at him until he frowned and said, "But you don't look so fine, Miss Victoria. Don't they never let you out? You're pale as a ghost, and you look about as 'appy as one too."

"You ought to be the expert on that, my lad," she said merrily, ignoring his comment, very well aware that she hadn't sufficient peace of mind or outdoor exercise to look her best, but determined to divert him from something she could do nothing about, "since all the chatter here is about how the Hall is chockablock with ghosts. I'm all over envy," she sighed sadly, rising from her knees; "we haven't so much as a headless midnight mouse to disturb us here at the Manor."

"Then I can't imagine why you 'aven't been sleeping," Alfie commented, still looking at her critically, in his usual terrier fashion not sidetracked in the least from his major concerns. But then something in her face must have answered him, for he shrugged his shoulders before he said, with more animation, "Aye, it's all the chatter at the

'All too, so it's a major disappointment to me that there's not been a sign of 'em about."

"Oh, too bad," Victoria commiserated, stooping to pick up her fallen pattern, "but it's early days yet, you might still *'appen* upon one."

"Aye, 'appen I might." Alfie laughed before he went on more seriously, becoming quite coherent in his enthusiasm, "For I've been told of all sorts of haunts to expect in the night—there's supposed to be an ' 'orrible curse' on the family, you see. S 'truth," he said, crossing his heart and looking much offended at Victoria's quizzically lifted eyebrow. "Even Mrs. Haverford said so."

She grinned at him, for no matter what game he was up to, he never omitted the H in his benefactress's name, and it was apparent from the way he spoke it that he thought of her in almost sanctified fashion. Although the Stanleys were supposed to be nominally in charge of Alfie and his siblings, there was no longer any doubt that they'd become Mrs. Haverford's charges.

"Well, I don't envy you," Victoria said with a shake her head. "There's a great many things here in the countryside that I hadn't known in London town, from badgers to bees' nests, and I delight in them all, however odd or dangerous they might be, but you can have the ghosts, my friend, every one of them."

"Nothin' to 'em, Jack says," Alfie went on, following Victoria and watching her resume her intricate tracery. "If you meet up with one, just cross yourself and say, 'Peace be with you, friend,' and they'll sail right past you with a nod, like meeting the vicar when you're out for a walk. Unless," he said consideringly, "of course, they've got a curse to work off, or a score to settle."

"Thank you," she said firmly, "but I'll leave that sort of sociability to you."

"Scairt of them, are you?" he asked in a suspiciously light voice of unconcern. "Is that why you don't never come see us at the 'All then?"

From the way the color came and went in her cheeks, he had his answer, so he went on to say in the same blatantly artificial accents he used whenever his real emotions were involved or he was up to something.

"The earl, 'e's been asking after you. Oh, aye, 'e's been at the 'All for a few days now, seems 'is mama don't like the feel of the place when she's alone there. Not that she's ever really alone, mind. Not with us and all the servants and Mrs. Stanley and 'is wife and Old Comfort 'overing about all the time. But she's the only real Haverford in residence, and so maybe the ghosts are only after 'er, though she swears not.

"But 'e's back, and almost first thing, 'e's asking after you. Seems 'e even wrote letters asking after you. But she says as 'ow you never 'ave time to come, no matter 'ow often she invites you, and," he added, dropping his voice to ape elegant phrases and a false soprano, "that she can't bear the Ludlows enough to come back to see you. But," he went on, sufficiently agitated to lapse into thick accents again, "she says as 'ow she came here twice anyways, and never got a peek at you neither time. Now, that's odd, Miss Victoria, you never tole me 'bout it," he said in a rough aggrieved little voice, "and it do sound like you've been doing a disappearing act better than the ghosts we're supposed to 'ave cluttering up the place over at t' 'All."

"I am very busy, I assure you," Victoria said, staring at the pattern again, with her stub of charcoal arrested over a line of it, "and it seemed pointless to mention that I didn't see someone. How is he?" she asked quickly before she realized that she would.

"Why, that you'll see for yourself, and soon,"—he grinned— "for 'e's come with me today. In fact, I think I 'ear 'im coming now, wiv your employers too."

As Alfie laughed, Victoria looked up, standing frozen in place like a deer hearing hunters nearing. Then she made out the faint and distant sound of many voices and light laughter and then footsteps coming nearer on the hardwood hall floors that separated every room on the main level of the Manor. Victoria looked about, her face very white, her hands clenched so hard upon her paper pattern that it buckled in her grasp, and the bit of charcoal crumbled in her fingers.

"I must go, Alfie," she murmured. "I've no choice really, please say nothing, please understand," and so saying, she bent to kiss his cheek lightly and then stepped to one of the doors that led into the hallway. But she drew back quickly, as though she'd met a wall of fire instead of only the approaching sounds of the company. Then she spun around, and as Alfie frowned in incomprehension, she went quickly to the wall by the side of the fireplace mantel. He thought she was going to pull the bell rope that hung on the stretched silk wall covering there, but she bypassed it and her small white hand reached out, visibly shaking, to touch a carved wood rose upon the paneling to the side of the hearth. As Alfie gaped, he saw the paneling swing open to reveal a low and narrow doorway, and just as the last sight of her gray gown whisked through the opening, he regained his wits and leaped after her, so that as the door swung closed again on her hem, he was also inside the narrow passageway he discovered her to be bent within.

It was a dark bare wooden passage, and he could see that it stretched out into the darkness on one side, while a faint flickering wall lamp illuminated the long narrow tunnel that spread out in the other direction. It was cold, even on this summer's morning, and dank, with enough cobwebs to please any ghost from the Hall. Although he fit within comfortably enough, he could see that Miss Dawkins, although of no great height herself, had to crouch down to fit, and though of no great bulk, had scarcely enough room to turn herself about. But she didn't even attempt to do so. She only stood very still with her eyes closed.

" 'Ere," he said angrily, "what's 'appening?"

Before he could say more, she put her small cold hand over his mouth and bent so that her lips were near his ear.

"Ah, Alfie," she whispered, both the pain and the sibilance in her words and the sighing of her warm breath causing him to shudder, "please. Say nothing. They mustn't see me or hear me. It isn't just my wish. It's the rule here, you see. Now we must stay, or we'll be heard, until they leave. Please be still, for me."

He stood with her in the dimness, and said nothing. Not

a word. Not even when he heard the earl's laughter, or heard him wondering in some annoyance as to where that rascal Alfie might have taken himself off to. Nor even when he heard the squire's lady ask where the governess was, or when he heard Miss Sophrina giggle that she might be so deep in one of her fusty old books that she hadn't hear the summons, or even when Miss Charlotte, after thanking the earl for his pretty compliments, opined that the way London-bred servants were, her absent companion might be on her back in the wine cellar for all they knew.

For a half-hour on that bright summer's morning, Alfie stood silently at Miss Dawkins' side in a ragged aura of small flickering light, and heard the company at their play as though he were in the room with them, instead of impacted in the skin of the walls around them. And at the last, when he felt a drop of wetness fall upon his cheek, he didn't even look up, for though he knew it was not his tear that had fallen there, it just as well might have been. For there in the half-darkness he'd found another old companion, one that he'd thought he'd left behind forever, but it was only despair, his old playmate, come to call again.

Pretty, giggly little Miss Sophrina, the earl thought as his horse trotted down the gravel drive, should be strangled, and if her sister didn't do it as she so clearly wished to, he would be happy to hire anyone who might. And Miss Charlotte, he mused as he steered his mount through the long meadow that separated his property from the Ludlows', for all her lovely little bosoms that she so frequently accidentally almost let peep over the top of her little white debutante's frock, and with all her violent eyelash play, wouldn't net half so much in a week at the trade which seemed most suitable for her as Melissa Careaux would in an hour. As for the squire, the perpetually sozzled head of the neighboring family, he, the earl thought sourly, belonged in a bottle. That way he could be totally immersed in the same spirits which already filled him to the brim, and it would not only save him time, it might spare his company the bother of trying to make sense of what he slurred to them. And if the Manor had no specters, such as his own Hall supposedly harbored, Mrs. Ludlow's overpainted face and artificial smile would do just as good a night's job of terrifying the unwary, he decided bitterly.

Colin Haverford was in a vile mood as he rode through the long sunlit meadow. He didn't blame his mama in the least for declining to accompany him on this visit, and though he was put out with Alfie for his sudden disappearance, being both surprised and disappointed at his desertion, he could at least understand the boy's reluctance to do the pretty with that lot of fools he'd just endured a polite hour with. He grew even more depressed when he thought that he'd have to return again, perhaps even many times again, if he ever wished to discover what had happened to Victoria Dawkins.

She hadn't wanted to see him, that was manifestly clear, he thought, scowling fiercely as he rode through the sweet clover. He hadn't wished to pursue her either. But he'd discovered that with all the diversions that London offered to a gentleman of his new rank and fortune, he could neither get the thought of her out of his mind, nor the sight of her from his mind's eye. And, he admitted, it seemed no wine or more tangible substitute could take the taste of her from his mouth. He might have stayed on in town continuing in his attempts to effect such a mental and physical erasure, but, he supposed on a sigh, it was all for the best that his patience had run out before his health had. He enjoyed wine and women very much, but there was no question he disliked feeling as though he were being forced to constantly partake of both.

He had, in the end, after waking to yet another morning with a throbbing head and an unappreciated bedmate, to admit he was either ensorcelled or obsessed by Miss Dawkins. And what amazed him the most was that he hardly knew the girl. There was no mystery as to why he'd been attracted to her at first sight—he had eyes, she had undeniable assets—but he wasn't such a boy as to lose his head over that. He believed he'd become interested in knowing her because he'd admired her courage, compassion, and honesty after seeing the way she'd handled her impoverishment, his dishonorable offer, and the Johnson children's fate.

But all the while, he understood that it might be that after an hour's calm conversation he'd discover her to be underbred or undereducated, or he might find himself bored, or even put off by her chatter. Even though he'd obviously been haunted by the memory of her, he knew that he never knew her at all. Achieving firsthand knowledge of precisely who Miss Victoria Dawkins was, was clearly the first step he must take to resolve his problem.

But this was difficult to do if the chit had resolved to hide in the Ludlows' attics every time he showed his nose at their door. She'd been cast from his own house because of the talk her proximity to him would cause in light of the fact that there was no longer any real reason for her presence in his household, and because, he had to admit, of his realization of how true that gossip might turn out to be if he remained that proximate to her. He'd attempted to illustrate that very salient point to her when they'd last been alone together. But now, as she wouldn't even meet with his mama, how he'd get to hold that essential exploratory conversation with her, short of moonlight abduction, he did not know.

The earl's thoughts were all gloom on that bright morning as he rode through the fields toward his newly inherited home. The thought of that legacy to which he was returning made him even more despondent. There was nothing essentially the matter with High Wyvern Hall—it was majestic, it commanded hundreds of fertile acres that rolled all the way down to the gleaming sea. Famous men had worked and visited there, it had beautifully proportioned chambers which held multiple treasures, and certainly no more drafts than any other stately home in the land.

But though he hadn't seen any of the spirits said to hold uneasy vigil there in the two months since he'd opened the Hall again, there was still no doubt that it was, inexplicably, a depressing place. The high-ceilinged rooms seemed shadowed even in sunlight, and even that sunlight seemed paler once it had tentatively crossed over the windowsills in its futile attempt to lighten the atmosphere. He would have thought it was only because he remembered the previous earl and that nothing associated with him could bring him pleasure, but the Hall affected everyone so, from the least kitchen skivvy to his own irrepressible mama. Even Alfie, although awaiting a glimpse of his first ghost as eagerly as other children awaited Father Christmas, couldn't deny that the place seemed "sad-like, and queer."

Thoughts of the perfidious Alfie piqued the horseman even further, for the boy had promised to try to flush Miss Dawkins from her hiding place for him today but then had vanished himself. The earl had left instructions at the Manor that the lad be driven home when he turned up at last, but now he narrowed his eyes as he caught sight of one lone little figure trudging through the meadow ahead, with bent but undeniably brilliantly golden head glowing in the morning light. The earl nudged his horse to overtake the truant.

"Good morning, Master Johnson," he called, slowing the horse to a walk to match the boy's when he came abreast of him. "How very pleasant to see you. And yet, how odd that I did not when I was at the Manor this morning."

Alfie didn't lift his head, and it wasn't like him to remain in silence as long as he then did as he continued to walk along, for with all his sauciness, he was never presumptuous, and never forgot that the earl was a gentleman, and he only a boy.

" 'Ow nice," Alfie finally said when he and the horse had walked on side by side in silence for a few minutes, " 'ow honored I am that the great lord, the master, 'is 'igh lordship 'imself, deigns to walk wiv me, and even talk wiv me, who is just a scurvy peasant."

"Been hitting your history books, eh?" the earl remarked pleasantly, "but 'scurvy churl' is, I believe, the phrase you were seeking. It's in that green picture book, the one Comfort's been lately torturing you with, isn't it?

It used to be mine," he added, "or one very similar. Depressing how history never changes."

"No, it don't," Alfie agreed, nodding as he stared down at his boots as they trod down the clover, and then volunteered nothing further.

"It's a long walk," the earl remarked presently, "since, thank God, we've a lot of acres between us and the Ludlows'. Care for a leg up?"

Knowing how much the earl enjoyed his daily ride, Alfie had argued against taking the curricle out for such a short trip just because he was coming along. And he'd flatly refused to take the horse that he'd been learning to ride to the Old Manor, preferring to share the earl's mount, saying it was because he wasn't sure enough of himself alone on the beast as yet. But since the boy had taken to the horse's back as though he'd been riding since he could toddle, the earl thought it more likely that he wanted to be truly expert when he finally showed Miss Dawkins his new skill. The need to cut a dash in front of a fair lady being so much a part of the male condition at any age, the earl had quite understood. But he didn't understand when the boy shook his head and replied repressively.

"No, thank you kindly, my lord, I'd rather walk. Wouldn't want my inferior self cluttering up your saddle, would I?"

"What the devil's got into you?" the earl asked, with some justifiable annoyance. "I ought to be vexed with you, my friend, for running out on me, forgetting your errand, and leaving me alone with Miss Sophrina, Miss Charlotte, and their wonderful parents."

"You didn't seem in need o' me, my lord," Alfie said, throwing a bitter look over his shoulder to the earl, "and 'oo could blame you? If I was being called 'dashing' and 'charming' and 'so amusing' and what-all, plus being begged to come to breakfast, nuncheon, and dinner, 'anytime,' " he said mockingly, adding in perfect duplication of Miss Charlotte's breathy little voice, " 'since it's so exciting, really, too thrilling, having the Hall open once more, and with such a charming new earl in it too,' I wouldn't be looking for no other company, not me."

''Where were you, wretch?'' The earl laughed. ''Behind a curtain?''

''No,'' Alfie said seriously, ''in the wall.''

''What?'' was all the gentleman could muster in reply. ''Talk sense, lad.''

''I am,'' Alfie said sorrowfully, ''but I wisht to Gawd I wasn't.''

The earl slid down from the saddle, and taking the reins in his hand, paced along with Alfie, who'd never stopped in his forward march, as though once he'd set his feet in motion, they carried him along independent of his body.

''The place,'' Alfie said thoughtfully, begining to speak up as soon as he heard the earl fall into step beside him, and as it was important to him to communicate, abandoning his duplicitous use of slum argot and speaking as clearly as he was able to do whenever he deemed it prudent, ''is filled with hidden passages. Now, Miss Victoria explained that lots of the gentry don't like for their guests to see their servants, and don't care for the sight of their help themselves, for that matter. So, she says, in some great houses, the help has to turn their faces to the wall and freeze tight if they see anyone coming. Then everyone pretends they aren't there, so it's all right, 'cause it's like they aren't. Have you ever seen such, my lord?'' he asked, turning a troubled face to the gentleman.

''Once. Yes,'' the earl answered slowly, and just as seriously as he'd been asked. ''When I first came into the title and was invited to a duke's residence outside of London. I thought I was seeing things.'' He smiled now. ''Imagine what it feels like to enter a room on your way to the gentlemen's convenience and to see out of the corner of your eye some poor little female, clad all in black, not two feet from you, standing staring at the wall with her head down, just as you said, as though frozen in place. For a moment I thought she might be an apparition. Fortunately, I had a friend with me. So when I turned round and began to stare to convince myself that what I saw hadn't been brought on by all the port I'd been drinking, he quietly explained the matter and so saved me from embarrassing the poor creature further.''

"Ah," Alfie said softly, "so if it's all the crack, why don't you have us do that at the Hall, your lordship?"

"I shall not hit you," the earl replied tightly, "since I don't like striking someone smaller than myself. Remind me, then, to clout you a sound one for that when you grow up. If I allow you to grow up. Why, you miserable little wretch," he shouted, losing his temper and stopping in his tracks to confront his small companion, "how dare you think I need such trappings to convince myself of my excellence? Or that I would befriend anyone who did?"

"I didn't, not really, I was only checking," the boy apologized at once, and then, as they both began to move on again, he sighed and said helplessly, "but, sir, I had to be sure. You see, the Ludlows think like that, or at least, blame where it belongs, their granddads did. 'Cause the house is built full of passages, they're alongside every room, then go round and round the house, upstairs and down, long tunnels lit with little torches and wall lamps, all so that the servants can creep around the place and never bother the gentry. So when servants hear someone coming, if they can't get past them fast enough, they have to creep into the walls and go back that way, or else stand and wait in the wall until the coast is clear.

"I was in the wall of the gold room," Alfie said sadly, "with Miss Victoria all the time you were with the squire and his family, 'cause I followed her, not knowing where she was nipping off to when she heard you coming."

"I didn't know she detested me that much," the earl said quietly at length, shaking his head, "that she'd flee into the very walls at my approach."

"She don't," Alfie said. "She had to, or lose her post. That's the rules at the Old Manor."

"But she's a governess, not a lower servant," the gentleman protested.

"She's nothing but a servant to them," Alfie replied savagely, "but since she didn't want to get her dress all filthy, she didn't crawl all the way up the stairs to her room through the walls, like she could have done."

"How could she bear it?" the earl wondered aloud, his dark face wearing a black scowl.

"Oh, she done very well," Alfie reported, "for she didn't say nothing until everyone was gone. She just stood there all the while you was taking tea and compliments, with her eyes closed, even in the dark. But I almost drowned. Mind, she don't sniff, nor snivel like our Sally does, but it's even more 'orrible, 'cause she stands real quiet, and all the tears just keep falling like it was raining inside the walls.

"Imagine," Alfie said again, a long while later, after they'd walked on a distance in silence, "I went through the whole house that way afterward. Can you believe, sir, that they even got a tunnel behind the squire's bedroom wall? Now, how could you sleep knowing someone might be creeping about behind your pillow all night?" he wondered.

The earl was diverted from his own dark thoughts for a moment by the notion that there were a great many other things one might not be able to accomplish in one's bed with the thought of such a possible unseen audience in attendance, but all he said dryly, was, "I imagine it would be most inhibiting."

But then by Alfie's sidewise crafty smile he knew the precocious fellow had gotten there long before him, and he was glad of the opportunity to laugh aloud.

"Here, lad," he said then, as though the laughter itself had finally decided him, as lightly as though he'd rid himself of a burden, and so, he thought, he had, even if it meant taking on another one, "it's clear we've got to get Miss Dawkins to come back to us. By hook or by crook. Although the Hall is said to be haunted, I would think she'd be happier there than where she is right now. For I believe that invisible servants are far worse than visible spirits, don't you?"

"Absolutely, my lord," Alfie crowed, turning a vivacious face to his companion. "And now, if I may make so bold, do you think we might put that nag of yours through his paces? 'Cause if we all walk home together as equals, before you know it he'll be putting on airs."

"An excellent idea," the earl said, swinging up into the saddle again and bending to give a hand to the boy.

"Kindness to servants is one thing. But I will not allow my horse to get above himself."

"Very proper," Alfie agreed, settling himself on the saddle before the gentleman, and then he said no more, for they rode home so fast the wind quite took his breath away.

9

Miss Dawkins received two letters all in a day, which in itself was enough to make that day a memorable one for her. One came by post, and though it had come a long way, she realized to her sorrow that, as with all the others she'd gotten since she'd come to the Manor, it had been read and reassembled before it had ever been given to her. The servants at the Old Manor had no more rights or privileges than their counterparts did when the place had originally been built. But then, Victoria thought resignedly, they hadn't been called "servants" then; "serfs" was more likely to have been their designation.

She'd been attempting to teach this, as well as some other points of history, to her younger charge, but at about ten minutes into the lesson, when she was just dipping into some simplified feudal history, Miss Sophrina developed the most exquisite headache from the strain of staring at the picture book she'd been shown. After warning her tutor that Mama would be outraged if she should develop squint lines from gaping at such fustian, she'd waved her away entirely, declaring that she would take to her bed immediately to prevent any such outrage to her beauty.

As Miss Charlotte had made it clear that she did not require a companion in the morning, those hours being devoted to sleep and relaxation, Miss Dawkins had set about her other chores. It would have been pleasant, she'd thought, to have a word with one of the other servants she passed as she made her way down past the kitchens to get some new threads and needles from the housekeeper's stores, though when she received her letter from the woman along with the sewing supplies, it chased all thoughts of conviviality from her mind. But then too, it hardly would have mattered if she'd cared for a conversation or not. Although there were nine other indoor servants at the Old Manor, the truth of it was that there wasn't one she could have chatted with. Precisely because these were no longer the days of feudal servitude that she'd tried to teach Miss Sophrina about, the sort of person who, although born free, nevertheless opted to work at the Manor, was perforce the sort of person Victoria had little in common with.

The butler and the housekeeper held themselves too high to speak civilly to any other but each other and their employers, Cook ignored everyone and was happy so long as she got her due respect and five round meals a day, and all the other unfortunates worked like drones, bypassing any possibility of unity with their fellows because they were terrified of giving offense and so losing their positions.

And, as Victoria soon discovered, if one were constantly fearful of uttering a word out of place, then one could never place a word right. It might even have been that some of the others had been forced to their employment through a similar run of bad luck such as she'd experienced, but there was no way of discovering if that were true, since they all worked in silence. Tentative smiles and hesitant whispers were the most she ever received from any of them. Perhaps if she'd shared a bed with the other females, as the maidservants did, sleeping three to a mattress in their rooms under the eaves, she'd have heard their midnight fears and confessions. But as a governess-companion, she had her own small attic room in the nursery wing and it was as remote from other human habitation for her as was any mountain peak.

So she accepted the fact that her mail was preread, just as she'd had to accept Alfie's news of Mrs. Haverford's past visits, realizing that they'd been kept from her, in the same deadened spirit with which she'd accepted every indignity of servitude she'd been treated to since she'd come to this place, because she had absolutely no choice in the matter at all. If she didn't work at the Old Manor, she honestly didn't know where she would be.

She made her way quickly from the housekeeper's quarters after she'd been given her letter. For now that she also had her work to hand, she could slip off somewhere for a few moments to read it. Mrs. Finch had handed it to her with the hint of some vast pleasure in her eyes, and Victoria hoped that it signaled some good news that the housekeeper had discovered the letter contained for her. Victoria had never stopped believing in human compassion. And the missive was from her brother. It might be, she fancied, that it held news of his fortune finally made, and the housekeeper in her own peculiar fashion was pleased that at least one poor wretch could now escape from this place.

It was rising to a clear warm July day, so Victoria, who never had enough of the fresh clean air she'd discovered in the country, went out through the servants' door to the kitchen garden and took a garden seat to read her letter and breathe in the sweet summer's morning. But she stopped breathing entirely at the very first words she read, for they sloped off to the side of the page themselves in their excitement, and they spoke, amid hasty blots, of "great good news that could not wait."

She paused, she breathed in again, and laid her letter down in her lap, for, like all beings who are unaccustomed to much gratification, she wanted the pleasure of drawing out the pleasure as long as she could. Then, when she couldn't wait another second, she dried her palms on her skirts and picked up the paper in fingers shaking so visibly that she had to lay the letter right down again upon her lap to see it right, and only then did she read on. And then she crumpled the letter between her two hands and would have thrown it to the ground if she hadn't recalled herself at the last, remembering that she would want to refer to the letter again and again to convince herself that it was true, to torment herself with the proof that it was true, in all her long mornings to come.

For, ". . . you would love her," he wrote, and "seeing her, hearing her, you would understand at once why I could not wait upon matters," and "Had I not offered, she'd have gone to another, I know," he'd written, and "Had we not wed at once, I'd have lost her forever," he explained. And then, "With a family coming soon now, I know you and Mother will understand that I can no longer send very much to you, and with my future here with Amy, I doubt I can ever return to you. In time, when I've made my fortune, it might be that I could send for you one at a time. But first there's our new home I must pay for, and the baby coming with all its needs, and Amy cannot go in rags, it would not look well for me, so I know you both will understand that . . ."

Ah, but she did, she thought, smoothing out the letter and folding it neatly so that she wouldn't need to read further now. He'd been without Mama and herself for all of a year, and he'd forsaken all he'd promised them, because he, poor lad, had never been able to do for himself, and so could scarcely be expected to do for others; it had been their own folly to presume that age would bring him what had not been born in his bones. So now, Victoria thought, remembering Mrs. Finch's barely disguised smile, and knowing it for what it was at last, they could tell her to take up permanent residence within the very walls here instead of only crawling into them for an hour as she'd been forced to do the other day, and she'd have little option but to comply. Now she was truly alone, for once hope has been killed, the will either bends to the pressure or breaks entirely.

So when Alfie gained audience with her in the late afternoon, he was surprised to see her more pale and quiet and bereft of laughter and animation than she'd ever been, even when he'd feared that she lay dying.

"Sickening again?" he asked as they strolled down the gravel path in front of the Manor as they always did in clement weather, for from the first, even though she was always given leave to visit with Alfie when he came, he'd always taken care to have conversation with her far from any watchful eyes or listening ears.

"No, no, dear," she replied quietly, so quietly that he frowned as he stared up at her averted head, "it's only that I'm just a little weary today."

"Tibbet's not gone after you, 'as 'e? I'll sort 'im," Alfie growled, thinking of the butler he'd already decided was no match for himself.

The first laughter she'd felt in hours tickled at Victoria's throat as she thought of the bony, lofty Tibbet unbending so much as to touch another being, though perhaps, she thought, with gloves, he might. And when she told this to Alfie, he laughed as well, as much in relief for seeing her own amusement as for the jest, for unlike Victoria, Alfie was familiar with the baser ways of mankind in general, and had no difficulty picturing anyone touching anyone else.

"You've got the sullens, Miss Victoria," he said shrewdly, "but I've a thing 'ere that's a cure for them. Just cast your eye over this 'ere I brought for you, and then tell me you're feeling 'weary.' C'mon, read 'er, they 'ad me bring 'er so's no one else could see it. Since I tole 'em they never tole you Mrs. Haverford came to call on you, they don't trust nothing to the post, and that's only sensible. 'Ere, read 'er now, so's I can bring an answer, like I'm s'posed to do."

Victoria had grave doubts when she saw the letter Alfie thrust at her, for she'd had enough to do with those outwardly innocent pieces of paper for one day, or for one year, for that matter, but Alfie was not to be denied, so she took it from him. He watched carefully as she unfolded it and began to read. He saw her eyes widen as she scanned the lines; then he saw her read it again, and then once more, though it was a simple enough message, and he'd committed it to his gratified heart the moment he'd stood and peered over a broad shoulder, watching it being set to paper.

"Miss Dawkins," it said, in the same impatient hand that she'd seen before, "we find we must ask a favor of you. My mother's companion, Miss Comfort, has taken it into her head to visit with some near relatives. That being the case, and being new to this area, we discover ourselves about to be bereft of a companion for my mama, as well as for a tutor for the Johnson children. I know you are well established at the Manor, and can only ask you to come to us as a personal favor with the assurance that as the only governess-companion in residence, there should be no gossip about your presence here to disturb you, and with the promise that I will meet and surpass whatever wages you are presently receiving."

The word "No" was on Victoria's tongue, for weeks of maltreatment and mockery from the Ludlows were preferable to one more moment of embarrassment in front of the earl, and the simple syllable was almost out when Alfie said, "There's more, there at the very bottom, see?" and she read the hasty postscript: "Not only do I now ask you to come to live at my home, Miss Dawkins, I ask it as a personal favor to me."

"Well?" said Alfie. "You'll be ready to go in the morning?"

"Since I suppose I must pack and sleep first, yes," she said at once.

None of the Ludlows turned out to see Miss Dawkins leave in the morning, but all of them, save for the squire, who slept the sleep of the entirely castaway, wondered if they ought. It presented a neat social problem they were incapable of solving. It was true that Miss Dawkins was only an upper servant, which was precisely why no one but the housekeeper and the butler were supposed to be there to see her off, as was customary, to make certain no silverplate had been slipped into her baggage. But she was going to High Wyvern Hall and the Earl of Clune's carriage had been sent to take her on that short journey. It was also true, if the gentleman's story were to be believed, that she really was a friend of the noble family, which was why Mrs. Ludlow and her daughters watched her departure from behind their curtained windows, wondering at whether they ought to at least lift a hand in farewell. But then again, she'd left without proper notice given, which was reason enough to shun her entirely, if not to stone her through the gates, and yet again, she'd left upon the request of their neighbor, who was not only an earl but also entirely attractive, wealthy, and unwed, and so must be allowed his peccadilloes. His predecessors, after all, had been permitted far more.

The Ludlows weren't the only ones to be suffering from an admixture of feelings this morning. While the squire's family pondered their insoluble social dilemma, Victoria sat back in the carriage and tried to deal with her own excitement and fear so that Alfie, who'd come along to oversee her remove, would see neither. But he was too busy telling her about how thrilled the other children were at the idea of her return to notice her state of mind. Or, Victoria, thought on a little smile, perhaps that was precisely why he was so busily entertaining her with stories about them as the coach left the Old Manor behind.

She was beyond delighted to see the last of the Ludlows, far more than thrilled to be going to High Wyvern Hall, and thoroughly terrified as well. But it was never the rumored specters in the Hall she was going to that haunted her thoughts, for half a hundred ghosts could sail up over the carriage as she came up the drive and she thought it would not faze her half so much as the sight of the earl would.

It was difficult enough knowing how to behave at any new post; she'd always found that one of the hardest things to become accustomed to in her brief career. It was never easy to come into people's homes, get to know them intimately, all the while remembering to keep a distance and a cool professional attitude. It wasn't only failure to get along with the strangers that employed her that she feared when she began a new job. She often worried about what would happen should the reverse be true and she found that she suited a position well enough to remain permanently.

Dwelling for years among people she might grow to know as well and perhaps care for as much as her own family would present problems too. Because she knew that all the while, for all those years, she'd have to remind herself constantly that however dear to her they became, they were neither kin nor friends, but always and only her employers. Living that way for decades, she wondered, wouldn't part of her heart wither away for lack of use?

A paid servant could never forget her position so much as to show an excess of affection to her employers or she'd give offense and be considered presumptuous. And she could never expect a similar show of love in return, or she'd be considered addled. This constant girdling of the spirit, Victoria often thought, must eventually cripple it, and so she'd almost been glad that in her short career she'd never been with a family long enough to care enough, and so be hurt by them.

Now she was going to work for the earl, to tend to the children, whom she already loved far too well, and to companion Mrs. Haverford, whom she'd begun to feel a great fondness toward. And she'd be sharing a home, however huge, with a man she suspected she could come to care for far too well, far too soon, and for no good reason at all.

Would she have been better off, she'd wondered as she'd dressed this morning, if she'd taken on the position as his mistress immediately? She scarcely knew him, but couldn't deny how attracted she was to him; the mere thought of seeing him again had kept her up half the night with racing heart, alternating between delight and fright, despite all the stern lectures she'd given herself. There well might not be gossip about her presence in his home if Miss Comfort were gone, just as he'd promised. But of course he couldn't promise that his new foolish employee would cease to respond to the very sight of him. So if she were going to be hurt in any event, as she strongly suspected she would be, simply by constantly being near to him, then wouldn't a gentleman's mistress know him more intimately and thus more satisfyingly than a mere governess-companion in his household ever could?

When she thought of the things a mistress would come to know about a gentleman, and there were a great many things she could think of, since her father had insisted on an enlightened household, her grandmother had been forthright, and she'd observed a great deal in her weeks in Mrs.

Rogers' lodgings, then she believed she ought simply to have said "Yes" to him that day, and been done with it.

But then too, she thought, if a governess loyal to a family for twenty years still had to conceal her heart's pleasure in that family, then a mistress, who she knew seldom received the opportunity to turn in twenty months, much less twenty years of servitude, might also have to disguise any real devotion she might come to feel for her employer. And, she'd realized, a mistress might also be expected to have some skill in her field, even as a governess did. Although she'd been schooled in many disciplines, she'd only been kissed a few times (and most often on the run, at that) by various gentlemen who oughtn't to have tried to take advantage of a female on her own in the first place. These errant males had ranged variously from a schoolmate's brother who'd been whacked by his papa for it, to an employer who'd caused her to give in her notice, to the earl, who'd only turned her world upside down and made her think, even for a second, that solid bourgeois little Miss Dawkins could ever sprawl, all in satin on a recamier, playing siren or mistress to an earl, and not be entirely ludicrous.

"But o' course," Alfie said a bit louder now, "if you been struck mute, then I'll just tell the coachman to turn round, since I don't think a deaf female is what they're after hiring today."

"I have been thinking," Victoria said self-righteously, since she couldn't come up with a better defense for her total and unflattering abstraction.

"Been worrying," Alfie corrected her, and when she turned a smoothly innocent face to him, he went on smugly, "and for no reason at all. Everything will be fine now. Just think! There's over two dozen indoor servants at the Hall, now it's been opened, and not only does Mrs. Haverford know every first name of everyone of 'em, but there's not so much as one passage in one wall for them to creep into," but here he paused, looking momentarily regretful, before he continued on a note of triumph. "No, and they wouldn't need to, nobody has to face the wall like a lumpkin when 'is lordship passes. Why, if they did, they'd be sent off to be quacked before they could spit, for they'd be thought foaming mad, they would. If it's ghosts that's worrying you," he said consolingly, "might as well put that away as well, for there's not been a sniff of one about, and I prowled the place one night till I gave the footmen a turn, but nary a sight of 'em did I get. Between us, Miss Victoria, I s'pect it's all a hum the old earl started to keep relatives away. More haunts whipping about in the Tower in London every night, the earl says, and I believe him."

"Thank you," Victoria replied pleasantly. "Now I shall sleep tonight."

" 'Course you will. You don't have to worry about any other visitors in your bed neither, Miss Victoria," Alfie said blandly, " 'cause as for the earl 'isself, whatever 'e's thinking, 'e's a real gent, and 'e'll never do a thing with his mama and us about the place."

Victoria turned to her guide with an expression of shock, but before she could go through the embarrassing charade of denying that which she felt no small boy ought to think of, much less know so well, she caught sight of the towers of High Wyvern Hall in the window behind him, and so completely forgot all she was about to say.

"It is something, ain't it?" Alfie said as proudly as if the great house were his own, as he saw her stare.

It was, she felt, a good deal more than that, but at that moment she hadn't the words to express it, and indeed, it had taken learned men centuries to find the precise words for the ancient building. She'd read of its beginnings in the book about the Manor, whose chroniclers never forgot to detail its more famous neighbor, since the Ludlows, both quick and dead, knew very well that all their home's fame lay in the fact that it lay in the shadow of the enormous Hall.

Once, it was said, primitive men had built a fortress on the highest hill that overlooked the surrounding meadows. A Roman dignitary had built himself a home for a life of ease on the ruins of that, and when his house crumbled after his empire did, gentler souls, religious men, came and built a place to worship. But gentle men were not destined to command the hill, and when their world was toppled by quarrels of kings and princes of the Church, the first Earl of Clune, a most ungentle man, came to build himself a home.

He took an idea from each of the others who had failed before him. He planned to build a fortress, he would construct a luxurious home, and he decided to erect a great house of veneration. But all in one, and all for himself. And he would build one that would last the ages.

Ages had not passed since he'd set the first stone upon stone, but Victoria could think of nothing less than the Apocalypse which could topple his structure now. It stood on top of a hill in a leveled-off court, and it grew from the earth to reach toward the sky, and wrapped around the top of the rise to dominate the scene. Its highest windows could look out far beyond the landscaped grounds to the west, and to the east, to a ribbon of blue that was the estuary, and on a clear day to a further shining silver horizon that was the wide sea itself.

The first earl had begun the structure with stones stolen from all his predecessors, and wrenched the rest from the surrounding countryside. His descendants had added to it in the same spirit and material, and so the Hall was the color of red earth with salmon and gold tones intermixed. Because each successive architect had honored the first earl's concept, the building had kept to a form and so kept to its dignity and spoke in its every well-shaped line of strength, not mere weight, and of power, not simple size.

Victoria remained silent as the carriage went round the long drive, past trees and hedges, through hollows and over rises, losing and then catching sight of the Hall again in a mischievous game of discovery, just as Capability Brown had intended when he designed its approach for the fifth Earl of Clune. When the coach finally stopped in front of the house, Victoria stepped down in a daze, all the while keeping her neck craned back and her eyes on the most magnificent home she'd ever seen, and then found herself halted by a flurry of warmth and noise in the region of her knees.

"Miss Victoria!" Sally cried, hugging her legs.

"Oh, Miss Victoria," Bobby said hoarsely, trying to remain as cool as his brother would wish, while yearning to be as spontaneous as his sister had been, and so succeeding only in becoming quite red in the face as Miss Dawkins swept him up as well in her perfumed embrace.

When the laughter had stopped and the few errant tears been mopped up surreptitiously by all concerned, Victoria discovered Mrs. Haverford to be standing on the front steps with her hand outstretched in welcome, just as though she were greeting a Personage, and not just a governess-companion. It was then a while before Victoria could trust herself to speak.

So it was just as fortunate that she did not have to. The children wanted her to see their new home at once, if not sooner, and laughing, Mrs. Haverford agreed. They wouldn't be able to utter a sensible word with the children bursting with impatience anyway, she opined, since she told Victoria she'd discovered that even silent little Johnsons had the habit of shifting from foot to foot and looking so imperative you feared they might pop if you touched them when they had something they felt was important to disclose. The children, she decided, would take their new governess through the house while a maid unpacked for her. They would all meet afterward in the rose sitting room, for, as Mrs. Haverford said sensibly, it was quite a long jaunt, and as she added with a quirked grin that reminded Victoria of her son for one painful-pleasant moment, she'd already seen the place.

It was indeed a long journey of discovery that the children led Miss Dawkins upon. There were so many rooms that they passed through, looked in on, and remained in for a space to wonder at, that it was difficult to remember the whole of it even minutes after she had done with the tour. There were lavish rooms and exquisite ones, tasteful ones and some that delighted the children but caused Miss Dawkins to blink. There were rooms for dining and sleeping, rooms for playing and rooms for praying, rooms for reclining, rooms for tranquilizing oneself, rooms for entertaining others, glassed-in rooms for growing things, bricked-up rooms for storing things, rooms in which to paint or play instruments or act out plays or write them, rooms for gloating over amassed treasures, rooms in which to read about how to acquire more, there was even a room somewhere, she didn't doubt, for thinking about adding on more rooms.

Everywhere there were servants, and everywhere, unlike at the Old Manor, they smiled or bowed or curtsied as if it gave them pleasure to greet visitors, and never as though they simply feared giving offense if they did not. And they never seemed to mind, Victoria thought in glad bewilderment, that the visitors were merely children accompanied by a new servant. Cook gave the children bits of cakes and tastes of puddings and then scolded them lightly for ruining their appetites for dinner; the housemaids dipped their little curtsies like dropped giggles; the footmen grinned; even the butler, however imperceptibly, definitely smiled upon them.

There were some in the house that Victoria noted especially, for they looked so pleasant she wondered if she might not make some friends in her stay here. There was a hearty elderly fellow who had recently been hired on, he said happily, to restore the library, which had fallen upon hard times under the stewardships of the sixth and seventh earls; there was a charming couple who were similarly attending to the picture gallery, engaged to clean and document it; there was a merry-looking little female near her own age, niece and apprentice to the housekeeper; and there was another young woman Victoria spied drifting through the music room, an ethereally beautiful fair-haired creature who smiled tenderly when she saw the children excitedly leading their new governess about, before she wafted into an alcove and was gone from sight.

Then, high in the house, in the southern wing, they met Nurse, grateful to be summoned from retirement in the village to tend to Baby, who, while always a good child, as though he'd always known he lived on tolerance, now outdid himself. For he sat in her ample lap in the old nursery as quietly and placidly as though he quite understood how he was honored here, and feared to give one gurgle that might upset his new and beautiful applecart.

Then they met with Miss Comfort. She was busy packing her bags, but spared a moment for them. The country air hadn't seemed to agree with her. Seeing her again, Victoria felt ashamed of some of her own dark and private reasonings about precisely why the earl had summoned her to the Hall. Because it was clear that Miss Comfort really needed this sudden vacation she was taking. There was no doubt that the old woman had somehow aged even further, and even more unsettling was the fact that she was uncharacteristically subdued. She seemed a shadow of the acerbic and opinionated person she'd been. And just as when one hears that a noisy neighbor one's been complaining of has died, Victoria thought guiltily, in this case the absence of a nuisance was more unsettling than it was satisfying. Miss Comfort's new state was as depressing as she herself was obviously depressed. Since Victoria had seen her last, her face had grown more lines and become grayer and her movements were stiff and awkward. But she smiled at the children, and stroked Sally's fair hair with one thin hand, and even had a brief word and a small smile and a wish for success for Miss Dawkins, her replacement.

"Looks like she's seen a ghost, don't she?" Alfie said, shaking his head sadly as they left Miss Comfort's room.

"Shhh, Alfie, please," Victoria cautioned, fearing they were still within earshot of the diminished older woman.

"Oh, Miss Victoria," Sally breathed in alarm, "are you scairt of ghosts?"

"Absolutely," Alfie said blithely. "It's why she din't come to visit us here in all this time, don't you know?"

And so as they went down one arm of the long double central staircase to meet with Mrs. Haverford again, Victoria protested her innocence in the matter of her aversion to undead spirits, as Alfie teased her about her horror of meeting up with night-walking specters and to reassure her, both Bobby and Sally loudly voiced disclaimers of any knowledge of the merest shadow of any shade hovering within the great Hall. The several conversations ended abruptly when they reached the bottom of the stairs. For then both a spotted spaniel and some unidentified fuzzy moplike creature Sally vowed was a dog came hurtling, claws scrambling and sliding across the marble floors in their attempts to elude a panting footman, to achieve sanctuary in Bobby's arms. That they achieved bliss there as well was undeniable, for eyeing the roiling, tumbling beasts lapping at his brother's face, Alfie sighed, " 'E keeps finding 'em about the place and bringing 'em into 'is bed. 'E don't need covers no more, 'e don't, but 'e's starting to stink like a kennel for all 'e thinks 'e's clever spraying 'em with the bay rum 'e begged from a groom. Now 'e smells like a groom in a kennel what fell into a vat of flowers."

Victoria remembered a large black dog she'd seen trailing the children sometime during their walk through the Hall, but he'd gone by the time she'd turned around to ask them if he was gentle with strangers. She'd enjoyed the company of small dogs in the city, and always regretted there'd never been a place for one in London above an apothecary's shop. But she was city-bred and had never known a beast the size of the one she'd spied. Now she saw that Bobby likely had a collection of dogs in every size and style imaginable, and even some, she thought, eyeing the shaggy creature the footman was gently detaching from his new young master, quite unidentifiable.

As she then followed her eager young guides to the rose sitting room to meet with her new employer, Miss Dawkins thought in that moment she'd never been so content. It was not only due to the dazzling wonders of the great Hall, for the children, their laughter, even the merriment of the dogs, all contributed to her feeling of well-being, a sense of having found at last, after much travail, a safe harbor from the storm, a place where she could be herself and build a good life.

But there was no such place on the earth, she remembered suddenly, if there was no such place in her heart. For the door to the rose sitting room swung open and she saw the eighth Earl of Clune, dark-visaged and all in dark colors, like the shadow he cast over her realistic chances for happiness in the future, and as strong and substantial as the yearnings the sight of him brought back to her. And being unlike the rumored haunts of his house in every other way as well, he was thus as real as her fears of him and of herself were. Then, compounding them all, he smiled and came forward to take her hand and say, ''Welcome, Miss Dawkins, to my home.

''We're pleased to see you,'' he continued, as she rapidly withdrew her hand from his firm clasp before he could detect how cold it had grown. ''It's very good of you to come so soon—it will make it a smoother transition if Comfort's substitute arrives as she packs to leave. Thank you.''

Victoria averted her eyes from his long dark gaze and managed to murmur some polite agreement. She would have been far less frightened, although not a whit more comfortable, had she known that she herself would be packing in a sincere attempt to leave by the next afternoon.

10

Everyone was rushing in different directions. The footmen who weren't tearing off into the kitchens to find vinegar and spirits were being dispatched to the housekeeper's larders to unearth salts and blankets. Maids were dashing every which way, some waving their aprons like giant white fans in response to the earl's call for "air," and some, skirts held high, were running off to the stables to be sure the cleverest groom on the swiftest horse was sent to the doctor's straightaway. Only the children, Miss Dawkins, and of course Miss Comfort were absolutely still.

The earl was holding Miss Comfort in his arms, and though he'd held many another female close to his heart, it was fair to say that he had never disliked it so much before, nor ever been so alarmed or confused by it, no, not even when he'd been barely sixteen and beginning, with the help of an unexpectedly obliging dairy maid, to succeed in furthering his education beyond his wildest dreams. But the old woman had just begun to ascend the steps to the coach that was about to bear her away to her distant cousin Emma's house, when she'd stopped, staggered, and then fallen down insensate. He had caught her up in his arms just as she'd started to crumple, and now his mama was shouting instructions at all the household staff who'd come to see his now-insensible burden off on her travels, and the drive in front of the Hall was swarming with distracted people.

Finally, with a grimace of annoyance, the gentleman swung around and strode back into the house with Miss Comfort. "She'll do better in her bed," he called over his shoulder as he ascended the stair. As he approached the woman's room, he was relieved to note that she was still breathing, and as he placed her upon her coverlet, he was tangentially bemused by the fact that he seemed to be making a habit of carrying unconscious governess-companions off to their beds these days, but unhappily, they were either the wrong sort or it was for the wrong reasons.

He left Miss Comfort to the ministrations of his mama and the housekeeper and her minions, and went off to the study to wait upon the doctor's arrival. The children, he noted with approval, had all gone off with their new governess, so that they were neither underfoot nor over excited by the odd occurrence. He felt twinges of guilt as he waited for the physician, for he'd never cared for Miss Comfort and had been delighted at the thought of her absence from his mama's home, even if it were only to be for a few weeks or months, or however long it took for Miss Dawkins to find other suitable employment, as she'd agreed. Still, he couldn't deny he'd been grateful those years ago when he'd first left home to seek their fortune and his mama had written to say that she'd found a relative willing and able to come help with the other children. But he hadn't liked her when he'd finally met her, and didn't doubt the feeling was mutual. She suffered him, he imagined, only because he provided for his mama so handsomely.

Miss Comfort was the sort of female, he mused as he sat at his predecessor's desk and stared at papers he did not see, who made a man feel masculine in the worst sense of the word. Her femininity was used as a barrier to easy acquaintance, she caused males to be acutely but uneasily aware of their gender, and she was in some fashion like a spindly gilt chair or a frilled and pink boudoir filled with scent. In her presence a fellow always felt uncomfortable: too large, too loud, too ungainly. Her attitude toward males, he'd often felt, was very much like some females' attitudes toward dogs. He'd often heard charming young ladies sigh that they loved dear little puppies so, that it was a shame that they had to grow up to become great slobbering brutes. Even Theo, not the most observant chap, had reflected on how it was odd that Old Cold Comfort had seemed to like him when she'd first met him only a few years before, but now that he was a man, she appeared to disapprove of the transformation. Since that transformation had not been especially splendid, his cousin had forborne to comment, but there'd been truth in the perception.

But the earl certainly didn't wish the old woman any harm, in fact he so much wanted her well enough to go ahead with her plans that when his mama, accompanied by the physician, finally requested audience with him, he ushered them into his study personally. Then he stood and waited so eagerly to hear the doctor's pronouncement that the fellow could be forgiven for thinking the new earl had a sincere and pronounced attachment to his newest patient. Then the fact that his diagnosis of Miss Comfort's condition caused the earl's face to darken confirmed the doctor's diagnosis of the gentleman's fondness for the old woman, and so he said very quickly (for being a young chap just starting a new practice in the district, he wished to be pleasing).

"But with rest, sufficient rest and good nourishment, I see no reason, my lord, why she shouldn't be completely herself again. In my opinion," and here he paused, for he was still a very young man and regrettably also a small and thin one at that, so that he often worried that his opinion might not carry much more weight then he did, but then he went on hurriedly, "and I doubt I'm mistaken, although of course, you may call for another opinion, I understand you have a physician in London, but I hear nothing amiss with her heart, nor do I see problems with any other bodily part beyond that which her years might most naturally account for, and so it's simple and plain exhaustion, I believe. She hasn't been sleeping well, nor eating well either, you know."

"No, I didn't," the earl commented. "But how long before she can travel, for example?"

"Oh, Cole," his mama sighed, as the doctor said thoughtfully, "I see no reason why she shouldn't be able to embark on the trip she'd planned," and the earl's face brightened, while the doctor, being a punctilious young man, paused to give an exact estimate, but then became morose when the physician ventured to say at last, "oh yes, there should be no problem with that in, say, two or three months."

After the physician had left, most impressed with the compassion the earl had shown toward his servants, since there wasn't a doubt, the young doctor thought with approval, that the nobleman was most unhappy with the news that the poor old woman would have to remain bedridden for some weeks to come, the earl's mama, no more perceptive than the physician, but better acquainted with her son, sat and grieved with him.

"I blame myself," she sighed. "I do, Cole. For from the first, after I'd met Miss Dawkins, I hinted and hinted about how I wished I could provide sanctuary for her, but that of course I couldn't, not when I already had a companion. It was too bad, I kept saying, that a trivial thing such as our fear of gossip might mean the end to such a sweet young child's chances in life. I kept sighing over the inequality of it all, in that we could take in the Johnson children, and though it would be counted an eccentric deed, it could be dismissed as a mere act of charity, especially since we'd found someone to foster them, yet Miss Dawkins' very youth and beauty condemned her to our neglect. I kept harping on the fact that sheltering her, especially after those rumors about young Theo, would only fuel speculation about your motives, Cole, since everyone knew I already had the longtime services of a companion who was also a qualified governess. Then, I'll admit it, I mentioned Comfort's other relatives half a dozen times, and at least half a hundred times I just dropped a word, mind, just a word, about how she'd earned a nice pension, and kept wondering aloud about whether that cottage she was always going on about retiring to when the time came mightn't still be available.

"And then when you and Alfie told us about the Ludlows

and their ghastly walls filled with servants, Comfort saw how distressed I was. When she finally ventured to say that she might clear the way for Miss Dawkins by leaving to visit her relative until matters were settled, I practically leapt at the suggestion, and exclaimed over how clever it was until she sent word to them announcing she was coming. And I only offered the footman an extra guinea for an immediate answer, and when she got it, I actually helped her to pack. Oh, fie, Cole, I feel a beast now. Poor Comfort, as soon as she wakes from that potion the physician gave her, I must assure her that she is, was, and always shall be welcome here."

Her son refrained from replying "Is she?" as he was tempted to do, and was thinking of a suitable noncommittal reply when he heard an excited conference in the hallway grow louder when it arrived at his door. Before the tapping had even begun then, he called, "Enter," and saw three distressed young people obey his command.

"She's only packing. She's only set on leaving, and she won't stop, no matter what I say," Alfie reported in exasperation.

"Oh, poor dear," Mrs. Haverford cried, rising. "But the doctor said she mustn't set foot from her bed for at least a week. I must talk sense to her. She can't take on such a trip in her condition and at her age."

" 'Er age and 'er condition?" snapped Alfie. "It ain't like she's Miss Comfort or nothing. Fact, if she was like 'er, she'd be a sight safer, but where's a smasher like 'er going to find a safe place to anchor now she's burnt 'er bridges behind 'er?"

"It's Miss Victoria who's leaving now, ma'am," Sally wailed plaintively, as Bobby added in amplification, "Aye, my lady, she says as how she only came 'cause Miss Comfort was leaving, and now she can't stay on. She *mustn't* stay on now, is 'ow . . . how she says it."

"No matter what I says," Alfie said angrily.

"I must speak with her," Mrs. Haverford exclaimed.

"No," her son decided, "I must. And I shall."

"Ah, well then, now that's settled it," Alfie sighed contentedly as the earl strode past him to the door.

* * *

Miss Dawkins found her packing a very simple task. Her things, after all, hadn't had a long enough tenure in her bureau drawers or wardrobe to have gotten into the bad habits of sprawling or relaxing into difficult positions, and so were easy to refold neatly. And the one or two stray tears that fell into her linens and slippers scarcely took up any room at all. She hadn't bothered to close her door, and she stowed her things away again in her portmanteau in plain sight of the world, for the moment she'd realized that Miss Comfort was staying on, she'd decided she was leaving, and had hurried to finish packing before anyone was assigned the embarrassing task of telling the new governess she was redundant.

She had only the faintest glimmering of an idea as to where she would go, although she was ready to tell anyone who asked that she was exactly sure of her future course. The Ludlows' Manor was out of the question, of course; if life had been difficult there before her desertion, it would be impossible to bear after it, and likely impossible in actuality as well, since she doubted they would take her back at all. She could not, would not, land herself upon her mama, to jeopardize her already tenuous position. But she had some money saved, and she would, she imagined, go back to London, register with the Misses Parkinson again, find another rooming house similar to Mrs. Rogers', and perhaps she'd meet up with some precocious children and . . . And then she shook her head and took in a deep and resolute breath. For damp clothes, she decided with some real annoyance with herself, would be the devil to get wrinkles out of when she unpacked at last, wherever she landed.

"The Johnson clan is monstrously spoiled here, I know, but I scarcely thought they were that bad," a deep voice commented dryly and with the slightly slurred sibilance which had never ceased to echo in her mind. Victoria looked up to see the earl leaning against the doorjamb.

"It's never the children . . ." she began.

"No, I didn't really think so," he said, straightening and coming into the room after carefully closing the door a few inches so that while it was still open, they were more private.

Her eyes widened, and despite her desire to be cool, she backed a pace from the portmanteau she'd been trying to close as he loomed over her. He looked at her keenly and seemed discomfited himself for a moment.

"I don't ask permission to enter your room," he explained at once, taking his black gaze from her and looking around the chamber which she'd already stripped of all her personal belongings, "since obviously, it's no longer your room, is it? And I imagine," he said, lowering his voice, "it's not really anything to do with your duties here either. It's me, isn't it? I never explained matters fully to you, did I? But then, I've never had a moment alone with you since that morning in your delightful landlady's parlor, have I? Hush," he said, raising his hand. "Those are rhetorical questions. I should think that as a governess you ought to know them when you hear them.

"Really, Miss Dawkins, I assure you, you have less to fear from me now than you have from our famous nonexistent ghosts. It's true that at our first private meeting I did ask an impertinent question of you, although," he mused with a contagious smile lightening his dark face, "there are those that would claim an English nobleman can never be impertinent, not even with his creator, or else he'd never have been created a lord of the realm in the first place. And I hope," he added with unmistakable laughter now coloring his voice, "that there'd be a great many who'd rush to defend my further point that it was a flattering offer rather than a demeaning one. But nevertheless, no matter how you parse it, it was only an offer, Miss Dawkins. Never a command or a claim or a demand.

"You refused," he said softly, watching how she colored up and suddenly seemed to find her fingertips fascinating as he went on, "and so be it. It's regrettable, but it's forgotten, I assure you. I don't know what sort of employers you're used to, Miss Dawkins, and it's not pleasant for me to conjecture what you imagine my attractiveness to be to others of your sex, but I promise you I'm neither so driven nor so desperate a chap that I'd enlist my own mama and lure innocent children to my estate so as to better lay my hands upon you. I do need a governess for the children you saddled me with. No, don't bother denying it, you passed them on to me. From the moment they clapped eyes on me I've been in their thrall. They're rather like tar babies, aren't they? They stick to one's heart at one touch," he complained, "and I begin to think I'll never shake myself free."

She smiled at him then, looking up from her hands and smiling so radiantly that he wished to continue saying amusing things to her for hours, so that she'd continue to look at him so. But then something in his appreciative reciprocal smile caused hers to waver so he went on, in a parody of sorrow, "And my mama, although the most liberal parent imaginable, would not be best pleased if her eldest son took to creeping about the Hall, plotting and planning on how to seduce her new companion. I wasn't born to the nobility, but I was raised 'proper.' " He grinned. "I can't deny that I find you attractive, but neither can I forget that you're now my dependent. So you've nothing to fear but my admiration, and admiration's never assault. So you see," he concluded with a helpless shrug, "whatever my original goals, and I'll not deny that they were very different, please believe me when I tell you that now you are entirely safe in my home."

"But," she said very quietly, "you did say that you did not want me in your home."

"So I did," he admitted seriously, "because I didn't want gossip, nor did I care to contribute to such gossip. But now there is a good and valid reason for you to be here, which might still the tattlers, though nothing short of death, ours or theirs, will silence them, you understand. Then too, I believe that if I'm surrounded by infants and hemmed about by servants, and watched over by my mama, my lascivious nature might be bridled. Mind you," he sighed, "I don't say it will be changed, but I do believe it could be contained."

She had to grin at that, both at his self-mockery and at the picture of her own outsize vanity that his words provoked. As if, she thought in shamed realization of how foolish her previous fears and hopes had been, as if it were halfway likely that an earl, a gentlemen of his obvious intelligence and stature, would risk disgracing his name before his own family, simply for the sake of some stolen moments with a commoner he'd once briefly thought of as a bed companion.

"I was leaving," she said at once, as honestly as she was able, "precisely because of the possibility of gossip. I know, indeed, I can never forget, how kind you and your mama have been to me and the children, but I'm not a homeless child. I'm a grown woman. That's why I'm going. I understand that not only does Miss Comfort have nothing seriously wrong with her, but that she's staying. And if so, there's no more reason for me to stay on as well, except for reasons of your charity. And though I'm mindful of it, I can't accept it any longer. Indeed," she went on, less honestly, and thus in far cheerier accents, "there's no reason for me to do so. I'm well qualified for the position, I'll do very well for myself, I assure you."

She was exceedingly proud of the way she said it and of the way she'd managed to do so without once letting any emotion but sincerity peek through her words. But then, once she'd done, and he stood watching her with an unfathomable expression, she had to look down at her portmanteau and fuss with the straps on it to maintain her equilibrium.

"Very well, then," he said briskly, "you may start to unpack at once. Because you can't have heard the doctor's final ultimatum. Although fortunately she's not in desperate case, nonetheless Miss Comfort's to stay in her bed for quite some time, weeks, months perhaps. Unless the children wish to take up residence at her headboard and my mama wants to pass all her time at the foot, I believe they'll need a new governess-companion at once. What luck that we happen to have such a highly qualified one on the premises."

Then, as he turned to go, he paused at her door and said, in the lowest of voices, but with his words tempered by the wickedest grin, "And to think, all the while you were leaving because of Comfort! And I made all those rash promises to behave myself, and there was never a need for it at all.'' Then, shaking his head sadly, he left her to her unpacking.

''The boy was not only born to hang,'' the earl said pleasantly as he came up to the fence and rested his arms against it, ''it's clear he was born to ride as well. Have you ever seen such horsemanship? And he's only been in the saddle for a matter of weeks. Now,'' he said, looking down at the young woman who stood at the rail of the riding ring, ''if he could only learn to speak as well as he can ride, we might have the makings of a gentleman.''

Victoria flushed. She hated herself for not having a quick and amusing retort for him. She had rehearsed quite a few to impress him with over the past week, but she'd seldom seen him, much less had a chance to amaze him with her wit, since the day he'd persuaded her to stay on at the Hall. Now he'd materialized from out of nowhere in the afternoon sunlight and spoke at her elbow just as she was watching Alfie put a horse through its paces. Not only had he startled her, since for such a substantial gentlemen he could move very silently, she thought with some grievance, but he'd mentioned the slum accents Alfie used, the ones he could put on and take off like a cloak, and, as she'd also realized soon after meeting the boy, the ones he used precisely as a cloak for his true feelings. She could scarcely betray Alfie's secret, and yet if she didn't she knew she'd portray herself as a poor instructress. To sink her further, she knew that all the while she pondered how to reply, she was portraying herself as a ninny, standing gazing down at the grass before her employer, blushing and searching for words.

''The remarkable thing,'' the earl said gently as he leaned against the fence and contemplated the effect his remark had upon her, ''is how the boy manages to sound precisely like a gentleman when it's needful and yet can revert to a gutter rat whenever he deems it preferable or is unnerved, or had you noticed? No,'' he said, watching her closely, ''it wasn't fair of me, was it? But, Miss Dawkins, this is not the Manor either, you know. You may disagree with me from time to time. In fact, now that I think on it, considering how my own mama, Miss Comfort, and even Alfie treat me, you and the under kitchen maid—you know the plump one with the red hair and the space between her teeth?—well then, you two are the only ones who treat me with the outsize respect obviously due me."

He seemed to brood over this as Victoria stood tongue-tied, thinking of the several clever things she'd like to say in response, all the things she knew she ought not to say to any of the men she responded to: the nobleman, the employer, and the outrageously attractive gentleman, all of whom the earl personified.

"At any rate," he said at length, his voice now bored and smooth, as he glanced away from her to Alfie, "I just dropped by to see the lad, and to be sure lessons in the schoolroom were going as well as those in the riding ring."

"Oh, absolutely, my lord," Victoria replied readily, for she stood on firm ground when she spoke of her duties. "He's as quick and able a student as one would wish, and he's so enthusiastic about bettering himself, he sets a firm example for the younger ones. Bobby is just as able, although much more shy, and Sally . . . why, Sally is as bright as her face would lead you to believe. I'm most pleased with all of them—you may be sure I've no complaint. Is there anything else you wish to know?"

The Earl of Clune stood and contemplated her for a moment before he spoke, and she thought he was considering her question. He was, but only in the sense of wondering at the banality of it. Amazing, he thought to himself, incredible actually. What a poor judge of humanity I am become, how lucky I'm not a rash fellow. For, he mused, gazing at the pretty, demure female awaiting his reply, I'd thought her damnably attractive, she preyed on my mind, she'd half turned me upside down trying to sort out my emotions of lust, pity, and admiration. Yet the more I know of her, the less there is to know. She's bright, to be sure, but entirely conventional, and likely, once out of my bed, she'd have bored me to extinction in an hour. And as for bed, it was only her face which brought me to think of it, he realized. It was the thought of my asking her to that naughty place that lent her the only animation she's ever shown me, he decided.

Why, she's Comfort, he thought then in sudden amazement, Comfort herself, a generation past. If he could imagine the old governess young, he thought, he might as well concede she may have been beautiful. But beauty, to such life-denying, insipid, conventional creatures, he thought on an inward shrug, was entirely unimportant, and indeed, entirely incidental. In fact, the more he contemplated the prim and passionless Miss Dawkins as she stared at the ground awaiting his reply, the less lovely she appeared to be to him. Now he decided her cheek was not so much softly rounded as it was perhaps a trifle too plump, her nose might be considered a jot too short as well, and her upper lip, which he'd thought altogether enchanting and eminently kissable in its slightly outward thrust, now appeared merely flawed.

He felt a bit foolish for having entertained such lavish fantasies about such an uninspiring creature. But he was glad he'd discovered Miss Dawkins' fatal flaw. It was, he believed, only the absence of a personality. Then, somehow enormously relieved at his revelation, and continuing to gaze at her, acknowledging a jolt of disappointment as well, he became amused at himself for feeling blighted at being saved from distraction, aggravation, and worry, and so, smiling, he at last replied.

"No further questions, Miss Dawkins. I'm pleased everything is so well in hand."

He turned his attention to Alfie again, and had dismissed her so thoroughly from his mind that he was a bit startled to hear her voice at his side again.

"Ah, my lord," she said softly, "I have a question to ask of you, and though it was never important enough to seek you out for, since you seem at liberty at the moment . . . ?"

"Yes?" he asked, in a more abrupt fashion than he'd intended, since he'd been surprised.

She blushed. "It's foolishness itself," she murmured, but then she raised her head courageously, looked him in the eye, and said firmly, "Sally's been asking about the ghosts. You see, the boys have been teasing her mercilessly about them. They'd like nothing more than to be frightened out of their wits by one, you know. I believe it's only their disappointment at not having turned up any that's leading them on, but they've invented a pack of specters for their own amusment. It's gone too far, though, and poor Sally's afraid to put a toe outside her covers after dark now. Last night I came to tuck her in, and the poor thing was in some distress. Well, it seemed that she had to pay a visit to . . . ah, she had . . . she needed to use the necessary," Miss Dawkins ventured boldy, "but didn't dare step out of bed. The boys," she said ruefully, "told her a tale of one of your ancestors who likes nothing better than crawling along the nursery floor and catching hold of little girls' ankles. He was slain centuries ago, they said, by his little sister when he was on his way to the privy one night, and that's how he takes his revenge. Well," she said, and then she faltered, her sensibilities, the earl thought, too offended to go further, but then, to his amazement, he saw that it was laughter she was trying to suppress.

"They've peopled the Hall with all sorts of spirits," she continued in a shaken voice, "headless footmen and phantom coachmen, and even a governess who, because she could never get the first earl to listen to her, hides in the schoolroom and swells to twice her size in rage every full moon. Nothing that I, or Miss Comfort, or even your mama can say will ease her mind—really, my lord, they've invented some shocking tales. The one who sidles across the nursery floor looking for ankles is horrid enough, but some of the other ones are . . . positively inspired," she managed to say.

"Ah yes," the earl said thoughtfully, "the ankle-fancying chap, is he up to his old tricks again?"

At her wide-eyed look, he added pleasantly, "Though mind, the governess is the one most people complain of. No, I lie," he said thoughtfully, "the east bedroom, the one with the bay window and the yellow Chinese wallpaper, yes, that one has the worst of them. That's the room that has the fifth earl's spirit haunting it. It's a tragic story,'' he went on sadly. ''He died of a surfeit of pudding, yet refuses to lie at rest because he discovered there's no just deserts for him in the hereafter. His slurping, they say, is a ghastly sound at midnight, but I understand if one leaves a bowl of syllabub on the mantel each night it's quite safe. Why, that's your room, isn't it? Perhaps if you had a chat with Cook?'' he suggested solicitously.

Her laughter was a lovely sound, he thought. Alfie turned his attention to it, his mount's ears went back at it, even the groom with him smiled back in pleasure, for it was a young girl's irresistible laughter that rang out, rippling and rich and full-throated with nothing pinched and proper and governessy about it.

''Come''—the earl smiled—''we'll take a walk and talk about it where Alfie's horse can't hear us. That mettlesome beast's got his own sense of humor and will toss the lad off if he senses he's distracted. No, no, please, don't poker up, that's no complaint on my part, Lord knows this old Hall can use all the laughter it can get,'' he protested when her face became still, and he continued to smile at her until she visibly relaxed. Then he waved to Alfie before he led his governess away and down the path that led from the stables.

''I'll have a talk with Sally. I'll clear the Hall of any hint of a spirit for her, yes.'' He smiled down at Victoria, looking a bit shamefaced. ''I'm aware of the fact that she idolizes me. I can scarcely wait until she becomes old enough to see all my flaws, as all other adult females do. But if I can make use of her partiality for me to solace her now, I shall. For the truth of it is,'' he said thoughtfully, pacing along the bright flower-banked walk, ''that there *is* something about the Hall. Or do only we guilty Haverfords sense it?''

''No,'' Victoria replied seriously, all her fears about being too forthcoming with her employer fleeing in the face of a sensible query, ''I've only been here for a week''—she paused to get the words right—''but everyone speaks of it, from the housekeeper to the stableboys. The Hall is the loveliest noble home I've ever seen, not that

I've seen very many," she admitted on a depreciating smile, "but there's an atmosphere, a shadow, a sense of something, an uneasiness in the air that keeps it from being as beautiful as it might be . . . I cannot say it clearer," she admitted, "but I believe it might only be that with so many rumors of spirits, one keeps looking over one's shoulder for a glimpse of one. I understand that it was left deserted except for maintenance staff for a full year after the old earl passed on. I think ghosts breed in vacant rooms and phantoms thrive on loneliness.

"Perhaps that's why I never encountered any in London," she continued reflectively. "Space is too precious there, so we've probably crowded them all out, for surely just as many people die unhappy deaths there as do here in the countryside, but we haven't half the number of hauntings you seem to have. So just as the living displace the dead in London, perhaps now that the house is filled with children and dogs, the noise they make will chase all the old phantoms away."

He looked down and saw her tentative smile of tender reason, and realized that she was trying to reassure him just as though he were little Sally's age himself. But he did feel fractionally warmer for her smile.

"Thank you, Miss Dawkins." He grinned. "Now when I have, ah, that is to say, need . . . to use the necessary in the night, I can do so without stepping smartly and fearing for my ankles. Or was that only little girls my dreadful ancestor was after? If he was," he went on, his mood veering and his dark brows lowering, "then it was probably a true Earl of Clune the boys invented. Small wonder the Hall has such an evil reputation—a great many evil fellows ruled the roost here. That's not only hearsay. I met a few in my time.

"Perhaps," he said ruminatively as they strolled back to the house, "that's why I didn't open the house for so long. I've never felt at home here either. Likely all my predecessors are grumbling in the cellars and attics about the milksop that inherited the place from them, as well. I do feel their disapproval," he sighed, "but I've got the title and the house with it and it's my responsibility as I see it to hold all intact for the next earl. It might be that in time I'll sire some hell-raiser and that will placate them, because I begin to think that only in raising their spirits will I lower the spirits here." He laughed.

His companion only nodded at that, not sure whether she ought to make any comment on his potential fatherhood, and as though he realized this himself, he changed the subject quickly.

"Doubtless I disappoint them in a thousand ways," he said on a shrug. "I even cleared the place of their prize peacocks after I moved in."

"I know." Victoria laughed, feeling free to look up again at this. "Sally, I might tell you, regrets it almost as much as the boys do."

"Really?" he asked, frowning. "But I thought they detested the creatures as much as I did. I found them to be merely huge, glorified chickens. They spent half the night screeching at each other, and the other half fouling all the garden paths. They might have had lovely bodies, but their brains were sadly lacking. I spied one strutting in circles one morning, when there was no peahen about, exhibiting his tail in an effort to court a very bored pigeon. After they'd destroyed my sleep for a few weeks, leaping about on the parapets every night, mewling like cats to each other, I had them all herded up and gave them, every last feather of them, to Squire Hadley over in the next county. He sets great store by them and says they add dash to a gentleman's estates. But Alfie begged me to serve them up for dinner dressed in their own feathers, just as he'd seen in his history books, and Bobby said they gave him the headache, and Sally herself coveted their tails for a fan. Now you tell me they mourn their absence?"

"Only because they agree with Squire Hadley," Victoria laughed. "They're shocking climbers, you know. They feel their earl ought to have 'everything a gentleman ought to have,' as Sally says."

"I agree," he said with a nod of satisfaction, "but I draw the line at peacocks. But there, you see, my ancestors doted on the idiot creatures and I chucked them all out. Doubtless that raised up a surly Earl of Clune or two from the grave vowing to disturb my slumber more than his precious peacocks had done."

"I see," Victoria said, and then blurted, so amused at her sudden thought she was unable to stop herself, "then like 'The Princess and the Pea,' you feel they were some sort of test of your noble blood? But I never heard tell of 'The Prince and the Peacock,' " she added on a gurgle of laughter before she stopped short, aghast at her presumption. For he said nothing in that moment, did not even venture a grin at her jest, only stared at her, arrested. Then she remembered belatedly that a commoner ought not gibe with a nobleman, and neither should a servant rally an employer.

"Oh," he said at last, with a long slow smile, "but what a lovely idea—how I wish they'd put a few under my mattress instead of outside my window."

Then he roared with the laughter he'd suppressed, and all the way back to the Hall he laughed with her and joked with her, and quite made her forget her place entirely, and made her forget that she'd ever wished to leave this place entirely.

And all the way back he thought of how animated she was, how witty and how bright and lovely a creature she was, and realized that he had been right about that originally after all, and heartily regretted that he'd discovered it to be true again now, just when he'd convinced himself all his problems had been resolved.

11

"No," Miss Comfort said, "it is not done."

Victoria's shoulders slumped. It was, of course, the right answer—trust Miss Comfort to give the right answer—but it was the wrong one as well. The old woman, sitting up in her bed, decently clad in a ruffled bed gown with a bed jacket over that and a shawl added for warmth and for the propriety of receiving visitors, seemed to sit even straighter as she added relentlessly.

"I can understand that it would be pleasant for you. But I cannot think it would be wise. The Haverfords are an unusual family, you are a lucky girl to have fallen in with them. They are very liberal. I, for example, as Mrs. Haverford's companion, was always welcomed at her side at table, and at every soiree. If you were only her companion, I might say it would be permissible. But you are also and perhaps primarily a governess here, since though I am bedridden, I am still alive."

No smile lit the aged pale and serious face as she made this observation, and then, nodding at the silence it produced in her listener, Miss Comfort went on, "And a governess, my dear, never dines with the family in company, no more than their infants do, no, she has few more privileges than her charges in that respect in any household, however modern, or careless, it might be. I know you have occasionally dined with them over the past weeks," and here Victoria lowered her lashes over her eyes, remembering those delightful times when everyone ate and laughed together, the food never being half so delicious as the conversation, "since the Haverfords still live easily, not yet being accustomed to the title. Of course," Miss Comfort added, "it hardly mattered, since there was no one else about but other house servants to observe it. But tonight would be quite different."

Victoria didn't wish to seem as though she were pushing, she never wanted to appear to be anxious, so she said as lightly as she was able, in tones she hoped did not sound so much argumentative as thoughtful.

"But both the earl and Mrs. Haverford said that as they'd put it about that I was also a friend of the family, it would be quite correct for me to dine with them this evening. None of the company, the earl said, would think it wrong. Rather, he said," she added, more defiantly than she knew, raising her chin as she rallied her pride, "he said that they might even think it odd that a friend of the family did *not* dine with them on a social evening."

Miss Comfort sat very still and gazed at her young substitute. Miss Dawkins wore a light blue dress this morning, a simple thing, muslin, banded at the waist with a peach riband, with a trim of peach about the hem and at the closings of the wide sleeves. It was a perfect airy, cool drift of a frock for a summer's morning, and because the day bid fair to become a sultry one, she wore her light brown hair pulled back and away from her high forehead, caught up quite simply in the back with a narrow peach riband. All simplicity, dressed all for convenience, and she looked like a blooming rose withal, Miss Comfort thought, as only the young and lovely can appear to be without either artifice or ornamentation. The older woman remained silent, but it might have been that she sighed then, for the ecru lace at her thin bosom stirred.

"It is all very well for the earl to say that," Miss Comfort replied in the new trembling, faint voice she'd acquired since her illness. "He is a man, and a nobleman. But though he will learn that eccentricity is permissible in his new rank, he will also discover that he has his family to protect. Therefore it is up to us to protect him until that time. You are not a fool, Miss Dawkins,'' Miss Comfort said in a harder voice, ''or else you wouldn't have come to me for advice before you agreed to it. I suspect you already knew the answer before you asked my opinion. Roberta Haverford is kindness herself, and sometimes that overshadows her good sense. The earl is a man. You must use your wits. You are a young, attractive female, and one, moreover, with a certain history of scandal, deserved or not,'' Miss Comfort added, putting up one thin white hand to forestall Miss Dawkins' defense of herself.

The old woman drew her shawl more closely about her narrow shoulders despite the growing warmth in the room and said with finality.

''The correct thing would be to dine with the children in the nursery, saying that you feel more comfortable there. Then bring them down to visit the company after dinner. You may, however,'' she added at the last, almost as if against her will, after seeing Miss Dawkins' solemn expression, ''remain with the company after the children are sent to bed. That you may do, if you feel you wish to be seen as a friend of the family.

''I tell you only what is proper, although I understand what is proper is not always pleasant. Indeed, I spent most of my life teaching a generation of children just that, as you likely shall do as well. I am a friend of the family too, and more, for I am related to them. Yet I know my place, and always did. And poverty, my dear,'' Miss Comfort said, her voice becoming stronger and clearer, her face growing colder even as she seemed to be becoming more personal, ''poverty will always show you your proper place. Friend of the family or not, Miss Dawkins,'' she concluded with the twisted travesty of a smile, ''can you imagine how the Ludlows will feel if you sit down to dine with them?''

Victoria could, she had, and she'd told that to the earl immediately after he'd given her the invitation as they'd been walking this morning, watching the children tumbling down the hillside with their wicker baskets, searching for the wild strawberries they'd promised Cook. He'd been astonished that she'd known the family was planning a social evening with local gentry and yet had not planned on coming to table with them. "But, my lord, can you imagine what the Ludlows would say?" she'd asked at once, horrified at the thought of her former employers' reactions. And at once, he'd flung back his head and laughed at the very idea of their amaze. And as was so frequently the case between them these days, she knew exactly what he was thinking, and in his laughter she saw the awestruck faces of the Ludlows as clearly as if they stood before her in fact.

"Miss Sophrina," he'd managed to say at last, "eyes popping out as much as the front of her frock, and Miss Charlotte looking about wildly for a mirror to see if the fault lay in herself. Oh, Miss Dawkins, how can you think of refusing and ruining my evening? Bad enough I must do the pretty with the vicar, the squire, and the doctor, and even old Squire Hadley come all the way from the next county to break bread with his benefactor. Can you find it in your heart to leave me alone to endure his endless gratitude for those wretched birds? Doubtless he'll document egg production and feather loss to assure me as to their happiness all through my soup and on into fish . . ."

"And heaven help you if you serve an unusually large pheasant"—she giggled—"you'll have to produce the feathers to reassure him."

Then they both went off into laughter again, as they so often did on these morning jaunts with the children. For here in the countryside she could forget that the dark gentleman was a nobleman and her employer. Indeed, it was difficult to remember their relative stations when he was freeing her dress from brambles or carrying Sally on his back or sitting on the banks of a stream or lying back against a tree to tell his vastly entertaining stories of the islands to his attentive audience of children and their governess.

But there was nothing so odd in it, not out there in the sun and on the lawns and in the meadows. She was of an age and education to be conversant with him, after all. Who else should he seek out for conversation, she wondered, the grooms? the housemaids? his valet? He did spend time with his mama, and at times with the librarian, and the couple who restored his art gallery, and from time to time he rode out to visit with neighbors. But summer days were long and he was a long way from London, and he chose to remain in the countryside restoring High Wyvern Hall, and he adored the children, that was crystal clear, and their governess was always with them. Luckily, she often thought to herself; oh, luckily for her.

He was a perfect gentleman with her, had been for all these summer weeks, although she might choose to entertain herself by interpreting some of his looks and words differently in the velvety summer nights as she counted over her soft lovely lucky days before she drifted off to sleep. But she knew that was only a game she played, she knew that she must never blur the line between her present reality and true reality, or her reality and his. Although the idea of having dinner with him had seemed delightful and right early this morning in the meadow, this noon, she looked at the woman in the bed before her, shrunken and diminished by pillows and comforters, and knew this was actuality. She had to deny her fantasy and admit that in the end she had more in common with this frail old female than she ever did with the earl. For he was only a dear passing dream, and here before her lay a living example of her real future.

"You are quite right," Victoria said bleakly.

"Yes," Miss Comfort said vigorously, primming her lips in pleasure. Yet as Victoria left at last, promising to bring the children for an evening visit to show how well they'd dress for company, Miss Comfort stirred restlessly in her vast bed. As the door closed behind Miss Dawkins, Miss Comfort stared for a very long while at the back of it, and then at length breathed very softly, "Yes. And I am sorry."

The Yellow Salon was not the largest or most opulent downstairs room in High Wyvern Hall, but Victoria liked it best and was pleased to see that her hosts obviously did as well. For that was the room to which all the company had repaired after their long and lavish dinner. The two great fireplaces were aroar because it was such a large room and such an unexpectedly cool evening. But by no means was it cavernous, that was the charm of the Yellow Salon. The fire and lamplight lent more light to the saffron-silk-hung walls and cast bright glances at the nymphs and shepherds busily engaged in the painted medallions on the high reaches of the ceilings. The intricately patterned Eastern carpets lay like verdant flowerbeds beneath the rosewood feet of the many tapestry-covered chairs and lounges; these blossoms and bright colors made it the most glowingly alive room in all the Hall. Yet even so, Victoria thought, as she led the children in to the company, there was a dimness, a shadow here that no color or light could dispel. But perhaps, she thought on an interior shrug as she dipped a curtsy to the assembled guests, that was only a reflection of the shadow that lay over her own bowed spirit tonight.

There were almost two dozen people who swam up out of the ruddy moving shadows to return her greeting. These few she didn't know she assumed to be the peacock-fancying Hadleys, and two other family groups whose names she recalled to be those of near-neighboring landowners. The rest she recognized in turn as her gaze swept over the room: the vicar and his wife, the young doctor, the estate manager and his wife, the couple who supposedly fostered the children, the elderly librarian, the couple given a respite from their work in the gallery, and the Ludlows gaping at her so nakedly that Victoria suppressed a shudder and was very grateful for Miss Comfort's advice—until she noted Miss Comfort herself, expressionless, wrapped in as many blankets as a small mummy, snug in a wing chair by the fire.

Mrs. Haverford, at her old companion's side, smiled and immediately commented on how pleased Victoria must be to see how successful they'd been at getting dear Comfort down for dinner among company again for the night. So when the earl gave Victoria a dark reproachful glance as he came to take Sally by the hand to draw her into their midst, Victoria was too numbed to feel as betrayed as she knew she ought to be. There still was little doubt Miss Comfort had been right, she thought as she settled into a chair, even though, as it turned out, she herself had been misled.

Sally answered all the friendly questions with shy grace, she enunciated each word with such great care that those who did not know her might have thought her a creature of high birth and only as hesitant with adults as a properly raised little girl ought to be. Alfie and Bobby said very little, but stood with their hands behind their backs like a pair of half-scale footmen. But Victoria saw the subtle glances Alfie often cast toward Miss Comfort, who'd exclaimed over their attire only hours before, with never a word offered about how she'd soon see them in their glory in company for herself.

"Heavens!" Miss Charlotte cried, fanning herself as rapidly as she blinked. "What a charming little creature. One would never imagine that she's a charity child. How she's come on since I first saw her. But isn't there a baby as well that we've never seen, my lord?" she asked, with a sly inflection that could have meant she yearned to see the babe, although it just as easily might have implied that she wondered why the bachelor nobleman withheld the infant from view.

"Baby's sleeping," Alfie began truculently, until a look from the earl silenced him.

"Indeed he is," the earl said pleasantly, "but there's no mystery about him, I'll introduce you two any day you please. It's only that we scarcely thought him ready for such elevated company. He's not even got a year to his credit as yet, so his conversation, I fear, is not very enlightening."

There was a murmur of laughter among the company, and Miss Charlotte, flushed beyond the firelight's reflection, pressed on in a determinedly merry little voice in an effort to cover her lapse and show she was either ingenuous enough to be oblivious, or charming enough to be forgiving of the set-down.

"Ah, but I hear the Hall has several mysteries, my lord. The old earl shunned company toward the end, you know, and we were thrilled at being asked here again. Now, pray do not tell us we are to spend an evening here at long last and still hear nothing of the famous Haverford ghost? How shall I hold my head up in company after this?"

"But, my dear," the earl replied in amusement as Sally looked up at him with her eyes widened, "there's no need to hide that lovely face for any reason, for there's nothing at all to tell."

Miss Charlotte pouted prettily and Mrs. Haverford deftly changed the subject by asking after Squire Hadley's pride of peacocks. At about the time the company was growing heartily bored with descriptions of all the fascinating nuances of peacock mating behavior, the earl, noting Sally's yawns, took time to ask the guests to hear her and her brothers' good-nights. Victoria rose to escort the children to their rooms, but was forestalled when the earl summoned a footman and an upstairs maid to the task.

After the children had left, conversation limped on in such desultory fashion that Victoria wondered why she'd ever yearned to come down at all, and began to think herself fortunate for having missed dinner. She gazed down into her lap, thinking of all the time she'd spent deciding on what to wear this night before choosing her very best, a thin yellow velvet frock with rose trimmings, which, because of its lightness, was even more flattering than it was unseasonable. It was all a waste, she decided, as she smiled witlessly at a tale of an interesting misdiagnosis the doctor was regaling her with, for though she matched with the room, she felt about as entertaining and entertained as any other furnishing within it.

Then, as the hour grew late, but not so late that anyone could yet beg exhaustion as the children had and so escape the tedium, Miss Charlotte was heard to say again, in a high, desperate voice.

"Oh fie, my lord. The children are gone, and still you treat us all like infants. Everyone knows there are ghosts at the Hall, it's been gossiped about forever hereabouts. And yet you'll say nothing to us of them. Shame, sir!"

She might have been angling for more of his attention—

he'd been chatting with the vicar's spinster daughter—she might have simply been bored to tears, but Victoria doubted she expected her host's reaction. For, "Very well," he said, turning about, some imp of mischief flickering in his dark eyes (or was it the firelight?), "if you wish to hear about her, you may. But I can't promise you'll ever want to return to visit us here again, if you do."

This was a problem to Miss Ludlow, for she very much wanted to revisit the earl; in fact, it was becoming clear she wouldn't mind taking up residence with him. But to deny the story now was to make her motives look precisely like what they were. Yet to insist on hearing the tale anyway although he'd expressly said it might bar her from his home forever was perhaps to insult him. She was saved, fittingly enough, by the doctor. The young physician was oblivious of all the maneuverings within the room, and honestly fascinated by any stories he might try to disprove with science.

"Oh, marvelous," he said, sitting down and gazing up at the earl very like Sally had done, only with great expectation, rather than trepidation, clearly showing in his large light blue eyes.

After a few pleased exclamations and a general shifting of attention and positions so that everyone was soon seated and gazing at their host as though he were headmaster and they his attentive students, a silence fell over the Yellow Salon. The earl stood in front of a great fireplace, silhouetted by the flames behind him, his dark hair and eyes taking on demon red glints from it. His voice was low but carrying, the faint susurration of his speech perfect for conveying the faint unease of any good ghost story.

"It is said," he began quite seriously and very sadly, "that my ancestor the first Earl of Clune took to himself a beautiful young wife when he reached his middle years. His had been a misspent youth, and a riotously spent adulthood. In fact, the only good thing he'd ever done, in everyone's opinion, was to build this great Hall. But once it had been built, he found it empty, even after he'd stocked it with treasures and hangers-on, and passed time in it with great dinners and orgies. He must have had some idea of the sort of fellow he was, so he determined to find himself a wife as opposite to himself as existed on the green earth.

"Her name, it is said, was Lady Ann, but no one can be sure, for no trace of her remains in our time, save for her poor unquiet spirit which they say still walks these halls by night."

Here the earl paused and looked up at the stair, as though he saw something there, and though it was a cool summer's night, with no thunder or lightning or howling wind outside to supplement his eerie tale, all of the company gazed up at the staircase as well, in some dread of what they might see there. A few flinched, and there was one muted cry of "Oh!" at some perceived movement of something white between the oak rails, and the earl said softly as he continued to gaze upward:

"You may remain there, although I'm not best pleased with your deception, but then, I likely would have done the same in my time, at your age. So stay where you are, since you're no longer dressed for company, but only if you can promise me your sister is abed, with her door closed, and that you'll not repeat this tale to her."

"She is. I won't. Cross my 'eart," Alfie whispered fervently as Bobby echoed the same behind him from where they crouched together in their nightshirts high on the stair.

The guests shifted in their seats, both amused and a bit ashamed of their own gullibility. But, Victoria thought, looking back at the narrator, if he can make us this uneasy after only moments, how shall I ever get up to bed tonight when he is done?

"My ancestor was not an unhandsome man," the earl went on. "How could he be? He was a Haverford, after all." He waited until the relieved laughter was done before he continued, "He was extremely wealthy, since he was a warrior-knight who'd won many prizes for and from his king, but he was no longer young, he was not gentle, nor was he, from all accounts, in any way kind. The Lady Ann was not only surpassing lovely, she was, just as he'd wished, everything he was not, including very young. She was only fourteen on their wedding day. Which never means," he added at once, to the company's collective gasps, "that he was necessarily perverse. Such was the way of things in those bygone days, for people did not live very long and had to get on with life and the business of begetting life as soon as they were able.

"And Lady Ann behaved just as ought, being poor and lovely and obedient, for she bore her lord three children, all before she'd reached the age of one-and-twenty. Now, we might have no more ghosts here at the Hall than any village church, if it were not for the fact that the first earl was called away on his sovereign's business in the spring of the year, seven years to the day after his wedding. I suppose," the earl said softly, reflectively, "that if it had been the fashion, before he departed, my ancestor would have fitted his wife out with the sort of Italian contraption that ensures fidelity," and here he smiled slightly and glanced upward, so that the company would know it was for the children's sake he did not actually mention chastity belts, but after seeing the puzzled frowns that several of the ladies and a few of the gentlemen wore, and the bright grins he saw shining on the faces of the Johnson boys, the earl continued quickly.

"But they'd become obsolete, and indeed, he'd scant reason to doubt her fidelity, unless he judged her by his own evil standards, since she was the most docile, humble little creature imaginable, or at least, so she is in all the stories that have come down to us. And so she might have remained until her life's end, if she had not met her neighbor, young Sir Randall, yes, he whose family owned the castle that now lies in ruins not two leagues from here. He too was everything the first Earl of Clune was not, for he was radiantly beautiful to look upon, and young and noble and kind and good, and everything else the bards could get to rhyme in all their salutes to him.

"Of course, they met, and of course, they fell in love. Nothing could be more natural. And being the sort of young people they were, no more might have come from it but a great deal of frustration and bad poetry and a broken heart or two, if it were not for the fact that my ancestor liked his mission very well, and remained from home for a full two years, enjoying himself enormously with his royally sanctioned looting and rapine. And—terribly sorry, Vicar—but two years, and those two years passed alone together and yet not together, was, you may agree, far too long for even two such decent, noble young persons as the Lady Ann and Sir Randall were, to bear."

The vicar "tut-tutted" and "harumphed," but before he could think of a word to venture that was neither too sanctimonious nor liberal, the earl went on, suddenly more seriously and quietly, "Be that as it may, the fact is that when my ancestor at last sent notice of his imminent return, the two young lovers were faced with the reality of their predicament. And that reality was a newborn babe."

There were several muted exclamations; the company stirred in their chairs, their faces, in the flickering firelight, troubled and dismayed, and focused entirely upon the speaker. Colin Haverford gave out an audible sigh and went on, "There was no hope for it. The two young lovers talked it round the clock, they called in their faithful retainers for consultation, but there was only one option open to them. They knew they must flee across the Channel and then further, and never return to their homeland, and certainly never to this great Hall. For the first Earl of Clune was a hard and violent man, and they feared his rage, the more because they feared he would be right in it.

"Lady Ann had a constant heart, despite her infidelity. She insisted on bringing all her children with her in her flight. Did Sir Randall object? Did he want only his own get and not those of my wicked ancestor? One could scarcely blame him, but did he then desert his lady because of it? The bards disagree on this. We only know that he left first, to secure passage for her and the children, some say, to free himself of the entanglement, others say. I cannot say. His ghost does not trouble us. He died in France many years later and doubtless burns in some other clime, that is, if he does not prowl some castle by the Seine for eternity, just as his love walks here.

"For she was not quick enough," the earl said harshly, and several ladies and not a few gentlemen jumped at that.

"She left it to the last, poor lass, and was out there, on the inland sea"—he pointed in an easterly direction at a tapestried wall, and some of the guests gazed in the direction of his outstretched finger as though they could see the shining water there—"on the estuary, in a small boat, headed for the true coast, when he, my dreadful ancestor, came thundering after her. He'd heard about the babe, he'd come with a company of rough men, he stopped at the water's edge, and saw her in the boat and shouted. He shouted something at her, but the wind carried his words away. For there was a fierce wind blowing that evening."

All the company remained silent, and it seemed as though they huddled together, though not one of them dared make a move as their host said softly, so softly they had to strain to hear him.

"What was it he cried to her? Did he threaten her as she'd feared he would? Or did he repent his cruelty, and fear her leaving more than his loss of honor? We, the living, shall never know. Some say he too haunts this place. But we all know she does. For she died that night."

A gasp was heard, and no one turned to see who had reacted so, they were all so enthralled with the tale.

"Her boat overturned. And when they brought her home, here to the Hall, she lasted only until the dawn. But she lived long enough to know that all her children, all four, were brought back as well, but all cold, and all drowned."

Victoria was naturally a most sympathetic person, but unlike the other ladies, she didn't sob or catch her breath at this utterance, because something in the way the narrator pronounced it, drawing out the "cold" and lingering on the rolling R in "drowned," alerted her to the fact that he was enjoying ravishing his listeners with the tale almost as much as his wicked ancestor was supposed to have done with his ravaging the countryside. A glance to his mama's bemused face confirmed this, and so Victoria continued to listen to him with as much attention but with far less susceptibility than the others.

"We do not know," the earl continued ominously, "what he said to her in his grief and anger and anguish as she lay dying, although we can imagine it, since we who live in the Hall can never forget what she said to him. For it is said that with her last breath, she whispered''—and here he dropped his voice so low, all present actually bent forward to catch his soft words—'' 'There will be no peace for you, my lord Earl of Clune, and all your kind, no, never, not until you love a bastard child with all your heart and bring him to your bosom to let him lie in the heart of this accursed Hall.'

''Well!'' the earl said abruptly, returning everyone from that ancient death watch at the lady's bedside to the present, although it was only that he used his natural voice again. ''He never did any such thing, of course, which is why she still roams the place. He wed again, actually, producing another litter of Haverfords, from which all subsequent Earls of Clune, even I, descend. So there you have it, Miss Charlotte, our ghost. Lady Ann is the one who troubles our nights. For she is said to walk the length of the house and back each night before dawn, more often than that on rainy nights, grieving for her lost children, cursing her perfidious lover, reviling my ancestor, and making a general nuisance of herself. It's said she's doomed to walk until her own curse is lifted. Which should keep her trotting about, I should imagine, until the end of eternity. She doesn't bother ladies much, unless they're Haverfords, of course. And children''—and here it was to his credit, Victoria thought approvingly, that he never once flicked an eyelid up to where the boys sat as he said it—''are never bothered by her in the least, for it is said that, quite naturally, she quite likes them.''

''Ah, well then,'' Miss Charlotte said with a forced laugh, and in shaken tones, ''as neither a Haverford nor a man, I've nothing to fear then, have I?''

''Oh,'' the earl replied thoughtfuly, ''I don't know. She's only our primary ghost. It seems that once you've gotten yourself a haunting, it makes it that much easier for other spirts to crowd in. Something on the order of misery, even ghostly misery, loving company. Either that, or it may be that once there's a rip in the stuff of reality, there's an opportunity for a great many odd things to come crowding through. Many houses have multiple spirits, you know, and here at the Hall we've Lady Ann, of course, but the thumping in the attics is said to be the first earl by some, or a murdered footman, by others. Lady Ann's faithful dog is said to walk the Hall too, after he comes in from his nightly search of the shore, eternally looking for his mistress and the children. They claim it's because he was left behind, being too large to fit in the boat, and that he drowned attempting to save them."

The earl paused, and then Victoria did see his momentary glance up at the stair before he went on blandly, "But though disturbing, these are harmless spirits, causing more unease than actual hurt. We've others, less benign, of course. There's said to be an outraged governess who rules the midnight nursery, who swells to twice her size in fury, and a phantom coachman, and even another ancestor who creeps across floors catching on to living ankles."

Here Victoria could see that some of the gentlemen surreptitiously jogged their legs a few times, and many of the ladies drew their knees together as they picked their slippered feet up a fraction from the carpet, even as she heard muted stifled giggles from the vicinity of the stairs.

"But enough of that," the earl said heartily. "We don't wish to be recluses here, after all. I'll not utter another word about our unquiet visitors, or I fear we'll never have another living one to grace our salon. Come, Miss Charlotte, enough chatter about devilish things. Your mama tells me you have an angel's voice. Would you be so kind as to favor us with a song to lighten all our spirits?"

He might just as easily have said, "all the spirits," Victoria thought in secret amusement, for she noted that Miss Charlotte was exceedingly careful, and glanced all about herself when she walked to the pianoforte in the corner as the assembled company urged her to do. But soon after, she relaxed and played and sang. Although Victoria thought any undead howling would be an improvement on the sounds issuing from the singer and the instrument, as did, she noted, the Johnson boys, who disappeared from the stair after the first note rang out, the company stayed and endured encores. The only other spirit shown that night was when the singer's sister entered into competition with a recital of her own. But since Miss Sophrina's offerings were not quite as good as her sibling's, it wasn't long before the assembled guests began offering all sorts of excuses for their departures, after having gazed jealously at the Hadleys, who, living furthest from the Hall, had, after all, the most valid reason for fleeing first.

She should have been weary when the night was over, Victoria thought. She'd bade the earl and Mrs. Haverford good night when all the company had left, and left the Yellow Salon herself to the servants' attentions as they cleaned and cleared the room. But she lingered belowstairs, first on an errand to the kitchen to secure a tidbit she finally offered to one of Bobby's hounds that had eluded the footmen, and then on a trip to the library to get a good book to pass the rest of the night with, and then on a trip back to the Yellow Salon to look for a lost handkerchief that she wasn't even sure she'd brought down with her. It was only when she stood alone in the dim hallway on the first landing, dreading her necessary journey up another flight of stairs to her rooms, that she realized she'd been far more influenced by her host's stories than she'd thought.

The tales had not only chased sleep from her mind, but she discovered she was peering into shadows and starting when the floors creaked; and when a footman belowstairs coughed, the echo of it, she was sure, caused all her hair to rise vertically from her scalp. She was chiding herself on being extremely childish, nonsensically foolish and craven to the point of idiocy, when she heard the distinctly real sound of footfalls right behind her, and then remembered that the last time she'd looked around, a scant second before, she'd been quite alone in the hallway.

She would not scream, she told herself weakly, and only hoped she could find enough voice to muster the whisper "Peace be with you, friend," as she was rehearsing, when she heard a very mortal, somewhat shaken voice exclaim:

"Miss Dawkins! You ought not to stand in the dimmest reaches of the hallway, wearing diaphanous garments, after I've just passed the evening straining my imagination to the utmost inventing specters with which to frighten unwanted company away. You almost made me wonder if I'd actually conjured up Lady Ann."

"It's not diaphanous," she replied at once, relieved but abrupt because she was shamed at being discovered terrified by her employer, the admitted perpetrator of the original hoaxing. "It's velvet, not the stuff of shrouds. But did you make up Lady Ann entirely? I confess, I'm impressed, and," she added in a grudging little voice, "I was frightened. . . . A bit. Oh, not then, not in the salon. But just now, when I was alone. I congratulate you."

She could see him quite clearly now, for he'd come so close in order to see her better that she could make out every detail of his dark face glowing in the shadows, even to the deeper darkness of the small indentation at the bottom of his chin. But then she saw his even white teeth glinting in the half-light as he replied:

"Oh no. Sorry, but the Lady Ann is quite real, that is to say, she's been documented, although I confess I've never met up with her. But I thought I saw your gown drifting like shifting spiderwebs up here in the hall, that's why I crept up on you. Never say it's velvet, but, yes," he said, more softly, "you don't lie, though my eyes did, for it is, isn't it?"

He'd reached out a hand to touch her shoulder, to verify her claim, but once his fingers had met the short thick nap of the material, they lingered there and then spread out, almost of their own volition, to slide along her arm. She felt the warmth of his large hand dispel all the chill that had been in her mind and body, and when it widened its exploration to begin to stroke across her neck, now discovering the texture of her flesh as well as of her gown, she found she could not, or would not, think to say a thing to him, either to deny or encourage the strange encounter.

He felt softness leading to softness, the dense pile of her dress leading to the cool satin feel of her skin, the pleasurable sensation of stroking something furred and warm giving way to the familiar but always new and thrilling discovery of tracing surfaces that were curved and smooth and distinctly, deliciously female. But not just any female, he knew, for he could not take his eyes from hers, at least, not until he gazed down at her lips. Then his other hand rose to cup her neck and gently bring her still nearer to better see what he thought he glimpsed in her eyes, and then to see if those lips offered what he thought they did.

If she could not deny the pleasure she suddenly discovered in simply standing so close to him, as she'd so often imagined herself doing, she could not in all honesty deny the wonder of having him actually touch her and draw her nearer to him. And then, of course, she couldn't gainsay the joy in having his cool, no, now wonderfully warm lips upon hers, no, not even if she could have found the breath or the reason to say a word just then.

"Victoria," he whispered after he'd touched her lips only briefly, drawing his mouth back just far enough so that he could speak, "Victoria love, it's not enough to only accept me, no, join me. Here, love, open your lips just as I did for you, yes, yes, just so, yes," he breathed, before he made sure he could not speak again.

It might have been some small noise the great Hall made as it settled down for the night, a creak that sounded too much like a footstep to some small, guilty, still alert part of Victoria's dazzled mind. It may have been that she discovered too much pleasure in his clasp, or it could have been that his warm hands began at last to make her too warm, drew her that one fraction too close for her inexperienced senses to take in all at once, but too much of something made her pull back, and then dawning awareness of what had begun made her panic and attempt to give up and deny everything that had transpired.

"You said," she whispered then, her fingertips shivering against her own traitorous lips that had silently told him too much as well, "that you would be a gentleman with me."

"I was," he stated flatly, coldly, even as he reached for her again, "but now, my love, I find it far more entertaining to be merely a man with you, as obviously, oh so obviously, you do too."

12

The great house was still, but not quiet in spirit. It was as though the enormous Hall itself held its breath even as did the two people who stood facing each other in the night, upon the landing of the stair in the huge and empty upper hallway. The gentleman was dressed in dark evening clothes so that all that could be seen of him, if anyone else were afoot in the night to observe him, was the white gleam from his neckcloth, shirtfront and cuffs, and the indistinct blur of his swarthy face. The young woman's yellow velvet gown glowed as if lit by its own rich interior radiance, and her pale face was uplifted to his. He held her at arm's length as they stood in that moment, as still as the great Hall itself.

Then he dropped his arms from her, releasing her, though still she did not stir.

"So," he said softly, "it seems there are all sorts of spirits abroad tonight. For a moment there," he said on a sigh, looking down at her as though mesmerized, even as she stared at him as though he still held her with more than his dark unblinking gaze, "I think I was possessed by some of them. For I wasn't acting either as a gentleman or a man just then. No, I think," he went on, reaching out a hand to gently smooth back a lock of her hair that he'd disarranged, "I was acting precisely like a nobleman . . .

of the sort that used to reign here, in this damned great Hall of theirs.

"Now, there's a thought," he added more lightly. "Does the Hall make the nobleman? Were all my bold, bad ancestors decent men before they took up residence here? That would indeed be a greater curse than poor Lady Ann thought to lay upon the wretched place. Don't worry," he said more gently, "it's done, I've done, it's over, I'm sorry. Lord, shall I write it out for you? It would be kind of you to say something at this point, you know."

"It was my fault as well," she said quietly at last.

"Oh, certainly," he said, backing up a step, as though her words had broken whatever spell had kept him close to her, and thrusting his hands into his pockets like a boy, he said roughly, "Absolutely. Chap has to beware of pure, lovely young governesses sneaking up on him in the dark and pressing kisses all over his helpless person. My dear Miss Dawkins," he said wryly, "I merely acted like a savage, I simply was about to attempt your seduction, all the while knowing I was supposed to be your protector in the best sense of the word, and that had I deliberately forgotten that and harmed you, you'd have no recourse whatsoever, since I am pleased to be an earl now, and you are a young woman in my employ, with neither family nor fortune to help you wrack retribution upon me."

"Were you trying to harm me?" she asked, twisting her hands together as her eyes searched his face, fearing she sounded stupid, knowing she was stepping out of her place, but in the deep of this dark night, with the memory of his warm breath moving over her lips as though it were her own, suddenly no longer clearly seeing the lines that separated their places.

"No," he answered slowly, "no, not actually. Just then I suppose I was trying to please you. But all the while I couldn't help but know that the sort of pleasure I was trying to visit upon you would bring you nothing but eventual pain. Not just that sort of little pain maidens generally encounter in their first lovemaking, that's inevitable, and neither terrible nor lasting—or did you know that already, my little well-educated apothecary's daughter who still had to be taught how to kiss?—but rather the grander pain of abandonment, shame, and regret. For I was thinking of pleasure, Miss Dawkins, purely pleasure, and not permanence. Do you understand?"

"If you were an earl's daughter," he said harshly then, when she still didn't answer, "I don't know that I would have dared. Now do you understand?"

She nodded, incapable of any other sort of answer.

"And I am rather filled with self-loathing at the moment. Not that your kiss didn't please me, no, you improved out of all recognition with just a little prompting. But this damned place . . ." He laughed, he grimaced, he shrugged, he began to speak bitterly and low, as though he were attempting to explain himself to himself. "I suppose I can't put the blame on spirits, although no doubt my forebears were wildly applauding my stunning exhibition of lust and irresponsibility just now."

He paused, took another step back, and said in firmer tones:

"But it's done. Put it down to the active and inactive spirits of the night, and put about as much stock in it as you might one of my wilder stories of them told this night. And then forget it, please. But I can't order that, can I? I suppose you may yet regale your charges with it in future, remembering the night when the master of the house forgot his place. A lowering thought, but probably no more than I deserve.

"Now," he said decisively, looking down at her dispassionately, "please go to bed."

"I said *good night*, Miss Dawkins," he repeated in a harsher voice when she did not move.

He grinned a little grimly when it became apparent his request finally registered as a command, and she started as though from a reverie, and blinked. Then she backed to the stair and turned and fled up it without a good night or a backward look to him.

He watched until the glow of her gown disappeared at the top of the stair.

"Lady Ann," he said then with a skewed smile, when he was quite alone, as he bowed to the dark and empty air, "it seems I've still some honor. Terribly sorry, old girl, best purchase a new pair of walking slippers. For I refuse to be the earl who gets that bastard for you, to take to my own cold noble heart."

She didn't see him at breakfast, since she was careful to take it in her rooms with the children. Then in the afternoon when she discovered he'd gone riding with Alfie, she could relax. So she was pleasantly conversive with Miss Comfort when she delivered Sally for her French lesson, and had time and to spare to chat with the head groom when she brought Bobby to him so that the pair might see to the training of a pair of scent hounds. Bobby vowed they'd be the greatest addition to the autumn hunt that had ever been seen in the district, although from their size and lethargy, Victoria privately thought they were more likely to become the greatest boon to the welfare of fleas that had ever been known in the kingdom.

Mrs. Haverford was secreted in her rooms with a novel she couldn't bear to part from, the librarian was desk-deep in annotations to his list, the couple at work on the paintings had only just discovered a risky patch of canvas they couldn't spare a breath to disengage their eyes from. Since her known companions were otherwise occupied, Victoria decided to look up acquaintances she'd always meant to pursue further. The housekeeper's sprightly niece had the toothache, so Victoria went to the music room to hunt up the lovely young woman she'd often seen there. The housekeeper had said the fair-haired girl she'd described might be the young person from the village who did fine mending on the curtains, although since she was always dressed so well, in flowing white chiffon, Victoria believed Mrs. Haverford might be right in assuming her chance-met companion was more likely to be the gardener's niece, a pretty-behaved young woman who saw to the floral arrangements in the Hall. A disadvantage, Mrs. Haverford had sighed, of having such a grand Hall to keep up, was not so much the great number of persons one had to employ, as it was the fact that it was hard to acquaint oneself with each and every one of them.

When she got to the music room, Victoria was delighted to find the fair young woman again hovering near the harp there. But even as she began to speak to the girl, she was dismayed to see her rise, smile apologetically, and then, although with every apparent sign of rue for it, immediately fade into the shadows and out of the room, as though there was an errand she couldn't bear to let wait another instant. As a last resort, Victoria climbed the stairs to Nurse's quarters, for the old woman liked to reminisce, and did so charmingly, only to find her as soundly asleep as Baby, as they were both taking their customary afternoon nap.

It was only then, at that advanced hour of the day, that Victoria at last admitted she was forced to be alone with the one person whose company she least wished to bear—herself.

She left word with the butler in case she was needed and then prepared to leave the Hall, since the outdoors, she reasoned, held more things to divert her thoughts than her own room might. At the last, she made one more bid for some distraction from her thoughts and sought one of Bobby's dogs for company. She'd hoped that even a companion who'd only fetch a stick for her might chase away the specters of her punishing conscience and weak will, both of which had kept her awake most of the night with their fierce interior dialogues. But most of the dogs, from the spotted setter to the odd little cur with the quantity of fur, had followed their savior to the stables. Only the enormous melancholic black beast that followed the children everywhere, dogging their steps from a distance, remained within the Hall. Victoria frowned when she found him plodding down a hallway; it was only more evidence of her poor luck this day, for he was the most disobliging animal, never responding to any of her offers of friendship. She tempted him with a boiled sweet, she whistled and cooed, but though he followed her almost to the kitchen door, he hung back in the dim corridor when she stepped into the light, and not only wouldn't budge further, but disappeared entirely when she became insistent.

She walked alone to clear her head, she walked far to

evade her thoughts, but it soon became evident that no sunlit pastoral scene had the power to erase that midnight encounter from her mind. As was so often the case at the Hall, night again defeated the day, for as she walked past the gardens and statuary that enhanced the grounds, she never saw them at all, so intent was she on the remembered vision of that dark and shadowed face she'd actually touched last night.

She visualized him as she wandered past the knot garden, recalled his low voice as she strolled along the crushed-shell walks, felt his hands and lips upon her again as surely as she felt the soft breeze whisper past her hair as she picked her way down steep garden slopes. And so after she finally came to rest, midway across a Palladian bridge which watched over the small serpentine river that chuckled past the Hall, she didn't recognize reality immediately when she eventually heard that voice comment in amused tones:

"I thought it was Narcissus who fell in love with his reflection."

The earl ignored her sudden start in reaction to his actual appearance as he strolled to her side and rested his elbows on the rail beside her. "But there's not a chance of getting a good look, the water flows so swiftly here, so it can't be self-adoration you're after. It couldn't be self-destruction either," he laughed. "If you leapt from here, all you'd net would be an awkward landing—it's scarcely waist-deep, you know."

When she didn't reply, but only gazed at him as though he were one of the ghosts his Hall boasted, he went on in reasonable ruminative tones, although he looked down to the water and not at her.

"I've come to beg pardon, again. I might have let it pass, hoping time would mend things, but time's like this running river, it might carry things away, but as it's also always deepening its channel, it has a way of deepening insult too. I saw you from afar, just standing, just staring. You've walked a long way and been gone some hours, and you're obviously distracted. Since the guests are gone, Comfort's bedridden, and my mama's the soul of innocence today, if only because she's so rapt in her book, and the children are better behaved than I've been, I assume it's my actions that have distressed you. So I repeat, I beg pardon."

She noted how the clear light took nothing away from the firm features that had etched themselves in her mind, and then said with equally as much candor and honesty as she'd already used with the phantom Earl of Clune a dozen times over in her mind in the last hour as she'd stood watching the water bubble and slide down below her.

"No, it's true I'm disturbed, but not with you, my lord, it's at myself. Yes," she said as he turned slightly to show that he raised a dark brow at her, "me. You see, last night, as I said, was my fault as well."

"Oh, yes," he agreed, "I noted how well you stalked me."

"You're not the only one to have troublesome ancestors prodding you, you know," she went on resolutely, again forgetting her place, again remembering only her emotions. "I've a great-grandmother many times removed who was a king's consort, or so they said. And today I can't help but wonder at her influence over me. Because I could have run away from you, or fought you, or protested, and well I know it, I couldn't sleep last night for knowing it," she explained unhappily, dimly aware that she oughtn't to be confessing this to the man who'd caused her problems, but in her loneliness thinking only that he was the one person who might understand since he'd shared that experience with her.

"But you see," she admitted so quietly the rushing water almost swept her words away, and would have if he'd not moved closer, "I found, I believe, that I might have said 'Yes,' " she finally blurted.

"I wasn't insulted, or frightened, or even regretful. Do you understand?" she asked, staring into his dark and widening eyes, continuing to speak in the forlorn hope that he would, and so would explain it to her. "I was about to say 'Yes. Yes, my lord, I will,' to whatever you asked of me. At least, I think I was. Do you understand?"

"Yes," he answered softly, slowly, looking down into

her troubled, light-filled eyes, shaking his head as though shaking away some nagging thought. "Oh, yes," he said as he drew closer still, and "Certainly," he began to say until the word was lost against her lips.

He held her very close and his kiss was hard, almost hurtful, until he felt her surprise and slight withdrawal and then he gentled his mouth and his hands and she found herself moved along with him as though she were some light, insensible thing the rushing water beneath them carried in its wake. When he touched her breast she stiffened, but then even as he closed his hand over it, she discovered that she moved more closely toward him, as though to aid and abet him in her own seduction. She couldn't stop to reason why what should have alarmed her only drew her nearer, not while he held her and murmured how right it was.

And he, finding her so pliable, so trusting, so infinitely susceptible to his every word and motion, forgot his original motives entirely. It was only when he at last raised his head for a moment to look about for a comfortable place to continue that which he'd begun and take it to its natural ending, that he realized where he was, who he was, and what he was doing and about to do with the young woman in his arms. In that same instant, looking down again at her stunned pale face, drowning in the desire he'd created and only just beginning to show confusion at his lips leaving hers, he recalled what he'd known last night, what he'd tried to forget just now: that she had no idea of what he was about to do, nor of what she was about to begin with him. For whatever her willingness or her desirability, he was too experienced to ignore the awkwardness that clearly showed her innocence.

One of his hands had been wound in her hair, supporting her head as he'd kissed her. When he drew away, the first thing she felt after his lips left hers was the tug of his hand tightening in her hair.

"Yes?" he asked harshly, and her eyes flew open to see all softness fled from his face, his dark eyes no longer warm but rather burning now, his lips not full and tender but thinned and curling around each scornful word. "Yes?

You'd be a mistress as your ancestress was? Ah, but she consorted with a king in an antique age, and this is modern times. Well, and if you want the position, my dear, it's best I detail the duties for you. It's a high-paying post, I'll not hire on someone not willing to take on all her obligations.

"Now, it's a better financial proposition than that for a draggletail slut such as used to haunt your old neighborhood, but then, she has only to put up with her customer for a brief fumbling moment, a fleeting hour. It's true she works in a doorway or on a rented cot, while you, my sweet, shall have silken sheets and gilded rooms. But a mistress, oh, love," he said with nothing like love blazing in his eyes as his hand closed to a fist in her hair, catching it up and paining her as he spoke, although she doubted anything could hurt so much as his bitter words stung her, "silken sheets or no, she at least has some respite when she wants it, but you, why, you shall have to be ever and always at my immediate disposal. Those are the rules.

"Should you like me to come to you foxed?" he asked insolently. "Not just a trifle elevated, mind, perhaps even stumbling drunk, and then enter your bed and body? For I'd have every right to, at my whim, at any time, or in any condition. Perhaps I'd come at noon, or after an unexplained unrepentant absence of a month or so, or directly from a rival's bed, or from my wife's embrace. It would be my right. Or I might lend you, as a book or a sum of money, to a friend. Though I don't think I would," he snarled, "since I'm possessive, and people never remember to return things they borrow. But it would be my right, as well.

"Oh, there'd be grace notes," he said, refusing to allow himself to look away from her tear-filled eyes. "I'm civilized, you know. But you, Miss Dawkins, descendant of a mistress, so eager for the post, why, you'd have to be ever easy, ever loving, ever joyous in my company," he insisted, his slightly slurring accents dragging out the words and etching them in acid. "That's what I'd pay for, that, and not 'love,' which is always given, and never bartered."

"No, I never meant that," she cried, pulling away, but not running from him, knowing that he had only spoken truth, and horrified yet grateful that he had destroyed all her roseate childish illusions of glory with him, "that is never what I meant, I couldn't be that, do that. Don't you understand?"

"Yes, I understand," he said, suddenly releasing her. After turning from her and resting his hands against the rail, he said wearily, "All too well, my poor girl. That's why I'm leaving. Yes, I'm decided, I'm off to London. For a space. It's best. The children will regret it, of course, but I'll make a game of it and solicit all their orders tonight at dinner. If I promise to return with bags full of good things from the great city, I believe I can make my departure more of a treat than a loss. And what may I bring you?" he asked more lightly, glancing to her. "Or will my remove be enough for you?"

"I didn't mean to drive you away," she began, but he cut in, saying swiftly:

"You did not. I brought you here for your own safety's sake. I'm driving myself away because of it, and my own good opinion of myself, as well. Because I don't know that I was about to do anything respectable for you just now, no matter what my heated, belated, puritanical little lecture implied. And I can't seem to keep my hands off you long enough to find out.

"And I don't want to sour something so very new, and so very sweet. I was raised a gentleman. Forget my position—god knows I have often enough. I will not take advantage of yours. I'm your employer. If I'm to be responsible for you, I must first ensure that I can be responsible for myself. It's too easy to blame phantoms."

He gripped the bridge's railing until his knuckles showed white, and muttered, as though to himself:

"A grown man ought to know better than to mew himself up on his country estate for weeks on end, with few more attractive rumps to behold than those of his own sheep. Small wonder then he'd sink to pawing at the one presentable female servant who crossed his path, prodded by evil spirits or not."

The small sound of her quickly indrawn breath made him grimace:

"But you're far more than merely presentable, aren't you, Miss Dawkins?" he asked, glancing toward her with a twisted smile. "And we have a certain history, don't we? And yet we'd established a sort of domestic friendship in spite of it, hadn't we? Forgive me my rash act as well as my unthinking tongue. I hope you'll find it easier from a distance. I won't become a true Earl of Clune, no matter how this place pushes me to it. You're very lovely, but even though I was the only legitimate heir to my title, I can never forget how very many illegitimate ones there were."

And then, since there was obviously nothing she could say, and nothing he chose to, he bowed, and left her there.

There might have been several dozen dead but nonetheless overactive Haverfords lurking in High Wyvern Hall, but it was the absence of just one living earl that caused the house to feel so empty, and cast a pall of deeper gloom over the place. He left on a Friday morning, full of smiles and trailing promises behind him even as he threw his portmanteau into his carriage. He took with him his valet and his tiger, and the good wishes of everyone at the Hall who'd come to see him off, and he left a solemn fretful household in his wake.

The children took their lessons, did their chores and behaved well, but without the sparkle that had characterized their activity since they'd come to live with the Haverfords. It was obvious the earl was never far from their thoughts; they spoke of him often, even when they thought they were alone, lovingly detailing his smallest actions and comments as though they were the stuff of epic legend. They missed him so profoundly because all of them, including the usually cynical Alfie, Victoria thought, caught between amusement and a new and rueful cynicism of her own, seemed to believe that the sun set over the earl's left ear and rose over his right one each dawn.

His mother regretted his departure as well, but then, as she so often said, with a grin very reminiscent of her absent son's, the devilish difficulty in it was that it seemed poor parenting profited one more than good, since the more successful one was at raising one's progeny, the more painful it then was when one was done with the task. For while one never wished to have a dreadful child, of course, she sighed, the more charming one's offspring turned out to be, the more lonely it made one when they left to take their place in the world. And as the world was, of course, London, Mrs. Haverford had a sigh for absent laughter, but got on with her life, gracefully accepted the inevitable, and made sure to include the earl, in his turn, in her regular correspondence with her other children.

Victoria never brought up the earl's name in conversation. She smiled and nodded when she heard the children's tributes to him, and placidly agreed with Mrs. Haverford whenever his virtues were documented. But she never ceased to think of him, never while she was awake, and seldom when she was sleeping. Dining made her remember his favorite foods; when she bathed, the smell of the soap and spicy herbs the housekeeper provided made her recall the scent about him she'd savored when he'd held her close. A fleeting expression on his mama's face could bring him back to her with the force of a blow, and even the innocent darkness of night brought the touch and feel of him back to her senses. Yet all the while she knew, and kept reminding herself constantly, that nothing else would actually ever bring him back, at least never to her. He'd return to the Hall, she knew, but there was no forgetting that he'd as much as said directly that he was leaving it because of her.

Her only consolation lay in the fact that perhaps she'd have found a new position and so would be gone when he finally returned, so she'd at least have bright memories to bear away with her. She didn't wish to have those admittedly disturbing memories, which nevertheless she suspected would be the most important episodes of her life, ruined by further remembrances of him returning to the Hall and then going through the awkward painful business of attempting to avoid her, so that she in turn wouldn't remind him of that odd and rash impulse that had come over him that odd and rash day.

But thinking about the earl and all his reasons for those

strange and more strangely gratifying moments only saddened Victoria, and even that sorrow, she knew guiltily, was for all the wrong reasons. For thinking of his actions and her reactions made her feel not so much put upon as she knew they ought to do, so much as they made her feel vaguely ashamed of her temerity, and embarrassed by her morality.

Her own wicked ancestress, Victoria thought, the lady whose painted miniature likeness she sometimes stared at in her sleepless nights, would certainly have known what to do about such a strong attraction to such a troublesome gentleman. As a commoner who'd consorted with a king, her unhappy great-great-great-granddaughter thought, no doubt she'd have been thoroughly ashamed and scornful of a descendant with such watery blood trickling through her veins.

The one comforting, or irritating, fact, depending upon which night the sleepless sufferer thought on it, was that she could no longer even consider becoming his mistress, not now that she knew precisely what that demeaning role would offer. But unfortunately, she could scarcely bear to think of how she'd go on with her life without him now, now that she'd some idea of the delights his embrace could offer. At any rate, since he could be most persuasive if he wished, and yet had obviously gone out of his way to stress all the disadvantages of such an arrangement, there was little doubt he disliked any idea of such an arrangement with her. Whether the fault lay in herself, her stars, or her status, she didn't know, but it didn't matter, she decided, since he likely had filled that vacant position the moment he'd arrived in London town.

That depressing thought occurred to her often, so it was understandable that her eyes became heavy with missed sleep and she became overly familiar with the sights and sounds of the nighttime Hall, almost as much so, she sometimes thought sadly, as poor Lady Ann was supposed to be. In fact, since the day the earl had left, she often found herself wishing his Hall boasted a ghost or two, for she'd have liked company of any sort for those small dreary wakeful hours. There were even nights when she wished she could sneak off with a warm dog from Bobby's room, but he tried to keep them all safe from marauding footmen, behind his door. Even the one great independent beast, the massive black dog with drooping ears and eyes that Victoria still spied now and again trailing about the corridors searching for the children, remained aloof from her hesitant blandishments, regarding her with a quizzical stare before vanishing into some more interesting portion of the house.

But her days were well spent. The children were a joy. Mrs. Haverford was such an entertaining companion Victoria sometimes wondered just who was supposed to be companioning whom. Even Miss Comfort, she discovered, had a wealth of information to dispense. And since she'd made the further acquaintance of many persons at the Hall, there was seldom a daylight hour when she had to be alone if she didn't care to be. The librarian, Nurse, and housekeeper, the estate manager and his shy wife, and the Lawrences, who were restoring the art gallery, could all usually spare a moment for some pleasantry in the course of their crowded days. Some, she continued to see only now and again, like the housekeeper's perennially bustling, busy niece, or the lovely fair-haired girl she often encountered in the music room and elsewhere, but unfortunately still, so far, always just as she was almost gone from a room Victoria was entering. But even there, by the sweet sad smiles of regret she was always given, Victoria knew that there were still other relationships that might be pursued further someday.

But only if there were to be much more of a future for her here at the Hall, she thought, as she went to visit Miss Comfort in her room one fine August morning. A week had slipped into a month, and now, however tepid the Colfaxes' commendation, however reluctant young Theo's mama was to insist on a better one from her erstwhile ally, certainly enough time had passed for a substitute governess-companion to ask for an equally valid, enthusiastic one from Mrs. Haverford. It was only that the substitute governess-companion rationalized that not enough time had elapsed for her to bring herself to ask for it. For although the longer the earl stayed in London, the more she began to feel that her presence was keeping him away, the longer he stayed, the more she began to imagine that if she remained he might forget about her enough to return anyway. Perhaps she'd ask in a week, then, she decided resolutely as she tapped upon Miss Comfort's door, and then tried to put the thought behind her. Perhaps in a century, she admitted to herself in a burst of honesty, just before she was bidden to enter.

Mrs. Haverford sat at the bow window with her invalid companion and gave a genuinely warm and beaming welcome to Victoria when she came into the sickroom. By Miss Comfort's petulant look and forced smile, Victoria assumed the two had been at their usual gentle argument. Miss Comfort no doubt wanted to rise from her bedridden condition and get on with her duties, or her journeys, or her life again, and her employer no doubt was still insisting on her further rest for the sake of her complete recuperation.

"But, Comfort, my dear," Mrs. Haverford continued to say, too involved with her argument to give it up as Victoria took a seat, "the doctor has said that you ought to remain at rest, he even said so again just yesterday when he was here."

"And he said so the day before," Miss Comfort replied waspishly, "and the day before that. Really, Roberta, even you ought to acknowledge that I am not so ill that I require the daily attention that I've been receiving. I believe that the young doctor comes here as often to see Miss Dawkins as he does to visit me. And further," she said, as Victoria's eyes opened in shock at this tack the elder woman was taking, even as her cheeks turned a dim rose as she remembered the amount of unsubtle attention she generally received from that young man, "I cannot help but think that he has his own reasons for wanting me to remain in an invalidish condition. After all, he's likely realized that once I am up and about, Miss Dawkins will be gone from here, and I don't believe the good physician wants that."

"Comfort!" Mrs. Haverford said as her own eyes widened. "I can't believe my ears. Indeed, I cannot. Dr. Parker is a reputable physician, and although I can't deny he seems very taken with Victoria . . ." And here she shushed her new companion as she began a red-faced protest of her innocence in the matter, and overrode her comments by proclaiming, "As indeed who could blame him? He's young and unmarried and has eyes in his head, hasn't he? Not that I think she ought to encourage him, because I truly don't feel they would suit. It's clear she doesn't care for him in that fashion in the least, and I'm not gothic enough to preach that that sort of emotion would grow on her, for of course, it wouldn't. Not *that* sort of affection which is necessary for a true match . . ."

Mrs. Haverford frowned then. "Ah, where was I?" she asked, and then brightening, went on without the prompting that neither woman in her audience, one out of embarrassment, the other from pique, would give her.

"Dr. Parker, yes. As I was saying, I doubt such motives would influence him. Why should they? Because, Comfort, my dear, charming as they are, anyone can see that the Johnson children are a handful, and that Victoria's of a perfect age to deal with them. I certainly wouldn't burden you with their care when you're well again, especially not when she's here and able to handle them so well. And I scarcely think anyone, most especially not a physician, would think we'd ask it of you. No, I'm sure he doesn't for a moment believe your recovery would displace her, and so would have no reason to thwart it, even if he were such a conniving sort of character, which I'm sure he is not."

"So Miss Dawkins is to take on my duties with the children permanently?" Miss Comfort shrilled, rising unsteadily to her feet and clutching her morning robe closely together over her narrow breast with one thin gnarled hand. "I quite understand, oh, I do. I suppose you're waiting until I can walk safely enough to take myself off to a quiet retirement. Well, I assure you, Mrs. Haverford, I am well enough for that already. Doubtless your new broom will sweep cleaner. Doubtless she can cavort with the children, and amuse you, and your son, far more than a dried-up old creature like myself can do."

"Whatever are you thinking of?" Mrs. Haverford cried.

"I want you to remain with us, and Cole has nothing to say in the matter at all."

"Oh, does he not?" Miss Comfort retorted, swaying as she stood and glared at her employer and the new governess. "I have seen how he looks at Miss Dawkins, and I assure you, Mrs. Haverford, he never looked at me that way!"

Victoria didn't know whether to giggle or weep at the pronouncement, but before she could respond, Mrs. Haverford rose to her feet and put out a hand to touch the old woman, only to find her shrinking back as though she expected a blow. So she only said sadly:

"You certainly cannot be well, Comfort, to speak such nonsense. Cole thinks of you in the light of a mother . . . well, not actually," she mumbled, "rather more of an aunt, I should say, but you are of an age to be his mother. It would be reprehensible, bizarre in fact, if he should ogle you."

She paused to suppress a distinct giggle, as Miss Comfort said stiffly, "That is never what I meant," and then went on, in softer tones:

"Come, Comfort, be reasonable. He's young, Victoria's lovely, what more natural than he should appreciate looking at her? Has the doctor better eyes than he? But he's never the sort to fling you out of your house—and never doubt that wherever I am is your house as well, my dear—just so that he can continue to enjoy the sight. Be sensible, my dear, sit down and consider what you've said, indeed it doesn't become you and I believe you may even owe Victoria an apology for this morning's work."

"And if you encourage your son in his appreciation of Miss Dawkins, your family may find you owe her a deal more than an apology," the old woman retorted, "but it would be for the result of a night's work, and not mine, never fear!"

"Comfort!" Mrs. Haverford gasped.

"Miss Comfort," Victoria ventured, in a sort of anguish of embarrassment at the turn the conversation had taken. She'd been watching and listening to the two women like a spectator at a shuttlecock match, and hardly knew when she ought to put in a word. As the altercation grew louder, and most especially when the earl was mentioned, she became unhappily aware that the two had forgotten her presence entirely, and was even more uncomfortable when she realized she was afraid to interrupt and remind them, lest she miss a word. Now she also wondered if the old woman could read minds, or if she herself had been so transparent in her yearnings toward the earl that even a passionless creature such as Miss Comfort found no difficulty in reading her face.

But Mrs. Haverford saved her from further embarrassment by reminding her it was her son, and never her governess, who was being accused of lechery. For her employer dropped her kindly air, drew herself up regally, raised her handsome head, and spoke in such clear and measured tones that no one, not even Miss Comfort, would dare to interrupt her. In fact the older woman dropped back into her seat and seemed to shrink lower with each word uttered.

"Cole is an honorable man, Comfort, and he's never given you any reason to doubt it. He might think Victoria the most delectable creature on earth but he'd never forget she was his dependent. He's not the sort given to pinching servant girls. And indeed, Victoria is no low servant, either. There's been too much talk of the past here, too many tales of the supernatural shades of that past since we've come to this place, I fear it's clouded your perceptions as much as it's given poor little Sally the nightmare.

"The previous Earls of Clune might be famous for their cavalier attitudes toward their social inferiors, but don't forget, for I know he cannot, that Cole wasn't born to the purple as they were. He earned his bread by the sweat of his brow, and understands what it means to be at another person's mercy for one's health and welfare. He would never take advantage of his position for his own gain, of any sort."

"But what of Miss Dawkins?" Miss Comfort said weakly but tenaciously, holding on to her grim tone of grievance. "What is to say that she will not forget? Have you thought of that? With all this merry thoughtless encouragement you offer, can you forget that a young girl might break her heart at receiving a gentleman's attentions that society dictates can never go beyond jest?"

"Cole doesn't give a fig for society," Mrs. Haverford said angrily.

"He doesn't?" Miss Comfort replied in a tight and trembling voice, growing extremely white with anger and emotion herself. "Are you intimating that he would offer for a poor commoner in his employ when he's all the social world of wealthy and titled young females to pick and choose from? As if you'd countenance it either," she scoffed, her bitter laughter turning into a creaking sob of rage. "You do Miss Dawkins a disservice even to suggest it. Life is hard enough for a young person in her position without you giving even a careless moment's credence to such futile air-dreams. Useless dreams that would keep her bound to old women and other people's children, haunted by dreams of what can never be until it is too late for her to remedy. Better you packed her bags and encouraged her to elope with little Dr. Parker this night, than that."

"I will not. For whatever Cole wished for, he would see to it," Mrs. Haverford said, her chin held high. "And whatever he wished, I'd never object to. I wasn't born to this Hall either, remember," she said, giving Miss Comfort a haughty look. But in that look she saw how pinched and fragile, how spent from her bout with emotion the older woman appeared to be.

"But what are we doing?" Mrs. Haverford exclaimed in horror. "Brangling over Victoria's future, putting her to the blush with idle speculation, discussing Cole as though he were some sort of decadent monster, such as his ancestors were. This house must indeed be haunted! See how its cruel aura sets us at each other's throats. You've been in this room too long, Comfort, my dear. I'll ask the doctor if you may come outside to the garden this very day. And, Victoria," she said determinedly, "accept our apologies, and never mind our foolish chatter. We're old friends,

Comfort and I, even if we're supposedly employer and employee. But I suppose I haven't much noble blood, for I never had any use for that sort of rigmarole.

"Old friends don't mind their tongues when they're together, which is also precisely why, I suspect, I never wanted a 'companion' so much as I needed a friend. Just as I always told you, Comfort," she chided her companion, as the other woman sat down at last and sighed in resignation, shaking her head at her employer.

"We're well used to this sort of wrangling," Mrs. Haverford explained as she fussed with the older woman's shawl, trying to straighten it, even as her companion weakly attempted to shoo her away to do it for herself. "We're both hardheaded females. But it can't have been pleasant for you. You run along, child, and see to the children and spend this summer day more pleasantly than we began it for you. Never fear, I'll mend fences with Comfort here, whether she wills it or not, for I've an advantage. She's such a stickler for propriety, you see, she *has* to practice what she preaches and obey her employer and forgive her, if she demands it. And she does."

Victoria arose, and seeing that Mrs. Haverford had already coaxed a small smile from Miss Comfort, she was only too relieved to duck a small curtsy and escape the room. But she had a great deal to think about as she made her way to the nursery, where the children were awaiting her. So much had been said and almost said that her mind reeled. She was wretched at the discovery that both women seemed to know of her feelings toward the earl. She was surprised to have found that Miss Comfort, for all her spite, yet seemed to be genuinely concerned for her. But then, overriding all else was the incredible fact, both dismaying and delighting her, that the earl's own mother did not think a match between an earl and an impoverished commoner was unthinkable. But it was to Victoria. At least in the clear sane light of a summer's morning it was. Tonight, she promised herself, as another young woman might promise herself a sweet or a treat, tonight, when she was alone in her bed, she'd think on it. And there where the kindly dark made all wild thoughts possible, she might hug it to her heart.

But as it turned out, she had no time for it. For that night Sally saw the ghost. And the next night, Mrs. Haverford and the boys saw it. And on the third night, Victoria did.

13

From the vantage point offered by the high box tucked into the horseshoe-shaped wedge of the theater that projected out over the mass of the audience, a privileged patron could get a clear, unobstructed view of the costumes, shapes, and grace of the almost unearthly beautiful dancers. But if that privileged fellow were also an experienced one, he would know that what he saw from his high seat was not quite what was actually occurring on the wide stage below. It was not, after all, meant to be.

Thus, he would realize that the lovely faces he saw were painted on so that they might be seen even from the worst seats in the house; he'd know that the dancers, seeming to leap as easily as if they were floating, could hear each other grunting and gasping under the music as they exerted themselves; he'd accept the fact that the sparkle in their eyes was belladonna like as not, even as some of the sparkle upon those white shoulders might only be the dew from their exercise, running and reflecting in the dancing stage lights.

And so the Earl of Clune sat back and idly surveyed the crowd at the close of the performance, in no haste to get himself backstage, knowing, indeed, preferring that his chosen ladylove be able to freshen herself before he visited with her in the green room behind the stage.

"Aren't you coming, Clune?" his companion asked as he rose to leave the box.

"In time, there's time," the earl replied laconically.

"For you, sir, you've singled yours out already. I, however, am in the market for some company this evening. So I'm off. Dinner was amusing. Let's meet again, and soon," the gentleman said, offering his hand. The two parted amiably, and as the earl watched his erstwhile companion hurry through the curtains of the box, he had a moment's amusement, for he doubted he would ever pass time again with his new acquaintance, chance-met at his club this evening, if, indeed, he ever recognized the fellow again if they did meet.

But most of the gentlemen he'd met this past season that he might call "friend" were out of town now, this being the summer, the time when the *ton* customarily abandoned London as though the black plague raged through its streets. However, London was large enough to enable him to have spent the last weeks amusing himself anyway in both the highest and the lowest reaches of society. He'd gone to *ton* parties and low revels, often, interestingly enough, encountering the same gentlemen in both places. But for all his efforts, he hadn't been as diverted as he'd expected. He'd been, in fact, unaccountably bored and even lonely amid all the gaiety, though he believed this might well have been because no entertainment was quite as enjoyable without one's good friends in attendance. And his were not.

Most of his older friends, the ones he'd made before he'd come into his honors, were still out of the country where he'd first met them. Those few who were in England were still too intimidated by his new title to be easy in his company. He was, he reflected sadly, as he noted that the theater had emptied enough to make him conspicuous still lingering in his box, truly a man caught between two worlds just now.

Some of the men he'd met over the past year that he might like to befriend, he thought as he strolled along the narrow carpeted hall of the theater, like the lofty Lord Leith, who had also once worked for his bread, and the sly and amusing Duke of Torquay, whom he now spied caught amid a knot of sensation seekers as he was attempting to descend the stair with his beautiful wife, were already wed, and so had little time or inclination to make new male friends. As if to illustrate the point, after he'd greeted them, the flaxen-haired duke and his lovely lady informed him that they were in town on only a brief visit. The earl voiced his polite disappointment, and after sidestepping their invitation for him to join them in the countryside at his leisure, he gave them a pleasant good evening, and continued on his way. Then, reflecting upon their evident content, he considered, rather wryly, that many of his new friends who were unwed also seemed to be heading toward the parson's mousetrap this season. The Baron Stafford and the slightly disreputable Marquis of Severne were traveling in and out of town these days, both rumored to be occupied with affairs of the heart, affairs that kept them in a mental state of confusion, as well as physically apart from other matters.

It was singular, the earl thought as he took the long gilded flight of steps down toward the stage level, that a great many of the gentlemen he'd been impressed with were those who had slightly raffish reputations as well as lively minds. But they were the ones he'd discovered to be least likely to sneer at him for his beginnings, and most likely to have befriended him, then or now, title or no.

For although he was an earl, and wealthy twice-over, from his legacy as well as from his own efforts, those very efforts seemed to smell rank to those in society who chose to ignore the new spirit in the land, and the very idea of a gentleman dealing in matters of trade. He'd been admitted to Almack's, invited into those august and socially pure precincts so soon as he'd acceded to the title. But he'd gone there only once. He'd been sensitive then, he knew, but still, from the uplifted noses and quizzing glasses and the cool reception he'd gotten that night, he'd felt as though the haughty members of what he immediately perceived to be a marriage brokerage masquerading as a social club actually thought they could still detect the lower-class stench of the shop about him. Just as they believed a well-bred young lady of fashion ought to be pure of body and mind, they chose to believe that a gentleman of title ought to be innocent of financial affairs.

Truly, the earl thought on a reminiscent smile as he entered the crowded green room where the performers met with their admirers, it was another case of "The Prince and the Peacock" just as Miss Dawkins had giggled. And, he believed, the idea that a gentleman ought to be as idle and ornamental as a peacock was just as empty-headed and banal a concept as that which might occur in that bird's own dim brain. But the thought of Miss Dawkins led to thoughts which might ruin the evening he had planned, so the earl attempted to banish all thought from his mind as he entered the room. There was enough noise and activity within to make that possible, if not even preferable, to any attempt at cerebration.

Melissa Careaux was flushed with success, giddy with attention, and only a trifle elevated by the champagne that had been pressed upon her by someone in her crowd of admirers. Her inky curls were in delightful disarray, her ample figure was covered by a gaily patterned wrap that she'd thrown about her half-costumed person, although she kindly loosened her grip upon the front of it every now and again, when she laughed, just to be fair and display a peek of her lavish bounty to those not fortunate enough to afford to get a private viewing later on, closer up.

For Melissa was a kindly girl, and at the peak of her form in all ways, but a girl had to take care of herself, for Gawd knew, as everyone backstage said, that no one else would. She'd made her way out of the slums the only way many another female had, by vending that which nature had given her. But what she'd been given most of, although lavish, was purely physical, and so, as even she knew, was like any other sort of fleshly commodity sold at market or in barrow, in that when it was no longer fresh, it was no longer salable. So when she noted the Earl of Clune's dark face in the crowd, with its sardonic but admiring expression that was usually enough to melt the last of the buttons on her wrap, she grew pensive for a moment, before she sipped at her champagne to cover that lapse and then gurgled a giggle at some florid compliment someone threw to her like a rose. Because although she knew she'd give up a great many sensible things in order to gain the comfort of his arms, and even more to gamble on his longer-term patronage, in light of his hesitation so far to commit himself to even one full week, she wondered if she could afford such rash gaming.

But for all her resolve she was still young, and even women of pleasure can sometimes think of their own pleasure. So she gave him such a warm smile of greeting that Lord Hoyland, that fattish, baldish perennial denizen of the green room, sighed with resignation and looked about for another light lady to finance for the night, or however many nights she might grant him until someone more wealthy or expert happened along to steal her away from him.

"You were magnificent tonight," the earl said, taking her hand to his lips, although his eyes denied his words and she was too occupied with staring at his lips to mind his words.

"I danced for you," she sighed.

Her bramble-black eyes were moist with desire, she ran the tip of her little pink tongue over her pink-painted lips, and the look she gave him then was so replete with the promise of all the things she'd do to and for him later that poor Lord Hoyland, who'd chanced to glance back at her, was heard to gasp in wonder at the look that was never for him, and that indeed no female—even, or especially, his own wife—had ever given to him. But the intended recipient of that heated gaze looked back at her and could only think that he'd done it already, she was only reminding him of what had been, last month, last week, and the night before, and that, to his great and terrible shock, he really didn't care to go through all that all over again. At least not all that playacting, he thought defensively, not all that unbuttoning and posturing and emoting and exertion, he rationalized wildly, and all for nothing but a brief spasm of relief and a feeling of lassitude and a desire to be all alone again in his own wide bed at the end.

"Melissa," he said then, for he was now operating solely on instinct, as something hideous had occurred to him, only to be pushed back again to the unexpected depths it had sprung from.

"Melissa," he breathed, for he was proud of his quick thinking in all emergencies, "I only came tonight to tell you how much I enjoyed the perfomance. I only stayed so long, in fact, to tell you that much. And now I must leave you. For," he said, as amazed as she was by his words, although his face, at least, was trained not to show it, "it seems I have the headache."

After he had left the shocked opera dancer to the humble but expensive attentions of a dazed but abjectly grateful Lord Hoyland, the earl strode off into the night. He marched straight into his carriage and didn't give his driver his direction, even when asked twice, so that canny fellow contented himself with driving slow circles around Piccadilly until his master came to his senses.

After several long circuits, to prevent the horses from getting dizzy the driver headed the team toward the earl's town house. But by then his master had recovered himself a little. It was incredible that he'd offered a cozy, obliging armful such as Melissa Careaux an excuse he'd heard gentlemen quote from their disinterested, disheartened wives for decades. But he'd had time to work the thing out since he'd entered the carriage, and decided that it was only that he was of an age and of a temperament now to dislike sexual favors he knew he was paying for. It had to happen, he told himself with relief as he sat back in the carriage. After all, he'd been in a falsely domestic situation at High Wyvern Hall for weeks, among children and with his parent, and with a young woman very like the sort of . . .

"Here, John," he called to his coachman, "to the Swansons', on Grosvenor Square. If the soiree's still in full cry, I'll disembark there."

The soiree at the Swansons' was running at full tilt when the Earl of Clune was announced. It was summer, of course, but since chickenpox had struck their country home, the Swansons were marooned for a summer in town. The cream of the *ton* was in the countryside as well, at least those not venturing abroad now that Nappy seemed to have been bottled up again after his recent debacle in Belgium at Waterloo. But there were still enough socially important persons left in town for various other reasons, or at least enough to fill up the ballroom. And having produced a clutch of daughters, filling their ballroom had been a primary concern for the Swansons for years.

The earl had remembered the Swansons' invitation, indeed, he seemed to recall his valet telling him about one each day since he'd returned to town, although he knew that couldn't be true. But at least when in distress the name had floated to the top of his mind and he found himself exceedingly grateful for being able to escape from himself here, so grateful in fact that almost immediately after his arrival he asked the nearest of the platter-faced Misses Swanson for a dance. She refused him. She was to regret it a hundred times that night alone, and to build a great fiction of an infatuation on his part to warm herself with several years later, after she eventually married young Lord Bryant. But she really did have her card filled by then, by a dozen young gentlemen who also felt they owed a favor to her father.

The new-made earl took it for insult, however prettily the refusal was given. But he wasn't given to brooding, so he shrugged it off and waded into the festivities, determined to enjoy himself.

Another, younger Miss Swanson he solicited for the dance was passing fair and might have been a mute, he thought, for all the answers he got to his polite conversation, until her piercing giggles given in reply almost made him miss his step. Miss Darling was a pretty little thing, but her mama made all her conversation for her. Miss Chapman had a cat, she seemed to think it the height of wit to speak about it ceaselessly, but then, the Honorable Miss Lamont had a lisp, which she seemed to regard as equally enchanting. Miss Fontaine was not very handsome but she was very wealthy, indeed, she told him so several times, and the Incomparable Miss Merriman was incomparably lovely to be sure, and was as impressed by the fact of it as she seemed to hope he was.

By the time he'd passed an hour at the Swansons', he'd decided he'd encountered the cream of the current crop of debutantes still in London, and they appeared to be exactly like the ones he'd met when he first came into society, and all the ones he'd met since. And, he thought, for all he remembered or cared, they might well have been the self-same ones, at that. Although he didn't enjoy their company, he was grateful to them for reminding him just why he never sought them out, and was wondering how soon he could leave the premises without giving offense when a delightful vision swam into his view.

"Hallo, Clune," a slight young gentleman said at his side as he gazed forward. "I'm Grayson," he went on, offering his hand. "We met at Tattersall's, remember? Well, this is m' sister," the graceless fellow murmured, "Lady Honora. She was on fire to meet you. Lady Honora, may I present Colin Haverford, Earl of Clune. There, that's done. Don't look daggers at me, Horrie, I'm off. Ta," the young man said, and true to his word, he backed a step and evaporated into the press of people, leaving the earl to look down at the most charming young person he'd seen all night.

She was small and dark, just as Melissa Careaux was, but there all similarity between the two females ended. For although she was shapely with huge dark eyes and a curving pink mouth as well, Lady Honora was innocent of paint and powder, her dark hair was smooth and stylish, and her eyes remained downcast beneath thin brows and unusually long dark lashes. She was all that was demure and all that was dainty. The earl led her into the dance with great care, for everything in her aspect bespoke her delicacy of mind as well as of face and form.

But she had a great deal of conversation, although it appeared to be all in the form of queries. At first, like any male, he was vastly pleased and flattered by her interest in himself. Soon he found himself telling her, during the dance or on the sidelines, then at late supper and over ices, not only about his adventures in the Caribbean, but also all about his family and his holdings, from his London home to his hunting box to High Wyvern Hall itself. In fact, she was so full of questions that he soon grew weary with hearing his own voice. About then, he began to discover that the lovely young creature was more interested in knowing about property he'd acquired than time he'd passed in the islands, and far keener on hearing about his acquisitions than his opinions. By the time her untouched ices had melted, his own heart had frozen, and he had the vague, errant thought of offering her a note to his man of business so that she could document his fortune and dealings with more exactitude.

But she was an earl's daughter, and he was a gentlewoman's son, so he bore with her questions with fortitude, although his answers grew briefer and terser as the hour grew later. The admiration had gone from his eye, and watching her with unclouded vision as she chewed over the latest information about the acreage of his Scottish estate along with her bit of damson tart, he decided that she wasn't so much ingenuous as immature, she was not so much sylphlike as undeveloped, and not half so attractive as Melissa, whom perversely, he now began to long for.

He had to be called back from his reverie twice, the second time sharply, before he attended to her again.

"Terribly sorry, Lady Honora," he answered in a not terribly sincere tone. "What was it you wished to know now?"

"Oh no," she tittered, making so much play with her lashes that he wondered how she ever got to see anything if she always lowered them for effect whenever a gentleman looked at her. She'll end up marrying the wrong fellow, for she won't recognize him unless the vicar names him, if she doesn't take care, he thought whimsically. "It's only that it's so close in here," she pouted.

"The evening's at its end," he commented, pushing the crumbs of his cake into a triangular pattern, destroying the star-shaped form he'd previously created as she'd interrogated him about the number of rooms at the Hall.

"Oh, not yet," she said, putting one little hand at her breast in alarm. "Why, how time has rushed past us! I wouldn't have believed it"—she smiled at him—"but it's still far from over for me," she sighed, "for Papa lingers in the card room until he's won back all he's lost, or until they throw him out, and in either case that could be forever. Won't you accompany me out into the courtyard for a breath of air? I hesitate to go there by myself, my lord."

Because she'd made him laugh, and because she'd said it so prettily, and because she was an earl's daughter and he was trying to be a gentleman, he agreed at once.

And it was not too much longer than that before he desperately wanted to go back into the Swansons' house.

"Lady Honora," he pleaded as he held his head high and back from her searching lips and tried to extricate himself from her clutches, for the girl seemed to have become some sort of Indian goddess once the darkness had covered her and appeared to have grown herself an extra dozen pairs of arms, "I think you ought to go back to your parents."

It had been comfortably cool in the night air, and when she'd stopped strolling and turned to look up at him, he'd expected another dozen questions about his estates and had instead been shocked to find her flinging herself forward into his arms. He reacted by holding her as though she'd stumbled, to prevent her doing herself an injury, and then found her arms wrapping about his neck and her mouth seeking his, but fortunately finding only his chin before he'd actually taken a stumbling step backward himself.

He didn't have time to think of much but a fervent prayer that her father was occupied with losing his entire fortune and her brother had met with a fatal accident, for it would be worse than fatal for him, it would be wedlock, if he were discovered in her embrace. He hadn't the least desire to welcome her touch because of that dread thought. Then too, he'd had a surfeit of yielding female bodies since he'd came to London, he could have remained with Melissa for that, it was company for his uneasy spirit that he'd been after tonight. Then he had no more time for futile prayer, he had to concentrate all his efforts on freeing himself. He never would have guessed that such a slender girl had such strength in her slim arms. As he struggled, feeling more foolish by the moment, he was reminded of a grape vine that he'd once tried to unravel after it had encroached on his mama's favorite quince tree.

"Lady Honora," he breathed at last, stepping back a long pace so that she'd have to actually throw herself forward to reach him, and he'd still have a chance of dodging her embrace if she did, "it's possible you've had too much punch. It's possible it's the full of the moon. But whatever it is, I suggest you forget it. Now, you have a choice of either entering the house again with me, or going by yourself. But I'm returning now."

She seemed to fall docilely into step behind him and he dared not venture another word until he held the French doors open for her and achieved the lighted ballroom, which he now regarded as sanctuary in very much the same spirit in which a medieval felon with a howling mob at his heels would regard a cathedral.

He wondered what he would say to her, but even as her toe touched the floor, she wheeled around and snarled, "Capon!" at him, before she marched away.

He decided not to leave at once, feeling it would be better not to run if he'd committed no crime. So he stayed to chat for a few moments with a number of persons whose comments and conversation never registered with him, until he saw a florid gentleman, all smiles, with the Lady Honora's brother at his elbow, shouldering his way through the throng in order to step out the French doors into the courtyard. They returned a few moments later, the elder gentleman not smiling at all. He spat a few words at Lady Honora's brother before he stomped off into the card room again. The younger man stood back and eyed the crowd. Then, spying the earl in their midst, he ambled over to him.

"Papa's had the worst run of luck at cards for some time, you know," the younger fellow said softly. "I congratulate you on your footwork," he added coolly, "but then, I understand you actually worked in the fields once, so I suppose that explains it. Next time, I think we'll choose a true gentleman," he sighed, and bowing, left.

If it was meant to be a cut, it never even stung, and the earl was so blithe when he stepped back into his carriage that his coachman smiled at the way the soiree had cheered up the master.

Once home, the earl poured himself a libation and raised it in a toast to himself when he was alone in his bath. He celebrated his quick-wittedness and his continuing freedom. He'd recently said, he recalled with an ironic grin, that he didn't know if he would dare attempt an earl's daughter. As it turned out, he hadn't, but for very different reasons than he'd meant. He'd heard stories about the sort of entrapment he'd almost fallen victim to; unfortunately for the lady's family, they hadn't supposed he would have. He may have been new to his title, but he'd gone to good schools and the most interesting parts of his education had always come in whispers after midnight. Those half-believed tales had saved him tonight. For though he hadn't wanted the girl, had he not heard about how some impoverished gentlewomen snared wealthy, unwilling mates to repair their family fortunes, he supposed he might have stayed to cooperate with her, and be discovered by her supposedly enraged papa, if not because of lust, then out of vanity, or even for pity's sake. And then, of course, he would have shortly been a married man, or an outcast one. He shuddered then, even though the room was warm and he'd wrapped himself around with a towel.

It would have been a mighty high price to pay for some fumbled embraces, he thought, but then, though Melissa's attentions cost a good many guineas, and assurance of her fidelity might be worth emeralds and rubies, society put an even more inflationary value on the touch of noble womanflesh. Then, he wondered idly before he realized what he was about to contemplate, what the worth might be of a good woman's kiss, the value, for example, of a governess's love? But these were dismal thoughts, he decided, annoyed with himself at such sober reasonings, and it was late, and he was weary.

Colin Haverford made for his bed at last, as happy to see its white sheets in the moonlight as another man would be to see a lover awaiting him with wide-open arms. But once settled in its embrace, he lay there with wide-open eyes for many long hours. Until at last, he sighed as a man will with a broken heart, for he'd at last reached the end of his rope. He was lonely where he lay. It was in the end, after all his evasions, just that simple.

He wanted no more courtesans, expensive or faithful, nor did he want a society miss, chaste or not, conniving or not. He hadn't been tempted by Melissa or Lady Honora tonight, nor would he be again by any female who breathed, from any sphere, because he'd already found what he most desired. He acknowledged at last precisely what it was he wanted, and whether she was an earl's daughter or an apothecary's daughter had never been the problem. He had only wanted his freedom until now, until just now, when he finally accepted that he'd lost it long since.

Then, at last committed, he fell to sleep as he at last could admit he'd done for all the past weeks: with her name on his lips and her face in his mind.

But in the morning, it was Lady Malverne's face he had to contemplate.

"My lady," he said, bowing properly, as he received her in his study, before he waved her to a chair and took a seat safely behind the polished surface of his desk himself. Then he took care to smile down at her with just the right amount of boredom and annoyance at her arrival at his house unbidden that he thought she deserved and would expect from the head of her family. But she knew the game very well and managed to hide her own impatience and anger as well. She was of an age with his own mama, but was a smaller, rounder person, and though dressed in the height of fashion, was done all in pastels like her son Theo, from her pale blue eyes to her ash-gray hair. She might have been pleasant to look upon in a faded fashion, if it were not for the fact that her pale little eyes held a sharp expression and never left off evaluating her viewer.

He'd kept her waiting an hour while he dressed, gave orders for his packing and travel to his servants, had a light breakfast in his rooms, and pondered the reason for her odd early-morning visit. A bit of fear that the aborted episode with Lady Honora might have had some repercussions gave his greeting a chill edge, and the remembrance of his visitor's role in losing Miss Dawkins her original post lent his attitude a certain tension. He scarcely knew what to expect from the lady and yet was surprised to hear the immediate challenge she did issue.

"Good morning, Clune," she said. "And what have you done with Theodore now?"

"Nothing that I know of. Why, what's he done now?" the earl replied warily.

"Only hared off to High Wyvern Hall. I understand you've that governess there. Has she got him in her coils again?"

"Assuredly not," he replied, making sure his voice retained its bored accents, as he riffled through some letters that had been left out for him.

"Then," his relative persisted, "why did he fly there? One moment he was off to visit with you here. Then he came tearing home yesterday, sent a volley of messages off to his friends, and then flung his clothes together, collared his valet, and fled for High Wyvern Hall, as though it were on fire."

"One hopes it is not," he replied without a pause or a discernible emotion on his dark face. "And did your dutiful son not tell you the reason for this trip? For I assure you, he didn't inform me of it, as I didn't see him here."

"I was not at home," she answered with chagrin. "He left word that he was going, of course, and some muddled story about some message from your mama being delivered whilst he was here waiting on your return, and that it was a conversation he had with the groom who'd brought it that decided him on his immediate course of action."

"A letter from Mama?" the earl asked, now genuinely concerned. "Ah, here it is. I came in too late last night to be told of it, although I am sure," he said, almost to himself, "that if it had been urgent Simpson would have waited up for me to tell me so. Ah," he breathed as he began to read it. "Aha!" he said as he read it. "Well," he said at length, when he had done and Lady Malverne had tested her upbringing to the utmost, having managed somehow to restrain herself from snatching the missive from out his hands long since.

There was an unreadable expression on his wicked dark face, the lady thought, as he arose and looked down at her. It might have been excitement, it might even have been laughter, but as she rose and took in a breath to demand an answer, he said:

"Content yourself. Theo's only chasing after thrills and excitement again, as might be expected of a lad his age. And it is a lady whose presence accounts for his absence all right, but it's one of high birth and rank. Theo's obviously on fire to meet her. The only problem is that she's dead. And has been for several hundred years. My ancestors seem to be stirring. It appears," he said, "we've got a ghost afoot in the Hall."

There was only so much haste a good team could make, and so much time it took them to travel, even if they were sprung and then changed at a posting house halfway on the journey. And since that journey could not have been set out upon at dawn, it having been decided upon after breakfast in the first place, and there being a necessity to stop at Lady Malverne's house to collect up her things and her maid and leave a message for her brother wherever he might be, in the second, the journey had been delayed. It had been delayed further by the heated argument that had ensued, ending only when the lady had threatened to cast herself in front of the earl's horses if he left without her.

It was not the scandal, he vowed later, when he sealed her into the coach with a mumbled good riddance, that prevented him from preventing her. It was, he said bitterly, before he mounted his own horse to travel outrider style, the thought of the mess in the street. Thus assured of her welcome, she sat back in his carriage, having gotten as good as she gave, now convinced that there might be some worth to the new earl after all.

Although two days' journey had been compressed into one long haul, it was still night, and deep night, at that, when the coach and riders at last pulled up in the courtyard in front of Wyvern Hall. Exhaustion made unlikely camaraderie, and the earl gave Lady Malverne his arm as they made their unsteady way up the stairs to the great oak doors. Even then, when the doors swung wide to admit the master and his guest, they exchanged weary and compassionate grins with each other, acknowledged survivors of a mad ride, as they crossed the portals into the grand hall. But the blackness within caused the earl's smile to fade.

"What new economy is this?" he demanded. "Is this the bottom of a coal scuttle, or the entrance to my home?"

"We lit the lamps up as usual, my lord," the butler said, appearing gothic as he stood in the gloom with a branch of candles in his hand. He continued, with a hint of distress in his voice, "We lit them at dusk, only to have the order countermanded, and then we put them out again. Thrice, my lord. Your mama wanted them on. But she went to bed and young Master Theo ordered them out. Up she rises," the butler tried to explain, forgetting his hard-won accents in his attempt, "and on they come again. And so it's gone on all night, my lord. We are glad to see you, indeed we are."

"Then light them all, and see me," the earl commanded as he strode into the grand salon, where he heard voices rising in dispute.

There were several people in front of the fire. His mama, Theo and two ungainly-looking young sprigs, one deranged-looking old gentleman in his night clothes, several servants, and Alfie and Bobby. But his gaze ran past them until he saw the one face he'd been seeing in his dreams, waking and sleeping, since he'd left her. She stared at him wide-eyed. She left off arguing with the elderly fellow to simply stand and look upon him as though he were a spirit himself. Alfie was at her side, with a jacket thrown over his nightshirt for propriety. When he saw the direction of his governess's gaze, he took a step forward. The earl's mama had been nearby to them, in heated debate with the truant Theo, but as she saw Alfie's defection from her cause, she stopped, and then saw her son at the door. Those arguments having been silenced, the others turned to see what had happened. And then a great hush fell over the room.

"We saw a ghost," Alfie explained to the newcomers.

"I am not one," the earl said smoothly, "and I don't believe in them."

"There, then that's settled it," Alfie said with a sigh.

And then the echoes of a wild and eldritch laughter rang out through the room, around the room, and through the great hall, though all the while no living person in the room dared breathe, much less make a sound.

14

The company was served cakes and toast and chocolate, coffee, tea, and warm milk in the grand salon. This was not the common practice at any stately country home, especially not at two hours into the morning of a new day, but no one among them seemed inclined for sleep, and their host and his mama agreed that it was better to have them together than to have them roving singly about the Hall. Or, as the earl so succinctly put it, "Light every lamp, feed them and soothe them, and maybe they won't go rattling around the house all night."

The household had been wakeful and stirring even before the earl or the weird laughter that had greeted him had come. There had, in fact, been a hot debate raging. Theo had been planning on sitting up with the lights off, waiting for the Haverford ghost to show itself, some others that he had invited were all for only dimming the lights and holding a séance to speed matters along, and a minority opinion, held by the beleaguered Mrs. Haverford and her governess, wanted all the lights on, and all the guests in their beds.

The earl's arrival had ended the discussion. Immediately after the wild burst of eerie laughter that came on the heels of his entrance had faded away, a search of the house, led by the earl, some of his staff, Theo and his spiritual twin, Mr. Colfax, his friend, Georgie Burton, and an elderly gentleman discovered to be father to that young exquisite, revealed nothing about the source of the infernal disturbance. It had been a vigorous effort, but much to the guests' disappointment, it had revealed nothing to them but the excellence of the Hall's housekeeping staff. It was such a well-run, well-organized household, in fact, that not even a dust ball was found behind the one curtain discovered to be swaying in the music room, and that movement, it transpired, had only been caused by a window left a fraction of an inch open by a zealous but forgetful housemaid who had cleaned it that afternoon. The scuffling in the corridor behind the search party was discovered to be caused by one of Bobby's spaniels, going along on the ghost hunt in the proper spirit of adventure that a good gun dog ought to show, and the rattling in the upstairs rooms turned out to be Miss Comfort fumbling at her door to see what was amiss, her face pale beneath her nightcap, newly woken, as she then complained, from her slumbers by the very mortal sounds of the wild hunt passing along her corridor.

It was a very large house, and there was an enthusiastic band of volunteer detectives, but nothing was found, and by the time they straggled back to the grand drawing room, the refreshments awaited them and were fallen on with the same enthusiasm that the missing phantom might have been. Now the warmth given off by the beverages, light, and company seemed to thaw the last of the terror from the marrow of the most fearful among them, and since there hadn't been one ghostly intervention since that single screech of laughter, even the timid became bold enough to join in the discussion of the phenomenon. Indeed, it was become, as young Lord Malverne was heard to declare around his mouthful of saffron cake, "actually a jolly good way to spend a night. Great fun!"

This estimate of the evening's activities won him a sour look from his mama, and he subsided. But his young guests silently agreed with him. It was an informal group that congregated in the salon; almost every guest and member of the household was there in various stages of disarray. Some were still formally dressed for dinner, and some looked as though they'd been roused from their beds by the disturbance caused by the earl's dramatic arrival. Miss Dawkins, the earl noted with some regret, was dressed quite completely, her proper gray gown buttoned up to the neck as befitted a governess. But she looked as weary as he felt.

Baby and little Sally were not present, for as Nurse and Miss Dawkins reported after peeking in at them, those two were lost in the easy innocent sleep of childhood. Nurse lumbered back to the nursery floor soon after making her announcement, her own sleep, she declared, being far more important than any ghost's wakefulness. And though there might be some who envied or disparaged her unfeeling response to the spectral visitation, all would agree that it would be a very bold spirit indeed who dared to interrupt that good woman's slumbers.

"Actually," commented the spindly old gent, Lord Burton, who was wrapped round in a voluminous night robe, his white hair standing on end as though he'd just seen a spirit, although it was only that it was disarranged after having been lifted from his pillow so quickly, "there are some persons, you know, who would not notice if a troop of ghosts frolicked upon their bed. There are others, of course, who are rather like lightning rods. They receive the slightest of vibrations from any psychic emanations, willy-nilly, want to or not. It's a question of sensitivity, you see," he explained expansively.

The old gentleman had been pleased to introduce himself to the earl as they'd gone about the house together searching for clues to the disturbance. He was parent to a young blade Theo had summoned when he'd begun his flight to investigate what was happening at High Wyvern Hall. Old Lord Burton had packed on the instant and scrambled into Theo's carriage after notifying some of his cronies as to his destination, so that they could envy him. For he and they were members of a select gentlemen's club, and one of their fondest avocations was the investigation of ectoplasmic manifestations, or "ghosts," as he'd condescended to explain to his unwitting, unwilling host.

"Aye, and no wonder," Alfie had whispered to the

earl, and he was close enough to do so, as he'd never left that nobleman's side since he'd appeared, wraithlike himself, in the doorway to the salon, "since the old gent's like to be one of them any 'our 'isself. No wonder 'e's so keen to find one."

"Hush," the earl had said. "Uncharitable stuff, lad."

"Aye," Alfie had grumbled, "but 'e's a selfish old puffed-up thing, my lord, 'e is. You 'aven't passed time with 'im, thank your lucky stars. Wants to find 'is bugbear, 'e does, and don't care if 'e scares everyone else to pieces going about it. Asked Sally questions 'ad her eyes crossing until Miss Dawkins shooed 'im off and barred the door to 'im. And 'e thinks 'e's smarter than anything that ever drew breath, 'e does. I'd like to ' ave Lady Ann meet 'im all right, and take 'im 'ome wiv 'er, too. Only likely, being a lady, she'd 'ave better taste than that."

It hadn't taken long for the earl to agree, albeit silently, with Alfie's estimation of Lord Burton. But the fact was that he'd come home to find his house littered with people he'd like to have dismissed on the spot. His mother had begged forbearance, it being neither correct nor kind to fling persons from one's home in the middle of the night. And as two were also persons from society, Lady Malverne added in a firm undervoice, having edged close to the earl and his mama's whispered conference, it would be politic to let them stay the entire week, invited or not. Then, after a glance at the earl's face, she'd sighed and opined that as they'd not been asked to High Wyvern Hall by its owner, she supposed it would be enough to let them stay long enough to catch their breath before they were hinted to, then flatly asked to go on their way. Perhaps just one more day then, she finally offered, though from her it sounded more like pleading, and then the earl nodded terse agreement.

Although, the earl thought, reconsidering, as Lord Burton discoursed at length about spirits to the company, now it might be better to let them stay until he had successfully routed the ghost, so that there'd be no more talk, and no more curiosity to bring more unwelcome visitors down upon the Hall. Even as the elderly gentleman described the known habits of haunts, the earl thought on who could be responsible for the incident. Because however convincing the old gentleman's soliloquy, the earl nevertheless devoutly believed that the culprit would eventually be discovered to be among the living.

"Oh no, my boy," old Lord Burton chortled, delighted that his son had just said something that he could correct, "many of the unfortunate beings are quite ordinary-looking. Why, a quite famous gray lady at Sudeley Castle is frequently taken for a housekeeper there, as indeed she must have been in life, for she always seems to disappear just when she's asked for an extra towel," and here he chuckled merrily, having displayed both his erudition and his opinion of servants in one statement, but before he could go on, young Mr. Colfax gasped.

"You mean, one might see them in the daytime?"

"Oh my, yes," Lord Burton replied on a rich chortle. "What is time to a being who dwells outside of time? Some are always present, but like the planets, they are easier to see in the night. Others seem to manifest at particular hours, perhaps because they stubbornly cling to earthly habits. Most, however, are most frequently active between midnight, the witching hour, and the first hour of the new day."

As some in his audience covertly consulted timepieces, the old gentleman continued happily, "Ah yes, and many are nondescript and so can appear at midmorning tea and be overlooked, and mistaken for servants if they're not scrutinized too closely. The gentleman spirits as well, for the monk at Chingle Hall, the monks at Beaulieu Manor and Bolton Abbey, most of them in fact, are shortish, fattish little persons, nothing horrific in their aspect at all, even in the middle of the night.

"Actually," he went on in condescending tones, misinterpreting the earl's grimace, "there's nothing to fear from the poor things at all, although I'll grant some few are said to be fairly awesome-looking. For they can't actually do anything to one, you know. My fellows and I are not such great heroes"—he smiled, as though denying what he was saying about his virtues—"for as we always say, they can impel, but not compell, us to dire things. No, they're just poor lonely beings, cut off from heaven and hell, eternally alone. Most of them, except for some instances of monkish choirs I've heard of, are quite isolated, even though their domicile may contain several other different shades as well. But there's no such thing as a fraternity of spirits, for they seem to go on, each haunting and walking its own well-worn road in perdition, never aware of each other's presence at all. We believe they all exist on very different planes from each other, never mind us poor mortals. So there's nothing for the dear ladies to fear.

"And speaking of the fair sex, few of their shades are exactly exquisite either, for they're almost always described as 'gray' in their sustained manifestations. It takes a great deal of ectoplasmic energy to produce vivid color and shape, you know," he said, as though someone had challenged him, although no one else had spoken, "and most of the poor things simply do not have it in them. Some are so deficient that they appear as half-persons, legless, headless, or even incomplete, like the one recently seen at Longleat. Energy, energy's the key. Great love, or great grievance, might provide it. So this one here at High Wyvern Hall," he said, rubbing his hands together, "is one we have high hopes of. It's obviously malign, for one thing, as witness that maniacal laughter, and it's very active, as well."

"*Suddenly* very active," the earl said wryly, and Alfie looked up at him at that, "which is quite all right for spirits, ladies and gentlemen," he went on, "but as we are all mortal flesh, I believe it's past our bedtimes. And as Lord Burton said ghosts are usually most active between midnight and one, our specter has by now doubtless tripped off into the crypt for a good long snooze. I suggest we all do the same. Only, not in the crypt of course," he added, so that laughter might temper his dismissal of them.

The guests straggled off to their rooms. Theo was happy to nip off with his cronies so that his mama might not stay him, but that lady was preoccupied and only too pleased to leave with Miss Comfort, so that as her room was being made up, she might be advised, firsthand, and in terms she would understand, as to the shocking state of affairs that held sway at the Hall. Mrs. Haverford kissed her son on the cheek, gave him heartfelt thanks for having come riding "like a knight to the rescue," and on a relieved sigh, sought her own neglected bed.

Victoria tarried because the boys had seemed unwilling to leave, and she was very glad of that excuse so that she might have a chance to stay on a few more moments to look at the earl and hear his voice again. But now that there was only herself and the boys and the earl left in the salon, she lowered her gaze and said softly:

"Alfie, Bobby, please. Come to bed now. The earl must be weary and it's shockingly late for you to be up."

The earl stared at her until Alfie called his attention back if only by the stress the gentleman heard in the gruff young voice. "Yes, Miss Victoria. But I'll not sleep a wink till I know . . . Here, my lord, I got to know. It's not us you think's up to nothing, is it? For I swear it ain't. On my solemn word, sir."

"And mine, sir," Bobby echoed very earnestly, very unhappily, as he stood next to his brother, both now pale and regarding the earl with equal intensity.

"What's this?" the earl asked, shaking his head after tearing his gaze from his governess. "I am weary, to be sure, possibly even exhausted, or else I don't believe I'd think I was hearing such nonsense."

"It's not nonsense," Alfie said stubbornly, "and well you know it, my lord. It's clear you don't believe in ghosts, and if you don't, why, then you got to believe it's someone living causing this mischief. And wherever there's mischief, grown folks always think there's kids, don't they?"

"Not always," the earl laughed. "There's that business that occupied us for the last decade, you know, and I don't believe Napoleon was a boy when he started that. No, lad"—he smiled, ruffling Alfie's fair hair and putting his hand on his brother's shoulder—"I never thought it was you, nor you, Bobby."

"But I been thinking," Alfie said earnestly, "and maybe

it's the work of someone wants it to look like it was us. So we'd get the blame and have to go. Or maybe it's being done more clever-like, by someone wants to scare us into leaving this place. Maybe even it's the exact opposite, maybe it's no one wants us gone. Since it began when you left, maybe it's someone wanted you back here again."

"Why, Miss Dawkins," the earl said with a wicked little grin, addressing her for the first time since he'd returned, although he'd seldom ceased looking at her since then, "what a naughty scheme! But I confess, I'm flattered. Thank you."

"It's never her," Alfie scoffed, "though I know you're pulling her leg. Why, she was six shades of green after she saw it t'other night."

"I apologize then for my conceit, though I regret your innocence, my dear," the gentleman said, pausing a breath so that his comment could be taken both ways by her, his dark gaze regretting nothing but the distance between himself and the young woman he spoke with. "And I'd apologize for my ancestor's lady as well, but I don't think it was her at all."

"Neither do we," Alfie began eagerly, but the earl cut him off by laughing.

"Neither do I," he agreed, "but in truth, I'm too tired to think of who it might be tonight. So please, chaps, do go to bed, and I'll speak with you both tomorrow. I promise. And, Miss Dawkins," he added, smiling now, the most alarming look in his eye, something between tenderness and threat, "I'd like a word with you then as well. Alone. Quite alone. Tomorrow."

Then Alfie, showing where he'd recently lost a tooth, grinned as hugely as if he'd been given the answer to all his problems as he breathed, "So that's the way of it!" to himself. And then hitting his brother on the shoulder, he ordered him off to bed.

But Miss Dawkins looked back at the earl once as she ushered the boys out of the salon, and saw him regarding her with an expression of deep thought upon his solemn face. And then it was no unquiet spirit but her very own that kept her awake for several more hours, as she lay in the dark, haunted by the question of whether, jest or not, he really suspected her of impersonating Lady Ann's ghost herself.

Sally confessed her crime, first thing after breakfast in the morning. After the earl's breakfast, that was, for, as her governess reported in a quick aside, the child hadn't been able to consume a morsel of her own, she'd been so anxious about her coming interview with the earl. He'd hit upon the idea of summoning each child, in turn, in private, to his study so that he could speak to them alone, and so that they could answer without prompting or prejudice from any adult or each other. But then Sally's quivering lip and her quick frightened glances about the huge book-lined room changed his mind.

"Come, lass," he said then, rising from his chair and offering her his hand, "it's a lovely morning. Most of the old London slugabeds haven't woken yet. Let's go for a walk in the gardens as we talk."

Once there, in Sally's favorite place, the rose garden, she sat herself upon a bench beneath an arbor, smoothed her skirts around her, and looking down into her hands in her lap, confessed.

"I was not in the nursery when I saw the ghost lady," she said so quietly the humming of a nearby honeybee almost drowned out her soft voice, "and I wasn't in my room neither . . . either, my lord. I was going to see Miss Victoria, so I went to her rooms. But she wasn't there so I sat on her bed and waited. And then I seen . . . saw it. But I know I wasn't s'posed to leave my room at night, and I did anyways. I'm sorry," she said. "Truly."

"Oh, Sally," the earl said softly, gathering her up and sitting her on his lap, never minding how her tears were falling, splashing and leaving great wet spots upon his pristine dove-gray inexpressibles, only worrying that she would tear herself apart with her great gulping sobs. "Oh, Sally, Sally, my dear, why are you weeping?" he asked as he tried to wipe her eyes with his handkerchief. "Did Miss Victoria scold you? Has anyone scolded you for it?"

"No," she wailed. "They were very n-nice. 'Cause I was so scairt, I 'spect," she sniffed, subsiding a bit in order to explain, for she was a Johnson, and so though very young, still never a fool. "And o-only a beast would scold a little girl what's . . . who's crying," she said, exhibiting an honesty that had long been her oldest brother's despair. "But I wasn't s'posed to go there by myself at night, no, I'm not 'lowed to leave the room by myself at night. And I'm very sorry," she wept, going off into a new freshet of despair.

"Because you saw the ghost?" the earl asked, bewildered.

"No," she cried. "Because I'm scairt you'll be so mad I was bad that you'll throw me out. Oh, my lord," she begged, looking at him with huge damp violet-blue eyes whose power to melt a gentleman's heart she'd not yet even imagined, having grown up with two strong-minded brothers, "please don't throw me out."

After the earl understood the heart-wrenching fact that her fear of being made to leave his household was a more profound terror than she could ever feel for any grave-grown specter that could confront her, the interview went much better. For he assured her that she could stay with him until she was so old she'd have to be pushed in a bath chair through the corridors of the Hall, that she could remain with him until she was so ancient that she frightened little girls herself, that she could live with him for so long as he lived and then stay on to comfort his own ghost, as well. He promised, he crossed his heart and kissed his little finger, and then he vowed to swear it on any Bible she cared to produce. Only then, reassured, comfortable, giggling, and dry-eyed again, did she tell him about that other specter that had haunted her, the Haverford ghost.

She had heard some moaning and rattling, and then she'd seen the ghost for only a moment before it vanished again into the wall from whence it had come. It was a female, because it had skirts and long snarly white hair, Sally said. It was tall, but then, the earl thought, who was not to Sally? And it was all gray and floaty. But she couldn't see its face, for it was hooded. She did feel cold too, she offered, when she'd run out of details about the brief visitation to inform him of, but determined to be honest, she confided that she hadn't realized it until later, when that old gentleman had asked her if she'd felt the sensation of a graveyard chill. But who would not, the earl pondered, meeting up with a ghost in the night?

He thanked her courteously, and sent her skipping off to fetch her brothers to him. For he discovered himself more comfortable in the rose garden than in the study, and decided there was little sense in interviewing those two rogues separately any longer, especially since they'd been together when they saw the ghost. He really had no need to question them at all, he thought, absently nodding approval at a butterfly's taste in yellow roses as he awaited them, for his mama had been with them as well that night, and she had told him about the ghost over breakfast this morning with as much precision, as well as elaboration, as a man could wish for.

The thing had come sailing down the hall at them as she and the boys had gone to ask Miss Dawkins to join them in the kitchen for a stolen late-night snack, since no one could sleep anyway after the previous night's happenings when Sally had seen the thing, his mama had explained, so absorbed in the tale she dripped honey off her toast into her coffee cup. It had been gray and shifting, and when it saw them, its cowled hood slipped down to its shoulders as though it were melting, and it shrieked. A long banshee yowl, in fact, she said with relish, stirring the honey into her coffee as though she intended it to be there. And yet, his mama had said at last, fixing her son with a long stare, it was mightily odd that a ghost would run from them as it had, for even as they shrank back, it did, until it disappeared at the top of the stair.

It mightn't have been odd at all, he'd commented blandly, not if she'd had her hair up in curl papers as she was wont to, and certainly not if she still affected that tatty red robe he'd begged her to give to charity years before. He'd only escaped breakfast intact because his mama was a lady, and he smiled remembering it now.

No, he sighed, there was little need to ask the boys

about the ghost; they'd chased it, he understood, but it had eluded them. No, he waited for them now because his interview with Sally had made him ashamed, and he knew it was necessary. So he wore a grim face when the boys presented themselves, and as they'd learned to watch adult expressions and be human weather vanes in order to survive in the past, though they'd come laughing up the path, they now stood still and sober before him.

"Gentlemen," he said, "be seated."

They sat on the bench beside him, quiet and calm, two pale fair-haired children with uncommonly knowing eyes, silent and white as two statues; all that was needed, as he told them, was a fountain for them to guard and he'd be glad to pay them by the hour to ornament his garden. But they did not smile at his weak jest, and so he rose from the bench and strode a few paces and then turned around to confront them.

"I've spoken with Sally," he said, something shadowing his dark face further, and so making their own fair visages even paler, "and something she said disturbed me mightily. My lads," he sighed, as they held their breath, each wondering what crime it was that he was about to accuse them of, each also beginning to wonder now—for they'd both always known that it could never last, hadn't they?—how they would be able to manage to live in Tothill Fields again now that they'd dwelt in heaven, "our association began so oddly, so spontaneously, that I never had time to think it through. But obviously, it's neither fair nor right of me to let things go on as they are. There's too much indecision in it, I'm too precise a fellow, I cannot like it.

"When you came here," the earl continued thoughtfully, "we put it about that you were being fostered by my estate manager and his wife, but we never formalized the scheme. It was all done to forestall gossip anyway. That was a foolishness."

"Then you're sending us off to live with them somewhere else, my lord? Why, that's very kind of you, sir, and we're grateful for it, never think we're not, for the little ones need looking after," Alfie blurted with false brightness the moment that the earl paused, for although he shrank at being an object of pity, he still had his family to think of and was trying to secure something for them still, even from out of the ruins of everything. The gentleman might have become bored with them—he'd never doubted, he told himself fiercely, no, not ever, that it would come to this. For that was the way of the gentry, that was the way of the world. But if they could stay on in the country with some other family, there would be that, at least there would be something salvaged from this adventure.

So he went on, with such a determined look upon his face to prevent his smile from cracking, his features set so tight that the earl stared hard at him, "It was kind of you to take us from the slums, sir, and we'll never forget you," and he edged the shocked Bobby with his elbow until he too said, "Oh yes, sir, that's true, sir, thank you."

The earl narrowed his eyes and then he shook his head.

"This is the first time I've ever known you to be entirely, completely, and absolutely wrong, Alfie," he mused, and then he grinned and said, "and I'll treasure the moment. I don't think I'll ever let you forget it. Doubtless it will serve me well in the years to come, since I don't think you'll ever be so wrongheaded again. Alfie, you dunderhead, I'd be angry at your estimate of me if I didn't know why you had to have it. It's my own fault for not speaking sooner. Here, lad, if it's all the same to you, I'd rather keep you chaps on for as long as you care to stay. The devil with gossip, is what I was about to say, before you so rudely tried to butter me up to my ears and bid me farewell. For I don't worry about gossip any longer, whether it is me or my family that's the target. Because this past month I at last held my breath and then immersed myself in society in London. And I learned that in polite society they'll talk about every evil thing you've done, and if they don't know of any, why, then they'll make it up. But they'll have you in to tea anyway, so long as they think you can afford not to have it."

He smiled down at the two boys. "In short," he said, "I'd like to live as I please, as I did before I became an earl. And I shall. So what I was about to propose was in the nature of a more permanent arrangement. I've had a word with my man-at-law. As I can't see how I'll ever be able to be shut of you, I believe it's useless for me to try. So I'd like to make you my wards. My legal wards. Would you agree to this?"

Bobby looked to Alfie, as his elder brother slowly stood and faced the earl. He was staggered, he was dumbfounded, but he was Alfie Johnson, and he had learned how to fall on his feet.

"My lord," he said steadily, for this was business, and business was something he could handle, even if it was likely the most important business he'd transact in all his life, and he knew it, "we would be pleased to become your wards."

"Mind," the earl warned, "please don't be wounded, but I don't offer adoption, because I might be moved to have children of my own someday. But if you were my wards, I'd be entirely responsible for you anyway, in every way."

"I understand," Alfie said proudly, and then for once spoke entirely truthfully. "And I wouldn't say yes to adoption, my lord, or at least, I'd rather not. 'Cause then we'd be Haverfords. Which is a fine old name, and a proud one too. But we are Johnsons, my lord, and would like to remain so, if it's all the same to you. But it would be a great honor to be your wards, indeed it would be."

He put out his hand to the earl, and they shook hands just as well-brought-up English gentlemen should. But something in the earl's face changed that, and it was as well for everyone's dignity that there was no one else about to see the amount of hugging and sniffling and back-slapping and general carry-on there in the rose garden, before proper decorous order was restored once again.

" 'Ere, what about the ghostie?" Alfie asked suddenly after the three of them had strolled along the paths on the grounds of the Hall in silent peace.

"I think we can put a stop to that tonight," the earl said solemnly.

"Ah," Alfie said, nodding wisely.

"Yes, I believe we'll lure Lord Malverne and your favorite, Lord Burton, and their ghost-hunting cohorts into the west wing, to keep them nicely out of the way. Then you and I, my lad, will hunker down in the hall, where we're likely to catch her—that is, if she's still of a mind to walk tonight—and we'll put an end to it."

Alfie became sober-faced then, and he was about to speak again when the earl said, "But we'll speak of it later. For now, I asked for a private word with your governess. Do you happen to know where she is?"

"She's waiting in your study, my lord. I saw her there before we left the house," Bobby volunteered.

"And where were our other three lovely ladies—my mama, Lady Malverne, and Miss Comfort—just then, would you know?" the earl inquired pensively.

"Mrs. Haverford and Lady Malverne were having a coze in the morning room, and old Comfort was lying doggo up in her room, trying to escape from Lord Burton. But it ain't nothing irregular he's after with her"—Alfie grinned—"it's only any ghost stories she knows that he wants her to come across with for him."

Alfie received a light cuff on the ear for the information, with the mild admonition, "Respect for ladies, my lad, whatever their age or station," but then the earl grew more grave as they walked along.

"Then offer my apologies for the inconvenience, and then please fetch Miss Dawkins to me. I'll be waiting near the boxwood maze. I'd rather speak to her somewhere far from the house," the earl said seriously.

"You don't think it's 'er!" Alfie cried, aghast. "I thought you knew the way of it. I thought—"

"Lad!" The earl spoke sharply as Bobby looked up at them with amazement. "Whatever it is that you think you know, it would be best if you said nothing of it to anyone now. *Anyone*. If you value me at all, I ask you to trust me, I ask you to be patient . . . and I asked you to bring Miss Dawkins to me."

"Yes, sir," Alfie said very quietly, and, deflated, he went to do the earl's bidding, dragging his confused younger brother with him. For he did value the Earl of Clune.

But having learned in a hard school that trust is life's most expensive commodity, he gave it stingily, out of a heart he'd schooled to be a miser's, and so had less taste and more apprehension about his errand with every moment that passed.

15

The boxwood maze was a long way from the Hall itself. It might have been ordered so originally because it was more of an amusement than a decoration. But the bygone Earl of Clune who designed it had more reason for its placement than that; the Earls of Clune, after all, had always had hidden reasons for everything they did. This one had deliberately placed it so that his visitors would have to travel a long way through his extensive grounds before it was reached. In this fashion, the visitor, if he had eyes, could then be counted on to be so thoroughly awed by the grandeur of High Wyvern Hall before he ever attempted to discover the secret of the maze, that the earl would be assured of having him at an additional disadvantage. That way, no matter what the amount of the wager, it could easily be won by the owner of the Hall himself. Winning had ever been important to the Earls of Clune.

And the new earl, the eighth one, standing at the entrance to his great dark green evergreen maze, waited for Miss Dawkins as he saw her stepping down his crushed-shell walks, and hoped the ultimate secret of the maze, beyond that simple matter of where its dark heart lay, which was the secret knowledge that its owner always won, still held true.

She wore a simple green-and-white-striped percale frock, and the sun lingered at the tips of her hair, and as she stepped toward him he gazed at her in her entirety, from her graceful figure to her lovely face, and was again amazed to find he was more stirred by her here in the blatant morning light than he had ever been by any other woman in the dark of night in the dim, flattering shadows upon his sheets.

And she hurried forward as he came into clearer sight, so that he would find her breathlessness at their meeting quite explicable. He was dressed in dove gray and olive green, and the dark green background of the boxwood maze he was posed against swallowed up the morning light. So when she reached him and looked up from her curtsy to his black and searching eyes, it was as though it were still night to her, or at least still that night he had encountered her on the stair and thieved her heart away from her. She did not demand it back again, for even if she could she didn't know what she would do with it any longer, so she only said, very softly, very properly, "My lord."

"Come," he said seriously, giving her his arm. "Please. We have to talk and not be overheard. Come into the maze. Never fear, I know my way out, and my responsibility to you, so I'd never desert you there, or harm you there, but there at least we can have privacy, for no one will find us."

Once inside the maze, she understood his words, for looking about, she could only see a dark-sided tunnel, and as they walked, although they passed other entrances and exits, whichever one they took, they all seemed to lead to the same gravel path and high shorn boxwood walls. It was as if they walked nowhere, though they continued on for a long while, the only sound the gravel crunching beneath their feet. She'd been lost instantly, long before she'd ever entered the maze with him. So she said nothing, not knowing what she could say. Neither did he speak again until they at last reached a small circular clearing containing a pair of benches across from each other with a topiary boxwood sculpture of a female form between them, in the exact center.

"Please sit," he said then, leading her to a bench.

"We've come to the secret heart of the maze and won't be heard or seen here."

But he didn't sit; instead he looked about them and said in lighter tones, "Again, I disappoint them, my poor illustrious forebears. Can't you feel it? That sort of melancholy, that brooding sense of outrage? But since they haunt the house and not the grounds, there's nothing they can do about it here. Still, how furious they must be, for I understand that they none of them would have allowed a beautiful young woman into the maze simply to lead her to safety and a comfortable chat. No, they much preferred to let the poor creatures try to flee from their embraces for as long as they pleased, while they sat here and laughed all the while, until at last they'd gather them up, like fallen leaves, spent and, I'd imagine, willing by then to do anything to obtain their freedom. Oh, it wasn't so bad as all that, I suppose." He smiled. "I'm just being gothic for effect. Most of them were willing and too bad for those who weren't. Any female entering such a place with an Earl of Clune deserved what she got, don't you think?" he asked, staring down at her.

"Unless he'd given his word," she said quietly, half-afraid he'd go back on his word, half-afraid he wouldn't.

"Ah, his word." He sneered, the expression odd and alien to him. "You've heard of my ancestors. What good is the word of an Earl of Clune?"

"But you're not only the Earl of Clune. For you never expected to be one," she protested, not for her own safety, but to ease his obviously troubled mind. "Your mama said you were raised to be Colin Haverford, gentleman, and that nothing would alter that. You cannot take on a man's temperament with his title. I can't believe that. I'd sooner believe in ghosts than that," she said bravely, for his face was dark and forbidding as she spoke.

"Precisely," he said with relief, smiling like the sun coming from behind a cloud.

"It wasn't at all easy to play vile old Earl of Clune," he explained gently, "but it was important. I brought you here, just as I said, for privacy. But also to illustrate a point, for we Earls of Clune always have ulterior reasons, you know. My ancestors built this maze for purposes I could not, cannot, enjoy or approve. But I am not them; I am, as you so rightly observed, Colin Haverford, who just happens to have become the Earl of Clune. But only in name. And it's scarcely fair to punish me for that. Now, you see, I find I want something badly, and perceive that I've been held back from achieving it by that title and all the nonsense that goes with it, both in reality and in my own mind.

"Miss Dawkins," he said bluntly, staring at her, "it should come as no surprise that it's you I want so very badly."

"No," she agreed at once, but before he would say more, she turned her head away. "But the last time we met, you explained it by mentioning sheep's bottoms."

"Ah yes." He smiled. "So that stung, as I intended, did it? But, my dear, then, if you'll recall, I spoke more like a horse's bottom myself, I'm afraid. That's just it: I was afraid. And I tried to terrorize you as well because I was so afraid of losing my freedom. I didn't understand then that it was already a lost cause. At least for me, it was. Victoria," he said in somewhat strained tones, sitting down beside her, and possessing himself of one of her hands, "I want you, as I said.

"I want to marry you, in fact," he declared. "I'll have you no other way, my dear," he warned, "for I've come to understand I'm indeed no proper Earl of Clune, and I know now that you are a proper female, and never the sort who could come to me in joy any other way. And it's joy I'm after. Yours and mine, and for a very long time. Why else do you imagine I'd detail the duties of my mistress so joylessly? I'm not such a bad bargainer as that, you know, not when I want something. And I do now. You. And honorably. Hush," he said quickly as he went on. "You're an excellent governess-companion, but I don't believe you're a good enough actress to have feigned what you felt for me last time we met. Am I wrong?"

"No, but . . ." she began, as he said sternly, "Hush, I'm not done. I rehearsed this thing to the letter and you've got to hear me out. I just wanted to be sure my perceptions weren't clouded by my ancestors' vanity. You do love me then, I'm sure of it. Ssh," he said again, smiling, "don't be so impatient, I'll give you a chance to tell me so in a moment. I've kept you solitary here at High Wyvern Hall while I was out in the world tormenting myself. But I understand the young doctor's making courting noises, and now Theo's brought other young eligibles around. I have to move quickly.

"Now," he went on, as she stared at him and wondered if she were possibly hearing what she believed she was, yet though his voice was light, his face was as serious as she'd ever seen it to be, "remember, before you reply, if you are an apothecary's daughter, I am a soldier's son. We've both nothing more to do with earldoms than coincidence would have it. But we'll do the best we can. I honestly can't see how we could do worse than the general run of the peerage is doing.

"Did you know," he asked quizzically, "there's a duchess who makes Bobby look like an animal hater? The Duchess of Kent has ninety-nine dogs, they say, and all have free run of her home. Her bed is very like a kennel, I imagine, which may be why it's said her husband hasn't visited it in years. The Duchess of Oxford, on the other hand, doesn't need her husband; she's said to have all her children by different sires. True or not, were you listening closely? For I said, as everyone in the *ton* does, 'they say,' and 'it's said,' and so it is. Constantly. Gossip covers every one of them. And there's a duke I won't name who actually does have fleas, which he scratches at incessantly, in all sorts of vulgar places, not only interminably, but in company too."

He smiled down at her smile. "That's only a sampling of the beau monde I've encountered. Do you think we can do worse? It's clear to me now that I'd be gossiped about whatever I did. But I've learned it also would make no difference, except if I cared. And I don't. Nor should you. What a flat I'd have to be to marry just to be acceptable to society, and then have to listen to gossip about the length of my wife's nose, or her manners, or whatever else they'd care to invent forever, anyway. And what a goose you'd have to be to deny me out of fear of them too. Now. Will you marry me, Miss Dawkins?"

"Your mama—" she said, as he replied instantly, "Loves you and only worries that I'll marry some 'society idiot' instead."

"I don't know how to be a countess . . ." she began.

"Good. I don't know how to be an earl," he answered.

"I'm your dependent," she offered, feeling giddy, not wanting to come to her senses enough to think up objections any longer, gazing at him and wanting him to interupt her ruthlessly now, just this once wishing he'd behave as one of his wicked ancestors had, so that he might seize her up and kiss her until she had to agree to whatever he proposed.

"I work for you," she elaborated, her eyes growing very wide when he did not answer at once, fearing that she had at last named a real, insurmountable obstacle.

"No you don't," he said on a gleaming smile, gathering her up in his arms at last. "I'm afraid you've just been dismissed again, thrown out of your post, without a character too. Tsk, tsk," he said happily. "What a coil. Now I don't have to keep to my word either, for at the moment, and just for the next few weeks, mind, you're not my dependent any longer. Just my entire world," he breathed as he at last kissed her.

"Enough," he said raggedly a long while later, drawing back from her and taking a deep and steadying breath, "or rather, not enough, but enough for the moment."

As he helped her smooth her hair and gown, he smiled at her and commented, "There are some things I'd rather not begin in a maze of my ancestor's making, one of them being my line of descendants, but I'm very heartened by the fact that the thought didn't occur to you. Yes, you may well blush," he laughed. "Nonetheless, love," he said earnestly, turning her face to his and ensuring that she could look nowhere but into his dark, serious eyes, "you haven't answered, not really. I can't hold you to a kiss, although I promise I will continue to, but not in a court of law. I need a clear and audible answer."

"You are sure?" she asked very solemnly.

"More than that," he answered without a trace of humor, "or I would not have asked. I'm very sure I don't wish to go on with this lonely business of life without you."

"Then yes, of course yes," she whispered.

It was a while longer before he allowed her to speak again, and then there were a great many murmurous things said before he forced himself to draw away from her again. But as soon as he felt it would be sightly for him to arise and give her his hand, he did so, saying simply, "Enough of this placating my ancestors, my love. Let's go back to the Hall. We've business there this evening to prepare for."

Then he hesitated, and said, "Victoria, I asked Alfie to trust me earlier today; now I ask it of you. I'm aware that I've given you no token of my intent except for my embraces, but the omission was deliberate. Can you keep what's occurred between us to yourself, only just a little while longer? Only until this wretched ghost business is resolved?"

She'd forgotten everything in his embrace, but now the real world flooded back to her and she felt a chill very like that of a spectral presence as she gasped, remembering, "But you never asked me about what I saw that night."

"I had better things to do," he replied with a grin as he took her arm. But when he noted she was trembling, he asked at once, "Was it so very frightening, then? I understand it was a gray lady you saw in your room, with a gray hood and yards of straggling hair."

"No. Yes, it was," she said, shaking her head, "but now I wonder why you haven't asked me more. My lord, is it possible that even after all you've said, all we've done, all we plan to do, that you believe I played out a masquerade to bring you home, as you once jested?"

" 'Colin,' " he corrected her, before he said, "no, it's not possible. In fact, tonight I hope to prove it, for tonight, with your cooperation and with the help of Mama and the boys, I do believe we'll nab a ghost."

And if you don't, she thought with ineffable sadness, as he began to detail his plan while they walked slowly back to the house, drawing apart slightly as they left the maze so as to keep their new status as secret as the place where they'd decided it, if she doesn't walk tonight, will you ever quite believe that it wasn't me trying to call you back, after all? Will you, my lord? Will you, Colin?

It was a night made for roving spirits. Everyone said so. Lord Burton rubbed his thin hands together in glee as the wind picked up; the doctor, come from the village to observe, allowed as how it could not be better atmosphere as he shook the rain from his high beaver hat; and even the housemaids refused to venture anywhere in the Hall except in pairs with a footman at their back for insurance, as soon as the first long, rolling peals of distant thunder were heard.

Dinner was consumed but scarcely tasted, and there was almost a carnival atmosphere as the company assembled in the Yellow Salon to await their host and hear the plans he had for their evening. Theo and his friends had opted to station themselves around the music room, although Lord Burton was clearly indecisive. Since the ghost had previously manifested itself in the governess's room and in that hall, he ruminated fretfully, one ought to stay there. However, since two undermaids had sworn they'd seen a ghostly presence in the music room, and moreover, since the harp playing itself off-key there had sent them flying from the room this very afternoon, he agonized over which would be the hottest, or rather coldest, spot to be in this night.

When the earl entered at last, after having paid two giggling young undermaids handsomely and giving them the evening off besides, all speculation ceased, for the gentleman had a resolute air. And, as Theo had pointed out to Lord Burton and his cronies, as his cousin had instructed him to do, there was such a thing as manners. It was, after all, his cousin's Hall, Theo claimed, and his own ancestor's wife who was the lady in question.

That argument seemed to carry some weight, for it wasn't long before the Earl of Clune had everyone's acquiescence to his plan. Matters of breeding and chivalry aside, another fact that he lightly but definitely touched upon, which was that he could dispossess anyone who disagreed, doubtless lent his words some additional weight. With only a minimum of further grumbling, ended by the *sotto voce* comment by their host to the effect that he who owned the pack, dealt the cards, Lord Burton, Theo, and the rest agreed to station themselves in the music room. Miss Dawkins would keep to her room, and the earl himself, with his chosen stalwart assistants, would prowl the upstairs hall.

At midnight, the interior of the old Hall lay unnaturally still. The thunderstorm had passed and only a gentle rain misted down upon the grounds. The gentlemen hovering in the music room scarcely dared scratch for fear of frightening away the apparition they awaited. The footmen and other servants had either been sent to their rooms or watched breathlessly at their usual stations. Sally had been barred from the proceedings, but she scarcely minded, for she was enjoying herself enormously, pent in her room with Mrs. Haverford and Lady Malverne, with a clutch of maids for company and a manservant outside the door to guard against their uneasiness, as well as their restlessness. And the earl and his chosen stalwart assistants settled comfortably in a corner of the great dark hall. The gentleman sat in the shadows in a small gilt chair, his head laid back against the wall; his stalwart assistants sat at his feet.

After several moments passed in silence so absolute that each could hear the blood singing in his own veins, Alfie ventured a whisper so low that the earl had to incline his head to hear him.

"My lord?" Alfie breathed. "May I say something?"

"Certainly," his trustee answered softly.

"Well, then, do you really believe in ghosts?"

"Oh, I believe anything's possible," the earl answered.

"But not here, not tonight?"

"No, lad," the earl sighed sadly, "unfortunately, no, not here, not tonight."

"Aye, me too," Alfie sighed just as sorrowfully, as his brother nodded solemnly too.

Victoria sat alone in her room and resolved not to be a ninny. She had every reason to be joyful this night, every reason to be ecstatic, in fact. But the problem was that she didn't quite believe in anything tonight. Not in the reality of what had happened in the boxwood maze, although her lips still tingled and her flesh still yearned for that amazing touch it believed in even if she did not, nor did she believe in the existence of ghosts, and not, unhappily, in the nonexistence of them either.

She'd been too embarrassed to request one of Bobby's four-legged companions when she'd been told to remain within her room all night, but she'd seen his enormous black dog wandering the hallway before she'd closed her door, after the earl and the boys had seen her safely there. She'd attempted to lure the great melancholic brute in, even sinking so low as to offering him a ratafia biscuit she'd put in her pocket against the more easily satisfied hungers of the night, since Lord Burton had claimed that dogs were very sensitive to spirits. Sensitive or not, he was certainly a very large and doubtless protective beast. But he'd only stared at her again and drifted off, never letting her lay so much as a finger on his broad black head, being, she decided uneasily, before she shut her door again, a very disobliging, unnatural sort of pet.

Now she attempted to bravely face the night alone. Not three days before, she remembered, something very like a ghost had appeared from out of nowhere in front of the silk-hung wall she stared at now, and it had moaned and she had almost perished from shock before she'd fled the room, moaning herself. She tried to remember the pudding-crazed ghost the earl had once fantasized for her, and then she remembered him, and then she tried to believe that he had actually held her and told her he loved her and that it was possible he would do so again, and within the bonds of matrimony at that. The idea was still so revolutionary that she was lost in contemplation of it, holding it up to the light of reason to better see all the holes in its logic, turning it this way and that to find its flaws so that her spirit would not be completely flattened when sanity returned to her, or to him, that she did not at first see the thing that stepped out of her wall.

So it stood irresolute, that gray and hooded apparition, as if awaiting her screech of terror. When it did not come, the thing, almost as if against its will, stirred slightly and then hooted.

Victoria looked up at it and stopped breathing. She could not scream. She'd been raised as such a good and obedient girl that she never could screech as satisfactorily as spoiled children could, and so as the thing approached her, all she could do was to rise, and back away, and wish with whatever wit remained to her that she could at least utter a last word before she died of fright.

But then, because she wouldn't run this time and couldn't scream as a proper young lady ought, the thing came nearer. And in her panic, Victoria did the only thing a proper young lady ought not to do, would not be expected to do when confronted by a spirit: she reached toward it to stop it. To her astonishment, her hands did not disappear in a chilling vapor, but rather touched and clutched onto cold but definitely living, cringing flesh. And then there was a fearsome shrieking heard. But it emanated from the ghost.

For as Victoria drew her hands back, the awful hood came away, and although she dreaded looking up from her hands to see a headless thing, or a ghastly decomposing thing, she found herself staring wildly at Miss Comfort instead, who stared wildly back at her.

"Oh, Miss Comfort," Victoria cried in pity and distress, as the earl and Alfie came bursting into the room, her first disordered impulse, irrationally, being to calm the poor old lady, who'd obviously been frightened by the ghost. It was only when the earl barred Miss Comfort as she turned and began to flee back to the wall that Victoria slowly realized why the older woman wore such a flowing nightrobe, and why she'd combed her hair so high and let it stand in such unruly fashion about her distracted and strained white face.

"Ah, Miss Comfort," Victoria at last breathed, "did you hate me so much, then?"

"No, no, my dear," Miss Comfort answered coolly, when she could, when the earl had steered her to sit and pressed his hand against her shoulder to signify she should remain so. "No," Miss Comfort said then with remarkable control, for even as she spoke, Mrs. Haverford and Lady Malverne appeared wide-eyed in the doorway, "no, not at all. I think, in the end," she said, her voice shaking only a little, "it was rather because I liked you too well."

When the boys had been sent off to keep Lord Burton and his crew from the vicinity, with a tale of a sleepwalking servant to swear by, and the door had been closed against any other curious souls who might have heard the stir, Miss Comfort sat in a great chair. She held on to the glass of water the earl had gotten her as though it were her sanity itself, and quietly and reasonably explained her imposture. So sensibly and calmly did she speak that despite the hour, the strange circumstances, her madly disordered hair and bizarre nightrobe, with its bit of sheet cobbled onto its neck to improvise a ghostly cowl, she had presence, poise, and a certain terrible dignity.

"I resented you at first, my child, as why should I not have," she asked rhetorically, "when it seemed obvious to me that your advent meant my decline? I'd lived with the Haverfords for eight years. Eight years ago, my dear, you were not yet a woman, Lord Malverne was still in shortcoats, our dear Sally had not yet been born. That is eight years, if you wish to find a means of measuring it. I'd grown to care for Roberta deeply, and had envisioned ending my days with her. Yet, you forced me to see that which I had forgotten, what a governess-companion ought never to forget, which is that she is not a member of the family, and so, unlike a disagreeable or infirm mother, daughter, or grandmother, she must leave when her usefulness is done."

Victoria knew only too well what Miss Comfort was saying and thought she was the only one who did, but Mrs. Haverford spoke at once, anger almost overriding the sorrow in her tone. "But, Comfort, I told you, and told you again, that I wanted you with us, no matter how long Victoria stayed on."

"So you did, Roberta." The older woman nodded, as though Mrs. Haverford were an especially apt pupil who'd gotten a difficult problem right. "And I'd begun to believe you, but then I took to watching Miss Dawkins, and that was when the plan to frighten her away took hold in my mind. I decided it was imperative that you leave here, child," she said seriously, gazing at the young woman in her nightrobe, sighing then, "but because of what I saw in you, and what I saw when I looked in my mirror.

"I was," the older woman said then, raising her chin, looking so imperious that it was as if her bizarre raiment fell away and she were clothed in regal robes, "once young, and once very lovely. I know," she said with a hint of laughter in her thin voice as she glanced to the earl, "that is scarcely believable, and that any old wreck of a person may say it if there's no one to gainsay it. But it is nevertheless true. I never lie. Not overtly."

But the smile fell away as she continued. "Yes, so I was. I had fair hair and a fair face and form to go with it, and I was not unremarked by the gentlemen. I'd once worked for a noble family, you recall my telling you, Roberta, long before I took any of the succession of unexceptional positions I held before I volunteered to come to you. And, I might say now, after all those tedious posts, I'd decided that it was a choice of coming to you or going to my eternal rest. Although I admit that had I left the planet as I planned to then, I suppose I too would have been doomed to eternal roving like the poor Lady Ann I impersonated. But I was disappointed with life.

"There'd been a gentlemen, you see," she said proudly, "in that noble house, and he was a nobleman, handsome, clever, and all any woman could ask. And I'd loved him. For fifteen years. For fifteen unswerving, devoted years, although I knew that as I was a servant, there was no hope for any lasting alliance between us. When he died, there was nothing left for me, no matter where I went. And I did not want that to happen to Miss Dawkins."

"Ah, poor Comfort," Mrs. Haverford cried. "But Cole would never compromise a good young woman."

"I understand," Miss Comfort retorted a little testily, "but that was precisely part of the problem. My gentleman never compromised me either, you see."

As everyone in the room stared at her in confusion, she went on, more rue than pride in her voice now. "He was entirely noble. I was entirely safe in his household. He'd sigh at me, look at me longingly, he'd go to his wife's bed with a backward glance at me, he'd go out to his mistresses and his revels after yearning over me, and then come back to spend long hours discoursing with me, feeling noble, no doubt, at how he'd withstood temptation with me. But I was in his thrall nonetheless. It would have been nobler perhaps had he made me his true mistress, not his chaste one. For when he'd gone, I had not even memories, only regrets. I cannot say with certainty if that is true either. After all, I was what I was, and could be no other thing. But I didn't wish such a fate for Victoria, who was incontestably a good and lovely creature. And who seemed, daily, to be becoming as I was. Hence"—she laughed, more wildly now—"as you see, a ghost for a governess. A governess for a ghost.

"And it's likely," she went on, quickly regaining control, as though she realized what her audience was thinking, "that it was just as I've taught children for a generation: a lie leads to worse lies. For had I not feigned illness so as not to be sent away, I would not have been closed in my rooms for days, and would not have fretted and become restless, or heard the children speculating on Victoria's fear of ghosts, and after hearing of the hidden passages in the manor, would not have discovered the same sort of secret corridors, obviously long forgotten, linking the nurseries, schoolrooms, and upper servants' rooms here in the Hall. And so would never have had the means to attempt my wild ruse."

"The first earl disliked seeing servants in the corridors as much as the Ludlows do," the earl put in quietly. "He had passages constructed so that his children might be cared for by 'unseen' hands. The man deserved ghosts. It was the librarian who told me of it, having found a reference in one of the Hall's oldest histories," he added almost apologetically.

"So you knew?" Miss Comfort asked.

"I thought I did." He shrugged. "I couldn't believe Miss Dawkins would walk my midnight halls—there was no reason for it, when she knew too well she could have me back in a trice with a word. The children might have been suspects, but Alfie banished the idea with one look at me. Still, I hesitated to drop a word to save you further exertion for fear of offending you if I were wrong, for I couldn't imagine why you'd terrify Sally."

"Unfair, my lord," Miss Comfort said, turning very white. "I never suspected she'd be in here, as I never expected to encounter your mama and the boys in the hallway. It was all for Miss Dawkins."

"And so it was all wasted," the earl said softly, "for I'm going to marry her, Miss Comfort. I've asked, she's agreed, but I didn't dare let it out for fear it was dislike of her that was spurring our ghost, and I didn't wish to make matters worse."

"How could they be?" Miss Comfort laughed brokenly. "At least for me. I congratulate you, but I'm not sure, no, I'm not sure at all that it makes me feel very much better, though of course I'm pleased for her. But as for me?" Her voice trailed off; she looked very old and pensive, but there was too much excitement in the room for anyone to notice.

"Oh, how splendid!" Mrs. Haverford cried, embracing Victoria, embracing her son, even, in her delight, embracing Lady Malverne.

That lady stood very still, and when the earl cocked a brow at her continued silence, as his mother began to look very put out at it, she spoke slowly and thoughtfully.

"I can't say I'm delighted," Lady Malverne mused. "No, Roberta, I cannot. For I'd plans for him and a certain heiress. No doubt it will be difficult for me to live down the fact that he's marrying his governess. An Earl of Clune and a governess . . ." She shook her head doubtfully. Then, "Oh," she cried at once, as though she'd crossed a sharp tack in her ruminations, suddenly appearing very animate and very like her son Theo, "the very thing! It will do, my lord. Congratulations," she said in a sprightly manner, taking his hand and pressing it, before pressing her cool cheek to Victoria's flushed one and almost singing, "my fondest felicitations, it will do!

"For it occurs to me," she said happily, "that it is like to be the most shocking thing Clune will ever do in all his reign as earl. He is the most disastrously sober fellow, a somber footnote to the history of all those riotous predecessors of his. Those of us, his relatives who live in society, rue it, you know, for if nothing else marks him as not born to the title, and a par . . ." But there she paused just before her lips formed the complete word "parvenu," and aware that she'd been about to stumble, she pulled her thoughts up and said, "Ah . . . perfect. This will make him appear to be much more in the direct line, you see.

"An Earl of Clune," she said to Mrs. Haverford's mystified expresion, "is always scandalous. It's expected of him, it's fitting. My dear Roberta, rejoice with me. I can hold my head up again in society—there is a tale to be told of him now."

"So pleased," the earl commented, his dark face becoming cold, even as his mother drew herself up to defend her new daughter-in-law, "to be able to live up to my name without having to despoil dozens of maidens or youths. How fortunate that I met Victoria before I might have had to find some really exotic addiction. Although I might have taken up with some *fille de joie* and then married my mistress, would that have done?" he asked coolly, a bit of steel in his voice as he sent one significant glance toward his new fiancée.

"That would have been going too far, my lord," Lady Malverne said, after meeting his eye and aknowledging his stern hint by nodding slightly before saying, "gossip being one thing, infamy another."

Aware that he had won a concession, for in the circles Lady Malverne traveled in, a governess was actually rated a rung lower than a mistress, the earl decided to end the night's conversation before shock produced further gaucheries. As though in silent agreement, the ladies began to file out from Victoria's room.

Mrs. Haverford supported Miss Comfort and said, as they neared the door and she put her arm round the older woman so that servants might not see the odd nightrobe she affected, "But you will stay on, Comfort, that is essential."

Miss Comfort paused.

"I think it would be better if I did go to my cousin Emma's for a space," she said softy. "I'm well off now, you know, and can afford to lord it over her there. I need time to sort matters out. I was very foolish, you know."

"But, Comfort," Mrs. Haverford protested.

"My dear Roberta," Miss Comfort replied haughtily, with an ironic smile, "my name is actually Mary. Mary Clothilde, to be precise, as my mother was French, you see. But you never knew that fact, and have forgotten the other. That was only correct after all, for related or not, I was only a servant to you. But it's been a great many years since I last answered to my own name. Yes," she remarked quietly, putting her head to the side as though listening to an echo of her words, "yes, I believe I should go for a space, yes." And she left the room very slowly, as one who is indeed, as she must have been, very weary.

When no one but the earl and Victoria were left, he smiled at her and asked simply, "Can you sleep?"

"No," she replied

"Good," he said. "We'll see the sunup together. Throw on a robe to prevent talk, we'll meet in the morning room to satisfy propriety, and then, although we still can't do all I'd wish, yet we'll talk all we please. And we've a great deal to talk about. I think fifty years might be able to encompass it all. Now, I'll settle Theo and his crew, and see you there very soon."

The earl took the stairs as quickly as one of the boys might have, but when he reached the music room to rout the ghost-hunters there, he was surprised to find it unnecessary, since a sleepy Theo and his two weary friends, a vastly contented Lord Burton, and a glum Alfie and Bobby, were clearly already on the move, leaving even as he entered.

"Ah, there you are, my lord, we waited for you. Thank you so much," Lord Burton said with satisfaction. "It was the thrill of a lifetime. I shall be eternally grateful, and when my article appears in our little journal, be sure I'll send you a copy."

"Capital show, Cole," Theo agreed over a vast yawn, as his friends nodded agreement, "although can't say I'd care to see it if I were all alone. Still, smashing place, this. Great fun," he said as he dragged himself up the stair to ready himself to sleep until noon, and his companions straggled after him.

"They never heard nothing Comfort done," Alfie said in disgust when they all were lost to sight. "Too busy down here. They say as they saw a ghost here. A young and beautiful lady all in shining white, they said. Fairly killed themselves with excitement, and drank themselves silly afterward congratulating themselves for it. Prolly a trick of the lightning, I say. Oh no, they say, Lady Ann, to the life. Or death. People," Alfie said shrewdly, "believe what they want in this old life, don't they, my lord?"

"Indeed," the earl agreed, "but I'm grateful for it, lad. Comfort's got enough on her plate as it is. Now, off to bed, chaps, well done."

He turned to leave them and hasten to the morning room, when Alfie said softly but imperatively, halting him in his tracks.

"Ah, no, my lord. I can't. Bobby, you get yourself up and kip out. I'll come later. I've got to have a word with his lordship."

"It's very late," the earl said, with some futile yearning, looking down at Alfie as his brother flew up the stair. "Wouldn't tomorrow do as well?"—all the while knowing, from knowing his man, that it was only wishful thinking on his part.

For, "No, my lord," Alfie said very sadly, shaking his head. "I can't sleep on it one more night, sir. It's like a lump won't go down when I swallow. It's like a rock in my pillow. I've got to say it now, or bust."

"It's a night for revelations," the earl sighed. "Let's have done with all of them, then. Have a seat, Alfie, and we'll have it out in a twinkling, as the tooth-drawer says."

When Alfie didn't smile in reply, the earl said gently, "Come, lad. It can't be so bad as all that."

"It can, my lord," the fair-haired boy answered, now seeming very young, now seeming his true age at last as he shuddered in the thin late-night air, and looked up at the earl hopelessly. "And it is."

16

The music room seemed to hold an extra silence, as rooms will when a large company has lately left them. The earl offered the boy a seat, but Alfie only shook his head, sending his light hair dancing, and stubbornly held on to the back of a chair, as though that would be a moral as well as a physical prop in what he clearly looked to as a coming ordeal.

But the earl sat, lowering himself into a green tapestried chair, so that his eyes would be on a level with the boy's own worried ones. Then he crossed his legs, and with a lazy ease of manner that belied both his impatience to be gone to his lady and his growing worry about what the boy wished to disclose, he said, "Come, Alfie, it's late, I'm quite old, you know. Out with it before I grow too old to care."

"You've dealt square with us, no one could be better to us. It's not right not to tell you," Alfie said tersely.

"Probably not," the earl agreed. "Is it that you've done away with one of my guests? I might reward you, Alfie, but don't try to up the price by drawing the matter out."

"Please, sir," Alfie said, his own face white as a ghost's might have been in the scant remaining light in the room.

"All right, Alfie," the earl said, now all seriousness,

almost as somber as the boy, "I understand. I'll be silent until you're done. But go on with it, please."

"I wanted to tell you from the first . . . almost from the first," Alfie amended, "but time passed, you know. And I told myself it didn't matter. Until today, when you said you was going to make us your wards. Even then, everything kept happening to keep my mind off it, keeping the others away from Miss Victoria's rooms, hunting down Comfort, I'd all but forgot it again. But tonight Lord Burton was going on about his ghosts again. He was saying as how they listened to everything went on in a house, which was why Lady Ann appeared where people were waiting for her. He said that if they could read minds, why, they could say 'Boo!' to you in your sleep, and save themselves the trouble of haunting, but as they couldn't, they had to listen sharp to everything everyone said. He called them 'silent company.' It were interesting drivel, my lord, but that ain't it.

" 'Cause then he said something important, and it fair killed me. He said that nothing is ever lost in this old world, everything has an 'aura' or an 'emanation.' And so even a secret never dies, since even if only a wall hears it or sees it, it's recorded and down, somewhere, so someone can always ferret it out. And then I knew I couldn't hide the truth no more, and that I'd only make myself sick for trying.

"I think, my lord," he said then, an expression of such naked vulnerabilty on his face that the earl scarcely recognized him, "that you're such a fellow as wouldn't give us up for what I have to say. You mightn't make us your wards no more, no. But I believe"—and here he paused, as if to reassure himself of the truth of what he said—"I do believe you'd never give us up entirely for it."

"Thank you," the earl said softly, knowing the best compliment he'd ever received in his life when he heard it, even if he didn't know its reason for being, or if it would even turn out to be true.

"Our mama, she wasn't no seamstress," Alfie said in a rush. "No, nothing like. Which ain't to say she din't try it, but she was no good at it, so when she came to town after our da died a few years back—and he *was* a sailor, my lord, and they *was* married, I got their marriage lines still—she turned to the only sort of work a female with three kids to grow could do down there where she wound up, with no penny in 'er pocket.

"Well, she sold 'erself, my lord, is what she did," he said as lightly as if it hadn't, as he'd said, near killed him to get it out, "which is why she took a place with two rooms, much as it cost 'er. But not only did old Mrs. Rogers keep a sharp eye on 'er trade, so she had to sneak all the time, we was getting older and she was feart we'd know too much and catch wise to what was going on in t'other room. Some of us did," he admitted as an aside, before he hurried on, "so she took to the streets and did her trade there in doorways. I worked and I worked," he said in impotent fury, hitting the back of his chair with a small fist, "but it wasn't enough, so she snuck out again. But after Baby was born, she was different. She was sickly and she din't look too good and she never really got better from 'er lying-in. So though she did end as I said, in the streets, it wasn't collecting piecework she collapsed from, my lord, no, it wasn't that at all."

"I'm sorry for it," the earl said after a space in which Alfie didn't speak, "but I'd be a poor piece of work if I changed toward you for it. If that's what's been bothering you, lad, I'll agree that it was a wretched business and a great shame, but I can't say it matters to me, except that I'm sorry for the harm it did to yourself and to your mama. But even as I can't repair it, I can't blame you for it. Child, it's a sad history, but it's just that, a history."

"It's not all of it," Alfie said fiercely. "Else I'd not have bothered telling it. But you din't listen close, my lord, for I said she come to town a few years after my da died, and that she 'ad a time supporting the three of us. And the three of us it was, for a long time. Baby . . . well, sir, Baby," he said, even as the earl realized what it was he was struggling to say, "she got Baby through 'er line of work, you might say.

"That's why 'e got no proper name. She din't want 'im. 'Oo could blame her?" He laughed bitterly, slipping deeper into the voice of the streets with each word. "She took all sorts of things to be rid o' 'im, that's why she did so poorly after 'e was born, I think. 'E ain't got no proper name, 'cause after 'e come she wasn't 'erself no more and she'd call 'im a different name each day, sort of like a bad joke on 'erself, 'cause she din't know 'is father's name.

"But the thing of it is," he declared fiercely, "is that we love 'im. We do. We could o' been shut o' 'im after she went. Nothin' simpler, think on it. But 'e's all we got left o' our mum, and so 'e's one of us. So we can't stay on if 'e can't too, and I know how people feel about babes like 'im. 'E's nothing. 'E's just a bad word Comfort near killed me for saying once. He's nothing but a bastard, my lord," Alfie said clearly, drawing himself up and staring at the earl with defiance and entreaty, "but he is ours."

The room was very silent; the night held its breath.

"Indeed," the earl drawled, at his most urbane. "Then, you're right, that is too bad, Alfie. For I'd rather hoped you'd share him with me.

"Clunch," the earl added gently, as he held the trembling boy close so that he could help him conceal his tears, knowing how important that was to a lad, "as if it mattered. He's one of you. I shall love him too. As will my wife. Oh yes, you didn't know? It's to be Miss Victoria. Now, what do you think of that, you expert on social matters?"

"Alfie," the earl said a while later, as he held his governess-companion a great deal closer and quite differently than he had the boy, as they sat before the fire and waited for the dawn, "approves."

She giggled.

"Well, it's a relief to me, I can tell you," he said, his cheek brushing against her hair. "He's a fearsome lad. We decided too, before we parted for the night, that he'd think on a career in law. I'll need a sharp man-at-law in my dotage, you see. Bobby's too gentle for the military, so some sort of career in animal husbandry seems the ticket, Sally will have a dowry to attract whomever she pleases, and Baby, why, since Baby is the best behaved of the lot, it's clear he's headed for the church. He can be the one to marry our children off. All our children," he whispered. "Remind me to tell you something about him someday," he added, as she reminded him of something else entirely that made him complain after an interval:

"Not a day more than two months from now, no matter what Lady Malverne says about getting space at St. George's. We'll wed from right here, if we must, in the music room, so that Lady Ann can be bridesmaid."

"I do hope," Victoria mused, from the safety and luxury of his encircling arms, her voice a purr beneath his chin, "that all the uproar in the music room didn't frighten that lovely girl that I always see there. The fair-haired one," she explained. "I've never learned her name. The beautiful one. Strange that you don't know the one I mean," she teased as he began to look at her oddly, "for I was sure you, a lecherous Earl of Clune, would have remarked her. I see her all the time," she went on, "although we've never spoken a word to each other. Why, I mean the absolutely beautiful, ethereal-looking girl who keeps drifting in and out of there, she positively haunts the place . . ." she explained, before she put one hand over her mouth and stared at him in sudden wild surmise.

The children were asleep, Mrs. Haverford and Lady Malverne too; even Miss Comfort, with the help of the doctor's potent potion, slept, fortunately, and dreamlessly. Even the servants were abed; only the earl and his promised bride were wakeful as they sat and whispered together in the morning room, waiting for another morning to arrive to bring them that much closer to their wedding day.

But in his cot, high in the nursery wing, Baby stirred.

He opened his eyes to dark and complete night. He was, indeed, a very good baby, almost as though he'd always known he lived on sufferance and had to be. But perhaps because in some fashion he knew now that at last he was guaranteed continuance, perhaps because he'd grown accustomed to a warm and nourishing presence attending to him if he so much as coughed out of tune, perhaps because at last he was learning to be a real baby, he looked out into the dark and began to fret. It was a different darkness than the one he'd lately left before entering into the world, and it was frightening in its immensity and silence, and he was, in that moment, acutely aware that he was only a little scrap of a thing, and altogether alone in the great ocean of night.

So he thrust out his lower lip and a tear appeared in one wide blue eye and he drew in his breath and let out a little preliminary sob. It was never enough to waken Nurse, he'd never disturbed her in the night anyway, and so she didn't listen for him then. But before he could signal the full extent of his new unhappiness, the lady appeared at his door.

She came straight to his cot and looked down at him. And although he'd just begun to learn to focus his blue eyes at all well, he stared at her amazed, for even he could see, in the clear bright light she emitted, that she was very lovely. Her long fair hair streamed about her, and gazing down at him, now knowing what he was, she threw back her head and laughed. And it was lovely to see, even if it all was soundless. Then she bent and lowered her lips to his forehead, and although all he felt was a soft cool breeze, it comforted him.

She gazed all about the room then, with a sort of wistful satisfaction. Then she looked quickly to the window, but although the dawn was near, it was still quite dark. Then she smiled once more, relief and sad remembrance intermingled upon her ethereally lovely face, and she began to drift back toward the wall. And then she stopped and stared at the door. For a huge black dog with drooping ears and eyes stood poised there, and his bulk filled the entire doorway as he stared back at her.

He regarded her intently. Then he stopped panting, he ceased all movement. His great shoulders tensed, his entire body contracted and then he leaped at her. And she dropped to her knees and embraced him and he foundered at her feet like a great wave that had broken on the shore as he tumbled over and over at her little slippers while she laughed and hugged him, and their bright margins devolved into each other's as they greeted each other, while they neither of them ever made a sound.

Then the lady rose to her feet, and after glancing to the window once more, she looked down at Baby once again, and her smile was like a benediction and a final farewell as she began to move slowly toward the wall again. She had almost reached it when she paused and beckoned to the dog as if to call him home, as though to summon him to his home with her, to give him rest from his lonely wanderings at last. He looked around just once and then leaped up, and they vanished into the wall together.

It was the darkest hour of the night, for dawn was only a blink away. But Baby gave out one contented silvery little gurgle before he settled down to sleep again, and it was a thrilling sound, like a carillon chiming to welcome the morning. It was still the darkest hour. But now it was already lighter in the great Hall than it had been for centuries.

About the Author

Edith Layton has been writing since she was ten years old. She has worked as a freelance writer for newspapers and magazines, but has always been fascinated by English history, most particulary by the Regency period. She lives on Long Island with her physician husband and those of her three children who are not involved with intimidating institutions of higher learning. She collects antiques and large dogs.